Dorothy Allison is the author of *Trash*, *The Women Who Hate Me*, *Skin: Essays on Sex, Class, and Literature*, *Two or Three Things I Know for Sure* and *Bastard Out of Carolina*, the acclaimed bestseller and a finalist for the National Book Award. She lives in North California.

'*Cavedweller*'s evocation of rock stardom is a hoot, and Allison clearly knows small-town life first-hand. She has a fine ear for the way Americans talk, and delivers some wicked dialogue'
TLS

'Family drama meets Southern Gothic'
Arena

'If *To Kill a Mockingbird* came drenched in hell-fire and whisky it might be read like the coming of age that takes place for Delia's daughters'
Express

'Allison writes with mesmerising force'
Red

'Gentle, eloquent, touching and brilliantly written'
Minx

'Dorothy Allison's characters are so real that you can feel the searing heat of a deep Southern summer'
Eva

Also by Dorothy Allison

Cavedweller

Dorothy Allison

An *Abacus* Book

First published in the United States of America by Dutton 1998
First published in Great Britain by Abacus 1998
This edition published by Abacus 1999

A CIP catalogue record for this book
is available from the British Library.

ISBN 0 349 11105 7

Printed and bound in Great Britain by
Clays Ltd, St Ives plc

Abacus
A Division of
Little, Brown and Company (UK)
Brettenham House
Lancaster Place
London WC2E 7EN

For Wolf and Alix, my son and my beloved.
They have taught me all I know about healing the heart.

Cavedweller

Chapter 1

Death changes everything.

It was a little after dawn on the twenty-first of March 1981 when Randall Pritchard torqued his Triumph Bonneville off the 101 interchange southeast of Silverlake. The seventeen-year-old girl behind him gave a terrified howl as she flew off the back of the motorcycle, cartwheeled twice, and slammed facedown on the pavement, breaking both wrists and four front teeth and going mercifully unconscious. Randall never made a sound. He simply followed the bike's trajectory, over the railing toward the sunrise, his long hair shining in the pink-gold glow and his arms outstretched to meet the rusty spokes of the construction barrier at the base of the concrete pilings. A skinny, pockmarked teenager from Inglewood was crouched nearby, rummaging through a stolen backpack. He saw Randall hit the barrier, the dust and rock that rose in a cloud, the blood that soaked Randall's blue cotton shirt.

" 'Delia,' " the boy told reporters later. "The man just whispered 'Delia' and died."

Delia Byrd had been up for an hour, walking back and forth in the tiny garden behind the house in Venice Beach, thinking about the local convenience store, where the liquor was overpriced but accessible twenty-four hours a day. Eyes on the sunrise, fists curled up to her midriff, she was singing to herself, stringing one lyric to another, pulling choruses from songs she had not sung onstage in five years and segueing into garbled versions of rock and roll and folk. She told her friend Rosemary that there was real magic in some of those old melodies, especially the lesser successes of groups like Peter, Paul and Mary and the Kingston Trio. Rosemary laughed at the notion of a mantra in the mundane, but Delia found that after a few dozen repetitions of "The MTA" she could unfocus her eyes and laugh at the desire to drink.

"Oh, he never returned," Delia was singing softly as Randall's head dropped forward and the dark blood gushed one last time. She stopped then. Something may have passed her in the cool morning air, but Delia did not feel it. Focused on the muscles in her neck and upper back, the ones that ached all the time, she wrapped her arms around herself, gripped her shoulders so tightly she started to shake with the effort, and then let go abruptly. The release was luxurious and welcome. A little of the weight lifted, the weight of more than two solid years of trying not to do what she still wanted desperately to do, to sip whiskey until the world turned golden and quiet and safe, until Dede and Amanda Louise, the daughters she had left behind, ceased whispering and whimpering from behind her left ear. She hadn't had a drink since November, and the strain showed.

I'm tired, Delia thought the moment Randall died. A garbage truck rumbled up the narrow alley behind the cottage. A shabby gray cat jumped the fence with a yowl. Delia's neck pulled tight again as a shaft of sunlight cut through the tattered palm fronds by the fence. "I want to go home," she said out loud, and the two girls in her memory lifted their shadowy heads and turned hot eyes in her direction.

Behind Delia, in the little house, ten-year-old Cissy stirred in her sleep and burrowed deeper into the sheets. Her daddy was riding his motorcycle into a red-gold circle of flame. He was laughing and extending his arms high into the bright burning light. He looked so happy that Cissy almost woke up. He hadn't looked happy in so long a time. "Daddy," Cissy whispered, then slipped sideways into a dream of the ocean, the water sweet as the rum and Coke Delia let her sip when she was too drunk to say no.

*   *   *

Rosemary called at nine with the news, but Delia had already heard on the little radio she kept set low in the kitchen that opened onto the garden. Within minutes of the report, she had pulled down all the shades and barricaded the front door with a mound of dead plants and old newspapers, hoping the mess would make the house look empty.

When Cissy got up, Delia gave her daughter a bowl of strawberries and a toasted muffin, watched her eat, and then sat down to tell her girl that Randall was dead.

Cissy laid down her spoon and looked at Delia. "I don't believe you," she said. "You're lying. You'd say anything to keep my daddy away from me."

"Oh, baby, you know that's not true," Delia said.

"No!" Cissy threw off Delia's arm and pushed her away. "It's your fault!" she screamed. "It's your fault! He should have been with us. I hate you!"

Delia said nothing. She had lost count of how many times Cissy had said those words in the last two years, ever since Delia had moved them out of Randall's house. Keeping still and letting Cissy shout had become second nature to her.

Cissy pushed herself back from the table. "You killed him," she said. "You killed my daddy."

"Cissy, please," Delia said. "We're going to need each other now." Delia was still struggling for control. She crossed her arms over her breasts. "And that's no way to talk to me," she told Cissy.

"How am I supposed to talk?" Cissy's tone was sharp and wheedling. "Please, Mama, don't fall down drunk on the floor. Please, Mama, don't pass out at the breakfast table. Or please, Mama, don't forget what day it is and send me to school when nobody's there."

Delia flinched as though she had been struck.

Cissy glared at Delia's pink face. "I hate you," she said. "I hate you more than Satan and all the devils." She turned away to hide the tears she couldn't keep back any longer.

Delia forced herself to look at her daughter. The shape of Cissy's profile seemed to alter as she watched. "You don't even believe in the devil," she said softly.

"Oh yes I do," Cissy sobbed. "I believe in the devil. He's the one made you."

Delia felt the bones in her neck turning to concrete. She wanted to weep at what she saw, the child's face lengthening and closing against her. The left eyelid drooped a little as it had since the accident, but Cissy's eyes were Amanda Louise's eyes, her mouth the exact shape of lost baby Dede's.

Slowly Cissy, the daughter Delia had always sworn was pure Randall and none of her, had grown more and more like the babies Delia had left behind. With every day Delia was sober, Cissy became more pale and cold, more angry and hurt. In Delia's dreams her girls became one creature, one keening source of anguish, one child monster damning her name.

"I hate you," Cissy said, and it was as if Delia's three girls spoke in one voice. "I hate you" became the chorus that slowed Delia's pulse until she felt as if she were swimming a mud tide, the thick scum of her guilt clogging the chambers of her heart. For two solid years, Delia had scoured her own insides trying not to be what she knew she was—hated and deserving hatred in full measure. She had abandoned her babies and spent most of a decade drunk on her butt. Even the daughter she had tried to protect despised her.

Every time she went back to the bottle, Delia sang the same song. She called it the hatred song, the I-deserve-to-die song. It had no words but Cissy's curse, no melody but Delia's own pulse. Sunrise-sunset-goddamn-me-to-hell song. Delia sang it the way she had sung for Mud Dog, with her whole soul and every ounce of her blood. People said that hearing Delia Byrd sing in concert was like hearing heartbreak in a whole new key. Her voice could make you sweat, make you move, make you want to lift your hands and pull justice out of the air. But the song Delia sang inside herself was meaner than anything anyone ever heard onstage. It was almost meaner than she could stand.

* * *

When Rosemary came over that afternoon, Delia was sitting on the hassock near the big leather couch, turning over the same six photographs and humming "Puff the Magic Dragon." Three of the pictures were in color. One showed Delia leaning back against a lazy-eyed Randall, the infant Cissy cradled in her arms. Another showed Cissy at five, riding Randall's neck with a big smile and bigger eyes. The third, dated two years later, captured them in the same pose, but Randall was noticeably thinner, his face gray and lined, and Cissy wore an awkward bandage over her left eye.

The other three photographs were black-and-white snapshots with cracked edges. Delia fingered them tenderly. In the top one she was holding a baby exactly as she held Cissy in the color photo. A solemn-faced toddler was beside her, and leaning in over her shoulder was a man with washed-out features and stunned, angry eyes. Delia put her thumb over his face and stopped singing. "Damn you," she said, and looked up to find Rosemary watching her.

Without a word Rosemary picked up the two remaining photos. That man—Clint Windsor—lifting the toddler, Amanda, in front of a small frame house with a bare dirt yard and a porch half shaded by an awkwardly hung madras bedspread; and then baby Amanda, with her wispy blond hair pulled staight up into a knot at the top of her head, and baby Dede, hair just as blond and fine barely visible in the faded photograph, the two bracketing a dark-haired older woman whose hands were linked into a clumsy praying fist. The woman's eyes were on her hands, but the girls were looking straight out at the camera, eyes enormous and fixed.

"What are you going to do now, honey?" Rosemary asked, handing Delia the photos.

"Go home," Delia told her. "I'm going home to get my babies." From the back of the house came the sound of Cissy's heartbroken weeping.

"Oh, Delia." Rosemary shook her head. "Lord, girl, you do not want to do that. Those children are half grown now. They an't seen you in more than ten years. Nobody there is going to welcome you, honey."

"You don't know that. I got people there. I got friends." Delia rose suddenly, nearly overturning the hassock. "And they're my girls. I'm their mother. That don't go away. They'll be mad at me, yeah. But I can handle that. I been handling it here."

"But you got Cissy to think about, Delia." Rosemary looked toward the back of the house. "Listen to her. She's just lost her daddy, and you know how she is about Randall. Child thinks everything that happened is her fault, that he never done nothing wrong in his life. Take some time, Delia. Take some time and let yourself think about what you're going to do."

"I am thinking about Cissy. I'm thinking about all my girls." Delia's shoulders were shaking. The pictures in her hand crumpled as she tugged her elbows in tight to her abdomen.

"Rosemary, this is what I'm meant to do," Delia said. "It's what I should have done years ago. I don't belong here. I never have. Whatever I loved in the music an't got nothing to do with living here. I hate Los Angeles. It's the outer goddamn circle of hell."

Rosemary bit her lip. Delia's face was red and sweaty, but she did not smell of drink. She smelled of fever and grief and salty outrage.

"Honey," Rosemary said, and put her hand on Delia's wire-taut shoulder. "All I'm saying is you don't have to rush things. Just give Cissy a chance to absorb what's happened." But Delia was not listening. She's going to leave, Rosemary thought. She's going to go back to Cayro and fight those crazy people for her daughters. Her hand on Delia's shoulder reluctantly stroked and soothed. She looked down at the creased pictures in Delia's hand, the two girls' faces as bleak as her friend's.

"Oh, Delia," Rosemary said one more time. "Please, just take a little while to think."

The funeral made all the papers. All and all, it was a decorous affair. The Columbia Records executive who called about sending a car for

Delia was astonished when she told him she was not going. "I'm not about to let you see me crying," she said. "Let them take pictures of that girl Randall nearly killed, get a shot of her without her teeth." But in the end, though she told Rosemary she would rather have chewed dirt than put on that black dress and drive over to the church in Glendale, Delia could not refuse the grieving Cissy. A plot at Forest Lawn had been donated, but no one could swear that Randall would wind up there. Booger, solidly sober and twice the size he was when he had been with the band, drove down from Oregon to handle the arrangements for the burial and he was stubbornly closemouthed about what exactly would happen to Randall's body. "Leave that to me," he said. "Just leave it to me."

"Bet he's going to haul Randall's corpse out to the Mojave Desert and cremate him over brittlebush and dried yucca," Rosemary told Delia.

"That'd be about right," Delia said, but kept her voice low so Cissy wouldn't hear.

Cissy cried all through Booger's mumbled eulogy and the unfamiliar service. Delia sat dry-eyed and silent. Some of the band members stood up to speak, but they kept it brief. Delia kept expecting someone to say what they were all thinking—that Randall's death was as close to suicide as made no difference, that half of them had not spoken to him in the last year and the other half only when they needed money, but all the speakers looked over at Randall's sobbing child and visibly rethought their remarks. There was more "God bless" than "goddamn," and people joined in on the gospel songs with real emotion. It was as close to a Pentecostal service as could be managed in an L.A. Episcopal church.

"Wasn't too bad," Delia told Booger on the steps after, and he nodded in agreement. They both knew Rosemary and a few of the band members from the early days had chosen the music, mostly blues, and the flowers—great stands of gladiolas and ridiculously cheerful giant sunflowers imported from Brazil. "One last thing we can charge to the record company," Rosemary said with a big grin.

They had also managed to block the sermon the minister was determined to deliver.

"Randall weren't exactly religious," one of the brass players told the minister, prompting boisterous laughter from the other band members.

Standing on the steps, everyone said the same thing. "Wasn't too bad."

"Not at all."

The wake was something else again. Rosemary described it to Delia contemptuously as a goddamned carnival. "Rock and roll is dead" was the refrain, and the catering was done by a discount liquor mart. Most of those who came were already drunk or stoned when they arrived, their faces slack and eyes sheathed protectively in black shades. It was a mistake, one of the Columbia guys said, holding the event at Randall's place. Rosemary agreed. All of the old band members left in the first few hours. The open house drew the new crowd, the roadies and session players, the dealers and users who had been Randall's constant companions, and all those women who had trooped in and out of the house since Delia moved out.

"Rock and Roll is DEAD!" the crowd shouted repeatedly all evening. The drunks got angrier by the hour. People wandered through the house, picking up mementos and just as often setting them down. Around midnight someone dropped the crystal guitar Randall had been given after Mud Dog passed the half-million mark with *Diamonds and Dust*. The accident sparked a general melee, people smashing things just for the satisfaction of watching glass fly.

"Where's Delia?" one of the drunks demanded.

"Oh, she's pretty broke up," he was told.

"Well, goddamn it, so am I!"

Ignoring the weeping girls and cursing men, Rosemary went upstairs to look through Randall's closets. The seventeen-year-old who had been on the back of the bike swore at her awkwardly with her broken mouth but could do nothing with her pitiful hands encased in casts. Rosemary went about collecting what she had come for: all the pictures of Delia and Cissy, and a few pieces of jewelry from the big teak box on the burl table where Randall had always thrown his things.

Downstairs, a late-news repeat of a Reagan speech came on the television after the videotape of the funeral coverage clicked off. Those thin lips moved soundlessly while the roadies roared obscenities and poured beer into the back of the big-screen television set. When it finally blew up, everyone laughed helplessly as sparks sprayed the rug. Rosemary skirted the smoldering carpet as she left. The fire that flared up just before dawn probably started in that rug, abetted by the thirty or forty candles set up all over the living room with its gossamer curtains. The revelers swore the fire was Randall's creation, the flames trailing behind the ghost they saw walking the rooms in that dawn hour.

"He took his house," a roadie told the reporter from *Rolling Stone*. "He took it right down to hell."

Already Randall was becoming a legend, magnified into what he had never been, the Doomed Prince of Rock and Roll. Snakeskin boots and suede jacket, dark glasses and flashing teeth—the ghost of Randall Pritchard took the house down, his last act leading that crippled girl onto the lawn before he sparked out in the smoke and stink of the morning. The record company knew what it had. They quickly issued a memorial edition of *Diamonds and Dust* that sold far more than the first printing. The new cover was all Randall, snakeskin and teeth and night. Delia and the band were cropped and gone.

"Randall would have loved it," Delia said when Rosemary finished her account of the wake. She was sorting Cissy's clothes and drinking black coffee, her face puffy from tears and pale from lack of sleep. Since Randall's death, her talisman songs had sunk to wordless hums and whispers, snatches of folk and Laura Nyro and Spanish lullabies Randall had taught her when Cissy was born. She still hadn't had a drink, but there was no sense of accomplishment in the act. It felt to

Delia that if she did not get on the road, the beast would reclaim her and she would go down to the beach with a bottle. Going home was the answer. Making amends, getting her girls, that was the answer. It was all she could think about, all she would let herself think about.

"Cayro," she told Rosemary. "When I get to Cayro, I'll be all right."

Rosemary nodded, knowing better than to argue with a desperate woman. Somewhere in Delia, grief was waiting, and when it hit, she would wilt like all those flowers in the heat of the church. Then she would need someone to prop her up, and who was there in Cayro to take that on? Rosemary shuddered. No, not even for Delia would she move to Georgia. Whatever was going to happen would just have to happen.

"Hell, girl," Rosemary drawled in a deliberately exaggerated Valley accent, "you and I both know Randall would have preferred that all of Venice Beach go up." She gestured at the *Times,* where a news photo showed the blackened frame of Randall's house. "Man always did have a taste for that scorched-earth scenario. If the Columbia building burned down, he'd probably come back to piss on the pyre."

Delia laughed, then shot a guilty look at Cissy, who was sitting on the couch in a daze, sucking on a strand of her dirty red hair and hugging a silver-framed photo of her daddy that Rosemary had brought her. She had sworn she would not cry anymore, though that was all she wanted to do. She had also decided to ignore Delia, but that was proving harder still. Her mother had been packing like a madwoman, stripping the books off the shelves and the prints off the wall, giving everything that would not fit in the car to Rosemary. She talked continually about going home, as if Cissy was supposed to be happy at the idea. Now she came over to the couch and began her litany again.

"Don't worry, baby. It will all be different in Cayro," Delia said. "It an't like here. People are different there. They care about each other, take time to talk to each other. They don't lie or cheat or mess with each other all the time. They're not scared, not having to be so careful all the time. They know who they are, what is important. And you'll be with your sisters. You won't be alone, honey. Not being alone in the world, that's something you've never had. That's something I can give you."

"I won't go," Cissy said, the same futile words she had hurled at Delia when they moved to Venice Beach.

"You'll be happier there." Delia's eyes glittered like the rocks near the ocean. "It will be like I always wanted it to be. You and me, Amanda and Dede, all of us together. Your only living kin in the world are in Cayro, yours and mine, your sisters, your granddaddy."

Cissy hugged Randall's photograph tighter and looked at Rosemary like a cornered animal.

"Your sisters," Delia said fiercely. "Your sisters are going to be amazed how much you look like them. You won't believe it yourself." A tear glistened at the edge of her left eye, hovered briefly, and slipped down her cheek.

Cissy kept her focus on that wet streak. Her sisters. Amanda and Dede. Dede and Amanda. There had never been a time when Cissy did not know their names, how terribly Delia grieved for them. The lost girls, the precious ones. Delia was always saying that Cissy's hazel eyes were the mirror of Amanda's, her red-blond hair the exact shade of Dede's when she was an infant. Birthday presents, Christmas presents, Easter baskets, back-to-school packages, all testified to the same legend: "From your sisters." "From Amanda." "From Dede." "Until we see you." "See you soon."

What was Cissy to believe? That the sisters she had never met dreamed of her, wrapped those presents, and signed those cards? No. The same packages and tokens were sent in her name, and Cissy knew how little she cared. She signed at Delia's direction, printing out the message Delia dictated in careful block letters, impersonal and precise. The tears, the passion were all Delia's. She never seemed to notice how Cissy turned her face away at the mention of Amanda and Dede.

"Oh, Cissy." Delia's voice was thick and husky. "It is going to be so good to get home. You'll see. You'll see."

Cissy put her lips to the metal edge of the picture frame, tasting the sweet alloy with the tip of her tongue. She had loved to climb up Randall's back and press her face into his neck. Her daddy had always tasted smoky and sweet, like no one else in the world. When Delia had hugged her tight at the funeral, her neck tasted like flat beer. She could stay sober forever and it wouldn't matter. Bitter and mean, that was how Delia tasted. Cissy looked over at her mother and sucked harder at the metal against her tongue.

"When we get to Cayro, I'll call you from Granddaddy Byrd's," Delia was saying to Rosemary, who was looking at Cissy's blank face, as empty as the wall behind her.

Cissy knew about Cayro. Cayro was where her crazy mother was born, the back end of the earth. Cayro was the last place Randall Pritchard's daughter ever wanted to be.

"I won't go," Cissy murmured again.

Delia put her arms around Rosemary's neck. "Oh God," she said. "This time I'm going to make it right."

Rock and roll, in Delia's opinion, might as well have died back in 1976, when Mud Dog stopped touring. That was the year Randall trashed his agent's office and spent a couple of weeks drying out at a sanitarium in Palm Springs. By 1978, the year the Rolling Stones cut a disco track, Randall had gone off whiskey and settled into what he called his Keith Richards solution, boosting his heroin with just enough speed to keep himself mobile and charming. Columbia was coaxed into putting Delia back on contract and financing another studio rental, but that spring Randall flipped the T-bird in Topanga Canyon, nearly blinded Cissy, and broke the last of Delia's love for him.

When she decided to leave Randall, Delia told him to his face. She thought of writing him a letter, but what she wanted to say would sound absurd on a page. Dear Randall, you almost killed us. Dear Randall, you're on your own. Dear Randall, you've broken my heart. Instead she tracked him down at the studio annex, where he had one of his girls with him, a child not even twenty and stoned out of her mind.

"You got a name?" Delia said when she came to the door.

The girl just blinked.

"Go get Randall," Delia told her.

A few minutes later Randall came out, his pupils huge and glassy. He stood in the sunlight and gave her that grin of his.

"What's up, sweet thing?"

"I'm moving out."

"Moving?"

"We can't live with you no more."

"Damn, Delia." He squirmed inside his loose denim jacket. "Don't I take care of you? Don't I treat you and Cissy right?"

Delia looked at him until he blushed, but his smile never faded.

"There's that house in Venice Beach," he said finally. "That one Booger and me bought. It's pretty messy, but it's empty. Booger didn't like the neighborhood. We could clean it up. You could go there."

Delia hesitated and looked away. The girl was watching them from the annex. "All right," Delia said, "all right."

"Do you need anything?" Randall asked, one hand pulling money out of a pocket.

She shook her head.

"Ah, Delia." Her name was thick in his mouth. "Honey," he said, slurring even that.

For a moment Delia hated him. She wasn't just another girl he'd picked up on the street. She was the mother of his child, the woman who had thrown everything away for him. He had no right speaking her name with that sleepy smile. She stood there and let him see the contempt on her face.

Randall held out the bills. Delia slapped him hard, then bent forward to kiss his cheek. The smell of his skin startled her.

"I'm sorry," he said.

The whole time she was packing, Cissy sobbing in her bedroom, Delia kept wiping her face and remembering how Randall smelled that day, the tang of him. What surprised her was how little pain his death caused her. He had been dead to her so long that it was hard to mourn all over again, hard to keep in mind that all the time when they had so rarely seen him he had been going on with his dying. Somehow, in the middle of everyone else's living, Randall had given up on his own life and started dying. That he had nearly taken Delia and Cissy with him was what stayed with Delia, the memory of shattered glass burning her skin, and the smell of the man she loved turning bitter. He had never expected her to get sober or leave him. He had never expected anything to change.

Delia taped a box shut and kicked it hard. She had loved Randall from the first time she saw that angel smile bright under the spotlights. It had seemed a miracle when he pulled her up into his tour bus, the blood from her abraded palms black on his cream shirt.

"Girl," he had said. "Lord, darling, look at you."

Delia's memories of that moment were as golden and smoky as two inches of whiskey in a thick tumbler. Jim Beam in a bar glass, a mound of crushed ice in a hand towel, the pervasive aroma of marijuana and patchouli oil. From the instant Randall helped her into the bus, Delia felt numbed and fragile. The whiskey he gave her warmed her belly, while the icy glass soothed her bruised temple. But it was Randall's soft embrace that made the difference, the open, easy way he wrapped her around. She shouldn't have trusted him, shouldn't have been willing to let him touch her with the mark of Clint's rage darkening steadily along the line of her face and neck. Maybe it was the whiskey. Maybe it was the bus wheels spinning clean and sure, taking her away from the nightmare behind her. Maybe it was that she had been wanting to run away for so long. But maybe it was just Randall and the way he had about him.

Delia wanted to scream at the figure in her memory, at Randall's body so long gone, so much of him wasted even when he was alive. He had been so beautiful when he took her in his arms, so strong and tender when she was so hurt. He had felt like the one man on earth she could hang on to and be safe with. How could she not have loved him? She loved him more than her life.

After the accident in Topanga Canyon, trying repeatedly to get sober, Delia stopped going over to Randall's place at all. Even when she slipped back into drinking, she wouldn't let herself be cajoled into climbing into one of the limos sent around by record companies hoping to sign her to sing on her own. She didn't like the parties anymore, and she'd never enjoyed talking business. Drunk or sober, Delia lived in the small town in her heart, ignoring the world in which all her love had turned to grief.

Once they moved to Venice Beach, Delia tried to behave as if it were just another small town too, a place like Cayro. It did not matter that behind her house loomed thousands of others, postage-stamp boxes layered across Los Angeles County up from Santa Monica or south to Long Beach and all the little suburbs that trailed down to San Diego. Delia rarely went outside her neighborhood, and as long as she stayed off the highways, she could pretend they were cut off from the world. When she took Cissy over to Randall's place in West Hollywood or went to the studio annex in Santa Monica, the sight of greater Los Angeles stunned her. The glass structures along Wilshire, the grotesque mansions in Beverly Hills, the interlaced freeways that Randall prowled, none of that was Delia's world. Her world was the cottage and its tiny garden, the convenience store a few blocks west, and Cissy's school two blocks past that, with the occasional trip down to Rosemary's in Marina Del Rey.

"It's strange. Every time I take a drink, I go back in time," Delia told Rosemary not long after she left Randall. "I imagine I am back on the bus, going nowhere in particular, just cruising with the band."

"Uh-huh." Rosemary blew smoke out her nose. "Cruising back to the toilet to puke your guts out and curse Randall with every heave of your stomach? I remember you pregnant and sick as a dog. I remember those bus trips."

Delia pushed a strand of hair out of her eyes and shrugged. "In my imagination," she said, "it's always 1971 and we are all young and happy. It's like a dream, a good dream."

Rosemary shook her head. "Nothing like the dream life, huh?"

Delia was the only member of Mud Dog who had loved the road.

While everyone else grew pale and exhausted, she blossomed, catching naps during the day and sleeping easily backstage. She drank a lot but ate little, mostly fruit and rice, and avoided the pills and powders that kept half the band wired and sleepless and sick as dogs. In the midst of the tour chaos, Delia was serene. She would drift up the middle of the overloaded bus with a smile and a bottle in her hand, trailing her long fingers over the greasy Formica storage cabinets as if they were flowers and sweet-smelling vines. Sometimes she just stood there, steadying herself with one hand, eyes almost closed. To her it seemed like dancing, balancing there while the bus swayed and rolled along. She would laugh at the thought of herself almost motionless yet hurtling forward.

What Delia did not love were the motels and the parties, the obsequious roadies dealing drugs behind the luggage vans, the hysterical fans who pounced on her before she could get away. There were always people coming up on her from behind, wanting to talk or to touch her, following her every move so closely she would start to shy away even from Randall or Rosemary or Booger, or Little Jimmy the drummer with his shy nudge. Her skin seemed to wear thin, to the point where she hesitated sometimes before following the band out onstage. After a while the road wore you down until you lost the satisfaction of the music everyone came to hear, and Delia knew that the only thing she loved without reservation was the music in her head. The road itself, the two-lane blacktop and the six-lane freeways, the truck stops where the only things you could be sure of were the eggs and the bottled beer, that was not something you loved. The road was something that took you over unawares—the unexpected poetry of road signs and the reassuring glint of reflective markers counting off miles, the backbeat of the wheels whooshing along the asphalt and the song it awakened in the back of Delia's head. She got drunk on the road the same way she did on whiskey, a gentle drunk, an easy binge, smiling and loose and careless as death on two legs.

Delia dreamed on the bus like nowhere else, humming with the wheels, drifting, her eyelids open just enough to catch the shine of the road lights. In that condition, neither asleep nor awake, Delia dreamed of home, of Cayro and Amanda and Dede. Sometimes she dreamed of them in their bodies, the babies growing into girls while she watched and cared for them. When she dreamed that dream, she would weep with relief as everything that had happened after Dede's birth erased itself. In that dream there was no band, no house in Venice Beach, no Cissy, no third girl child with Randall's lazy mouth and her own dark red hair. In that dream Delia was the good mother kneeling on the clay path near her old house in Cayro, her fingers cupping Dede's baby face and her tears burning her own cheeks.

Sometimes the dream would play out the years differently, Delia sweeping in like an angel the week after she climbed into Randall's bus and ran away. In that dream she snatched up her babies, pulling them to her throat as their arms reached to embrace her, her shoulders sprouting wings that carried them all high and far, like the Santa Ana winds over Southern California.

"Mama," the dream girls would say in one voice, "Mama," and Delia's heart would lurch in her breast. The dream children cried her name and held on to her: "Mama. We knew you would come." Their cheeks were hot and flushed, their hair smelling earthy and sweet, the way Delia's palms smelled when she worked in the garden. She breathed them in and felt her insides tremble as the scent filled her. But the arms that reached out to Delia were phantom arms. The dream daughters were ghost girls, imaginary creatures. The road that went everywhere never went to Cayro. As the scent faded, Delia would jerk awake, her face streaked with tears and her muscles straining to hold what was not there.

Sober and fully conscious, Delia knew these dreams for what they were, a comforting lie. If her daughters dreamed of her, they would not be loving dreams. Raging, angry nightmares, that's what her girls would dream of Delia. But in the weeks after Randall's death, she dreamed again her road dreams, Dede and Amanda Louise dreams, Mama dreams, guilt and hope dreams.

Emptying the closets of the little cottage, Delia picked at the raw sore of her conscience. It had been ten years. Dede and Amanda were not babies. They were eleven and thirteen, nearly grown, but what if they didn't hate her? What if her girls hoped for her as much as she hoped for them? From "what if" she fell to maybe, then to might be, could be, oh God! surely so. It was the way Delia thought when she was drinking, as detached from the real as anything could be. It was the voice in the back brain, the voice that swore one drink would not kill her and another was all right too. The devil or desperation, that voice whispered steadily and drew her on. Delia swore she would never drink again, but her girls were not liquor. Her girls were real. Cayro was real. Cayro was home. Maybe no one could earn forgiveness, but listening to that whisper, Delia Byrd packed everything she owned and decided to try.

Chapter 2

To Cissy it always seemed that one minute they were in the little bungalow with the bright pink flowers around the windows, and the next they were flying down the highway with all their stuff piled up in the backseat of the old Datsun.

They left before dawn fifteen days after Randall died. Delia shut the front door, pushed the key through the mail slot, and turned to Cissy with a smile. "All right, we're gone."

Cissy stared at her in outraged grief and refused to climb into the car. "I won't go!" she said in her refrain.

Almost before the words were out of Cissy's mouth, Delia picked her up as easily as the boxes and bags she had been hefting, and tossed her onto the passenger seat. She slammed the car door and glared briefly into the window.

Shocked, Cissy curled up on the seat. Delia had never hit her, never spanked her. Even when she was drinking, she had religiously taken the time to talk her daughter out of bad behavior. Reason, she always said. You have to use reason. This was past reason. This was madness. Cissy stared helplessly back at the little house. It had been her home for two years, the only place where she felt safe. That Delia was taking her away from it was incomprehensible. The act was one in Cissy's mind with her daddy's death, her whole world ruptured and remade in a design she could not puzzle out. When Delia turned off Venice Boulevard and took the ramp up to Highway 10, Cissy began to sob into her fists.

"For God's sake," Delia said in a smooth, tired voice. "There's no reason to cry."

Four months sober showed in Delia's face. All the puffiness was gone, but her eyes were shadowy, and there were new lines etched at the corners of her mouth. She had started smoking again and had hacked her long red-blond hair short the night before. She told herself that everything would be fine as soon as they got on the road, that by the time they got to Cayro she would know what to do next.

When Cissy went on crying and the engine made that familiar knocking sound, Delia paid no mind. She hummed to herself and kept her eyes on the road. The knocking diminished, but every time the speed dropped below 35, the front end would start to shimmy. "It'll be fine once it warms up," Delia said cheerfully. When she lost patience with the car and Cissy's sobbing, she beat her palms on the braided-leather steering wheel cover, missing as often as she hit, slamming her hands down on her thighs with satisfaction. "We're going home. Goddamn it, just shut up, we're going home!" Delia pounded on the wheel and revved the engine, keeping her face pointed straight toward Georgia.

"Put your glasses on," Delia said, shifting gears while Cissy wiped her eyes.

"I'm all right."

"Put your glasses on!"

Cissy scowled, but dug in the bag at her feet until she found the glasses. As much as she hated them, they cut the glare and eased her burning eyes.

Delia sucked angrily at her cigarette and blew smoke out the window. "I swear, Cissy, you'll do anything to get to me. You know you need to wear your glasses in this bright light. It's not going to do either of us any good when you're laying back with a sick headache."

Cissy kicked at the bag on the floor. She already had a sick headache from watching the road roll by, the exit signs looming up and passing.

Highway 10 was first the Santa Monica Freeway and then the San Bernardino Freeway, and then just Highway 10 again. "It will be 10 for a long time," Delia told Cissy. "All the way to Tempe."

The highway was raised for a long stretch, and Cissy could look into people's backyards, tiny green gardens hidden under bushy trees, garages and clotheslines and lawn furniture. It was like all her dreams of catching a ride and running away, looking down on the everyday world where people could only look up and see her pass by. Cissy's fantasies had buzzed with excitement and pleasure and contempt for the people below. Now she was the one who wanted to stop, to grab a mile marker and pull herself back to earth.

The exit sign for San Diego flashed by, and Cissy remembered the rare times she had been allowed on the bus with Randall and Delia and the band. Mostly she had been left behind with Sonny and Patch, to eat healthy food and sleep in the trundle bed with their boy, Wren. It had been exile, no matter that Randall swore it was for her own good and Delia insisted the road was no place for a child. For years Cissy dreamed of traveling, of eating the fried cheese sandwiches Booger made on the propane stove and stopping at diners in the middle of the night, of watching people stare openmouthed at the big blue bus while she sat on her daddy's lap. The bus was another country, one where Delia smiled and sipped whiskey and combed out Randall's hair and plaited Cissy's into a thin shiny braid. Peaceful, the bus was peaceful, the lights always low and music always playing, two or three different tape players going all the time. It was paradise to a child, and Cissy never forgave Randall or Delia for banishing her from the bus. Her fantasies of running away were always road trips where her feet barely reached the pedals of some big wide-seated vehicle with sleek dark windows and a radio that never stopped playing all her daddy's old songs. Somewhere Delia was crying her name and grieving, Randall was writing a song about losing what he had never known he could not live without. On the road Cissy-child was making her own song, riding a smooth, glossy braid of highway, licking grease off her fingers and swinging her hair to the beat of a band that would someday be her own.

When the freeway dropped down, there was one shopping center after another, Mexican restaurants and discount shoe stores, gas stations and little markets with bright kite shapes in the windows. But gradually green overtook the shops, trees became thicker as they moved out into the valley. After an hour the process reversed itself as the trees thinned to desert landscape. When they reached Palm Springs, the green came back again, but the landscape made Cissy's eyes ache and she kept pushing her glasses up on her sweaty face. Delia didn't stop for gas until the needle hit empty. Cissy got a Coke and a bag of Doritos. If Delia had stopped at a diner, Cissy wouldn't have had the heart to order grilled cheese. This was not the road as she had dreamed it.

"We're making good time," Delia said when Cissy came back to the car. She waved at the bright sky. "And look at that. Not a cloud in sight. April is the best time for this trip. No snow but not too hot. It should be clear all the way."

Cissy licked the powdery orange surface of a Dorito and bit off the triangle corners one at a time before eating the part that was left. Then she took a sip of Coke and began the ritual again.

Delia shrugged and turned on the radio, spinning the dial for something cheerful. Christopher Cross's "Sailing" was playing on two of the stations. "Nothing like a hit," she drawled. It was the kind of music Delia hated, with lyrics that could mean anything and therefore meant nothing. That roar of sound behind Cross's plaintive wail would have bothered Randall, all muddy brass instruments so loud the notes were indistinguishable. He'd once kicked over the stereo when Rosemary had put on a Rod Stewart album. "Son of a bitch needs a strong bass line," Delia muttered, then looked over at Cissy, who was still munching Doritos. Delia sighed and twisted the dial until she found a disc jockey doing an all-day tribute to John Lennon. "All right," she said, but after a few miles it became obvious that the guy was only playing the *Double Fantasy* album and making the obligatory rude comments about Yoko Ono.

"Son of a bitch. Man's only been dead a few months and already they're talking bad about her again. A rock-and-roll widow. Everyone thinks she might as well be dead if she's not going to turn herself into a priestess for the man that's gone." Delia had never met John Lennon, but she had once watched Yoko sit patiently through the kind of numbing interview she had never been able to stand. She turned the dial again and stopped at a surfer channel doing a reprise of Beach Boys and Jan and Dean hits, "Little Deuce Coupe" sung in a resolute falsetto.

After Palm Springs, there were Indian names everywhere. Reservation signs appeared past Indian Wells and Indio, billboards that promised turquoise and authentic native pottery, and giant lush renditions of Las Vegas showgirls in rhinestones and little else. The Cabazon Indian Reservation sign had been knocked sideways near one that announced the Colorado River Aqueduct. Cissy wondered if the aqueduct really had water in it. How could there be water under ground so flat and white and stony? A cloud of yellow dust rose, and Cissy's eyes burned. She looked back at the shadowy basin where a pipe jutted out from the sand. People lived on the street. Some even slept in culverts. Was that where she would wind up? Sleeping in ditches with Delia and stealing hamburger scraps from the garbage cans outside McDonald's?

"So much desert," she said. She could see her face in the side-view mirror. The whites of her eyes were crossed with tiny red lines like the map on the seat beside her.

"Oh, this isn't the real desert." Delia skimmed sweat from under her eyes with her left forefinger. "Wait until New Mexico. That's real desert. Saguaros and tumbleweeds. Every time I see those Roadrunner and Coyote cartoons, I think of New Mexico."

"I got to pee." Cissy kept her eyes on the mirror.

"Oh, for God's sake, Cissy. It can't be much more than an hour since the last stop!"

Cissy turned to stare at Delia.

Delia floored the gas pedal. "You can pee in Arizona, damn it. I'm not stopping again until we're out of California."

Arizona was much like California, more wide-open baked desert landscape. But just off the road near Quartzsite there was a vast parking lot and a big aluminum sign announcing a rock market. The lot was bumper-to-bumper, and cars were parked all along the highway. Delia slowed and pulled into a Chevron station. She climbed out of the car, rubbing her back.

"You can pee here," she said. "And don't go nowhere." She limped toward the station with money in her hand.

Cissy started toward the adobe walls of the building, shit brown and crumbly, with little bits of grass sticking out all over. Dusty logs protruded from the walls a few feet above the doors, some sporting faded orange pennants hanging limply from yellow plastic cords. A Coke cooler was sitting open and empty next to the bathroom door. Cissy held her breath and went inside.

She was surprised at how clean the bathroom was. The sink shone silver and white, and the paper towels had green borders. A dark purple plastic vase contained a spray of paper leaves in autumnal shades of orange and brown. A bright poster for a kachina exhibit at the University of Arizona covered one wall. Cissy quickly went about her business and washed her hands, sniffing but not using the eucalyptus-scented soap on the counter. When she stepped outside, she saw Delia standing at the open hood of the Datsun with a mechanic who was holding the oil gauge and shaking his head.

There was a loud pop, and Cissy turned to see a bunch of red and blue balloons tied to the Rockhound Camping sign, bouncing in the warm gusts that swept trash along the ground. The balloons were faded, though not so much as the blankets and tarps that shaded the camper vans. The desert was a place full of color, but it was a whole different palette from what Cissy knew, everything bright bleached to a smoky pastel. Cissy could see row after row of flea-market stalls past the vans. People moved through the dust as she watched. A few flat, seamed faces turned in her direction. Without thought, Cissy walked toward them. These were ageless people, tanned dark, with black or white or gray hair and ropy muscles on sturdy bones. Many sat on lawn chairs in front of mobile homes, behind card tables displaying dishes and strings of roughly polished rocks. Cissy stopped under a blue tarp shading a table stacked with glittery stones. She touched a strand of dark red.

"Red tourmaline." The woman's breath smelled of anise and lemons. She grinned at Cissy, revealing big, perfect teeth.

"Where do you get them?" Cissy could not imagine where all this rough beauty had come from. Hundreds of strings of beads of every gradation of red and black were piled in front of her, fifty or sixty beads to a string, twenty or forty strings knotted together, all arranged so that they lay in sensuous curves like giant snakes covered with gemstones.

The woman lifted her shoulders and bobbed her head, riffling the pink scarf that was tucked under the band of her eyeshade. Her whole body seemed to quiver and bounce on springy thighs.

"Go all over. Trade. Buy at discount, sell at a little less discount." She angled her head at the camper behind her. "Sometimes get something wonderful, never sell it at all." She lifted one hand to a polished oblong of jade at her throat, green with yellow light trapped inside. Cissy leaned over to see the stone more closely.

"You like?" the woman said. She grinned again and reached up to push her teeth back in more tightly. "You got good a eye. What you want?"

Cissy looked down at the table. There were beads cut in odd shapes, stars and moons and faceted balls. She put her hand on a string of black stars. It was warm and almost soft under her fingertips.

"Good eye. Volcano spit from Italy, bloodrock from Tennessee. Nice for not much money." The woman nodded crisply, then caught Cissy's shoulder and pulled the girl in close to her face. She sniffed three times, quickly and deeply, and let her air out in one long breath. "Ah." She smiled and released Cissy.

"Black diamond is good heart stone." The woman gripped a jagged piece of hematite and dragged it across the white paper beneath it. Two thin red lines followed the stone.

"Oh." Cissy resisted the urge to back away from the table.

"Scratch with it, it scratches red. Grind it, make blood ink. Heart sign." The hand dropped the stone, lifted, spread, and hovered over the piles of strings. The sharp eyes came up and looked directly into

Cissy's face. Green eyes, Cissy saw, faded a little, like the grass near the spigots under the camper's tie-down. The woman smiled as if she could hear Cissy thinking.

"What you like, moon or stars?" The hand wavered.

"Stars." Randall had a hatband studded with silver stars. The hematite burned silver-black in the sun.

"Ah." The old woman thumped the card table, and all the stones moved. "Hematite is special. Egyptian mummies had headrests made of hematite. You know that? Special. Draw your hatred out." She gathered a string of cut stars, lifted it, and extended her hand. Cissy looked into the green eyes.

"Heal your heart, girl."

Cissy walked back to the car with a string of stars looped twice around her neck.

"Where the hell have you been? And where did you get that?" Delia snarled the words, relenting only when she saw Cissy's face fall. "It's nice," she said. "Common as dirt, but nice."

Mine, Cissy thought, flushing. She fingered the stones as she curled up against the passenger door. The necklace still felt warm and soft, but when she tried to press a nail into the shiny surface of one of the stones, it took no mark.

The engine growled loud when Delia started the Datsun. Maybe it won't last, Cissy thought. Maybe it will stall and we'll have to stay here. Her eyes, when they showed above her glasses, were obsidian in the hot light. Maybe we will wreck, she was thinking. Maybe she'll run us off the road and roll the car. Her hand stroked the seat belt where it snugged into her belly. Delia's belt was lying unfastened beside her on the folded map. Maybe she will go through the window, break her neck or cut her throat. If she were dead I could . . . What? Cissy's stomach cramped so hard, she almost retched.

Cissy twisted around and watched the parking lot and all the campers slowly dwindle away. A sign for Big Horn Trailer Park loomed up, stained red and tan with dust and blown sand. Cissy wondered if it was named for Little Bighorn, where Custer died. Cowboys and Indians, she thought, and rubbed her eyes.

"We'll have to cut up toward Flagstaff," Delia said. "Drive the long way through the Navajo reservation. Monument Valley is up there, the Painted Desert and the Petrified Forest. We'll be able to see some of the hills from 40. All those cliffs against the sky. If there's any moon, it will take your breath away."

Cissy kept her face turned to the window.

"Randall and I went up to Monument Valley once." Delia's voice was careful. "It's amazing. Like an open cathedral. Something to see."

Cissy watched the sign for Buckeye coming up on the left. A cathedral, she thought. She looked out at the far red rocks, the purple and gray mountains in the distance. It was all a cathedral, open and pure and wide as death.

Delia took 17 up through Phoenix to pick up Highway 40. She spread the map to show Cissy the route. "This will take us most of the way. Forty is like Ten, goes on forever. From here to Nashville anyway."

Cissy remained silent, and Delia put on the radio again. Twice she found stations playing Mud Dog, but twisted the dial past them as quickly as she could. She didn't want to hear any of that. She found a stubborn rock station in Tempe playing Captain Beefheart and Steely Dan as if no one had ever died, and settled on that one as long as it would come in.

Late that afternoon they crossed Arizona into New Mexico and Cissy saw more and more Indian names. After Gallup there were Laguna Pueblo signs, with little hand-tinted posters advertising good turquoise jewelry and traditional blankets. Was Albuquerque another Indian name? Maybe it was Spanish. It didn't matter. Delia told Cissy to close her eyes and take a nap. She wasn't going to stop just to sleep.

* * *

Cissy dreamed of culverts and big concrete pipes, of stars and moons shining in black water, and of dark-haired women bending to scoop up beads of tears. She woke up with her eyes crusted and swollen when Delia stopped near Tucumcari. They had been making good time in the good weather, but both of them were tired and sticky with dried sweat. When the Datsun fishtailed in the slipstream of a passing semi, Delia noticed that her arms and legs were starting to feel rubbery and numb. She realized suddenly that they had not had anything but chips and Cokes since leaving Los Angeles that morning. New Mexico was dotted with diners and low mud-brown stucco buildings that proclaimed themselves "family restaurants." Delia chose a big truck stop and pulled in close to where the semis were parked.

Salad of iceberg lettuce and tomato quarters with cubes of bright yellow cheese, chicken chili, and Texas toast. Cissy gave the food all her attention and drank three glasses of iced tea. Delia picked at her scrambled eggs and stared longingly at the men drinking beer at the bar.

"We'll get to Amarillo by midnight," she told Cissy.

"Why are you in such a hurry?" Cissy's necklace glowed red-black against her throat in the fluorescent lights.

Delia used her napkin to wipe condensation off her tea glass. "Your Granddaddy Byrd is expecting us." She looked into the glass.

Cissy put her fork down. "You called him?"

"He's expecting us," Delia said again. "Cissy, please. All I have ever wanted you to know is that you are not alone in the world."

The table was dark wood shellacked so thickly that Delia could see her reflection in the surface. Her face looked like it was underwater, slightly out of focus, the murky image of a woman who had never known how to say what she was thinking. She remembered how Granddaddy Byrd had looked at her when he took her to live with him, the sullen rage beneath the grief. She remembered when she had started to sing to herself to fill the world with more than loneliness. She wiped her hand across the image on the table.

"Having family," Delia blurted. "Even sisters you've never met.

It's a blessing, Cissy. You're part of something bigger than just your-self alone. Growing up, all I had was Granddaddy Byrd." She shook her head. "Way he was, sometimes that felt worse than being alone. Man was just about the closest thing to a rock I ever knew."

"A rock. Well, that's good. I can't wait to meet him," Cissy said.

"He didn't mean to be like that." Delia shifted in her chair. "He was too hurt to comfort himself or me. And he was old, too old to take on raising a child."

"Then why did he?"

For a minute Cissy thought Delia was going to slap her. Then she said, "He had to. There wasn't anyone else." She wiped the table with her napkin. She could not smooth her image.

Cissy stirred her bowl of chili. She had thought chicken chili would be something special. This wasn't special. The chicken was stringy and tough, the tomato tasted bitter, and the chili powder made her tongue feel spongy. The best thing on the table was the lettuce, and what was that? Water.

Delia got up to pay for the meal. Cissy rubbed her fingers along her necklace and pulled her elbows in tight to her ribs. In her night-mares, Amanda was a sharp-beaked, black-winged crow cawing loudly right behind Cissy's bent neck. Dede was a wire-haired boar with razor-tipped hooves dancing close to Cissy's bare pink feet. Cayro, Georgia, was a pit of red dirt and gray clay sloped so steeply that Cissy could not crawl free. And Granddaddy Byrd was a rock. She put her hands over her eyes and pressed hard. Stars bloomed in the dark. The backside of nowhere, the ass-end of the universe, Cayro, Georgia, and the family Delia loved more than she would ever love Cissy.

The back window of the Datsun had been smashed in. The trunk was popped open. There was nothing left but a box jammed between the spare tire and the jack, and the half-full Styrofoam cooler with the crack down one side. Cissy leaned over the backseat from the open door and picked through the debris. The thieves had dumped a bag of clothes on the floor.

"Probably used the bag for the tapes," Delia said. She was looking at the front seat, where there remained only a smashed cassette of Jefferson Airplane's greatest hits.

"They took everything!" Cissy said. "Everything we had."

"No. Not everything." Delia hugged her purse to her hip. "We'll get more. Maybe they need it worse than we do. Like coyotes, panting after what little they can get." Delia stood by the car with her hands curled up under her chin. Her cropped hair was sweat-dark and limp.

Cissy gaped at her. Who cared what the thieves needed? How about what she needed? Her clothes, her books, the little box of pins and sparkling beads her daddy had given her for her last birthday. "I want to go home. You could call Rosemary. We could stay with her." She blew her nose on a piece of paper from the car floor and looked up at Delia pitifully.

"We *are* going home," Delia said. She felt lighter and freer without all that stuff, absurdly philosophical. She pulled out a kerchief and used it to brush away the broken glass, then shook it and tied it around her head. She sorted through the clothes on the floorboard until she found a shirt big enough to tie over the window from the clothes hook to a rip on the seat cover.

"We'll be fine," Delia said firmly. "When we get to Cayro, you'll see. We'll be fine."

"No we won't. You don't care about me. You're stealing me," Cissy shouted. "You're kidnapping me."

About ten feet away a trucker was watching them from the open door of his cab. He was chewing a sandwich and holding a bottle of soda. Delia looked at him and shrugged.

"You got hit," he said, his mouth full of bread. "Happens out here." He took a drink, then reached behind his seat and pulled out another soda, which he quickly opened. "Here," he said. "Give her this. She's just exhausted. Get lots of fluid in her and let her sleep.

Heat out here is bad enough without getting yourself robbed. Got a few more sandwiches too—meat loaf. You want one?"

Delia walked over and took the bottle. "Thank you, no," she said. "We just ate. But the soda's a good idea."

The man jerked his chin at Cissy, who had stopped yelling and was slumped against the bumper. "I got one of my own. They'll drive you crazy." He took another bite, keeping his eyes trained on Delia. "Don't I know you?" The words were clear even though he was chewing.

Delia looked at his face. He was squinting in concentration. No, she thought. Oh no. "Don't think so."

He swallowed and nodded. "You know who you look like?"

Delia waited.

"That singer, the one with the long red hair?" The man was frowning. "That one that died," he said. "Janis, right? Janis Joplin. People probably tell you that all the time."

"Oh, yeah." Delia smiled and nodded at him. No one had ever confused her with Janis, but she didn't want to get into that. She wanted to get back on the road. "Thanks," she said again.

"He knew who you were." Cissy's face was stained with tears and sweat.

Delia shook her head and handed Cissy the soda. "Honey, he'd have never heard of Mud Dog. You can bet every button on his console is set on a country station. He thought I looked like Janis Joplin."

"Janis Joplin is dead." Cissy wiped her nose. "Been dead forever."

Delia's face was unreadable as she opened the passenger door and motioned Cissy to get in the car.

Cissy ignored her. "We got plenty of room now," she said, climbing into the back.

Sandy grit rubbed into her bare arms and calves as she lay down on the seat. It might have been rock or grains of safety glass. Delia made up a pillow for her out of a pair of jeans, but Cissy pushed them aside. She lay with her face tucked into the crook of her elbow and cried softly once they were back on the highway. She knew Delia couldn't hear her over the wind whistling past the shirt pinned above her.

"We'll be fine," Delia kept saying, but Cissy knew she was talking to herself. Like a crazy person, Delia was talking just to hear herself say the words. Cissy put her fingers in her ears.

The back of the car remained open to the wind and dust and any other thief who might come along. It was a sign, as far as Cissy was concerned, but Delia just taped up cardboard when the shirt came loose. "You were getting too big for most of those clothes anyway," she said. "We'll buy you some nice stuff when we get closer to home, some shorts and sundresses that you'll like." As if clothes were the point, Cissy thought, as if they were not broken open themselves, broken open and whistling in the wind. Between the two of them the rage hummed loud as the engine.

Cissy slept through the Texas Panhandle. "You didn't miss anything," Delia told her.

"I want to stop," Cissy said.

"No stops. We are going to make time, girl. Time."

Cissy put her necklace in her mouth. The hematite tasted salty and dark. The sun was just over the horizon, and the ground was blue-gray and flat as a saucer. Oklahoma looked like New Mexico, occasional patches of farmland with low, unrecognizable plants interspersed with vast stretches of rock and desert, hills always silhouetted in the distance. Green, Cissy wanted green lush plants and bright hot flowers, Venice Beach and all those hidden gardens. When they first came into Oklahoma City and she saw the lush green trees, Cissy thought she would cry with relief. She stuck her head out the window and pulled in great breaths of cool air. It smelled like it might rain or had rained recently. Damp and rich and wonderful, a different cathedral.

On the eastern outskirts of the city, Cissy threatened to flag down a highway patrolman. Delia just patted her purse. "I've got your birth certificate right here." She blew smoke out the open window and laughed. "Besides, look at you. You think any sheriff wouldn't see you belong to me?"

Cissy leaned out the window again. She knew she was Delia's miniature, red-brown hair and hazel eyes, muscles that rode the bones in the same pattern, every inch her mama's girl. She remembered Thanksgiving, when Randall had come over too late for dinner. He had hugged Cissy and told her how much she looked like her mother. "Only thing of mine you've got is my mama's name and my teeth, my soft old milk teeth," he said. "You're going to have to keep an eye on those teeth, little Cecilia." He slipped his plate down and wiggled it with his tongue.

"If you changed your habits, you might keep the rest of those teeth." Delia had been sober for two weeks that holiday. By night she would be drinking again, and they all knew it. Randall smiled at her indulgently and let Cissy sip his whiskey. Delia jumped up from her chair. "Don't give her that. An't you done enough?" she shouted, and Randall walked out the door.

"You hurt his feelings," Cissy complained when Delia put her to bed.

"I'd like to hurt more than that." Delia spit the words. She said she had moved out of Randall's place to stop drinking and be a good mother to Cissy, but for most of the two years after they left him she matched him drink for drink. Every time he came around, she would start again.

In the backseat of the car, Cissy opened her eyes and watched brightly lit neon signs flash in the windows. If Delia got drunk, she would check them into a motel and let them both sleep it off. Drunk, Delia was no trouble at all. Drunk, she would sing along to the radio and make big fruit salads and giggle to herself. Sober was trouble. Sober, Delia was angry and miserable, scolding Cissy and constantly rubbing the back of her neck. Sober, Delia had headaches. Drunk, she felt no pain at all. A wave of cigarette smoke blew past the flapping cardboard.

"I'm thirsty," Cissy said. "I'm drying up back here."

Delia said nothing.

Cissy sat up and leaned over the front seat. She rested her chin on the sticky upholstery and sighed. "Don't you need some cigarettes?"

Delia turned her head slightly and shrugged.

"I could get you some, and me something too. A Coke, or orange juice with lots of ice." Cissy licked her lips. "I'd love to have an orange juice with lots of ice, maybe slices of orange in the glass."

Delia changed lanes smoothly. There was a lot of traffic on the strip, people in a hurry going somewhere.

"Juice," Cissy said. "We could stop anywhere here."

"In one of the bars maybe?" Delia tossed her cigarette out the window. Sparks flew back toward the rear bumper. "Get you some juice, me something too while we're there?"

Delia leaned down and tugged at a brown bag stuck under her seat, tearing the paper when she finally got it out. Two cartons of Marlboros thudded on the passenger seat. Delia looked left at a big Oldsmobile crowding into her lane and speeded up to pass it.

"When we need gas, I'll get you some juice," Delia said. "Get you some ice too, and maybe another cooler. But I an't stopping when I don't have to. I'm getting us to Cayro, Cissy, the fastest way I can."

Delia stopped at a Quick Mart near midnight, filled the gas tank, and then cruised the grocery shelves while the blinking clerk watched her. She bought another Styrofoam cooler, a carton of juice, an economy pack of luncheon meat, two boxes of saltine crackers, half a dozen chocolate bars, a big bag of peanut brittle, and a small bag of ice.

"Sustenance," Delia said to Cissy when she put the cooler on the floor of the backseat. She paid no attention when Cissy glared at her, just tore open a chocolate bar and revved the engine.

All the way across the rest of Oklahoma, Cissy chewed peanut brittle. A couple of times she crawled up front to get away from the wind that poured across the backseat, but she did not speak. Delia turned on the radio. Cissy turned it off. They rode in silence as they sped across the spring landscape. Just across the Arkansas line, Delia's adrenaline finally gave out, and she steered the car over to the side of the road. The two of them slept fitfully for several hours, Delia gripping her keys tightly as if she feared someone would steal the car.

Once they reached Tennessee, Delia drove as if her sanity depended on it. She made peanut butter and white bread sandwiches on the bumper for Cissy, rinsed fruit from roadside stands with service-station hoses, poured peanuts into twenty-eight-ounce bottles of RC Cola and chugged as she drove. They made steady progress, but not fast enough to suit Delia. She kept rubbing her neck and grinding her teeth.

At a service station near Chattanooga, Delia untied her head scarf for the first time since New Mexico and fought a wave of nausea from the overwhelming smell of gasoline. Whoever came through before them had spilled gas in a puddle next to the pump. They should clean that up, Delia thought, glancing at the rearview mirror. The attendant was staring at her, but why shouldn't he? She looked like hell. There was a band of pale skin across her forehead where the scarf had been. Her lips were cracked, her nose bright pink and peeling. The collar of her blouse was stiff with sweat, and she had rubbed the back of her neck raw. She closed her eyes and felt the world wheeling around her still body. Cissy pumped her heels at the dash, and Delia turned to her. The girl looked as bad as her mother, sunburned and filthy and miserable. Delia saw with a shock that Cissy's left eye was puffy and red.

"Christ," she said. "Where are your glasses?" She rummaged through the junk on the seat until she found the thick, dark lenses. "Put these on right now." For the first time Delia registered the desolation on her daughter's face. She reached over and patted her shoulder.

Cissy flinched. "Don't touch me." She got out of the car and crawled into the backseat.

Delia set her jaw and filled up the tank. She looked at Cissy once in the mirror, put the car in gear, and drove.

When they were on the highway again, Cissy considered tossing the glasses out the broken window, but she knew that Delia would back up a mile to get them.

They came into Cayro late that night. Cissy was sound asleep in the backseat. Delia pulled in behind the Motel 6 on the Marietta side of town and curled up under the steering wheel. "I'll just sleep for a little, just a little while," she whispered, and immediately fell unconscious.

Cissy woke up toward dawn as the light brightened and the traffic noise increased. Delia was asleep in the front, the torn and wrinkled road map sticking out from under her right hip. Cissy lay there listlessly until an awful grinding made her lift her head and look out the window. A big yellow and red Dixie General label shone on the side of an eighteen-wheeler steering slowly past the Datsun. Cissy wondered briefly just what the General was shipping, then stretched and unlatched the door. Her face was dirty and creased from the plastic seams on the seat cover. She rubbed her left eye and looked around. A sign across the highway advertised a Maryland Fried Chicken two exits away. Another sign, this one green and white, directed traffic toward Atlanta with a sharp arrow. Limping slightly from stiffness, Cissy walked toward the motel.

"Morning, honey."

The woman had tightly curled hair and was wearing a white uniform. Maid, Cissy thought. Then she watched her go into the little restaurant at the side of the motel. Waitress.

Honey. Cissy mouthed the word, mimicking the accent. Georgia. They must be in Cayro. Cissy was here because her daddy was dead and her mama was crazy. What was it like to be grown and crazy? Cissy looked around the parking lot. Probably lots of crazy people around here.

Honey. Cissy stretched the syllables, the way Delia talked when she had been drinking. Southern accent, honky-tonk twang. Randall had loved it. Cissy hated it.

Cissy headed for the restaurant. No one stopped her, so she went on into the bathroom and washed her face and hands. That felt so good she pulled down a wad of paper towels and rubbed soap and water up under her T-shirt and down into her shorts. She wanted to take off her clothes and scoop water all over herself, but she was afraid someone would walk in on her. Instead she pulled down more towels and scrubbed herself until her skin burned. She tried to comb her hair out with her fingers, but it was dark and stiff with sweat, so she stuck her head under the faucet until her neck got cold. Then she dried off with the last of the paper towels. In the clouded mirror over the sink, with her hair wet, she looked different—older, almost a teenager, a brunette with big brown eyes and a few freckles. "Honey," she said to the teenager, then laughed, surprising herself. She sounded like Randall.

When Cissy came out of the bathroom, the waitress was standing by the open back door near the telephone, smoking a cigarette. She looked Cissy up and down but said nothing. For safety's safe, Cissy did not try to go past her but cut left and went out the front door. She walked completely around the motel. In the breezeway at the back she found an ice machine, took two handfuls of chips out, and went to sit on the Datsun's bumper. She sucked ice and watched the day turn brighter and hotter, going back to the machine twice more, until Delia stirred on the front seat.

Honey. Cissy drawled the word once more around her ice chips. Deliberately she turned her head away from Delia's sunburned, swollen face. She was not going to speak to her mother. Not today. Maybe not ever. People were going in and out of the restaurant, opening the motel doors and carrying out luggage. They gave Cissy a quick look and then went on. Her hair was drying loose and tangled, and the sun was starting to glare into her eyes. She didn't have the energy to glare back. She was so hungry she was flat in the middle.

Cissy had hated the third grade, begged almost every day to stay home, but as she looked around the motel lot, she felt like promising never to miss a day of school again if only Delia would drive them back to California. How could Delia do this to her? Cissy wiped her arm across dry eyes. No one listened to kids. Grown-ups could do what they wanted. Delia could pick up and go anytime she felt like it. Cissy could lie down on the concrete and cry until her bones melted, and no one would care.

The ice in her mouth was gone. Cissy looked at Delia, who had struggled out of the car and was standing in the sun, blinking like a bird that has just run headlong into a window.

Delia rubbed her eyes and turned to her daughter. "Come on, let's get something to eat. You must be starved, honey," she said, and Cissy cringed.

Delia got Cissy settled down at the restaurant counter, ordered her a fried egg sandwich and a glass of milk, and went to the washroom to clean herself up. She had to ask for fresh paper towels and did not notice the look the waitress directed at Cissy.

To spite Delia, Cissy wanted to ignore the food, but was not able to stop herself from devouring every bite, including the pickled red apple on the side of the plate. She could have eaten more, but she wouldn't ask. She looked around at all the people eating their breakfast and reading their morning papers. The men had tired faces under pushed-down caps with sun bills peaked over their eyes. All the women seemed to wear their hair pinned up with little colored barrettes.

Delia came back with her hair combed and a fresh blouse brightening her face. She signaled the waitress and asked for a doughnut and a cup of coffee, counting out quarters and dimes to make a good tip.

"Long trip?" the waitress asked when she returned.

Delia smiled. "Too long." The doughnut had cinnamon sprinkled across the top, her favorite. She ate it quickly before picking up the coffee.

"Good appetite," said the waitress, clearing Cissy's plate.

"She's a good girl," Delia said.

Cissy scowled.

"Kids, huh?" The waitress had the grin of a woman who had raised her own.

"Uh-huh." Delia drained her coffee cup. She had never liked the coffee in California. It was too strong. This coffee she could drink all day. It was right, like the smell of the air was right, the humidity soothing her parched skin. Delia had to stop herself from laughing out loud. She was home. This place smelled and felt like home.

"I know you." The cook was leaning through the window behind the counter, soft white arms slung over the edge. "I know you," she said again.

Delia felt a shock go through her. She had not thought about this, being recognized here in Cayro. For a moment she hesitated, and then that brief signature smile crossed her face. Randall had trained her to smile, say thank you, and move on when people stopped her to gush. "Give them as little as you can," he always said, "but give them something. They make our life possible." Reflexively Delia ran her palms down her hips. There was nothing in her pockets, no pen to sign an autograph. She looked to the waitress with an embarrassed shrug.

"You that bitch ran off and left her babies." The cook's voice was loud and definite.

The waitress's eyes widened. Delia felt her knees go weak. Cissy stared at the cook, transfixed, half outraged and half hoping she would call Delia a bitch again.

"You took off with that rock band. Did all right for yourself, did you? Had yourself a good time? Well, don't think people don't remember. We remember. You the kind we remember." The cook crossed her fat arms and nodded her head.

The man sitting at the counter beside Delia twisted on his stool to face her, his starched uniform crackling as he turned. The long hair at the back of his collar was bound with a little rubber band. "Delia? Delia Windsor?" His eyes swept up and down her body, and his mouth crooked up at one corner. "Well, damn!" he said. "Damn!" He gave the cook a stern glance. "Don't pay that old cow no mind."

Delia backed away from the counter. The waitress's face was white and angry. Everyone was staring. Someone said, "Who is it?" and got a whispered reply. The people in the booths stood up to get a good look.

The waitress lifted her right hand. The change from Delia's tip was cupped in her palm. Quarters jingled against dimes, and then the hand opened and spilled the money on the linoleum in a loud rain.

Delia's mouth flooded. She pulled Cissy off her stool and tugged her away by one arm.

Everyone watched as they headed for the door. Every person in the restaurant watched Delia's staggering, stubborn walk. She had never walked off a stage weaker or resisted a drink with more grim determination.

Help me, God, Delia prayed as she dragged Cissy along. Help me.

Cissy wrenched her arm free as soon as they were outside. Delia turned vacant eyes on her and walked on toward the Datsun. Cissy looked back at the restaurant and saw faces at the window, a crowd pushed up close to the door. This was Cayro. This was home.

Until the day she died, despair for Cissy would taste of ice chips and sweat. Fear would wear a pushed-down cap with a stained sun bill. Shame would sport bright-colored barrettes and a tight mouth. And the word "honey" would be a curse.

Chapter 3

You'll love Cayro. People are different there," Cissy sneered once they were safely in the car.

Delia stared out the windshield. Her face was pink and flushed with heat. Her mouth was slack. She gripped the wheel of the car and looked back at the diner. There were two posters in the window, one announcing a fish fry sponsored by the local fire department and another proclaiming a welcome week at Holiness Redeemer, with a guest preacher from Gaithersburg. She could see the waitress looking out at them above the sign for the church.

"Nothing a bullet in the brain won't fix," Randall would say. "A bullet in the brain, a couple of lines, a shot of tequila." Delia swallowed hard.

What had she been thinking?

After all this time she could still taste it, tequila oily on the tongue. She had never cared for the lime. Didn't need salt. She liked the way tequila crossed her palate, burning away the dross. Randall would suck limes and put that powder up his nose. Randall would screw half a dozen girls and race cars on twisty oceanfront highways. All Delia ever needed was a drink in her hand. A bottle of beer, a glass of something, that scalded sweetness at the back of her tongue.

Cissy shifted on the seat beside her. Reluctantly Delia turned her head to look at the child, pale beneath her sunburn, her hazel eyes so dark they picked up the red-black of the hematite stars at her throat.

What have I done?

Delia closed her eyes. Randall had warned her. "Cayro, Georgia, an't never gonna love you," he'd said. "If you want those girls, we'll have to steal them." She had never listened. She had never believed.

But those faces in the diner, hateful and hard—they had looked at her like she was a monster.

I should not have come back.

"Are we going?" Cissy's voice was breathy and thin. Her left eye was watery and bloodshot.

I'm no good for her, for any of them. No good at all.

Delia's pulse thudded in her neck, the cars in the lot shimmering to its beat. That song was picking up again, the do-not-deserve-to-live refrain.

Delia nodded her head fiercely, picking up the melody. God-god-god-god-damn. Ought to die, want to die.

"Are we going?" Halfway across the country, Cissy had wept and stormed, but what sounded in her voice now was at a higher pitch. Hysteria threaded the syllables. The child was worn out. The child was at her last nerve.

"We're going," Delia said as calmly as she could.

A shot of tequila or a bullet in the brain, it was the same thing when you came right down to it. But Delia had dragged Cissy all this way and she hadn't even seen Dede and Amanda. She started the engine, shaking her dirty hair out of her face. She'd get Cissy settled, make sure her girls were all right. Afterward she could think about the alternative—one blue metal bullet or a glass of tequila straight up. This was not California. This was Georgia. In this county alone there were two dozen places she could get a gun as easily as a bottle of Cuervo Gold.

Driving across Cayro to Granddaddy Byrd's place took longer than Cissy expected. Twice Delia sat at stop signs so long that people started honking. Her knuckles were white on the steering wheel, and her mouth hung open as if she could not get enough air, as if air was not what she wanted.

"You all right?" Cissy finally asked when they sat so long the second time. A part of her wanted to enjoy Delia's obvious misery, but another part was frightened.

"I'm fine," Delia said. "Just fine."

Cissy shrugged uneasily and turned her attention to the scenery, picking at a bit of toast stuck in the gap in her front teeth. She thought about the people in the diner. Nothing she had imagined on that long trip across the country had prepared her for them. They were everything Randall had ever said they were, hard-faced and cold-blooded. They were the people who had made Delia; they were her match. She glanced over at her mother and quickly turned back to the window.

Cayro, Georgia, was just another wide patch off the side of Highway 75. Most people on their way north from Atlanta never saw it. Downtown consisted of a triangular intersection no bigger than a good-sized basketball court. There was a sign that read WELCOME on one side and COME BACK SOON on the other. The cutoffs at each corner of that intersection were marked with little directional arrows on which someone had drawn smiley faces. The road north led back to Highway 75 and the route to Nashville, but another smiley-face sign indicated that it was also the way to the county hospital. The route south was marked MARIETTA, but the road west was a mystery, with only the silhouette of a chicken beside the smiley face.

"Where does that go?" Cissy asked.

"The river," Delia said. "Farm country. Your Granddaddy Byrd's place and a lot of truck farms."

"What's a truck farm?"

Delia shrugged. "I don't know. Farms. People have always called them that. Maybe they're places where people truck produce out to the markets." She rubbed the back of her neck. "Never been much industry here. Mostly dairies and chicken farms and peanut fields."

"What does Granddaddy Byrd grow on his farm?"

"Dirt." Delia gave a wry grimace. "He an't farmed in thirty years. He bred dogs for a while, good hunting dogs, people said. But that takes a lot of energy and getting around to talk to folks. He ran out of both around the time I moved in with him. He was living on savings and selling off pieces of land when I got out of school. There may not be much of the farm left."

Delia drove along slowly, rubbing her neck every couple of minutes. She pointed out Cayro Junior/Senior High School, from which she had graduated. Past that was the brick hospital that had replaced the one that burned down. Cissy stared glumly. Delia turned the car abruptly and drove them back through Cayro, past the courthouse and the Methodist church. She cruised past the church parking lot, looking around intently, and then swung the car back toward the center of Cayro.

"Aren't we going to Granddaddy Byrd's?"

Delia stopped the car in front of a little shop with a dirty picture window and a hot-pink sign, Bee's Bonnet Beauty Salon. "We'll get there," she said. She leaned out of the car to peer into the window, which was full of dead plants.

"I worked there before your sisters were born," Delia said. "Mrs. Pearlman owns it. She was always good to me."

When they finally pulled up in front of the little farmhouse, it was going on noon. The dusty porch was bare, the windows shadowed by faded blue curtains. Delia sat clutching her purse and gazed around with big, dark eyes.

"Don't look like he's here," Cissy said.

Delia shook her head. "He's here. He's always here."

The screen door swung slowly open. An old man stepped out into the hot sun and gave them an angry glare. Slightly bent, chin thrust forward, shirt unbuttoned, he had wild gray hair all over his head. He came down the steps hesitantly, as if he had to tell every separate muscle what to do, but once on the ground he walked toward them firmly. Delia got out of the car and stood waiting by the fender.

He is *not* expecting us, Cissy thought as he gave her one long look and slowly walked all the way around the chalk-green Datsun.

"Pitiful excuse for a car, Delia." He wiped his face with his sleeve.

Delia smiled tentatively and reached for him, then dropped her arms as if her energy had run out. Standing there in the heat, she started to cry. The old man winced as she leaned into him and sobbed on his neck. From the front seat of the car Cissy watched, awestruck. She had never seen Delia cry.

"Slow down now, Delia," Granddaddy Byrd said. He patted at Delia's back with one hand, his knuckles knocking her spine like a salesman's at a strange front door. His eyes shifted to Cissy in mute impatience, as if he expected her to come take her mother in hand. Cissy stayed where she was, pulling her legs up on the front seat and resting her chin on her knees.

"Now, Delia," the old man said again, and Delia grabbed him even tighter. Then she pushed herself back and wiped her eyes.

"I'm sorry," she said. "It's been a long trip. Feels like I've hardly slept since we left Los Angeles." She looked at the car. "Cissy, come over here."

Cissy sighed and got out of the car. She was painfully conscious of what she must look like, her hair blowing across her sunburned face and her wrinkled clothes covered with dust. "Hello," she said carefully.

The old man turned from Delia to Cissy, his expression as distant and stern as any stranger's. "Girl." He nodded curtly, then did something funny with his mouth so that his lower lip moved down and pulled flat. "Harrumph." It was not quite a grunt. Maybe it was some Southern expression, some Cayro code for welcome, but Cissy didn't think so.

"I wasn't sure we'd make it." Delia pushed her hair back. She looked almost drunk with relief. "I swear, Granddaddy. It felt like we were racing against fate, like the ground was going to open up and swallow us if I didn't get home as fast as I could. Like you wouldn't be here." She gazed at the blue-white empty sky.

"Where would I be?" Granddaddy Byrd's voice was a scratchy, irritable whisper, as if he were out of practice talking to people. "I don't go running around. This is where I always am."

"I know, I know." Delia's hands swiped through her hair again and gripped the back of her head. "It didn't make sense, you know? It was like Cayro itself wouldn't be here. Like one of them terrible television shows where people and places just disappear and you think you're crazy." Delia dropped her hands. "Nobody ever talks about how long it is, driving all the way across the country."

"I don't have no television set," Granddaddy Byrd said. "I don't know what you're talking about."

Delia said, "No, of course you don't. It's all right. I'm all right. I'm just tired." She turned to face the house. "And I'm filthy. Let me get a shower, make us all some tea." She looked down at her dusty sandals.

"You want some tea, Granddaddy?"

The old man shook his head. "I don't need nothing," he said. "You go get yourself cleaned up. And be careful of that shower. The pipes are backwards, the hot handle turns on the cold."

Delia grinned at him. "You never fixed that? All this time and you never fixed that?"

He shrugged. "What's to fix? It works."

Delia opened the screen door tentatively and stepped inside as if she were afraid the floor would give way. Cissy bit her lips. Granddaddy Byrd took a seat on the front steps and dragged a folded bag of Sharpe's tobacco out of his shirt pocket, not even bothering to move up into the shade of the porch. Cissy sat down beside him, trying to make herself small and unobtrusive but wanting to look at this man.

Granddaddy Byrd shot her a narrow glance. Cissy dropped her head and kept her eyes on his hands on the tobacco bag. None of what was implied in the word "granddaddy" seemed to fit this craggy-faced reptile. His fingers were thin and long, with big knobby knuckles, the nails ragged and black. As she watched him work the tobacco paper, she saw that the left hand shook slightly, a steady palsied trembling, though the right was firm and he spilled not a flake of the crumbly reddish brown tobacco. His technique was to cup the paper against that firm right hand and roll it deftly with the fingers of the trembling left. He did it slowly, with great care, and the loose cigarette he produced took the flame easily.

"Pretty good," she said admiringly.

"Harrumph." A language all his own. He held the cigarette with his left hand and Cissy wondered briefly why he didn't use the right.

From inside the house came Delia's voice: "Cissy, you want anything?"

"No," Cissy called back. She canted her head and looked again at the right hand, which still held the Sharpe's bag. Something strange there. The long, skinny fingers with the swollen knuckles lay precisely against each other, ending in an even line. Cissy flattened her own hand against her thigh and immediately saw the difference. Her middle finger extended more than a quarter of an inch past the two on either side of it. On Granddaddy Byrd's right hand the fingers were the same length all across, the nails of the middle three flush with the nail of the pinkie. In each he was missing at least the length of one joint.

Cissy looked up at his face. He was looking right back at her. She flushed with embarrassment. Those fingers hadn't been chopped off, the nails were intact. No, Granddaddy Byrd had been born without those joints, and she had been staring. She dropped her eyes. She hadn't meant to hurt his feelings, she hadn't known.

Cissy curled her fingers into fists and locked her gaze on the mock-Indian face on the tobacco bag. "Looks like you," she said, her voice sounding unnaturally high. "Just like you."

"Humph!" Granddaddy Byrd used one of those short fingers to flick tobacco flakes from his lower lip. "Don't be stupid." His tone was flat, his glance indifferent. Cissy remembered then what Delia had said about him, that he was old when he took her in. How old was he now?

When he had smoked the first cigarette down to a nub, he took his time rolling another. Cissy sat there, unable to look at his hands and unable to look away. She kept comparing him with the Indian on the label. The feathers of the headdress above those painted features were fat and tapered like unsmoked cigars. The features themselves were sharp, angular, and shaded to catch the eye. The Indian was handsome, with his prominent cheekbones and pale blue-gray eyes. Granddaddy Byrd was not handsome. His cheeks and eyes were sunken like the faces of the mummies in some pictures Randall had once shown Cissy after a trip to Mexico.

47

"It is so dry down there," her daddy had told her. "It's so godforsaken parched and dusty, the dead dry up and last forever. They turn to statues that get leaned up against the walls of the caves near the missions. It's something to see, all the dead lined up wearing the same expression, openmouthed and tragic. Makes you think. Makes you think how precious life is."

Granddaddy Byrd did not look as if he thought his life was precious. He looked impatient to be past it. A walking dead man.

Cissy studied the little warts in the cracks and wrinkles that ran down his neck. She shuddered. Ugly, she thought, ugly and older than God. She waited for him to say something, but he didn't. He watched. He had a way of watching as though the eyes of the world were in his head—an infinitely cruel world. I know who you are, his eyes seemed to say, while his lips remained pressed together, flat and thin. I know things you don't know. I know how cold and mean the world is.

Cissy felt her insides shift. Fear tickled below her belly. The embarrassment she had felt earlier, the faint thread of pity, had steadily burned away and become anger. This old man had called her stupid. He had pushed Delia off him like a stinky dog. Now he stared straight ahead as if she were not even there, contempt radiating from him like the heat still rising from the hood of the Datsun.

Creepy old man, Cissy thought, but her anger did not quite cover her fear. She kept her head down, not wanting to be seen by those eyes, spoken to by that caustic tongue. Delia had told her the man was hard but fair. No. He was mean, just mean.

"He's had a hard life," Delia had said. Granddaddy Byrd looked hard. Just as hard as the parched red dirt of his empty front yard, the kind of hard that only accumulates over a lifetime. There was no crack in him. He was of a piece, this old man, a piece of flint.

Granddaddy Byrd's hands creased and recreased that tobacco pouch. His eyes flickered off to the distant horizon and then came back to Delia's Datsun. So far he had taken more interest in the car than in either Delia or Cissy. In the kitchen Delia made small noises, the clink of a glass, a splash of liquid, a cabinet opening and closing.

A slight breeze picked up dust from the yard and brought it up to pepper the steps. Granddaddy Byrd's tongue snaked out to lick his lips.

Lizard, Cissy thought again. Granddaddy Byrd stared at the Datsun as if he were thinking on how to get them into it, longing for the steady quiet he had treasured before they drove into his yard. Grimly Cissy pushed herself up off the steps and walked across the yard. She heard Delia's shoes slap on the porch as she came out of the kitchen and sat down beside Granddaddy Byrd, who slid away a few inches.

"You sure you don't want something?" Delia's voice was softer. Her skin shone, her hair was smoothed back, the collar of her blouse was damp and open. She looked almost like a girl again.

Granddaddy Byrd eyed Delia for a moment, then cleared his throat with a rough hawk and spat. "Why'd you come back?"

Delia took a deep breath. "The girls," she whispered. "I want to see my girls." Cissy realized suddenly how skinny Delia was, all bones and angles. Her knees and elbows stuck out. Sitting there beside Granddaddy Byrd, she looked like a cartoon creature, a Halloween skeleton in a short skirt and T-shirt.

"You spoke to Clint yet?"

Cissy stepped close to the Datsun's bumper. She heard a pinging from inside the engine as it cooled, and the clinking of the glass on the steps as Delia set it down.

"Naaa." It was as if the breeze had stretched the word out, not Delia. The bright, fresh look of hope disappeared.

Granddaddy Byrd coughed angrily. Cissy watched the color drain from Delia's face. She looked even worse than she had in the restaurant.

"Naaa," she said again. Her eyes shifted to Cissy. They were a shade lighter than Granddaddy Byrd's eyes, but like his they could go hard. Now they glinted like the shale that flashes from under the ledges of old mountains. The hollow in Delia's throat pearled with sweat and pulsed with heat. The muscles there flexed as she swallowed, but she said nothing more.

"You can't avoid the man, Delia. Specially not if you want to see those girls."

Granddaddy Byrd did not seem to see what his words were doing, the way Delia was folding into herself. He talked like a preacher, Cissy thought. Randall had always warned against preachers, men who talked as if the Bible were propped against their breastbones, God's truth a razor beneath their tongues. Randall's daddy had been a preacher. "And he was an evil old man," he said. "Died blaming his sins on his children and his wife, my mama, who was the sweetest woman you'll never get to meet. That man ran her into the grave. What I am saying is, don't trust preachers, Little Bit, don't let them get after you. You got to keep yourself away from those razor tongues."

"You'll have to talk to him," Granddaddy Byrd said, his voice gravelly. He kept his face forward, as though Delia were somewhere out in the yard instead of right beside him.

"I don't know." Delia reached for her glass and tapped the bottom lightly on the step. "Don't think Clint's necessarily going to want to see me." Her head was bent. Blown dust settled over her hair, her skirt, her bare arms and calves.

"Clint's still your husband." Now Granddaddy Byrd was looking directly at Delia. "He didn't choose to divorce you, did he? No, he held on all the time you were gone. And he heard, everybody heard, what you had done." His crippled hand gestured in Cissy's direction. "Likely once he knows you're back, he'll expect you to come see him."

"I don't know that."

"Delia."

They were facing each other now, bodies rigid, eyes locked. Cissy saw Delia slowly angle away from the old man, saw her shoulders hunch and settle. She got smaller and smaller, but her head did not turn, her eyes did not drop. She might crack, but she would not soften. A slight vibration moved down Granddaddy Byrd's long frame, from his leathery neck to his outthrust bony knees, as he clasped his hands in front of him and pulled his elbows in to his sides, like a mantis bent in prayer. Nothing in him leaned toward Delia.

"You got to talk to Clint." That preacher's voice.

Cissy turned away and squatted on the rough tarmac. She watched a line of ants circling a sun-heated piece of broken glass. Behind her Delia's voice was choked with misery.

"Granddaddy, don't. You know Clint an't gonna let me see my girls."

"Well, how you expect to see them if you don't see Clint?"

Delia rocked back and forth on the porch step. "I'd hoped you'd help me," she said. "I thought you might speak to Clint."

"What have I got to say to him?" Granddaddy Byrd spat again.

Cissy looked at the spot in the dust where his spit had landed. There was a barely a mark. The dirt looked like gray powder, but it was unyielding.

"Delia. You never did listen to a thing I said. Wouldn't think you'd start now. But you should. You should." Granddaddy Byrd rolled his tobacco bag between his palms. "You married the man. Clint Windsor might have been a son of a bitch, but there's lots of sons-a-bitches around. You married that one. You made babies with him. Then you run off and left him like you were never coming back."

Delia covered her mouth with one hand. The other remained locked around her shins.

Granddaddy Byrd glowered in Cissy's direction. "Hell," he said, "you can't just waltz back into Cayro and think you gonna get what you want. An't a soul in this county thinks you got any right to those girls. Not a soul."

He got to his feet slowly, straightening up as if in pain, and grunted again once he was standing.

"You won't help me?" she said, so softly he could have pretended not to hear.

"No." He stopped. Without looking back, he spoke again. "You go talk to the Windsors. They're the ones you should go see. You get down on your knees and tell those girls what you been doing all these years. Don't tell me."

Cissy gritted her teeth and took up a rock. Delia sat rocking as Granddaddy Byrd went across the porch and through the door. If she hadn't been so angry at Delia herself, Cissy might have run after him, thrown herself at the old man, and screamed out all the pain she could feel growing in Delia's body.

"Cissy. We got to get going." Delia stood up abruptly and headed for the Datsun.

Cissy ground a line of ants into the hot tar surface of the old driveway, tossed the rock aside, and followed Delia to the car.

Chapter 4

About the time Delia left Granddaddy Byrd's house, Marjolene Thomasina Jackson was pulling into the driveway of her newly ex–husband Paul's house. Six carloads had shifted M.T.'s property to her own new place near the high school. There were a few dishes and curtains left, but it was the delphiniums that drew her back, the cut and prepared seedlings and the box of garden gear beside them.

"Curtains and dishes are easy to replace," she told her sister Sally, "but damned if I'm leaving my rootstock to Paul and whatever he's gonna bring in."

A seventh trip across town then, without Sally. M.T. left her sorting boxes and helping the twins, Ruby and Pearl, make up their new bedroom. She did not want Sally to see what she intended to do to the perennial bed by what was now, legally, Paul's kitchen.

M.T. was a big woman, muscular under soft pads of flesh. She grinned widely as she took her spade to the tall delphinium spears and reduced them to a gray-green mash.

"Man got twelve years off me. Thinks he got the best of me. Stupid son of a bitch." She chopped and tore into the plants, pouring all the rage she had never directed at Paul onto those loved green shoots. "Son of a bitch," she cursed. "Stupid man. Show his ass." When she was done, her eyes were full of tears, but she was satisfied.

"Something might come back here," M.T. said to herself as she turned toward her car, "but it won't be pretty." She was swiping at her dirty cheek and arching her aching back when a green Datsun pulled into the driveway.

Later M.T. would tell the story as if she had known them instantly—her lost best friend and the daughter at her side. But sodden and heartbroken, skinny and desperate, Delia did not look like the girl M.T. had loved. For one never-to-be-admitted moment, M.T. thought that the woman driving up was another of Paul's foolish girlfriends and that the child beside her was one of his numerous little bastards. God knew the man had been cheating on her at least that long. Maybe this woman had shown up to demand fair treatment from M.T., something she knew she would never get from Paul. If a legal wife could be done so badly, what could a girlfriend expect? Then Delia turned her face to M.T. and their eyes caught.

"Goddamn!" M.T. dropped her spade. "Delia," she shouted as she ran toward the car.

Delia opened the door, and they fell into each other's arms while Cissy wiped sweat out of her eyes and prayed someone would get her a cold drink.

"Damn, Delia. Goddamn." M.T. shook Delia loosely and burst into tears. "Damn," she kept saying, the word soft and reverent, a prayer of thanksgiving.

Delia spoke only once. She mouthed M.T.'s name, and then she began to sob.

"Another minute," M.T. would say after. "Another minute and I'd have left. Delia was in such bad shape, you cannot imagine. She was almost gone. She was almost lost to herself."

It was true. If M.T. had not stopped to tear up her garden, they might have missed each other. That would have been terrible, because it was not that Delia was almost gone. Delia was completely gone. Somewhere in the short drive from Granddaddy Byrd's to M.T. and Paul's old house, Delia had lost the part of her that could fight back, take care of business, and do what she had to do. The Delia who fell into M.T.'s arms was childlike and broken.

"Hold me," Delia whispered to her old friend, and M.T. took her at her word, enfolding her like a rag doll, kissing her face and weeping onto her cheek. For several minutes M.T. kept her hands on Delia, one still on her shoulder even as the other reached for Cissy's cheek.

"Oh, look at you," M.T. pronounced, "look at Delia's girl."

When Cissy scowled and shook her hair down over her eyes, M.T. only laughed and packed them both off to her new place—a more difficult prospect than it first appeared, since Delia seemed in that moment to have lost the talent for driving a car. "Never mind," M.T. said, and loaded them into her old Buick. She placed a dirty box of cuttings on Cissy's lap and cuddled Delia to her shoulder on the front seat.

It took years for Cissy to learn all that lay behind the friendship between Delia and M.T.—rivalries and resentments as well as rescues and impassioned loyalty. Eventually there were tales of the time M.T. hid Delia in her own honeymoon cottage and of the terrible night in 1978 when just one phone call to Delia brought a check from Randall, no questions asked. But of all the things that happened that day, the one Cissy would never forget was the welcome M.T. made them, the joy on her face when she recognized Delia and the matter-of-fact way she took them in. When they got to her home, M.T.'s voice rang out like a bell. She pulled them out of the Buick and displayed them to her sister like prize puppies.

"Look! Look!" she shouted. "Look who is here. It's my best friend, my best friend in the world. My Delia has come back."

M.T. sent Sally over to get Delia's car while she put Delia down in her own bed. "You need to rest," she said firmly, and took Cissy into her half-unpacked kitchen. M.T. fed the girl cold chicken and corn relish on slices of white bread and quizzed her about the long trip across country.

"I'm sorry about your daddy," she said when Cissy mentioned Randall's death. "I never met him, but I know what it is like to lose someone you love."

Cissy looked at M.T.'s wide, gentle face and suddenly felt like crying herself. Her daddy was dead. Her daddy was dead and she was stuck in the back end of the world.

"It's all right." M.T. came around the table and pulled Cissy's head into her belly. "It's going to be all right, honey. Your mama and I will make it all right." She soothed and whispered while Cissy cried fiercely for a few moments. When Cissy started hiccuping, M.T. took a wet washcloth and squatted down to wipe her face. "It's going to be just fine. We're going to take good care of you, sweetheart. Good care."

Cissy held her breath. Her tears were bad enough, but the hiccups were humiliating. Around the bulk of M.T.'s body she could see two girls watching from the kitchen doorway.

"I'm sorry," Cissy said.

"Nothing to be sorry about." M.T. was placid and easy on her feet. She stood up effortlessly and tossed the washcloth onto a pile of laundry near the sink. "You've lost your father, and you've just come all the way across the country in less time than it takes most people to go across the state. I'd say a few tears are justified. More than a few, and you can cry around here as much as you like. I'm tender-hearted myself, and so are my girls." She gestured at the twins. "I was wondering where you were. Cissy, I want you to meet my treasures, my Ruby and my Pearl."

M.T. pulled the two girls in close to her hips. They were as thin as she was wide, narrow-faced and sharp-chinned, with dark brown hair in matching bowl-like cuts above their ears. They were not identical twins, though they were the same size and had the same coloring. They were easily four years older than Cissy, big girls, teenagers, and they were nowhere near as good-natured as their mother. Ruby was the sharper of the two, her eyes zeroing in on Cissy like twin rockets ready to flare.

"Your daddy was a guitar player, huh?" Ruby said. "Famous, huh?"

"Famous, huh?" echoed Pearl.

Cissy opened her mouth, then hesitated. Delia had told her that Randall was nowhere near as famous as he'd liked to have been and that Mud Dog was just famous enough to get by. But she could tell from the look in Ruby's eye that she dared not say anything like that.

"A little famous," she said. "He's dead."

Ruby gave her sister a thump on the arm. "That's a shame."

"A shame." Pearl nodded.

Ruby looked Cissy up and down and smiled. "Well, never mind," she said. "Welcome to Georgia, Cissy Byrd. What Mama won't tell you, we will. Anything and everything about Cayro."

"Everything," said Pearl.

"You girls," laughed M.T. "Why don't you go show Cissy your room."

A little shudder of dread went through Cissy. They were not going to be any help.

"**R**eal friends take care of each other," M.T. said that night, after checking on the exhausted Delia for the dozenth time. "Real friends never forget each other. Your mama and I are real friends."

Cissy stared numbly. She found it tiring and frightening to be so important to someone she barely knew.

"Lord, girl, why are you still up?" M.T. said suddenly. She led Cissy back to the bedroom and tucked her into Pearl's narrow four-poster bed with a kiss on the forehead. Gratefully Cissy closed her eyes and prayed for sleep.

"You lived in Hollywood?" Ruby's voice was a whisper from the other bed.

"What's it like in Hollywood? People really rich there?" Pearl chimed in.

Cissy almost moaned out loud.

"Did you know any famous people, movie stars and all?" Ruby propped herself on an elbow. The two girls were lying head to foot on her bed, and when Pearl sat up a second later, Cissy felt as if she were facing a courtroom.

"No," she said. "No movie stars."

"I heard your daddy had this big old fancy bus that your mama caught a ride on, and that was how they met. Your daddy let you go with him on the bus?"

Cissy closed her eyes. She had only been on the bus a few times, and she was not about to say so to Ruby and Pearl. She tried to think of something that would satisfy their curiosity, but nothing occurred to her. All she had ever cared about was her daddy and spending time with him at his house, but Delia had not let her go over there much the last few years.

When Cissy had no ready answers, Ruby and Pearl quickly lost patience. They already resented the child who was forcing them to share a bed. What business did Cissy and Delia have coming in on their new place, turning everything back to front and getting their mama all excited?

"Why is it the famous people always have such stupid kids?" Ruby asked, head in the air, as if she were speaking to no one at all.

Pearl joined in happily. "Yeah, it's like fantastic numbers of them kill themselves all the time."

"I heard that too."

Cissy ran her tongue over her teeth. The sharp edges of her molars reassured her. She turned over on one hip and looked toward Ruby. "What's your mama's real name? Don't she got a real name? And why'd she give you two those silly damn names?"

"Don't say nothing about my mama," Ruby hissed.

"Yeah." Pearl was louder than her sister. "Don't talk about Mama."

"Oh, I like your mama," Cissy said. She put her thumb on her lower lip and rubbed thoughtfully. "I do. But it's a bit much, don't you think? Ruby and Pearl, your mama's little jewels?"

"You are a bitch," Ruby said.

"Worse than your mama," Pearl added.

"Stuck up." Ruby flopped back on the bed.

"Full of herself," Pearl agreed. She lay down at Ruby's side. For a moment the two girls glared at Cissy and then turned their backs to her together.

I want to go home, Cissy thought. But she had no home. Stubbornly she bit into the cotton pillowcase. She was not going to cry. She listened to Ruby and Pearl whispering softly so that she couldn't make out what they were saying. When they fell quiet, Cissy rolled over, keeping the pillow between her and the other bed like a shield.

* * *

Maybe if M.T. had not been there, Delia would not have fallen so completely apart. It was a kind of permission, having M.T. to cook them country fried steak, enroll Cissy in school, and take her downtown to get a few clothes. It was M.T. who found them the house out by the river, the one that belonged to Richie, who worked with her in the meat department at the A&P. She did not tell Delia how much persuasion it took to get that house.

"I don't know," the man said. "An't she that woman run off and left them girls?"

"She's my dearest oldest friend," M.T. swore. "And you know me, Richie. If I say she's all right, she is."

"M.T., you are about the silliest thing. That's what I know. And you an't going to talk me into renting to no woman couldn't be trusted with her own babies, much less my old house."

"Oh, Richie, you don't mean that." M.T. batted her eyes and smiled and coaxed until she thought her face would break. In the end, Ritchie rented the house to her, not to Delia, and made her swear he would never have to meet the woman, nor do any work if anything went wrong.

"My wife is gonna skin me," Richie complained.

"She's going to be happy to get the money," M.T. reassured him, hoping Delia had more savings stashed away than she had mentioned so far. Twice in the decade Delia had been gone she had sent money when M.T. asked for it, no questions asked and no mention of repayment. But every time M.T. had mentioned money since she found her friend out at Paul's house, Delia started to cry as if she had no more than the little roll M.T. had already seen in her bag. That could not be right, M.T. told herself. There would be money coming sooner or later. Delia couldn't have left California with so little to show for all that time.

It would take a few weekends to clean the place up, M.T. said when she drove Delia and Cissy out to see the river house, but it would be nice. When M.T. started opening windows and dusting, Delia sat down on a chair in the kitchen. A couple of times she got up as if she would help, but she sat back down before accomplishing anything. After a while she stopped getting up at all and just sat there watching as M.T. chattered and swept out the whole house. "We'll get my sister to help," M.T. promised Delia. "She'll get this place fixed up in no time." But Sally was too busy to come, and the weeks stretched and became a month.

Every time M.T. walked in on Delia lying in bed and crying, she would coo and nod with sympathy. This was the kind of thing she had felt when Paul took up with that dancer from Augusta. No one had understood that when it was M.T. lying in bed.

"Sometimes a woman just needs a little time," she told Cissy.

"Harrumph," Cissy replied. She watched Delia pull a pillow over her head and draw her knees to her chest like a baby curled up in a crib. She told herself she was learning the family language, "harrumph" and contempt and a sneer. Delia could cry. Cissy did not dare. She had already made it through her first few days at Cayro Elementary on sheer tight-lipped determination, ignoring the whispers and pointing fingers.

No, Cissy did not dare relax, did not dare loosen her tightly clenched fists, her closely pressed lips. She took to chewing her fingernails down and picking at her ragged cuticles. She went to school because she could not think of a way out of it and because it was better than staying in the house with Delia crying in bed, and Ruby and Pearl making ruthless fun of her every chance they got, and M.T. patting her head carelessly on her way to get Delia a tissue or a drink of water. Cissy felt as if her nerves had broken through to lie exposed on the outside of her skin. She slept in a tight little ball—under the bed after the girls poured water on her in the middle of the night—and walked around with her arms crossed over her chest, rebuffing even the few people who tried to be friendly, two other new girls in her grade and the teachers who pronounced her name "Cece." If Delia was going to cry, then Cissy was going to disappear.

The album covers had been passed around at the school, *Diamonds and Dust* with its long shot of the Hollywood Hills, and the original *Mud Dog/Mud Dog* with the bus hung all over with flags and flowers. Everywhere she went, Cissy was confronted with her daddy's band, boys who asked her if she'd ever done any drugs, girls who sang a few bars of the music she didn't really know and the words Delia had never allowed her to hear. Everyone knew her name, her mama's name, all about Randall and the band and California and more—all about Clint Windsor and the sisters she had never met. She started wearing her dark glasses all the time, not for protection from the light but to discourage questions she did not know how to deflect.

Bumped into the fourth grade for the last month of school, Cissy sat unblinking at the back of the room the first day, her eyes obscured behind the thick lenses. When the teacher asked her to "tell everyone about California," Cissy stood rigidly at the blackboard while the whole class focused on her stern face.

"California is the thirty-first state. The capital is Sacramento," she said, and returned to her desk.

Marty Parish leaned over Cissy's desk when the bell rang. "Full of sass, an't you?" he said. His glance drifted across the open notebook under her hand. Cissy had written "Cayro" over and over down the middle of the page. "You got your mama's talent?" he asked her. "You sing nasty songs and shake your butt when you do it?"

"Leave me alone."

"Hey, girl. You know stuff, I can tell. You could teach me some stuff, right?" A small group had gathered between Cissy and the teacher, who was rummaging through her desk at the front of the room. The grinning boys and one wide-faced nervous girl looked expectant, as if they hoped Cissy would start crying or run out of the room.

"Women in your family supposed to be good," Marty said with a leer. "Real good. I heard your sister Dede is real hot."

Cissy pushed herself up. Slowly she tucked her notebook between her elbow and her side, keeping her eyes locked on Marty's face. "Get out of my way," she said to him.

"Marty?" The teacher's voice was loud. She closed her desk drawer and stepped toward the rows of desks. "Is there a problem?"

"No problem. No problem." Marty shook his dark head and took one step back from Cissy's obstinate stance. "We were just discussing Cal-i-for-ni-a." He smiled at Cissy and gave an elaborate shrug.

The teacher looked to Cissy, but her face was blank. Everyone started for the door, but Cissy made a point of stepping close to Marty. "I know stuff, yeah. I been with the band. I been on the bus," she whispered in his ear. "I've been places you'll never get in this life."

Since that morning at Granddaddy Byrd's, Delia had stopped talking about Amanda and Dede, hadn't even spoken their names. It was Ruby and Pearl who made sure Cissy knew all about her sisters.

"Oh, they're looking for you," Ruby warned gleefully one night. "Everybody knows that. I'd think you'd be dreaming about them all the time, them sneaking through the bushes, climbing in the windows. Carrying rocks and razors with your name on them. You just lucked out getting here after Dede went to seventh grade. If she was still going to Cayro Elementary, she'd have kicked your butt three times over by now."

"Four times," hazarded Pearl. "Your whole family is crazy, but them girls are genuinely disturbed."

"Disturbed, yeah." Ruby beamed at Pearl appreciatively. "Old Amanda is like this century's only Baptist Pentecostal nun. Goes around all the time in them high-neck dresses in the hottest weather, wearing them white socks and Mary Janes like she was a first-grader or something."

"Always praying and telling people they're going to hell," Pearl put in.

"And that Dede is like so different you can't believe it."

"Oh Lord!"

Pearl put her hand over her mouth and giggled. Ruby nodded wisely. They looked at each other and then gave Cissy slow, pleased smiles.

"Everybody says she's done it."

"Uh-huh. Everybody."

Cissy frowned in confusion. "Done what?'

"It. It. Sex." Pearl was bouncing on Ruby's bed.

"She an't no virgin, you can be sure," Ruby said. "And her going off to Holiness Redeemer with her sister and grandma every Sunday. Lord should strike her dead. What is she, twelve?"

"I don't believe you."

"She sneaks out of her grandma's place and goes driving with boys. Everybody knows." Ruby's voice was adamant, her smile enormous.

Cissy crossed her ankles on the mattress and put her hands behind her neck. "Well, it's nothing to me." She closed her eyes. "I an't never met them and an't looking to meet them."

"Oh, you'll meet them." Ruby kicked at the side of the bed once, inspecting the room as if she wanted something else to kick. "Like I said, they're sure looking for you."

Cissy kept her eyes closed. She didn't want to give Ruby the satisfaction of seeing that her words were having any effect. The truth was that Cissy did dream about Amanda and Dede, did watch for them. The truth was that she had already run into Dede. And she had Ruby and Pearl to thank for that too.

Every Saturday afternoon for the last month, Cissy had been going downtown to Crane's, the paperback resale shop, to trade in the books she was steadily pilfering from the twins. Their books were the only things they had that Cissy envied. She had left most of her own books behind in Venice Beach, and the few that Delia let her bring had been stolen. It was a simple matter to run her fingers along their careful stacks and pull a couple out now and then to tuck in a paper bag and hide in the trunk of the Datsun. Crane's had an inexhaustible need for the books the twins collected, the kinds of books Cissy thought contemptible.

M.T. and her girls shared a common passion, Regency novels full of tightly laced bodices, medieval tales of saints and courtesans, historical melodramas about Roman soldiers bedeviled by women who wielded trefoil daggers and called on the goddess to defend their lives, generational sagas of British aristocrats who chose badly in love or of serving girls who married up and made their children rich. There were boxes of books under every bed, romances of every kind. Pearl and Ruby were not of this world, and their taste in paperback fiction proved it. Cissy found the more contemporary romances— nurses with doctors, secretaries with gentlemen—only under M.T.'s bed. She never touched those, but it gratified her to take one of Pearl's beloved sixteenth-century Gothics, or one of Ruby's endless series set in the eighteenth-century Court of St. James, and exchange it for one of Ursula Le Guin's *Earthsea* fantasies. A world in which terrible curses could be cast on the wicked had a ready appeal for Cissy.

One Saturday Cissy was hovering over the trays picking through the thrillers and science fiction. Just as she reached for a prize copy of Vonda McIntyre's *Dreamsnake,* another hand closed over the spine, and she looked up to see a skinny blond girl looking back at her. They stood there, motionless, until Mrs. Crane dropped a stack of books and their heads turned together. Red-faced and shaking, Mrs. Crane bent to pick up the books without taking her eyes off the girls. Each of them frowned in the same way and looked again at the other, and each pulled back her hand.

Why hadn't Cissy said something? But what could she have said? Dede had looked like any other raw-faced teenage girl, blond hair pinned back, blue eyes piercing and cool. What bothered Cissy later was that her half sister looked so ordinary, that there was no aura of mystery about her, no electrical shock when they touched. In any book the twins owned, there would have been an ominous scent in the room, a flash of sisterly recognition. Cissy stood there wondering what to do. Were they supposed to speak? Dede took the book in hand and added it to the other she was holding, a dog-eared copy of Eudora Welty's *The Optimist's Daughter.* Her eyes went to Mrs. Crane, then dropped back to the bin of books. She moved down the aisle, not looking at Cissy again. Cissy put down the two books she had selected and left the shop without a word. When she got home, she went straight to M.T.'s makeup mirror to see if there really was a resemblance, if any stranger could tell at a glance that she and Dede were related. Despite her dark red hair and hazel eyes, she saw in the mirror what anyone else would see—that both of them looked like Delia, with her nose, her chin, and the same fine arched brows above clear eyes.

The immediate difference between them was that Dede was pretty. For the first time Cissy wondered what she would look like when she got older. Back in Venice Beach, Rosemary had once showed Cissy how she did her makeup, pointing out that they both had the same heart-shaped face. "Better than those square-faced ugly women," she laughed. "Makeup can only do so much. You wait. With that face, you'll be pretty as your mama."

Cissy had paid no attention. But gazing into the mirror with the memory of Dede's features still imprinted on her own, Cissy saw what pretty looked like. What she could not puzzle out was the other thing she had seen in that face. Dede had looked at her with curiosity, not hatred. Her face had been neutral, cool, and distant, not hostile. That face that was Cissy's face had been almost as unreadable as her own.

The river house was a furnished cinder-block structure with two bedrooms and a living room only slightly larger than the kitchen that opened out of it. The bathroom was a rathole squeezed between the bedrooms, a dark, smelly cubicle with a mildew-stained shower, one of those cheap plastic inserts, and one window covered with orange paint.

Over a June weekend, M.T. and Sally tackled the house in earnest and got most of it ready in short order. It was the bathroom that stymied them. They sprayed bug killer everywhere, let it sit a few days, and scrubbed down the floors and walls with bleach twice, airing the room out between cleanings. It still reeked.

The next Saturday, Sally stepped in, took a deep breath, and pronounced, "Crap!" She climbed up on the toilet, drew back her leg, and with two well-placed kicks knocked the window out of its frame. Light and air poured in, and a small army of roaches poured out. Sally nodded and called in her crew from Dust Bunnies, the cleaning service she ran. They pulled the rug out of the living room and burned it out back. Then they sealed all the windows with plastic and set off industrial-strength bug bombs. Two days later they took all the furniture out and scoured the place while Sally's husband put a new window in the bathroom. Using paint left over from various jobs, Sally and her crew redid the walls in the bathroom and kitchen and touched up the bedrooms. When they were done, they put the furniture back in and laid down a rug M.T. had provided in the living room.

M.T. drove Delia and Cissy over the next day with their few things and some new curtains, a bright yellow one for the bathroom. While M.T. told them how Sally had kicked out the bathroom window, Cissy nodded balefully and walked around the kitchen feeling the linoleum buckle under her shoes, wishing Sally had kicked out all the windows. She would rather camp under the stars than live in this horrible house, so ugly compared to the cottage in California. But Delia sat right down at the kitchen table and wept at how clean and bright everything was.

Sally offered Delia work with Dust Bunnies, and Delia took it gratefully. It was night work, and she didn't have to speak to a soul to do it. Every evening she went out in the same T-shirt and jeans to clean offices in Cayro's claim to an industrial park, and came home before dawn with her hair pulling loose from the rubber band at the back of her neck. She would sit at the kitchen table with her blank face until Cissy got up, then make the only breakfast either of them could stand, apple butter on untoasted bread. When Cissy went off to her room to read, Delia would put her head on the table and cry for an hour or so before she went to bed to sleep till late afternoon.

"Crying season," Cissy called it when M.T. asked her how they were doing. Some days Cissy envied Delia her free-flowing tears. Some days she hated her for them. Cissy's tears had dried up after that one outburst at M.T.'s.

Cissy passed her eleventh birthday at the river house, immersed in a biography of Elizabeth I that Pearl had grudgingly given her. When M.T. was moving them in, she had asked the girls to give Cissy some of their old books as a housewarming present. When the two went through their prized collections and complained loudly that their favorites were missing, M.T. caught the smirk that flickered across Cissy's face and quickly declared that she had borrowed them herself and loaned them to some of the ladies from the church.

"I'm sorry, baby," she told Ruby. "We'll see if we can't get you some new copies, replace your favorites." At her insistence, Ruby and Pearl picked out the most battered and boring titles they had, and M.T. cadged a couple of cartons of used books from friends.

"Delia's girl's a reader," she told people, "and you know Delia an't got a dime to her name." No one believed her—all Cayro thought Delia was rock-star rich—but they were willing to part with some worn paperbacks, a couple of King James Bibles, and a shelf's worth of Reader's Digest Condensed Books. That was fine with Cissy. Taylor Caldwell and A. J. Cronin weren't bad, and as for the rest, they were worth their weight in trade-ins for Kate Wilhelm and anything at all by James Tiptree. Cissy would never admit that she had read Ruby and Pearl's books before she took them to Crane's, but she spent most of crying season away in her head, talking Regency French and swishing her skirt, or Creole patois and fingering a knife. Now and then she made cat's-cradle designs with her fingers and tried hard to believe in the power of a curse.

Late one Sunday afternoon when M.T. was helping Cissy fix up her room, Stephanie Pruitt showed up with a big basket of vegetables from her garden. "I haven't seen you since you got married right after we graduated," she cried out, and hugged Delia like it had been ten weeks instead of more than a decade.

Steph asked Cissy for something to drink, "some tea if you got it, sugar," and settled down at the kitchen table to tell Delia all the gossip, ignoring M.T.'s warning looks. First on her list was Clint Windsor.

"Man has never looked well since you left," Stephanie said, smiling as though it pleased her to say so. "There's a lesson in that, you can bet your life. A lot of people blamed Clint for how you had to take off, you know. Everybody knew he was just like his daddy, only crazier."

M.T. leaned over and put a hand on Delia's arm. "Don't start worrying yourself now. Wasn't nothing you or no one could have done."

"That family's been stiff and mean forever," Stephanie went on. "Old man Windsor, holier-than-thou Louise, they knew what was going on, and what did they do, huh?"

M.T. squeezed Delia's arm again. "Steph's right, honey. You remember what Clint was like. He didn't change. Lord, none of us could keep up with Clint after you left. Everybody knew he was drinking, working out at the Firestone place and drinking himself into the ground."

"Yeah," Steph said. "Got all skinny and rangy like an old man, gray-faced and drunk all the time. I heard he was sleeping on the porch at your old house, showering in the backyard, not using the inside at all. Probably wasn't no room with all them empty whiskey bottles stacked up in there." She beamed at Cissy.

"Drinking men, they like to live alone, all lazy, messy, and evil-hearted, full of hatred for everything an't drunk or dead."

M.T. tried a grin. "Lord, yes, crazy drinking men. Only wise thing Clint did was keep it at home. It's good that the girls were with Grandma Windsor, Delia. She took care of them better than he ever would have."

Delia sat up and looked at M.T. as though she had just woken from a trance.

"I thought Clint had Mama Windsor come live with him," she said. Randall had hired an Atlanta lawyer. There had been investigations, reports, an official notice of abandonment, and rude letters from the county social services people. Old man Windsor had judges in his pocket and righteousness on his side. Nothing Delia and Randall did made any difference. But through the whole struggle Delia had always thought of the girls in their house, the old tract house on Terrill Road that she and Clint had fixed up together. As much as she disliked old lady Windsor, she had been comforted by the thought of her girls in that kitchen eating meals on those carnival-colored plates Delia chose when she and Clint first married. It was a fantasy, Delia realized now. It was all a dream she had created to ease her fear. All that time her girls had been with Grandma Windsor, out at that farm where Clint swore even the ground was dry and sad. Delia put her palms flat across her eyes.

"Way Clint was, old Louise probably saved your girls, honey," Steph continued blithely. "They're doing just fine, good-looking as you ever were, towheaded and smart. That Dede is your spitting image. An't that right, M.T.?"

Delia looked over at M.T. Her mouth opened and closed several times as if she wanted to speak but could not. Steph did not notice. "Well, I've got to get back. Did you hear I got a settlement from the fire we had? Got us a great set-up now, two trailers side by side, and a big old screened-in porch. You got to come see the place sometime." She drained the glass of tea, then set it down and wiped her upper lip.

Delia rose from her chair without a word and walked straight back to her bedroom. M.T. stared after her, her frown a match for Delia's stricken face.

"Well, Lord!" Stephanie stared blankly at M.T. and Cissy. "Was it something I said? Was it the girls? Lord knows she should be over that by now. How long has it been? Lord, must be at least ten years."

All through crying season M.T. used her hard-won capital for Delia. All the sympathy and understanding that came her way for how Paul had cheated on her and how she had stood up to him—all that she directed at her oldest, dearest friend.

Most of Cayro felt that Delia's condition when she came home—

the empty grief that burned on her face, the months she spent working on Sally's cleaning crew—was penance for a woman who had abandoned her girls. Opinion had not shifted enough in Cayro to forgive or understand the sin, not enough to consider that a woman in danger might have lost her girls running from a man who would have surely strangled her in Parlour's Creek if he had caught her before she climbed on Randall's bus. No, Cayro still believed Delia a sinner, and crying season was a penance they understood. They liked to see it, Delia with her mouth soft and her eyes sore at the corners.

M.T.'s smartest move was to drag the unresisting Delia to Cayro Baptist Tabernacle week after week. Every Sunday, Delia sat on that hardwood pew, sallow and pale, eyes vacant, hands raw and swollen from scrubbing floors and swooshing toilets.

"God surely keeps track, don't he?" Reverend Myles said to M.T. the first Sunday. M.T. linked her arm with Delia's and gave one careful acknowledging nod. She knew what she was doing.

On the tenth Sunday, Mrs. Pearlman put one hand on Delia's shoulder as she pushed herself painfully up the aisle. It was an accolade. No matter arthritis, hip replacement surgery, or pain past comprehending, Marcia Pearlman would never have touched the sinner without proof of repentance. It was a promise of forgiveness, if not actual forgiveness as yet. In the way of things, women screwed up just as men did, but women's sins were paid for by children and women friends. The debt had a ready and simple dimension. The woman who had run off and fallen into the good life could never be forgiven, but the woman who came back ruined and wounded, painfully sober and stubbornly enduring, the woman who suffered publicly and hard—that woman had a chance. That woman could be brought back into the circle.

Suffer a little more, girl, Marcia Pearlman's hand said, we understand this. It was fortunate that Delia was beyond understanding. Her pride could not have survived that touch. The Delia of Mud Dog would never have stood it. The Delia who had fought and fled Clint would never have endured it. Only the Delia of crying season could sit, head down, and never notice when the hand of God reached toward her. Not forgiven but understood. Not forgiven but enjoyed. Oh, the simple pleasure in seeing her like that. No woman in the congregation would speak it, but all knew. Look at her now, Lord. Look at her now. Marcia Pearlman's hand on Delia said more than all M.T.'s whispered justifying on the steps outside.

M.T. was a rock for Delia in those first months back in Cayro, proving her friendship by a hundred good works. There were times when Delia would not speak to her, but M.T. refused to take offense. She would check in with Cissy every few days, asking only, "How you doing?" It was a code.

"We're fine," Cissy would say, and M.T. understood that Delia was not better.

"That's good, honey. Just give her time. It takes what it takes."

Every day in Cayro took Delia back to her adolescence. She sank into herself and became again the wild girl no one dared approach. The odor of her own rank body never registered. The pitying looks she drew from the other women on Sally's crew passed her by. Delia had no energy to think about anything but moving one foot in front of the other. She wore the same loose T-shirt and cutoff jeans over and over, pulled them off and put them on again until Cissy switched them for clean ones. If she could have, Cissy thought, Delia would have showered in them and gone to bed wet.

Safe. What Delia needed was to be safe. Who would touch her in those clothes, her skinny, stooped body leaving its imprint in the shape of the worn cotton and faded denim? Who would speak to her, look at her, hair pulled back and face bare? Who was this woman? Not Delia Byrd. Leave this one alone, her look said.

In the county library Cissy found a book of martyrs. There had been saints, the book revealed, who went years in one garment. One robe. No mention of how or when it was washed. Perhaps it never was, or only incidentally, the face turned up to the rain, the body rolling briefly in a summer stream. The robe would tatter and rot and fall off the gaunt and fervid frame, to be replaced by another the same as the first. No vanity, no thought. No fear, no desire. The garment served to mask the flesh, not adorn it.

Maybe the saints had some disease, and maybe Delia had caught it.

Sleeping away the days in the little house by the river, Delia dreamed of her girls again. She dreamed Amanda and Dede and Cissy were babies pushing up to her breasts with open, hungry mouths. They were all the same size, shrieking for her, flailing their arms as she tried to lift them together, to pull them up into her embrace. Invariably one child slipped. One baby fell away. Delia screamed and reached to catch her daughter, and another one slipped, while the third gasped as if dying in Delia's grip. She struggled and struggled, but she could never hold them all safe. Waking from those dreams, Delia felt her wet cheeks and her aching arms. All she had was her need to shelter and care for her girls, no matter that Dede and Amanda were almost grown. All the way across the county, Delia could feel their hunger and persistent need. They're my babies still, she told herself.

Sometimes Delia's dreams were not nightmares but memories of what had been, the loved bodies as they had first been given to her. Amanda, still flecked with blood and mucus when the nurse handed her to Delia, was shockingly tiny and desperate. When the nurse shifted that elfin creature to Clint's hands, his eyes widened in panic.

"My God," he gasped, unable to believe that anything so vibrant and powerful had come out of the numbed and passive creature Delia became in the last months of pregnancy. He had thrust the infant back to her in a reflexive movement, then looked uncomprehending at the tableau of mother and resistant child. Amanda would not take Delia's bursting nipple. The baby cried and kicked and wailed while Delia sank into the overstuffed pillows and sobbed blindly, heartbroken. Their misery had drawn Clint back to the bedside, his callused hands awkwardly patting and comforting, first Delia, then the infant girl.

That moment was among the most awful and tender Delia had ever known. She could not make peace with the contradiction, the

bloody-minded horror of the Clint who stormed strange and dangerous through the house and the Clint who so feared harming Amanda
that he wept at the sight of his rough fingers near her baby-fine cheek.

Maybe it was the smell of milk and blood. At each birth there
had been that fleeting instant of tenderness. When Dede was born
and latched immediately onto Delia's nipple, her little fists bright
pink against the creamy breast, her cheeks pumping like bellows,
Clint leaned forward in awe, his hand coming down on Delia's hip.
She hissed in startled pain, dislodging the baby's mouth, the greedy
tongue still outthrust and hungry for the love-tit. Delia flinched when
the cool air struck the burning, cracked nipple, and Clint jerked
back, looking up at Delia's face with red-rimmed eyes. Their glances
locked, and Delia felt her heart thud stubbornly with hope.

Once he recaptured Delia's look, Clint had seemed oblivious to
those two yeasty warm bodies. It was Delia he breathed in and out,
Delia he bruised and dreamed of lying limp in his arms. It was her
wet, broken flesh that called to him, the children they had made together ghostly, distracting. Delia knew she was the only thing in that
house that had ever seemed real to Clint. Only when she was gone
did the girls register, and then only for the piece of her they were.
Clint had held on to Amanda and Dede because they were anchors
for Delia's heart.

"He doesn't want them," Delia told Randall after the judge in
Atlanta gave Clint full custody. She clutched her few pictures and
ranted like a madwoman. "What he wants is to hurt me, bleed me
from every pore. That is the sin God will judge him for, that is the
crime. The man could open his veins on the throne of heaven and no
mother would ever forgive him what he has done. He is damned, by
God, damned forever."

In the little house by the river, Delia dreamed Randall and Clint,
Dede and Amanda, her babies and her rage, and woke to lie in bed
with her eyes burning and her hands in her fists. How would she
explain? Her girls would have so many questions, and how could she
face them? Delia rocked in the bed, her breasts as swollen and painful
as they were on the day she left ten-month-old Dede dreaming in her

crib at the house on Terrill Road. "God," Delia prayed, "let them forgive me. Let me have the chance to make them forgive me."

Crying season ended suddenly and completely and without apparent explanation. One morning Delia came home from work pulling at the T-shirt, lifting the cotton and wrinkling her nose.

"Damn," she told Cissy. "This thing smells." She peeled the shirt off in the kitchen, balled it up, and wiped it once down her bare midriff. Her small breasts startled Cissy, too small, it seemed, to have nursed babies.

Delia saw Cissy's expression and laughed. "Nothing here you won't have soon enough." She dropped the shirt in the garbage and went to shower, staying under the hot water for a long time.

When M.T. came over later that day, she did not ask questions. She saw Cissy's face as she was walking up the steps, nodded, and said, "I'll get us a chicken. We'll cook something special."

Cissy had wondered what was going to happen. The old Delia had never been one to cry or fall on anybody's neck. The returned Delia wasn't either. She gave her friend one kiss and stepped back, and the surprise then was that nothing changed. It did not seem to bother M.T. that Delia no longer joined in her tears or held still to be comforted. M.T. wept and laughed and cooked her chicken, as happy with the recovered Delia as she had been with the tragic heroine. She didn't even mind when Delia refused to go to church with her that first Sunday after she came back to herself.

"Got things to do," Cissy heard her tell M.T. over the phone as she made a big breakfast.

"What kind of day you think it's going to be, Cissy?" Delia asked as she set a plate of ham and eggs in front of her daughter with a smile.

"Good day to leave," Cissy said.

Delia laughed. "Lord, girl. We barely got here."

Chapter 5

On her own, Delia drove over to Holiness Redeemer to watch the congregation gather three Sundays in a row. It was the one place she could be sure to see them—Amanda and Dede, and Grandma Windsor prodding them before her. Her eyes sought out her girls as soon as the doors opened at the end of the service. But just as Delia remembered, Grandma Windsor was always the last to leave. The old woman stayed in her seat until the pews around her were empty, eyes down and lips moving in prayer while everyone shifted and stood and wondered if they should sit back down and contemplate their sins. When Clint and Delia went to church with her the week before the wedding, Delia knew the moment she stood up that Grandma Windsor had been looking forward to her blunder. The woman had stared at her in pleased disdain, her lips curling slightly and her black eyes flickering to Clint's face to be sure he knew what Delia had done. Before then Delia had not realized how much Clint's mother hated her. Afterward there was no denying that Grandma Windsor was waging a war of contempt, that she would rather her son had gone to his grave than take up with the Byrd girl, who didn't know enough to sit quietly in a pew until her betters signaled that she could rise.

Delia watched people come out of the church two and three at a time, and when it seemed there was no one left, Grandma Windsor stepped out with the girls. She hugged her big purse and nodded once at the preacher, Reverend John Hillman, Delia saw on the sign out front, which also proclaimed, "Repent! Repent! The blood of the Lamb cries out." Amanda and Dede kept their heads down and made no move that did not mimic Grandma Windsor. Delia drew breath

75

as if there were not enough air in the world to ease her emptiness. Her eyes widened and followed the girls while her face went stiff with pain. They were exactly as she had imagined and nothing at all as she had hoped. Amanda was a taller, sterner version of Grandma Windsor, but Dede looked so much like Delia's own lost mother that it hurt her heart. Delia bent forward and pressed her chin to the steering wheel to keep from rushing out to embrace them. Her girls looked miserable. Her girls looked like they wouldn't know how to be happy if someone paid them to try.

Dede's mouth was swollen and pouty. She trailed after her grandmother and sister, with her shoulders angling away from them and her hips moving jerkily, like a mechanical toy yanked along by a string. Beside her Amanda hunched her shoulders and clung to Grandma Windsor's hip, though the old woman never looked back at her. Amanda appeared to be modeling herself on her grandmother, her hair tied back in a little-old-lady bun, her lips pressing her teeth in a practiced line of disapproval, her teenage legs stepping gingerly as if her hips were calcified and arthritic. Tears blurred Delia's vision, and all she could think was how much like her the girls seemed, like Delia at their age, angry and lonely and fighting all the time to keep what she felt from showing in her face.

God means this to hurt, Delia thought, as a bitter, prickly tingling ran up and down her arms. She could almost feel Dede's soft shoulders under her fingers, smell the soap-sharp scent of Amanda's flaxen hair. She wanted to jump out of the Datsun and run to them, and shake love into their wounded hearts. Her eyes tracked the members of the congregation, women she had last seen at her wedding and men she remembered sipping whiskey on Granddaddy Windsor's front porch. Not all of them had hated her. A few had looked at her with pity. But there would be no pity in them now. She was the fallen woman, the whore of Babylon, the bitch-whelp who had abandoned her young. No one on that lawn would let her near her girls. With one will, they would chase her away.

On the second Sunday, Delia's stomach lurched when Clint pulled up in his rusty white Chevy pickup before the service started, and leaned out to hand an envelope over to Grandma Windsor. He was thinner and older than she expected, his dirty blond hair scraping the collar of one of those white uniform shirts Delia had ironed so many times. She pushed the apple of her palm into her mouth and bit down hard as he turned his head in her direction and she saw the face clearly. No, not Clint, but some blue-eyed white man just about his age. Delia realized that she was shaking. She remembered Clint's charcoal eyes under that blond hair, the gray that darkened when he got angry. Those eyes had seemed almost black her last two years in Cayro. The man lifted a hand to wave at the minister, and Delia started her car too unnerved to think about seeing her girls again.

The third Sunday, Delia got out of the car and walked up the church steps behind the last of the congregation just as the choir broke into "All Blessings" and the organ boomed out over the worshipers. From the back row she could see her girls up near the front, their bowed blond heads right beside Grandma Windsor's tight gray bun. Delia stared at them, steeling herself to keep her seat once Reverend Hillman closed the service. She wanted to be sitting there when the girls walked past. She wanted to put her hand out and touch them, lift her eyes and see their faces when they realized who she was.

Tears slipped down Delia's face. She did not hear the sermon. She barely registered the choir. Only halfway through the service did she notice that the family in the pew across the aisle was looking in her direction, the father glaring angrily and the mother pick-faced and rigid. The two brown-haired youngsters with them kept squirming and looking up at their parents. No more than eight or nine, the boys had no way of knowing who Delia was, but there was no missing their parents' outrage. Their big, curious eyes kept shifting to Delia and back to their dad.

A flush bloomed on Delia's cheeks. Sweat broke on her forehead and beneath her dress. Her eyes roamed the nearby pews. A dozen people were shifting and craning their necks. Each glance was scalding. Each pursed mouth pressed a nerve. As the stir increased, more people turned to look. Delia locked her hands together in a double fist and kept her eyes on them through the rest of the service. She had told herself that she could stand it, the outrage and contempt, the likelihood that Grandma Windsor would slap her face and curse her—anything to stand close to her girls and speak their names. But at the benediction Delia stood up and walked out without looking back. She had been wrong. She was not ready. If these strangers looked at her with such loathing, what would she find in her daughters' eyes?

But as Delia was driving away from Holiness Redeemer, the hand of God reached out to her again over at Cayro Baptist Tabernacle. Mrs. Pearlman looked for Delia that morning and, when she didn't see her, spoke bluntly to M.T. on the church steps. The arthritis in her wrists and elbows had grown so bad that she was keeping the Bonnet going only through stubborn determination and a high tolerance for pain. Her stubbornness was limitless, but the flexibility in her fingers was almost gone. She no longer trusted herself with a pair of sharp scissors, and neither did her customers. Even her regulars had started to go over to Marietta, and her business depended on occasional strangers who didn't know better.

"Have Delia come see me," she told M.T. "If we can come to an agreement, I might have some work for her at the Bonnet." Her powdered cheeks trembled as she spoke, and her right hand settled more tightly on her cane, but her voice was firm and her words audible to the women standing around. M.T. nodded.

"Marcia, what are you thinking?" said Nadine Reitower, head of the Mothers' Relief Fund. "You don't want to take that hussy into your business."

Ruby and Pearl snickered into their Bibles, but M.T. didn't hear.

Mrs. Pearlman's eyes had sparked. "There's barely any business to speak of. I haven't even seen you this month. Have I, Nadine?"

Mrs. Reitower blushed. Her hand rose toward the little hat that held back her brown curls, but she stopped herself. "That woman's a scandal," she said. "No one will come to the shop if you put her in there."

Marcia looked around at the women standing on the church

steps. "Good Christians will," she said. "Good Christian women who know what it is to sin and ask forgiveness, I think they will come. There's no scandal in repentance, no scandal in working hard and paying your bills. And Delia Byrd used to work for me. I know what she can do. She was one of the best hairdressers I ever hired. Won't have lost that. Could probably even take care of that cowlick problem of yours, Nadine. Save you a bundle on hats and hairpins."

Nadine scowled and M.T. hooted. She herded the twins back into the Buick and drove directly to Delia's to tell her the good news. "Girl," she shouted happily when Delia met her at the driveway, "wait till I tell you what you missed at church."

Delia gave Sally two weeks' notice and started in at the Bonnet on Wednesdays and Saturdays. The rest of the week she worked at Beckman's department store in Marietta, in the tiny beauty shop behind the Misses' Dresses and winter coats. The first few people who came into the Bonnet and saw Delia there stared like she had two heads and the mark of Satan on each of them, but her old detachment had come back. She just nodded blandly at the outraged faces and walked away when they complained. This was work she could do with both eyes closed and half her mind engaged elsewhere. When she put her hands on a woman's head, Delia Byrd felt almost as powerful as she had when she stood onstage with Mud Dog. This was work she knew. This was work she was good at. It healed something in her soul to be doing good work, even if she did it on sufferance for way too little money.

Delia did her job. She did relaxed-curl permanents for women she had gone to high school with, tinting gray hair back to brown. Impassively she did modified punk cuts for the teenage daughters of women who wouldn't speak to her, ignoring their timid questions about Randall and the band. When Marcia told her she was a wonder and the lady at Beckman's started paying her more money, Delia didn't seem to notice. It was as if her brain was already overfull, too much to be worked out and too little time. She wore denim wrap-around skirts and cotton blouses right out of the Goodwill box, bought Cissy jeans from the Sears Roebuck outlet and plain white T-shirts sealed in plastic packages.

Once or twice Cissy came home to see Delia sitting at the kitchen table with her face stricken and empty, but as soon as she stepped in the door, Delia would be up and bustling around.

"What you want, Little Bit, something to eat?" Delia's voice was always loud and bright.

Cissy would shake her head and run back to her room. This was a new version of her mother, not the familiar stumbling Delia from Venice Beach and not that banshee who drove them across the country. Some days Cissy actually missed the weeping Delia in her gray stinking T-shirt. At least that Delia had left her alone.

John Hillman, minister of the Holiness Redeemer Church of God, lived out on the Poinsette Road southwest of town. Delia had already been out to his house one Saturday after work, when his wife told her he was visiting some sick folks out in the country. The woman had looked at Delia with a neutral expression, but her eyes were burning and intent, and her mouth reminded Delia of that cook who cursed her the first morning in Cayro. Probably hopes I'll burn in hell, Delia thought, keeping her own face as carefully composed as Mrs. Hillman's.

On her second try Delia spotted the minister on his way out to his car just as she was driving up. She called to him with relief. She had figured she could face his wife once, maybe twice more before losing her confidence.

"Reverend," she said, "I'm Delia Byrd." She considered using the Windsor name, but she could not bear to say it. Besides, she told herself, surely the man knew who she was as well as his wife did.

Reverend Hillman reached for her hand. "Mrs. Byrd," he said. "I've been expecting you."

Delia was startled. "You have?"

"My wife said you had stopped by." He smiled gently. "And I knew your people. I knew your mother."

Delia felt all her air leave her. Reverend Hillman's eyes were deep-set, sad, and compassionate. He looked at her like she was a child who had fallen and was turning to him to raise her up. For an instant Delia was that child, and then a wave of nausea flooded her throat.

"I didn't know that," she said, and swallowed painfully. "That you knew my mother. I didn't know that."

"Well, I'm not a young man." The minister brushed dust down the front of his trousers. "And I've lived in Cayro most of my life. I was away when you married Clint Windsor, I'm sorry to say. Didn't come back to take over the parish until after you had gone."

Gone, Delia thought. Not run off, but gone. "I don't remember you," she said.

"But I remember you." Reverend Hillman put his hands together in a steeple. "I remember you the Easter after your family was lost— the look on your face when you came to listen to the choir service. You came alone and you stayed at the back. You were just a spit of a girl, and so badly hurt I prayed for you with all my heart. But I was young and unsure of myself. When you didn't come back, I never went after you. I've regretted that for years."

"I was all right," Delia said.

"Were you?" Reverend Hillman leaned forward.

Was I? Delia wondered. Probably not.

"Are you all right now?"

Delia laughed. "Probably not," she said, unable to stop herself from grinning like a fool. She had not been prepared for this.

He smiled back at her. "Well, maybe we can do something about that."

"I want to see my girls," Delia blurted. "That's why I came to you. They're with Grandma Windsor."

"Louise Windsor, yes." Reverend Hillman nodded and looked over at his car. "It's been hard for her, I think. But they are fine girls, Deirdre and Amanda. Fine girls. And of course you want to see them.

Who would know better how hard it is to lose a mother?" He turned back to her.

"I saw you at church a few weeks ago, but you left early. Have you spoken to Mrs. Windsor yet?"

"No, I hadn't thought she would want to speak to me."

He studied the toes of his shiny black shoes. "Probably not," he agreed. "A lot of anger in Louise Windsor, a lot." He sighed. "You want me to speak to her?"

Delia felt as if her hips had turned to jelly. She had no idea how to stand when she was not wound up tight to argue or plead or fight off an attack. Was he really going to help her? "Oh yes," she breathed.

Reverend Hillman licked his lips and glanced at his car again. "I have to ask you, Mrs. Byrd. Are you going to be coming to join us at Holiness?"

Delia's hips locked. "I hadn't planned on it," she said. "I've been going to Cayro Baptist with my friend M.T., but I'm not sure what I'm going to do. Other than stay here. I'm going to stay in Cayro, that's for certain."

For a moment Delia imagined herself attending Holiness Redeemer, under the gaze of Mrs. Hillman and Grandma Windsor and all those old men who had done business with Clint and his daddy. The minister had surprised her by talking about her family, mentioning her mother. But no, Delia thought, she was not going to join his church.

Reverend Hillman's eyes were trained on her, sad and knowing. "Well," he said after a moment, "you should take your time deciding what to do, but I'm glad you're here to stay. There's good people here, some hard ones and some that are pretty worn down. But good-hearted people nonetheless—who will be watching over you. There are lots of those."

Delia's throat constricted. He wasn't going to help her after all. She pulled her hands up to her belly, pressing hard below her heart. "Thank you," she said, "for talking to me—I appreciate it."

"Oh, thank me later," Reverend Hillman said. "After I speak to

Louise. Maybe she'll listen to me. If she does, we'll see if you can't get a little time with your girls."

Delia gaped at him. Reverend Hillman ran his hand once over his almost bald head and walked to his car. "We'll talk again," he said. "Louise is not going to be happy to see me, so this might take a little time. We'll talk when I have something to tell you."

Delia watched him drive away and looked back at the house. Mrs. Hillman was at the window, her face like a storm cloud and her mouth like a seam. Delia dipped her head and smiled. Some days you get a little, she thought. Some days you get a lot.

Three months after Delia started working at the Bonnet, Marcia Pearlman had a stroke while locking up the shop one Saturday afternoon. She slid sideways and cawed like a crow just as Delia reached her car. When Delia ran back, Mrs. Pearlman kicked twice and rolled over unconscious.

For several weeks the Bonnet was closed while Marcia lay curled in a bed at the hospital. Delia visited her every other day, watching as she slowly regained the ability to speak and move. She was angry at the doctors and then angry at God. "Damn," she said for the first time in her life, tears streaming down her cheeks. She wanted to sit up, say what she had to say, and take care of herself, but her left leg buckled at every effort to stand and her left arm dangled uselessly, the wrist already turning in and the fingers going blue-gray.

The doctor told her she had done remarkably well. A stroke was an unpredictable thing. She could have been so much worse off, crippled for life and unable to talk. "Damn," Mrs. Pearlman said, "damn damn," and waved him away from the bed.

"I got nobody," she told Delia in a halting mumble. "Little Social Security. Little savings. Not much." She shifted her left arm. "Damn hand hurts. Damn."

"You got friends," Delia told her. "Good friends."

"Friends." Mrs. Pearlman sighed. "Need money. You can make

me some money." Her brown eyes were flinty and keen. "You got talent. I let you run my shop. You make me some money."

Delia frowned.

The shop and the building belonged to her outright, Mrs. Pearlman explained painfully. "But won't sell it. Lease it to you. Lease it to you, and you'll make me some money. And"—she paused and forced her lips into a smile—"you got to do my hair. Every week you got to do my hair."

"If I run the shop, people might not come."

"Who comes now?" Mrs. Pearlman shrugged weakly. "You're good. Time passes. They'll come. You'll make me the money I need." She closed her eyes, then opened them and fixed them on Delia.

"Anything you do to the shop, you pay for," she said. "I pay for nothing."

Slowly Delia nodded.

"Good." Mrs. Pearlman shook her arm again. "Damn damn," she said with a frown. "Damn damn."

Marcia's insurance man drew up a lease, and Delia called Rosemary in California to ask for a loan. If she was going to run the shop herself, she meant to repair what years of neglect had done.

"Just what I have always wanted," Rosemary shouted into the phone. "To be part owner of a white woman's beauty salon."

"Well, I won't exactly own it. I'll be leasing it, but I'll do your hair when you come visit." Rosemary could hear the smile in Delia's voice. "I'll read up on weaving and stuff, do it any way you want."

The Bonnet had been a beauty parlor for forty years and a garage before that. It was just a concrete-floored outbuilding for what had been the Cayro Hotel, but the hotel was long gone. The Bonnet was nothing much—one big room with a set of sinks in a section walled off by a low-hanging arch—but it was the first place Delia had ever earned a paycheck, the site, she swore, of too many of her beginnings and endings. From the back window she had watched the police take her uncle Luke away to jail and Granddaddy Byrd threaten the sheriff. From the front window, with its screen of dying plants, she had watched the sunset the night she knew herself ready to say yes to

Clint Windsor's proposal of marriage. And it was in the Bonnet's doorway that she had staggered and felt the wet stream between her thighs and known by the salt-sweet smell and the bite of pain that Amanda was about to be born.

When Delia decided to take over the Bonnet, M.T. quit her job at the A&P. "We'll do fine," she said when Delia protested. "You and me will do just fine. We'll get the shop open and going in no time. You wait and see."

M.T. read everything she could find on bookkeeping and tax accounting, signed up for a course at the junior college, and designed her own system around what Delia said she needed. "Real friends," M.T. told Cissy. "Your mama and I are real friends, and we know how to take care of each other."

"Well, I hope so," Delia said with a laugh. "We'll either do fine together or go to hell in a handcart. Either way, we'll take care of each other."

"Why you think Marcia Pearlman was so set on you taking the shop?" Steph asked. She had agreed to take a chair once the Bonnet opened—strictly on commission, of course, just like M.T.

"Maybe 'cause she and I both know it suits me."

"Yeah?" M.T. turned a page in her accounting book. "You think a building is you all over?"

"In a way. I think it is a weight," Delia said. "I think this place is something you carry. I know how to carry it, and I appreciate it, God knows. Couldn't make a living no other way, but I also know what Marcia Pearlman intends. For a Baptist lady, that woman is almost Catholic. She expects expiation, public and precise. This is where Marcia Pearlman thinks I should be. This is the price she thinks I should pay for all my sins, doing hair till I die and cursing her name with every water bill. I even think she means it kindly. In her own way I think she's ensuring my chance at salvation. I don't imagine she cares if I like what I'm doing. Happiness don't matter much in the Baptist scheme of things."

"You think the hippies care if you happy?" M.T. sniffed. She got defensive when Delia started talking about Baptists in that tone. For all her jokes, M.T. knew herself a good Baptist woman.

"No," Delia agreed. "An't no hippies keeping track around here either."

Delia and M.T. and Stephanie were working on the shop one afternoon when a big sky-blue Oldsmobile pulled up and Granddaddy Byrd got out. Delia had never seen the car before, or the woman behind the wheel.

"You got yourself a girlfriend?" M.T. asked when he came inside.

"Harrumph!" he said, but heat showed on his cheeks.

Standing at one of the sinks, Delia watched him come toward her. They hadn't spoken since she arrived in Cayro, and she couldn't imagine what had brought him to the Bonnet.

"I got some stuff for you." Granddaddy Byrd's tongue appeared and wet his lower lip. "Some curtains and stuff you had in boxes. Thought you could use them here." The color in his face deepened.

M.T. waved an arm at Stephanie. "Let's go get some Cokes," she said. "I'm choking on dust." The two women edged past the old man with a quizzical smile in Delia's direction.

"I appreciate the curtains," Delia said, "you bringing them by." She glanced out the window. The big square-faced woman in the car certainly didn't look like any kind of girlfriend.

"That's Mrs. Stone," Granddaddy Byrd said quickly. "The deputy told me I can't drive no more, and she's been helping me out."

"You have an accident?"

"No, no. Just bumped a little old garbage can at the post office. Nothing hurt." He licked his lips again. "There's some flowerpots too. In the car. I thought maybe you'd want to clean up that window, put in some better pots."

"That's real nice of you, Granddaddy."

"You an't spoken to Clint yet, have you?" he said abruptly.

Delia reached for the mop M.T. had left propped against the sink. "No."

"He's pretty sick," Granddaddy Byrd said. "Some people say it's serious. Somebody said it was bad enough he might die."

Delia's hands closed around the mop handle. Sick? What kind of sick? "I hadn't heard that," she said.

Granddaddy Byrd nodded at her. "I figured you wouldn't have heard. Thought you should know." He looked around the shop. "You're working hard."

"Why?" she asked. "Why did you think I should know?"

Her grandfather looked at her. "You went to talk to Reverend Hillman, didn't you? You went out to the church? Well, Clint don't go out there, and Louise Windsor an't about to tell nobody her business. Seemed to me you should know what's going on." He shuffled his feet. "You want to get those girls, you need to know what is going on."

They looked at each other, the old man with his flushed cheeks and his faded eyes, and Delia with her hands locked around that mop like it was holding her up.

"Thank you," she said finally.

Granddaddy Byrd dropped his head. "You got to help me, if you want that stuff in the car."

Delia was carrying the last carton in when M.T. and Steph came back.

"You all right?" M.T. asked her.

Delia put the box down. "He told me Clint was sick," she said. "You know anything about that?"

"Sick or crazy, I don't think anybody knows for sure." Steph dropped in her chair, pushed her mousy brown hair back, and looked at herself in the mirror. She had been talking about dyeing it red like Delia's.

"Somebody said he was sick last summer." M.T. was frowning. "But nobody has seen him in so long. I didn't know anything to tell you."

"An't he working out at Firestone?" Delia asked.

"Well, not the last year. He was for a long time." Steph turned her chair toward Delia. "Is it cancer? People talked about something like that, but I thought it was just gossip."

"The Windsors keep to themselves pretty much. You know that," M.T. said. "Clint an't been right in years, always drinking himself into the ground. Don't think I've laid eyes on him since his daddy died and his mama had that big service. I saw the girls then. I wrote you about that."

Delia nodded.

"Well, after that Clint went to live with his mama for a few years, straightened up a little. But he kept your old house, used the money from his daddy's insurance to buy it outright. I think his mama wanted him to stay with her and the girls, but he didn't."

Steph spun around in her chair. "My Lyle swears Clint can't stand his mama and that's why he keeps the house, so he don't have to stay where he can't stand to be."

"She is a hard woman."

"Yeah."

"It's a fact."

"But do you think he's really sick?" Delia stood up and grabbed the mop again.

"I don't know," M.T. said. "I just don't know."

"I'll find out," Steph promised. "Just give me a few days and I'll find out everything."

The plan was to reopen the Bonnet in February, and there were only two real obstacles. One was the effort required to get the shop itself ready, but Rosemary's check helped immensely, and neither Delia nor M.T. was afraid of hard work. Steph complained a lot, but she got down to it too, helping with the scraping and scrubbing while M.T. and Delia did the painting themselves. Most of the paint came again from Sally, who seemed to have endless stockpiles stored out in her garage, cleansers and paper goods bought at discount and bins of stuff other people had thrown out that Sally knew would come in handy someday. That meant that some of the paint was old and useless and all of it came in odd colors. Delia and M.T. experimented until they produced a great quantity of a curious peach glaze.

"I like it," Steph told them, and they took that as gospel. It was a good thing they all liked the color, because the greasy, stained walls of the old beauty shop needed three coats. It was also fortunate that they had a little money to buy white for the ceiling.

"Too much of a good thing is always a problem," Steph said. "And I think I would turn bilious if this was all there was all over everything."

The curtains Granddaddy Byrd had brought were faded and tattered, but Delia put the pots to good use in the front window, salvaging a few of Mrs. Pearlman's plants and buying new ones to create a fantasy jungle that would draw people into the shop.

Once the work was in progress, the other obstacle loomed larger. Nadine Reitower confronted M.T. on the sidewalk one afternoon, demanding to know what they thought they were doing giving over an institution like the Bonnet to a woman like Delia Byrd. Since she hadn't made any headway with Marcia Pearlman, she had decided to confront the beast in its lair.

"I didn't give her nothing," M.T. said, "though I would sure enough. You know perfectly well that Marcia's leasing the shop to Delia now that she can't run it no more."

Nadine plucked at the thin lace collar that protruded from her pink sweater, which was buttoned all the way up. "I told Marcia before I wouldn't have Delia Byrd touching me. Now that hussy's taking over the only place I've ever gone to get my hair done!"

"Nothing is going to rub off on you, you know," M.T. said. "You an't gonna take sin from the touch of Delia's hand."

"Marcia should never have given that woman the shop in the first place." Nadine tossed her head, and her hen-brown bun bobbed dangerously. She was showing the effect of not having been to a hairdresser for a while.

"She didn't give it to her." M.T. spoke impatiently. "It's a lease. Steep rent too, and money Marcia is going to need. Seems to me you should be more concerned with making sure Marcia gets her money out of the fallen woman than keeping the fallen woman from doing decent work. If she don't manage the Bonnet, what you think she's going to do? She won't have no choice but to offer sin and wicked ways at half price to support herself and her child!"

"You are a rude and vulgar woman." Nadine's forehead was shiny with sudden sweat.

"Yes, I am, and I'm late too." M.T. stepped around Nadine and marched to the Bonnet's door.

That evening M.T. and Steph discussed the problem over a plate of fried potatoes and shrimp at Goober's restaurant and bar.

"You think anyone will come?" Steph fretted.

"I think a few will come just because Delia's so scandalous," M.T. said. "And a few will never come no matter if Delia suddenly had a halo light up over her spotless soul." She dipped a potato stick in ketchup and popped it in her mouth. "Hell, if she hadn't run off to become rich and famous, Delia would own the Bonnet by now."

"She is good with hair," Steph agreed.

M.T. chewed happily. "We just have to remind everyone of that before Nadine Reitower can remind them what a sinner Delia is."

"It would help if Delia made up with Clint." Steph picked at her shrimp. They were pitiful, but Goober's made the best fried potatoes in the state. "I asked around, and it looks like old man Byrd is right. Way I hear it, that man might die."

"One thing at a time," M.T. said. "One thing at a time. How we gonna get these fool women into the Bonnet?" She bit into another potato. "What you think? Should we run some contest? Or offer makeovers to the home economics teachers?"

"Naaa." Steph swirled ketchup all over her shrimp. "Junior discount maybe. But all we got to do is get the girls to talking about how their mothers won't go to Delia. Make her sound really dangerous and scandalous, and they'll come to us. We'll get the mothers when they see what she does for their girls. And we'll keep our rates lower than Beckman's."

M.T. laughed. "Stephanie, you are one smart woman," she said, and ordered another plate of fried potatoes.

Chapter 6

Reverend Hillman drove out to the old Windsor farm three times in one month to talk to Louise about letting her granddaughters see their mother. He had known from the first it would not be an easy task; Louise Windsor was not easy about anything. It was a family characteristic. Old man Windsor had refused to go to church more than twice a year, the week before Christmas and the week before Easter—on the holidays themselves he kept at home—but Louise had been a reliable face in the pew three rows from the front. Always at her side were those two stern-faced little girls, in cheap matching cotton outfits obviously chosen by the grandmother. The older girl, Amanda, was a regular at vacation Bible school and weekly prayer meetings. The younger, Dede, came to Holiness Redeemer only because her grandmother dragged her, and never looked up at him when he tried to speak to her. She was the one whose image chided him, reminding him so painfully of Delia's mother that he was grateful for the days she wasn't there.

"It's a shock to see her," his wife declared one time, surprising him by saying exactly what he had been thinking. "She's just the image of Deirdre Byrd, isn't she?"

"Children are like that," he had replied. "Every now and then one will come out the dead-on copy of some relative or other. It's like God is making another run at getting the model right."

Mrs. Hillman sniffed. "Well, that's a family needs remaking. Didn't none of them live long enough to do much more than make a few babies and go on."

Only once in ten years had Reverend Hillman met the girls' father, and that was the week they buried the old man. Clint had given the reverend a brief inclination of his stiff neck and turned away before the service began. He had watched the burial from off to one side, hands on his hips, eyes fixed on the casket. At no point did he look at his daughters, though they looked at him often. The hunger Reverend Hillman saw in those two girlish faces pushed him to preach more adamantly about the importance of love and forgiveness. Afterward several people told him how inspired his words had been, but neither Clint nor Louise Windsor said a thing. All Clint did was give another abrupt nod and hand over an envelope that contained exactly thirty-five one-dollar bills.

The reverend's wife had shaken her head. "That was a fifty-dollar burial if I ever heard one," she said, "but the Windsors wouldn't know the difference. Bet that boy would have planted his daddy in his peanut field if he could and saved the cost of the coffin as well."

On his third trip out to the Windsor place, as he pulled up to the farmhouse, Reverend Hillman recalled his wife's words with a heavy heart. He had reproved her for her tone but had been unable to deny that she was right. Clint Windsor would probably have loved the notion of plowing over his daddy's bones every spring, and Louise would have come out to watch with glee. What would it be like, he wondered, to see that old woman smile? In all his years at Redeemer he had never witnessed it. But what, after all, had she to smile about? Her husband was a brutal drunk, and from all accounts the son had turned out just the same. Reverend Hillman wiped sweat from his brow and remembered how many times the woman had come to church with bruises on her neck or puffy eyes. He had never been able to get her to admit that anything was wrong. What made the kind of woman who would take that as her due? he asked himself for the thousandth time. And what kind of women was she making out of those two youngsters in her care?

"You're getting to be a regular visitor," Louise said when he came up on the porch. Behind her he could see Amanda, with her hair in a kerchief and an apron tied tightly around her hips. "But this is my boiling day and I haven't any time to sit and argue with you."

"Boiling day?" He sniffed the steamy, bleach-scented draft off the porch.

"Oh, you wouldn't know. Your wife's young for it, but some of us were taught a woman changes over her sheets and sheers when winter passes. February fifteenth, my mama always told me. By then you're supposed to have boiled your whites and be ready to think about spring. Some years I do it a little earlier, some a bit later." She looked into the house once and rubbed her lower back. "This year I got buds on my forsythia real early, so I'm pushing it a bit. It's been such a damp, ugly winter. Maybe I'm wanting to move on into spring earlier than usual."

Reverend Hillman smiled. "I think we all are," he said.

Louise shot him a suspicious glance. "You come around to nag at me some more?"

"I've come for us to talk again. And yes, I do want to talk about the girls and their mother."

"Mother!" Louise's mouth twisted. "I've been more a mother to these girls than she will ever be." She shook her head. "You're wasting your time, Reverend. Delia an't no mother. She comes around here, she'll just get the girls all upset. First little trouble comes along, she'll take off again. Then what, huh? She goes away another few years and comes back, you gonna come speak for her all over again?"

"She seems set on staying in Cayro," Reverend Hillman said. "I don't think she wants to do them any harm. And having them know she cares about them might do them some good."

Louise snorted. "Good! There's no good in that woman."

"There's good in all of us," the reverend said carefully.

"So you say, but I an't no preacher. I'm a working woman raising two hardheaded abandoned girls growing fast into women themselves. And I don't want her putting no notions in their heads. Got enough trouble now." She looked back at the house again, clearly not wanting the girls to be part of this conversation. Reverend Hillman looked past her and saw that Amanda was gone, maybe back to the kitchen and the boiling pots.

He cleared his throat and decided to try another tack. "Trouble," he said, his eyes slowly sweeping the yard. "I know you don't want no trouble. That's what I was saying to Deacon Hayman when he told me he was worried what might come of all this. None of us want to see no family fighting in court, lawyers telling everyone what to do, the county welfare folks getting in on it."

"They wouldn't have no say in what I do." Louise's face pinked at the thought of lawyers and county officials. "I'm raising these girls right."

"I would support you in that anytime, anywhere." Reverend Hillman nodded firmly. "If you have to go to court, I would tell everyone how hard you have worked with Deirdre and Amanda."

"I wouldn't have to go to court." Now she was truly alarmed.

"Well, I would hope not. But you know how bureaucrats are. I remember when the child protective people gave you all that trouble before."

"That was 'cause of that hippie she took up with, him and his money, him and his lawyer," Louise fumed.

"Well, lawyers do make trouble." Reverend Hillman watched her face.

She thought for a moment. When she spoke, her voice was uncertain. "Delia got lawyers now?"

"I don't know," he said. "But she seemed very determined when she talked to me. And I had hoped we could make sure there would be no trouble. She said what she wanted was to see the girls."

"She an't gonna take 'em," Louise said quickly.

"Well, how could she do that?" Reverend Hillman waited a beat while Louise grew more and more nervous. "Didn't the court give you custody?"

"They gave Clint custody. I'm not on the papers. I just been doing all the work."

"Well, Clint." Reverend Hillman shrugged. "That wouldn't be a problem, would it?"

. Louise looked him speculatively up and down. "You been talking to her a lot?" she asked.

"No," he said. "I've just spoken to her the one time."

"Well." Louise gazed off across the yard. "Maybe we could talk about her coming to see them once or twice. Long as that's all we're talking about."

The reverend inclined his head in agreement, keeping his eyes level with hers. "That's all we're talking about," he said. "She just wants to see the girls."

Louise's mouth twisted again, her lips drawing up into a grimace. As she showed Reverend Hillman into the house, he realized that she was afraid. Probably thought everyone was some kind of danger to her. And the problem was, of course, that she was partly right.

Dede and Amanda took the news of their mother's return with little visible response. To the reverend they simply said they would do what their grandmother wanted. What they said to her, he had no way of knowing. But they had grown up in that dusty yard, eating their grandma's grits and stewed tomatoes, swallowing her sour resentments and seething distrust of anything she could not bleach or scrub or bury in lye. They wore her expressions and hid their thoughts so carefully that they might not have known what they wanted anyway. Their days were full of Grandma Windsor's favorite Bible verses, Revelation and the whore of Babylon, not the parables but the fallen woman. Delia was the curse and the stink of their lives. Packages that came at holidays were refused or remained unopened. Cards were burned in the trash fire. Bitter jokes were told behind their backs or repeated purposely to teach them a lesson. The smell of homemade soap trailed behind them, and their classmates laughed at the clothes their grandma made them wear. The sisters breathed in rage like steam off soup. Their mother had not loved them enough. What did they care if she came around now?

Delia decided she would be ready to reopen the Bonnet by Valentine's Day. She and Steph and M.T., with Cissy's grudging help, put up banners across the window and signs on every pole downtown. M.T. took flyers to church, and Steph went over to Beckman's and put some up in the women's lounge. M.T. had not been paid for cutting and styling hair since the twins were born, but she hoped to do as well as Steph. Steph hadn't worked for a living since leaving high school.

"My family and friends will come to me," M.T. kept saying. Delia agreed with a smile, though she was still unsure anyone at all would come to any of them. It was a small town, and Beckman's with its two chairs was not that far away.

The first few days the three women kept the Bonnet's windows full of fresh flowers and the chairs full of friends getting free introductory haircuts and treatments. Early on the opening Saturday, before the customers came in, Delia served coffee and corn muffins with slabs of bacon.

"You must have got up early to make these," M.T. teased.

"Yeah," Delia admitted. "Couldn't sleep anyway. They're a little heavy. Don't have the knack for making muffins, never did."

"You should have gone over to Biscuit World." Stephanie spoke around a mouthful of muffin. "Old man Reitower has the knack. Makes the best biscuits you ever tasted, specially the sausage biscuits. Makes you appreciate coffee all over again."

"Good there's something worthwhile in that family." M.T. sipped creamy coffee and smoothed her skirt, which stopped well short of her dimpled knees. No matter how wide her ass became, her legs were smooth and shapely. She had stopped at Biscuit World on the way over and noticed both the owner and his son looking at her legs when she left. And what would Nadine Reitower think about that, that skinny full-of-herself old biddy?

"We get this place going good, I'll start paying for biscuits," Delia said. "Right now I can barely afford cornmeal."

"Thought you was supposed to be rich," Stephanie said to Delia, waggling her muffin in the air and scattering crumbs on her skirt. "Thought everyone in the music business was rich. Wearing them clothes, riding them buses." She grinned and pointed a finger at Delia. "Doing them drugs."

"Oh yeah, drugs." Delia shook her head. "Lots of drugs. Marlboros and Camels, Southern Comfort and Jim Beam, straight-up whiskey in a warm glass."

"Sounded like it sometimes," Steph said. "Way you got so hoarse on some of them songs, sounded like you were sipping something."

"I was doing more than sipping." Delia's tone was harsh. "I was drunk almost all the time I was in California." She passed the muffins around again and saw that Cissy was listening. "No sense lying. It was awful, but mostly I wasn't conscious for it."

"All of it couldn't have been awful." M.T. was uncomfortable. She turned her chair so she didn't have to look at Cissy or Stephanie. "Some of it must have been good."

"Yeah, that Randall sure was pretty that time I saw him. One handsome man." Stephanie blushed slightly. "And famous don't hurt a man. Rich and famous. He made a lot of money on those albums."

"Oh, Randall was never rich. He just looked rich. *Diamonds and Dirt* was the only album Mud Dog did that made any money." Delia blew on her coffee and seemed to forget for a moment where she was. "What Randall had was presence. He looked like a star, behaved like a star. He made people think he was the real thing." Randall had charmed record company men so thoroughly that he even got them to front the cash for the star lifestyle. Reporters and photographers following everywhere, fancy hotel rooms trashed, glazed eyes, everything done for effect. All those bills handed over to nervous accountants. All those drugs laid out on redwood burl coffee tables polished to mirror intensity. The star life, the star presence. No cash to hand, but lots of perks.

"There just was never any money," Delia said.

Stephanie raised her eyebrows in disbelief. "No money?"

"Not a dime." Delia leaned back in her chair. "I didn't even have a phone for the longest time. Couldn't make a call if I wasn't in somebody's office or hanging at Randall's."

M.T. and Stephanie just stared at her. It was unimaginable, what Delia was telling them. A life lived in luxury but without funds. How did it work?

"Crazy how rich you can behave when you an't got a dime in

your pocket. You learned to charge things to the company or borrow against your name." Old clothes had to be sent out to be cleaned by hotel staff, new clothes bought on credit.

"Underwear was the hardest." Delia pushed her hair back. "I could get a fancy dress for a show charged to some fancy store on Wilshire, but I couldn't get panties, bras, or socks. If it couldn't be charged to some record company account, it couldn't be had." In seven years she never had in hand more than four hundred dollars. Delia told them it was like living in the twilight zone. If she stepped away from everything, it evaporated in her hand.

"Can I get a salary?" Delia had asked Randall when *Mud Dog/ Mud Dog* was in production.

"A salary? Girl, you gonna be rich!"

"Yeah, well I'd like something I could count on."

"You can count on me."

"Randall."

"Girl, girl."

As a conciliatory gesture, Randall got Columbia to issue Delia monthly payments of a thousand dollars. "That's not much," Rosemary had complained on Delia's behalf. She was getting a percentage for writing some of the music, though everyone knew Delia was working with her.

"Delia don't need money. Everything is paid for. She don't got rent or grocery bills or car payments. She can charge anything to the band. Anything she wants I get for her," Randall snarled out the side of his mouth. "Delia's my woman! She don't need nothing. Shit. Shit damn."

The joke was, Delia told M.T. and Stephanie, that Randall was always "borrowing" cash from her. More to the point, when she left, she had only the car in her name and six thousand in her bank account.

"Six thousand for what? Eight or nine years?" Stephanie was pensive. "Me and Lyle are doing better than that."

"Well, I just never thought about the money," Delia said. "I trusted Randall. Even when I should have known better, I trusted the man. Maybe it was the drinking, but the truth is, Randall had himself a piece of magic. He didn't know how to use it, and he never cared enough to really work it. But if he turned those big dark eyes on you, you just naturally leaned into him. Couldn't imagine he was mortal and silly like the rest of us. Thought he was something special just because he could sing sweet enough to break your heart."

"Ought to rename this the Rock Star Shop." Stephanie was looking out the window, watching people walk by and look back at her. It was time to open.

The words startled them all. Until Steph spoke, Delia's nervous chatter had obscured the fact that she was doing what she had sworn to herself she would not do—talking about the years with Randall.

Cissy was right there listening all the time, rocking her shoulders against the arch and watching her mother from behind her dark glasses and thinking about her daddy. Delia had no right to talk about him in that casual, scornful way. Stephanie had no right to suggest trading on his fame.

"I like 'Bee's Bonnet,' " she said loudly. "It's got history behind it. It's been here forever." She waved a hand at the peach walls and the white trim. It had been a gray morning, but light was pouring in the window now, steam rising from the coffeepot in the nook by the door and covering the smell of fresh paint and ammonia. If Delia renamed the shop, Cissy would find a way to burn it down.

Delia looked at Cissy, her eyes bright with gratitude. "Good," she said. " 'Cause I an't going to waste no money repainting that sign." She stabbed a rat-tailed comb into a jar of blue disinfectant.

Everybody laughed. The moment when it all could have changed passed. Cissy thumped her hand against the arch and bit her lip.

The Bonnet's first paying customer was Gillian Wynchester, Cayro's excuse for a liberated woman. Gillian was famous for declaring to her bingo group that she could understand the impulse to burn a bra, that she'd rather swing free than squeeze herself into the scratchy, lace-bedeviled contraptions her husband was always bringing her back from his twice-a-year trips to New Orleans.

"Man goes in those titty bars down there," Gillian told her friends, "comes home with stuff he saw on them whores, and expects me to wear it for him. Most ungodly getups you ever saw. And look at me—I an't got nothing up top to speak of. What's the use trying to make gallon jugs out of teacups?"

Gillian smirked at the awed shock her words provoked. After that she made a point of telling everyone what a freethinker she was. "You can't tell what I might not do," Gillian swore, though the truth was that she had not refused her husband anything since the day she spoke her vows—not even coming to bed in the green satin bustier that just pushed her double-A bosom up out of her baby-doll nightgown, though she did make sure her girl, Mary Martha, was safely asleep before she would put it on. M.T. had predicted Gillian would be one of the first in the shop, but she had called even before the Bonnet was open.

"I want something new and exciting," Gillian told Delia as she leaned her head back over the sink. "I was thinking I might even put in some color while I was there, maybe some of them honey-blond streaks you always see on that weather girl on the morning news."

"Mmmmm." Delia ran her fingers through Gillian's skimpy brown locks. "Might could lighten you up a bit. Change your conditioner. Give you some body so we could do something different."

"Different, yes," Gillian said, sighing as Delia's strong fingers massaged her scalp. For the next hour she giggled and whispered and told scandalous tales about her husband while Delia murmured and smiled and worked magic with her hands. When Delia combed her out and turned her to face the mirror, Gillian was struck silent for the first time.

"My Lord," she said finally, patting at the hair that curved back from her features.

"You are a good-looking woman," Delia said, and used the tang of her rat-tailed comb to lift Gillian's hair a bit higher at the crown of her head. The style was the one Gillian had worn since her wedding, but for the first time it was cut to suit her narrow jaw and soften the impact of those shrewd eyes.

"I am, aren't I?" Gillian agreed. In the mirror beyond Delia's left shoulder, Steph gave a small nod in M.T.'s direction. By the time Gillian had bought a few groceries, picked up her laundry, and mailed a package at the post office, the phone at the Bonnet was starting to ring. By the end of the week the trickle of adventurous customers became a rivulet. By the end of the month it was a steady stream.

When women came into the shop blushing and dreamy-eyed, talking about getting themselves made over, Delia put a cool, damp towel on the back of their necks and handed them her special collection of magazines, the big spring issue of *Vogue* with its double-thick wedding section, the fall issue of *Mademoiselle* with all the schoolgirl haircuts. "You see something you like," Delia told them, "we'll see what we can do." No matter how great the disparity between the ads the women chose and the physical reality, Delia would find a way to narrow it.

"You haven't got quite as much to work with as she does," she would say to a middle-aged woman holding up the image of a sixteen-year-old girl with hair down to her ass. "But we can make that shag of yours look longer, give it a nice light rinse, make it a little fuller." And somehow she did, or she made the woman think she had.

"Blind and stupid and mad with lust," Steph would say as the women went out the door. Steph never talked about love, only lust. "Spring fever," she would say. "Look like you coming into heat. You can see it in your skin. No joke."

"You need to get yourself some, Steph. Perk yourself up," M.T. would tease. "A little heat wouldn't do you any harm. Pinks the skin and brightens the eyes. Better than a shot of whiskey or a nap in the middle of the afternoon. Truth is, honey, I think you better get you some or you going to lose the notion."

"You can talk."

"I can." M.T. would beam and Steph would blush. Everyone knew M.T.'s reputation.

"Well, talk to Delia. She's the one needs some."

"Don't drag me into this." Delia would wave her hand and laugh. "I'm doing just fine, thank you very much."

It was what beauty shops were about—dreams and lust and the approximation of a fantasy. For all the banter, the women of the Bonnet loved the game.

"You're love-struck," they would tell some girl who had barely known what she was feeling when she stepped through the door.

"He that fine?" M.T. would ask. "He make you sweat just to think about him?" She'd wink at Delia or Steph, and soothe her victim at the same time.

"Well, a little," the girl might say. "Makes me think, anyway."

With M.T.'s fingers on their temples and Delia's smile in the mirror, the idea was more exciting than embarrassing. A beauty shop was one of the places where such passions could be acknowledged with impunity. "He's pretty nice," they'd say, then add, "And nice and pretty," laughing openly at their own wit. A woman knew where to go when love caught her up. The women at the Bonnet were priestesses of appreciation and encouragement.

"Come on, girl, let's do you up right."

"Come on, girl, take a chance."

"You got to risk a little to get a man worth the trouble. Come on, girl."

Hair could be tinted, layered, frosted, teased, or made over with a permanent wave. M.T. could do nails in any color, lengthen them or round them off with a glistening manicure, even glue on extensions. Steph could demonstrate a new foundation, a moisturizer, or a way to make eyes look bigger in a dim light. Delia would smile and hand over her magazines, nod and advise and reassure. And the next Saturday, when the woman came in again, eyes swollen and skin blotchy with disappointment, Delia would dredge up another piece of hope.

"Come on, girl, let's do you up right. I've got an idea of something you might like."

Every now and again Cissy wondered if that afternoon in the Bonnet giggling and dreaming might not turn out to be the best part of the relationship. The perfume-scented sheen of love's onset would surpass the mundane reality of a couple of hours of sweaty wrestling in some old Ford sedan. The glowing devotion of the women in the Bonnet could make even heartbreak seem romantic.

The joke in the Bonnet was that if a woman changed her hairstyle she was almost surely changing her sheets. "Putting on pink satin instead of white cotton," M.T. said. "Madrigal Whiteman wants a hairstyle to go with satin sheets."

"Her?" Delia laughed. "She's worn that too-long pageboy just about forever."

"Well, as of this morning she's wearing a feathery cap like the picture of that actress you had on the counter."

"Uh-huh. Trying to look like a girl again."

"She said she wanted something easy to care for."

"Easy to wash up without a whole lot of conditioner or bottled stuff in a heavy bag. No bag, no notice. The motel cut. It hides a lot of sin. Wouldn't think Madrigal would take up something like that at her age."

"Heard she's been talking a lot to that assistant manager at the new Wal-Mart. What's his name?"

"You mean slick-and-pretty?"

"Lord, Delia, way you talk."

But Delia never changed anything at all. She never altered her look or her sheets. She wore her red-blond hair just to her shoulders, pinned back or up during the day, letting it down only in the evening. She would let it hang down long and loose when she sat on her steps after dark.

"I like to shake my head and feel it," Delia said when M.T. told her she should cut it.

"Easier to wear it short. Long hair is for girls."

"I wore it short when I was a girl. Granddaddy Byrd said it was too much trouble to keep after me, and when I got sick in junior high, he had Mrs. Pearlman cut it right up tight to my neck. Wanted me to wear that bubble cut she had on a poster on the wall. He thought that would do fine, the son of a bitch. Wouldn't listen when I said I wanted it long. Said long hair took your strength out of you."

"Some of the old people say that. Say you got to cut a child's hair when they run a fever more than two days. Say the hair pulls energy you need to fight a fever. Girls wore their hair long and braided till they got sick or took to being sassy. People said you cut a girl's hair, you tamed her wildness. Silly superstition."

"Granddaddy Byrd believed it, I bet. Surely wanted to tame me." Delia smoothed a few stray hairs up off her neck and threaded them into her twist. "Wanted to leave his mark, I think, prove he had the power to say what was what. Had my hair cut off even though I cried and cursed him for it. Never felt like myself until it grew back."

"There was a time when girls would cut their hair off to show they were grown. Or wild."

"Well, I never needed to cut my hair to be wild."

"No, you didn't. Didn't need to do a thing."

Reverend Hillman was exasperated. Louise Windsor had agreed that Delia could visit the girls, but she kept saying she needed more time to prepare her heart. Would he come and read the Bible with her on Saturday afternoons so she could study up on forgiveness? At first he was delighted; it was more than he could have hoped for from that stiff-necked old woman. He called Delia at the Bonnet and asked her to be patient a little longer. After a few weeks of endeavoring to focus Louise's attention on John 8:7, it became apparent that the woman was in no hurry. To everything he said, she had a ready reply. "Yes, but . . ." or, "What about . . ." She bombarded him with fire and brimstone, verses on the subjects of adultery and loose women, the whore of Babylon and the harlot who would walk before the Antichrist.

"I don't think she is sincere about letting Delia see her girls," Reverend Hillman told his wife.

"Just occurred to you, did it?" she said, and blushed when she saw his stricken expression. "Don't let her wear you down. Mention the lawyer again. She hates lawyers."

Reverend Hillman did as his wife suggested, but went her one better, searching out every biblical reference to lawyers he could find. There were a surprising number and most of them quite daunting. After ten minutes of that, Louise Windsor looked at him as if he were a snake.

"Fifteen minutes," she said, getting to her feet and tucking her Bible back into its place on the top shelf. "Next Saturday, she gets fifteen minutes and not a second more."

Gillian Wynchester was just coming to the raciest part of a long story about her husband's last trip to New Orleans when Reverend Hillman walked into the Bonnet. Delia turned at the sound of his voice, and Gillian covered her mouth with one hand. "Reverend," Gillian squeaked. "It's so nice to see you. Excuse me," she said to Delia, and ran for the bathroom, her ears as pink as the towel around her neck.

Delia stood with her scissors in midair while the minister spoke to her so softly no one could make out his words. But when he paused, she whooped and threw her arms around him, almost stabbing Stephanie, who had stepped over to try and hear what he was saying. "Thank you! Oh, thank you," Delia kept saying while Reverend Hillman walked backward toward the door.

"Glad I could help," he said, nodding once to M.T. and then to the unrecognizable woman in the chair in front of her. The flush on his neck was approaching the color of walls.

Delia spent the rest of the week in a daze, using all her free time to drive over to Beckman's and shop for gifts that might please her girls: lace doilies for Amanda, hair barrettes for Dede, a blouse and a scented candle for each. "I don't know what to get them," she told M.T. "I figure Amanda might like this high collar and Dede might want the lace. And candles should be all right, but I don't know.

Everything seems so impersonal." She ran a finger over a lace doily, her eyes shifting uncertainly.

M.T. put her hand on Delia's. "It will be fine," she said. "You know this isn't what they are going to care about. You're the only thing they are going to see."

"Dede took sick," Grandma Windsor said when Delia came to the door. "Been sick to her stomach since last night. Amanda's not feeling so good either. I think Dede's bug is coming on her too. Another day, perhaps." She said it with a smile. There were years in those words, years of old heat and old grief, of bravely held tears and late-night sobs, years of sorrow past and pain yet to come. Small revenge it might have been, but Grandma Windsor took it in full measure.

Delia hugged the bag of presents in her arms.

Grandma Windsor said, wiping her hands on the skirt of her apron, "I know you must be disappointed. But after all this time, what's a little more?"

Delia looked down into the bag. Sunlight glittered on the wrapped presents. "Sick?" she started, but Grandma Windsor gave her no time.

"Next week," she said, her face a study in satisfaction. "Maybe."

In the car, Delia's mouth worked but no sound came. Her hands on the steering wheel convulsed. Grandma Windsor watched from the porch while Delia sat there, unmoving, and the sun rose higher in the cold blue sky. Finally Delia relaxed her grip on the wheel and started the engine.

"Another day," she said, looking out the window at Grandma Windsor. She rubbed her neck, pulled air in, and drove back to the Bonnet.

"She didn't let you see them!" M.T. could not believe it.

"Oh, she's cold," Steph said.

"Cold, yes." Delia had left the package of presents in the car. She should have left them, she thought, but it was entirely possible the old woman wouldn't give them to the girls.

"Well, I think we ought to drive right out there and have a talk with her." M.T. wiped damp hands on her smock. "Go out there and show her what's what."

"Think we might want to wait before we do something like that." Stephanie turned to Delia. "Clint has quit working. He is sick, seriously sick, and he isn't even coming in to Dr. Campbell's office anymore. His nurse, Marvella, was here and said you wouldn't recognize him if you saw him. But nobody sees him now anyway."

"She's right. The Reverend Myles told Sally he'll be dead by Christmas." M.T.'s face was flushed and uncertain. "Said it's cancer of the spine, or bone cancer anyway. Horrible. Said he can't hardly walk and Grandma Windsor is carrying meals over to his house. She's looking for some colored lady who'd be willing to go out there and help him, but it sounds like everyone's been turning her down. She an't got no money, you know, and always has been cheap besides. And God knows what he really looks like."

Delia leaned back against one of the sinks. Her mouth opened and her eyes widened. "God," she said.

"Yeah." Steph nodded. "This proves it, huh? That there is a God."

Delia shook her head. "Cancer? I thought somebody would kill him. I thought he might kill himself. But cancer? I never thought that."

"Delia?" M.T. spoke carefully. "What's done is done. Can't do nothing about it now. But you need to think about this, honey. If Clint dies while that woman is keeping the girls, you'll never get them away from her in this life."

"I know," Delia whispered. "I know."

"Well, you got to do something, honey."

"I know."

"Another day."

Every time Delia went out to see her girls, she heard the same words. Grandma Windsor's eyes glinted black and proud like shale in the sun. Every weekend when Delia appeared, those eyes turned on her. Coming on, suspected, a slight fever or a mysterious chill, the two of them were sick or, oh sorry, out of the house, every time Delia came in the yard. Some days she thought she saw the curtains move, a shadow pass on the other side of the screen door. Once, she was sure Amanda looked through the window at her. But Delia never got past the porch, and they never came out to her.

Every time there was another story, another bland apology, another cold smile, some reason one or the other could not go.

"Dede is in no shape to drag off in the heat of the day. We'll have to think about doing this some other time."

"If she's lying down, I could just say hi." Delia considered forcing her way in, but she didn't want to frighten Amanda and Dede.

"That wouldn't do."

Blank eyes. Black heart. Amanda had a cold. Dede had her period, "and she gets it bad, you know." Upset stomachs, runny noses, migraines, and sprained ankles. And no, one could not go without the other. They were so close. You have no way of knowing, the old woman's eyes said.

"Oh, if you knew the girls, you'd understand."

Every time Grandma Windsor spoke, Delia's neck became more rigid, her head more perfectly straight. She was as stubborn as any old woman.

"I need the girls to help me with the garden. Another day."

I need. They need. The girls need. Something. Anything. Not their mother.

On the fifth Saturday, Delia shuddered and went back to the car. She gripped the wheel with all her might, let go, and turned the key. "Old woman, you have gone too far," she said.

The words were as flat as the stone-set pupils of Delia's eyes.

Old woman.

The wheels spun. Dust rose and the car moved forward. Delia had talked about her girls to Granddaddy Byrd, M.T., Stephanie, and Reverend Hillman. Now she talked to her own soul and made her plans.

Chapter 7

Delia drove straight from Grandma Windsor's to Terrill Road and the little yellow tract house she had shared with Clint all those years ago. She parked in the driveway and sat for a moment while memories flooded her. The place had been her home, but it was all run-down now, yellow paint flaking off the plank walls, the yard scraggly and bare in patches. There were two almost dead old peach trees out front, and a thoroughly dead hedge that had gone blackish brown. The porch was missing some boards, and the steps at the side were covered with plywood and hammered braces to make an awkwardly steep ramp. Everything was dirty and worn.

Delia thought of the river house, with its mildew and neglect. She had already scraped out a patch where she could put in a little garden once the weather turned. She planned tomatoes and squash and flowers chosen for their big, wide blossoms: sunflowers and dahlias and leafy zinnias. She had always loved to garden. What had happened to everything she had planted here? She lifted her head. Above the roofline she could just see the soft shadows of the pecan and walnut trees where she sheltered with her babies that last summer.

The door swung open. A tall gaunt man with ragged hair stood there gripping the jamb with both hands. He swayed a little, then steadied.

"My God." Delia's face was stern with shock. Dime-size spots of red showed on her suddenly ashy cheeks. Her head turned slowly from side to side, as if protesting what she was seeing, that body in the doorway, so familiar and so changed.

The two of them stood looking at each other, Delia motionless and Clint swaying slightly. His eyes were trained on her like search-lights on a moonless night. His mouth hung open, and his tongue, gray and thick, touched his lower lip.

"Delia," he said. "I wondered if you would come."

"**A**re you sure this is a good idea?" M.T. asked as she wrapped dishes and glasses in newspaper. She was helping Delia pack for the move to the tract house.

"Don't you remember what you told me? If Clint dies while Grandma Windsor has my girls, I'll never get them."

M.T. couldn't argue with that, but she was worried still. "Maybe he'll get better," she said. "We don't know how bad he is."

"I know how bad he is. I saw him. He might have a little more time than you thought, but not much. He's no threat to anyone any-more."

"Even a dying man can shoot you in the head."

"Clint an't going to shoot nobody." Delia looked tired. "Way it is, it's almost like he got religion or something. He's different. He's changed."

"Well, I hope so," M.T. said. "Son of a bitch was surely going to hell if he didn't change. You think the cancer put the fear of God in him?"

"I don't know and I don't care. All I know is that we have an understanding. We made a bargain." Delia shoved a handful of frayed dish towels into a plastic bag. "A hell of a bargain. He's going to help me get Amanda Louise and Dede, and I'm going to take care of him till he dies."

"**Y**ou lived here?"

Cissy was sitting in the passenger seat of the Datsun staring at her mother. She couldn't believe her ears when Delia told her they were moving in with Clint and insisted that Cissy come with her to meet him. Now she couldn't believe her eyes. The yellow tract house did not look like anywhere Delia would ever have called home.

"This is where we lived when your sisters were born," Delia said. "It was a sweet little house when we took it."

"How long ago was that?"

Delia shifted uncomfortably. She pulled a tissue out of the box on the floor behind her seat and wiped her neck. "You were born just after Dede turned two. She's a Taurus baby, May fourth. You're August twenty-eighth, a Virgo." She folded the tissue and blotted under her eyes. "Amanda was born March fifteenth, a Pisces. She's four years older than you."

Cissy could tell that Delia was trying to keep the shame out of her voice, to talk casually about what she never talked about at all. "How old was Dede when you left?" she asked, knowing the question would hurt Delia, wanting it to.

Delia looked at the house as if it were the only thing she could see. "Ten months. She was ten months."

"That's little," Cissy said. "Awful little, a baby still."

The moments stretched. Cissy could hear Delia's teeth grinding. She was wondering if her mother would ever speak again when Clint came out on the porch and stood looking at the car. Cissy's eyes flew to him. For a moment she was reminded of Granddaddy Byrd—the long, lean frame and the patient way the body hung motionless. But the dark eyes were shocking, soft and glowing and full of pain. And young, too young to be in that worn, pale face.

Clint Windsor did not look anything like what Cissy expected. M.T. had said he was a big old nasty boy grown into a big old nasty man. This man was not big, though maybe he had been at one time. He made her think of the first book Randall had read to her, a book about a stick cricket—a walking stick. This man was like that, long and odd, a walking stick that could no longer carry his own weight.

A roar went through Cissy then, echoes of all the stories she had ever heard about the man Randall called "that evil stubborn redneck son of a bitch." Delia herself had cried his name like a curse, pounding the wall by the phone as she talked with Randall's lawyers. "That son of a bitch! That goddamned son of a bitch!" So much rage and power. So many memories. All of it compressed into one stick-thin figure hanging in a doorway.

Cissy pulled her legs up on the car seat and hugged her knees. She wondered if Clint was strong enough to hurt her mother. He might be, but he didn't have to touch Delia to hurt her. He had been ripping her up for years. Cissy looked out the window to the roofline and the trees behind it. They had been living here when it all happened, when her sisters were born and he nearly killed Delia, when Delia ran off and Randall found her and everything started over in California. This was where the band started, where Cissy started, too, if she really thought about it. Delia was shaped here. Everything that happened afterward was because of what had happened in this house.

"Come on, Cissy." Delia's voice was loud in her ear.

Cissy swallowed and got out of the car. Together she and Delia walked to the porch.

"Cecilia," Clint said in a husky voice. "I've wondered what you would look like." His eyes lifted to Delia and then dropped back to Cissy. "You look like your mother."

"You look like a grasshopper," Cissy said.

Clint grinned. "Yeah," he said, " 'cept I can't hop much." His shadowed eyes found Delia again. "She's your girl," he said. "Your girl for sure."

On the way back to the river house, Delia pulled another tissue out of the box and blew her nose. "It's going to be hard, Cissy," she said, her eyes level, insistent. "It's going to be very hard. But it's going to be good too, living there with Clint and your sisters."

In California, when Delia said "your sisters," Cissy imagined figures from an overexposed photograph, strangers who did not matter, family, but not really. They were unimportant, distant, the kind of family you never had to think about or confront. After all, they had remained in Georgia with Clint. Cissy didn't know exactly what had happened between Delia and Clint, but she didn't care. Her world was Delia and Randall. The world was the three of them, and the friends who came around to hug Delia's girl and tell her how pretty she was, how much like her famous daddy, her beautiful mama. Maybe Delia was always drunk and Randall hardly ever there, but Cissy had never known anything different.

From the day crying season ended, Cissy's world was remade. Everything was about "your sisters." Everything was Dede and Amanda. The world was full of people who looked at Cissy like she was some dog who might bite, some girl who didn't matter at all. Granddaddy Byrd, M.T., Pearl and Ruby, Stephanie and the women who came into the Bee's Bonnet Beauty Salon—the world was suddenly full of people who did not love Cissy. From the first moments, Cayro, Georgia, had settled down on Cissy like a clamp on her heart, the weight and substance of two girls she had only known in dreams.

"Your daughters," she said to Delia. "Your daughters, not my sisters."

Clint's promise was good, the bargain exact. Even before Delia and Cissy moved into the tract house, he made the arrangements. It would take a little time, he said, but Delia would have her girls. He was the father. Grandma Windsor could not block him.

By the day of the move, Clint could no longer get out of bed without help. "There's not enough of him left," M.T. whispered to Cissy, "to make a woman do a damn thing. He's gotten so small, and he used to be so big."

Cissy wasn't so sure. When she looked at Clint lying back against that stack of pillows, all she could think was that he had to be planning to shoot Delia in the head first chance he got, maybe with one of his precious hunting guns that hung on a polished pine rack over his bed.

There were three bedrooms in the little yellow house. The big one in back was Clint's dying room. The smallest was for Delia. The one on the other side of Clint's room was for the girls. From the first day, Delia started getting it ready for Dede and Amanda. She squeezed three narrow beds along one wall and put a dresser and a shelf on either side of the closet.

"You'll have to share," she told Cissy. "And it will be a little tight, but it will work out. We'll make it nice so it does."

Cissy said nothing. The room wasn't large enough for three big girls, but she knew what Delia was thinking. Soon enough there would be another bedroom available. When Clint died, the house would open up like a puzzle box. Cissy crowded her stuff into a corner and let Delia enjoy herself making up the rest of the room for Amanda and Dede.

"Amanda will like these." Delia had found small earthenware lamps with matching pale green shades. "And Dede needs a reading light. M.T. says she's always getting books from that place downtown."

Uh-huh. Yes ma'am.

Delia cooked soupy, unseasoned meals for Clint's sore mouth and tender belly, mostly potatoes and rice reduced to a colorless puree. She scrubbed out the house, and swabbed down Clint's sickroom. Sally refused to lend her crew, complaining that she had done more than enough for that family. M.T. didn't press her. She was still unhappy about Delia's decision to move out to Terrill Road.

"M.T. thinks cancer is catching," Steph said. "She thinks it's like herpes or VD or something."

"I do not!" M.T. slammed the cash drawer shut. "I just don't like being around sick people. I never have."

"You were over at Billy Trencher's place every day for a week after he broke his leg," Steph said pointedly. "You were doing his laundry and cooking for him almost every night."

"Billy's an old friend, and he wasn't sick. He was injured. There's a difference." M.T. glared at Steph. "And I don't hear you offering to help."

"I never could stand Clint Windsor, not even when he was healthy. Wouldn't bother me if he drowned in his own piss."

"You don't have to do anything." Delia was embarrassed. "The house is fine. All that's left is the garden, and I'll do that myself."

From the back window Clint watched Delia's every move as she spaded and sowed. He had promised his help. She was doing her part. She would have her girls. If it took a lawyer, a judge, and a court ruling, she would have that too. Clint had promised, and Clint was the way through.

Cissy took care to avoid the spindly body pinned to that big, blond Hollywood bed in the back room. The larger bathroom was right next to his room, but Cissy used the little one off the kitchen. She'd have showered under the garden hose rather than pass under the eyes of Clint Windsor. For three days she washed herself in the sink in that tiny bathroom until Delia lost patience and shooed her into the old claw-foot tub. Cissy climbed in as carefully as she could, trying not to splash. The whole time, she imagined Clint lying under his gun rack on the other side of the wall, listening for any sound, grinding his teeth with his patient, awful hatred.

Cissy was almost twelve now and terribly full of everything she had figured out, everything she knew that no one thought she knew. She knew that Delia had left Clint for her daddy, Randall, knew it had broken the man's heart and that half of Cayro hated her for it. But Cissy also knew that the other half thought Clint had it coming, that as many people cursed him as had ever cursed Delia. She had heard from M.T. and Stephanie that Clint was just like his father, a man who put his wife in the hospital half a dozen times, and that any sane woman would have left him well before Delia climbed onto Randall Pritchard's bus.

Cissy thought she knew the story. Delia had been foolish in her head and Clint evil in his heart. She figured Clint was like Granddaddy Byrd. Every time he looked at her, he would see Randall in the bones of her face. He would be reminded that Delia didn't love him, that he had broken Delia's love and driven her away. It was only a little less complicated than one of the plots in Ruby and Pearl's romances, but a lot meaner. Either way, Cissy figured Clint had to hate Delia. He had to.

For a week Cissy stayed away from Clint, but one late Sunday afternoon when Delia was hanging out sheets in the backyard, Cissy heard him making low strangling noises in his room. She stood in the hall and listened, then tiptoed to the door to see him bent over the side of the bed, spitting painfully into a basin on the floor. He pulled himself up, fell back onto his piled pillows, and saw her, Cissy's big eyes catching his narrow squint, her pale face reflecting back his red one. Cissy remembered the photos M.T. had shown her, Delia and Clint at their wedding, their strong bodies and broad smiles. He had been a big man, not tall but thick and sturdy-looking. Now Cissy took inventory of the jut of his bones and the stretch of his scaly neck. There was no hate in his face, just an impassive gaze, old and tired.

"I could get you some water," Cissy whispered the words.

"All right." Clint barely nodded.

Cissy had to hold the glass for him. She looked down at his tangled hair, flattened against the sheet, and felt heat flame on her face. She had heard so many stories, dreamed so many bad dreams. He had been so big in those stories and dreams, wild and drunk and dangerous, breaking Delia's bones and cursing her soul. Chasing her out of Cayro and into the arms of another man, using her girls against her and never setting her free.

"You need anything else?" Cissy asked.

Clint wiped his mouth and shook his head. "No, no."

The next afternoon when Cissy came home from school, Delia was still at the Bonnet. The whole house was quiet and she went back to look in on Clint. He was sleeping restlessly, breathing hard in the stuffy room. Cissy opened the window and turned, leaning back against the sill. She saw Clint's eyes open and his mouth relax as he looked her up and down, and up and down again.

He said, "That's good."

Cissy didn't know if he meant the little sweep of the breeze that played through his hair, but she could see the pleasure in his face, the easing of pain. She could see in the glance he gave her that Clint prayed for something to pull him out of himself, even if only for a moment. It stopped her where she stood. In that instant she saw Clint Windsor as a needy, fragile man, someone she could comfort just by being present. Clint was a man starving for company, even Cissy's company. She was an unknown, another man's child, but she was also some piece of Delia. And more, she saw him as someone who could comfort her, just by looking at her with hunger and patient acceptance. Every time Cissy stepped into that room, his eyes ate her up, not hatefully but with something like love—something like Jesus' love earned through suffering and long patience. She remembered again all she had heard about Clint, and she knew that whatever he had been with Delia was gone. He was somebody Cissy did not know anything about, truly, except for one thing. She could make him happy by standing there in front of him, not hating him and not running away.

Grandma Windsor stalled as long as she could, but the day finally came when M.T. and Delia rented an orange truck, drove into that yard, and walked through the door. Cissy watched her sisters leave the farmhouse with their hastily packed boxes and glaring eyes, awed despite herself by the infinite patience and ruthlessness Delia had summoned to outlast one stubborn old woman.

There was a moment at Grandma Windsor's when Cissy felt almost sorry for her. Delia was dragging a big black sack of clothes, and M.T. was huffing under the weight of a box with one wet corner. Neither of them looked to the left or right. Neither was going to acknowledge Amanda's sobs or Dede's muttering. Cissy had stayed at the truck, so she was the only one who saw Grandma Windsor come out on the side porch, drop down on the steps, and let her head fall to her knees. After a moment she looked up, and her hands moved as if she were going to slap her own face. Her mouth pulled back and down in a howl, but she made no sound. She just rocked, grinding her fists into sunken eye sockets, the perfect image of grief.

Clint was the way through, but Clint did not matter at all. This was a war of women. No quarter. No mercy. The last box thudded into the back of the truck.

"Cissy!" Delia's voice was sharp, but she was looking past Cissy to the side porch. "Come on, girl."

Grandma Windsor stood up and looked back at Delia. Cissy turned away. She did not want to see what would come next, the awful damage the two women had done and were doing to each other. The screen door banged when Grandma Windsor went inside. The truck door groaned when Delia pulled it open.

"Get on, girl. You go in M.T.'s car. I'll take Amanda and Dede with me."

Bang. Bang. Doors slammed. A curtain fluttered. Dust lifted off that porch.

"Lord, I'd rather eat ground glass than cross your mama." M.T. wiped her face and started her Buick.

"You'd have a better chance of getting over it," Cissy said, watching as the kitchen curtains were pulled roughly together.

Neither Amanda nor Dede said a word the whole way to Clint's house. When they got there, Delia had to prod them into the bedroom where he lay limp and almost speechless. Cissy followed, breathing in Dede's slightly flowery perfume and Amanda's odor of starchy insistence. The girls stood and stared at their father. When Amanda bent over to kiss his stubbly cheek, Dede made a vague, impatient gesture.

"Girls. Good to see you here," the man whispered with clumsy grace, but his eyes wandered to Delia and Cissy, plainly more interested in them than in the daughters he had kept as his own for so long.

Dede stalked out, but Amanda stood by her father's bed until he finally met her gaze. "Daddy, you don't look well," she said then, in a tone darker than a curse. Clint flinched and blinked up at Amanda with her own piercing gray eyes.

That evening Delia sat them all down at the dinner table. Her face was stern and open, the girls' shuttered and blank. The air between them was electric with suspicion.

"You have to know I never wanted to be apart from you," Delia said.

Her words were stones dropping from a great height. Amanda laced her fingers on the table. Dede wiped the corners of her mouth with a forefinger. Cissy picked at her cuticles.

"I wanted you with me, every moment. I lost myself in California because I could not abide what had separated us. And I did not know how to get you back." Delia turned from Amanda to Dede and finally to Cissy. Her lips seemed to have thinned under the pressure of speaking precisely.

Delia took a breath and looked at Amanda. "Your daddy and I have reconciled. We're going to take care of each other, all of us." She paused. "You know your daddy is dying. He's going to take all my attention for a while. I expect to need your help. You'll all have to help, I think. And you'll regret it badly later if you don't spend some time with him now." She stopped again, her glance darting between Amanda and Dede.

"I know you don't want to be here. When you're of age, you can leave. Eighteen, and you can go where you will. That's not so long, Amanda. A couple of years is nothing. And the time will come when you will see how much I love you."

Amanda kept her eyes trained on Delia's. "I don't love you," she said. "I don't care nothing about you." Dede nodded almost imperceptibly. "You're nothing to me."

Delia flushed, but her gaze never wavered. "And you're everything to me. Everything. The two of you." She looked at Cissy. "The three of you. The three of you are all I want in the world. If you don't love me, I'm not surprised. If you hate me, I can take that too. But you're mine, all of you. You're everything I am. And whatever else happens, I am going to take care of you."

Cissy shifted in her seat. Dede's mouth was open and her color high as she twisted a strand of hair. Amanda clasped her hands more tightly in front of her, as if in prayer.

"God watches over all of us," she said. "You think He doesn't know what you are doing? You think we don't? A couple of years is nothing in the sight of the Lord."

Dede retreated to the bedroom that first night, the room Delia had so carefully prepared. She pulled on a set of headphones, covered her eyes with one arm, and lay back on the bed, the posture announcing that she was going to stay there until she was eighteen and could get up and walk out of the house a free woman. Amanda camped out in the living room, on the couch near where Delia liked to sit and read. Cissy stood in the doorway for a while, unsure whether to take her usual place on the couch or go read on her bed only a few feet from where Dede sprawled. Clint was coughing hard in his room. Delia had busied herself in the kitchen.

Never sparing Cissy a glance, Amanda got up and turned on the television set, rotating the dial until she located the news. Then she retreated to the spot she had staked out and shifted down so that she was sitting on the floor between the couch and the coffee table. She looked almost relaxed.

Cissy joined her, sitting down on the far side of the couch. She didn't know what she expected, not real conversation surely, but maybe a few remarks about the news, the weather, the local sports.

"This guy," she said, gesturing at the announcer, "is about the scariest-looking guy on television. Once, I saw his wig slide sideways, and he did the rest of the show like that. Somebody in the studio was giggling and snorting, but he never seemed to notice. Just kept talking with his wig hanging off."

Amanda ignored her. With enormous care she opened the backpack she had brought with her, pulled out a giant-sized box of vanilla wafers and an equally large jar of Jiff, and slowly began to spread the wafers with the peanut butter. Her attention was completely focused on the cookies and the television. When every wafer had been painstakingly covered with its layer of Jiff and they were all lying in a great open design on the table surface, she began to pair them, each pressed on top of the other, the edges precisely aligned. With one extended finger Amanda skimmed off the extra peanut butter that oozed from the circumference of each sandwich, and popped it into her small tight mouth. Cissy watched the whole process, unable to look away, until the coffee table was littered with a mass of joined cookies and the whole room smelled of vanilla and peanut oil.

Amanda gave Cissy one expressionless glance and turned back to her project. From the interior of her backpack she produced a large plastic bag and began to parcel the cookies inside. When the table was empty except for one lone cookie sandwich and a scattering of pale crumbs, she carefully sealed her plastic bag and tucked it in the depths of her pack.

Cissy discovered that her mouth was open. With a shake of her head she closed it and turned to watch the announcer. When she looked back, Amanda was munching on that cookie, her eyes fixed on Cissy's face.

"I despise you," Amanda hissed, her breath smelling strongly of peanut butter. "And her!" She pointed toward the kitchen. Her mouth barely moved when she spoke.

"Even if I have to go to hell for it," Amanda said, zipping up her backpack grimly. "God will understand." She hugged the pack to her breasts. "You'll be there, you know. You're going to hell for sure."

"I'm going to bed," Cissy said. When she went into the room, Dede had turned down all the lights and pulled a sheet up over her shoulders. Nervously Cissy put on her sleeping shirt and climbed into her own bed. Dede's body was close enough to touch.

"What's wrong with your eye?" Dede propped her head on one hand and peered at Cissy.

"Nothing."

"You crying?"

"No. I just get watery eyes sometimes."

"Only the one."

"So?"

Dede shrugged and lay back, falling silent when Amanda came in and knelt to say her prayers.

For four days Amanda ate her cookie sandwiches and refused everything Delia offered. Breakfast and dinner, peanut butter and vanilla cookies. She bought her lunch at school and threw away the wrapped sandwich Delia had made for her. Nothing belonging to these people was to be hers. When she went to sleep, she stretched herself taut, as if she did not want to relax on sheets that Delia had washed.

"You are going to hell," she told Cissy every morning, and "To hell," she said again, when they passed in the bathroom. Cissy said nothing in reply. What she felt was certainly not to be admitted. It was Amanda's expression, Cissy thought, her bright, determined eyes. Her voice was so sincere, her words, the smell of her—a girl who would not compromise. Against her will, Cissy was enthralled. Amanda was magnificent, and they were of the same blood. Amanda was Delia's girl, Cissy's half sister, someone to be proud of even if Cissy wished she had never been born.

Amanda and Dede were as different as Cissy could imagine, especially for children of the same daddy. It was just that the differences between them were not immediately visible. Seen side by side, asleep, they were almost identical, equally slender and lithe. It was also true that both of them had the same white-blond hair, without a hint of Delia's red. But Amanda kept her hair cut off above the shoulders, and Dede's was a long brush down her back. It was not even that Dede was beautiful while Amanda was not. Amanda should have been beautiful. Everything was there to make a beauty. Grandma Windsor had called the girls her Roses of Sharon, but it was Dede who was the bloom and Amanda the briar.

It was after you spent a little time with them that the differences between the girls became pronounced. People who knew them forgot the similarities. Though they had inherited the same frame, it seemed their bones were sorted out differently, Dede's finely carved and willowy, Amanda's awkward and heavy. She was within a pound of Dede's weight, but stood out like some thorny desert plant, all bristly angles and serrated edges. Amanda had those astonishing gray eyes, sharp as the ice on meat put by too long, while Dede's eyes were blue and deceptively placid, and though her smile was crooked, it was almost gentle. Amanda's smile, severe and fierce, rocked people. Amanda's smile made people look down to see what was unfastened, what was inside out.

"Skinny," people said of Amanda. "She's skinny as a rail." But turn them to Dede and a gleam would come into their eyes. "Look at that girl," they would say. "You see that pretty little thing?"

As she got older, Amanda's features became more austere. Her face lengthened until it was as flat as the backside of a shovel. Her nose jutted out and down in a line with the corners of her mouth. It was a face as sad as the grave, always downcast, so that she looked up from under her eyebrows. Dede's face was forthright, chin, nose, cheekbones, and brows protruding fearlessly, but the impact was cheerful. "Why, she's prettier than her mama," men said. Dede seemed always to be looking straight on, hopefully and curiously, and though she often pressed her lips tight together, she had none of the aura of repression that was Amanda's essence. In Dede the sadness was more subdued, not so awful. In Dede it was almost attractive.

That sadness, maybe, was what they got from Clint. That sadness, that suspicion, that fearfulness of spirit and deep sense of the fatefulness of life. They both expected trouble, Amanda head down and stubborn, Dede looking it in the eye and throwing her head back as if to say, What now?

Their silences were different too, not like Delia's, which were not quiet at all but full of humming, brief snatches of lyric, and muted music. Dede's moments of stillness vibrated as loudly as Delia's voice on the old records. And Amanda Louise could say more with a silent glance than most people could say in a string of curses. In her, quiet was a pool of great contempt across which only occasionally flashed a curse or a prayer. Cissy wondered sometimes about herself. She thought of herself as quiet, as a watcher, but she was not sure that was how other people saw her. Angry, resentful, and stubborn, M.T. had called her, and M.T. was rarely wrong. But Cissy had an object for her anger. Delia was the prism through which all her outrage focused. Delia was the fulcrum.

"Your sisters are too strange for this world," M.T. told Cissy after discovering that Dede had painted the ceiling of their room black and silver and pasted fragments of broken mirror all over it. "Every time I see 'em, I think how lucky I am to have my Pearl and my Ruby."

There was a part of Cissy that agreed with M.T. Dede and Amanda were difficult. Delia might be overjoyed to have her girls back, but she was paying for her triumph with every nerve in her body. The sisters did not so much settle into the house as take it over and remake it completely, but there was still no doubt in Cissy's mind that on the whole she preferred them to M.T.'s butter-mouthed, vicious daughters.

Dede not only painted the bedroom but hid cigarettes in Cissy's underwear drawer and communicated with stern eyes that she would be very displeased if Cissy told Delia. Amanda, who was a junior at Cayro High but seemed oblivious to the opinions of the other girls there, promptly organized a prayer circle whose sole purpose seemed to be directing God's special attention to her own heathen family. Cissy spent a lot of time in Clint's room, reading or hiding out.

When the sisters she had seen only at a distance or in photographs walked through the front door of Clint's house still smelling of the wild clover that grew all around Grandma Windsor's front yard, it struck Cissy that behind the facade of contempt and resentment she had already pieced out, there was still more that she knew nothing about. There was a world of justified rage in Dede's pale cheekbones, a simple iron strength in Amanda's tightly compressed lips. Dede was only two years older than Cissy, Amanda not quite five, both of them close enough to be recognizably family to Cissy, but they were nothing like her, and nothing like Delia. A little shiver went down her back when she looked at her long-lost sisters. All her life she had hated them. But from the moment they walked through Clint's door, Cissy lost her certainty. Delia had always said the lost sisters were a part of her, and for the first time Cissy began to see how that might be so.

Chapter 8

Nadine Reitower was beside herself. "That hussy, she's purely shameless," she told her new hairdresser at Beckman's. "Bad enough that place down the road's been an eyesore all these years, with that worthless drunk staggering in and out, but now she moves in with those pitiful girls of hers, and God only knows what's going on in there. And Lord, the youngest one, that devil child, going around in those dark glasses and always pestering my Nolan."

Nolan Reitower was Cissy's first real friend. "I think he's about the only young 'un around here," M.T. had said when Delia and Cissy moved in with Clint. "And his mama keeps him pretty close to home. She's a bit difficult, that Nadine Reitower."

Cissy never forgot the first few times she saw Nolan, planted on his mama's porch every afternoon with a different paperback book in his hand. It was the books that drew her. Nadine had sniffed at Delia's girl when she walked up to that porch and asked Nolan what he was reading, but Nolan just pushed his glasses up his sweaty nose and held out the book, a pristine copy of *Starship Troopers* by Robert Heinlein.

"You read *Stranger*?" Cissy asked.

"I've read 'em all. Only one I don't reread is *Podkayne*. That one got on my nerves."

"Yeah, it's like he wrote it on drugs or something. Most unbelievable girl in science fiction. I prefer Telzey myself. You know her?"

Nolan nodded. "Schwartz," he said, identifying the author.

There was a cough of disapproval from Nadine's chair as she pulled loose threads from a hem she was taking down.

"You like science fiction then?" Nolan asked.

"Yeah."

Nolan put *Starship Troopers* down with a scrap of ribbon marking his place. "Come on," he said, and led her around to the back of the house and down into the basement. Along one wall of the workshop his daddy rarely used there were four tall bookshelves built just to hold paperbacks. Each was crammed tightly, books sorted alphabetically by author and marked with little cardboard dividers.

"My collection." Nolan's voice was deep with pride.

"Lord." Cissy ran her fingers along the spines of some of the titles in the middle of one shelf: Harry Harrison, Robert Heinlein, Frank Herbert, Tanya Huff, Fritz Leiber, Ursula Le Guin, and multiple copies of the Julian May books arranged in sets. The bottom two shelves of each bookcase held magazines—*Analog, Fantasy and Science Fiction, Isaac Asimov's Science Fiction*—each boxed by year in labeled cardboard cases, though many were without covers and the oldest were stained and mildewed.

"This is serious." Cissy's voice was hushed, and she looked up to see Nolan smiling at her.

"If you want, you could borrow some." He said it casually, but Cissy knew it was no casual offer. A boy who sorted and shelved his books so meticulously but then had to put them down in the basement, that boy was not going to be casual about sharing them. Looking at Nolan's collection, Cissy understood more about him than his mama had figured out in years.

"I would appreciate you trusting me with your books," she said. "And I'd be careful with them, very careful."

Cissy and Nolan became friends in that moment. It did not even bother her when she realized that he was in love with Dede. A boy who reread Tolkien and Heinlein every summer had to be a romantic, and Nolan's first encounter with Dede was proof if more were needed.

"Lord, look at you!" Nolan was on his way up the front steps with a couple of new books for Cissy and walked right into Dede racing out the door. "You're beautiful," he blurted.

Dede laughed. "Well, look at you," she said back. "Bet you're your mama's little precious." She flashed a look of teenage contempt and walked away.

"What she say?" Cissy asked, coming to the door.

But Nolan just shook his head. He did not, fortunately, remember Dede's exact words, only the look and feel of her as she trained those crisp blue eyes on him. Magnificent, he thought, and blushed every time he saw Dede on the street. It did not matter that she was two years older and could not see him at all. Nolan was in love, heart-struck and imprinted. Dede could have cursed him up one side and down the other, and he would have stood there waiting for her to curse him some more.

Nolan was not the only one smitten with Dede. Young as she was, Dede caught the eye like something diamond-edged and precious. Boys would look over at her against their best intentions, be drawn in and made over just by standing next to her. It was something about the way she smelled. Good boys, churchgoing and respectful, would get a whiff of Dede and turn in a day to sucking Marlboros and spitting, talking bad and hoping for more than they could explain.

Ruby and Pearl had been right about Dede sneaking off with boys, if not about "it." For most of the year at Grandma Windsor's, she had been slipping away with the Petrie boys while Amanda was off at prayer meetings. She told Delia that they were teaching her how to drive. When they turned up at Clint's one day, Delia took one look at the rawboned sixteen-year-old twins, with their flushed features and shifty eyes, and knew they had been teaching Dede more than downshifting in that Chevy truck of their daddy's.

"You're too young." Delia kept her gaze on the nervous boys.

"Both my sisters been driving since they was fourteen." Leroy Petrie was trying to look Delia in the face. He knew that was what he needed to do to convince her he was harmless, but every time his eyes lifted to hers, a shock seemed to pass from his upper thighs to his navel. He looked over at his brother, but there was no help there. Clearly Craig was just as terrified as he was, both of them trying to hide the effect Dede had on them, and their fear that Delia would no longer let them see her.

"I'm a good teacher," Leroy said. "Really, ma'am. I'm careful."

"I have no doubt." Delia looked back at Dede, who was sitting on the couch with a magazine, a half smile showing on her face. She made no effort to join in the conversation.

Dede had lost interest in Leroy and his brother, though for months she had fought Grandma Windsor for every moment she could steal to wedge herself between them in the cab of that truck. She had learned to drive, but it was less to do with the boys than with her own hunger. When she thought about those months of practicing, it was the lessons of her body that resonated—her knees hot and bruised between the gearshift and Craig's thigh, her hip pressed to Leroy's, their hands drifting across her skin like little animals, hungry and heedless. The boys had not actually let her drive more than a few blocks at any one time. The height of her accomplishment with them had been to steer the truck and work the gas pedal while sitting in the middle of the seat, the brothers on either side of her, cupping her breasts through the sheer material of her blouse. Both of them were intoxicated with the smell of Dede's skin and hair, so much so that they panicked as she steered them down the road— afraid not that she would crash but that they would lose control of themselves.

"Dede's good," Craig managed to say to Delia. "She's got natural talent for driving. Real talent."

Dede grinned at him. It was Craig who had told her that their price for a real chance at driving the truck would be the removal of those layers of cotton and nylon that had so far obstructed their approach to her body. It was a problem. While Dede really wanted to learn to drive, she was not fool enough to give the Petrie boys anything more than they had so far managed—brief moments of access, severely limited and carefully accounted for, just like her access to the truck, but she had been yielding steadily as she coaxed more and more driving time, and sooner or later, the situation was going to get out of hand.

"I appreciate what you've done, boys. I truly appreciate it. But I can teach Dede what she needs to know just fine." Delia watched their faces turn to Dede, the longing so plain on them. She saw, too, how Dede smiled at them, the easy control her daughter had, and disdained.

"You want me to teach you, Dede?" she asked.

Dede gave a shrewd grin, turning from the boys to her mama. "In that beat-up old Datsun of yours?"

Delia tried not to let her disappointment show.

"I'd love to learn stick," Dede said, her face alight. "That would be great."

Delia turned to the stricken boys. "Leroy," she said. "Craig. Thank you for coming round." She eased them out the door gracefully, ignoring the mournful glances they kept shooting at Dede.

Delia always said the smartest move she ever made was teaching Dede to drive. It was the decision that broke the ice between them. She also said it was the scariest six months of her life. Craig was right, Dede was a talented driver. Her instincts were astonishing, her eye and reflexes extraordinary, but the girl had no governor, no stopping point, no fear. Delia's greatest challenge was to convince Dede that driving was not about racing or pushing the limits of the car.

"A car is a way to get somewhere, nothing else. It's no reflection of your soul, nothing you can use to prove who you are. You play games in a car, you're playing with other people's lives," Delia said, watching her daughter's distracted, careless face.

"You understand me, Dede? You understand?"

"Yeah, I know. But I was wondering, how fast can this thing go?"

Amanda remained unrelentingly hostile. She didn't even try to get Delia and Cissy to go to church with her, though she nagged her sister mercilessly. Dede was fascinated with the idea that a person could just decide on Sunday morning whether she would go to church or not.

"I can stay home if I want, right?" Dede asked Delia every Sunday.

"Yes, if you want," Delia said, and Dede would grin and go back to the bedroom. Then she might come out all dressed and ready, but there was no predicting.

"Cissy said you were Buddhist. Don't Buddhists believe in hell?" she asked Delia once.

"I wouldn't call myself a Buddhist," Delia told her. "And Buddhists have a whole different idea from the heaven and hell the preachers talk about. They think it's life that is hard. The goal is not to get to heaven but to get off the wheel of life."

"Wow!" Dede beamed. "You think I would make a good Buddhist?"

"I think you might want to take a little more time before you go jumping religions just to avoid getting out of bed on Sunday morning."

When Dede stayed home, Amanda blamed it on Delia. "You don't care if we go to hell, but I do," she said. "You don't even believe in your immortal soul, but God does." She went on and on, quoting Reverend Hillman and Grandma Windsor and various pamphlets she had read, while Delia nodded and shrugged and refused to argue, finally reminding Amanda that if she didn't leave soon she would be late. Amanda would plead one last time with Dede and then go out the door with a martyred expression.

If Dede did go to church, Amanda did not seem any the happier. "Well," she would say when Dede came out dressed for services, "won't God be surprised!"

It wasn't easy to get to Holiness Redeemer from the house on Terrill Road, but Amanda refused Delia's offer of a ride and doggedly took the bus. The first Sunday after the move, Reverend Hillman winced when Amanda rushed up to hug Grandma Windsor before the service and the old woman turned away. Sunday after Sunday, Louise Windsor rebuffed her granddaughter as if it were her fault that she was living with the harlot who had taken advantage of Louise's weak, worthless, dying son and sweet-talked him into forcing her to give up the girls. When Reverend Hillman offered to pray with her, Grandma Windsor turned glassy eyes on him and told him he had done enough already.

Grandma Windsor's coldness broke Amanda's heart, and she finally started going to Cayro Baptist Tabernacle. The congregation was big enough that she could avoid M.T., and she liked Reverend Myles. She had come to take a dim view of Reverend Hillman, the agent of her exile to Delia, and Reverend Myles reminded her of the minister at Holiness before Hillman came back. They had a similar style of preaching, heartfelt and loud. Grandma Windsor always said that the church was truly a church of the Word under Reverend Call. "That was a preacher," she'd declare, "a real Bible man."

Amanda remembered Reverend Call's big booming voice and the bright spots of color that appeared on his waxy cheeks when he got excited. He got excited a lot, so much so that Amanda was afraid of him when she was small. Reverend Call loved to preach on the world Communist threat and the perfidy of Washington liberals. He was a regular guest speaker at the Americanism versus Communism class back when it was required at the junior high, and he had never gotten over the school board's decision to redesign the class as Issues of Freedom about the time Jimmy Carter was elected.

"Issues of Freedom!" Reverend Call stormed from the pulpit. "God's issue of the chains on our immortal souls." As far as he was concerned, the Vietnam War never ended, and he was a mainstay of the MIA chapter in Marietta. The local papers printed his letters to the State Department passionately insisting that thousands of American soldiers were being held in the underground prisons of Hanoi.

"Where's Hanoi?" asked one of the boys in the Bible class at Holiness. The minister promptly turned as red as a beet, his eyes bulging and his neck swelling, and fell back on a gray metal folding chair.

Apoplexy, not a stroke exactly, more like a blow from God, the minister told his deacons later. "The children are being raised in ignorance. The devil is laying seeds in their hearts." Tears leaked from his bloodshot eyes.

"You're tired," one of the deacons said. "You need a rest."

"The devil never sleeps," Reverend Call intoned. His mouth was slack and wet. "God doesn't nap."

"Just a few weeks," he was told. He closed his eyes and put his hands over his face.

The vacation was not a success. The substitute preacher discovered that a great deal of money had been going to pay for subscriptions to magazines that came to Call in brown paper wrappers. The Ladies' Aid Group gossiped that the minister's wife was spending a lot of time visiting her mother.

Reverend Call was forced into retirement after his wife revealed that it was he who had been making late-night phone calls to the new English teacher at the high school. The reverend swore it wasn't true. He told the deacons that the English teacher was a member of the international Communist conspiracy, as was obvious when she organized a performance of *Jesus Christ Superstar*.

"A blasphemy," Reverend Call told Emmet Tyler as he picketed the high school auditorium. "Another nail in our national coffin."

"Oh, it's not that bad," Deputy Tyler said. "Some of the music is pretty catchy."

"You've lost all judgment," the reverend said sadly, and the deputy just nodded. No one wanted to argue with Reverend Call.

The deacons at Holiness put out a call that brought Reverend Hillman back. Folks said Reverend Call had moved to Arizona, where he was preaching on the radio in the dead of night, taking phone calls and continuing to inveigh against the threat of Communism. Some Sundays at Tabernacle, listening to Reverend Myles, Amanda would daydream about Reverend Call. He had appreciated her. He had given her a silver bracelet engraved with the name of a missing soldier and squeezed her shoulders when she told him how much she loved God.

"Stay strong," he said to her the last time he preached at Holiness. Grandma Windsor had baked him a butter cake and insisted that Amanda give it to him. The old man put his lips on Amanda's forehead when he took the cake. "You're an American child blessed by God," he whispered to her solemnly. She nodded and refused to wipe her forehead, though the spot he had kissed itched with the damp, rough feel of his tongue.

"I'm staying strong," Amanda promised God. In her imagination God looked like Reverend Call, but with Grandma Windsor's eyes and U.S. Army sergeant's bars on the wings of his white high-collared shirt.

Amanda didn't confine her evangelical efforts to Dede. At Cayro High School, she set herself to organizing a Christian Girls' Coalition that met in the cafeteria to plan a crusade against abortion and loose living. She told Dede that their high school was the front line in her struggle to spread God's love, and ignored her sister's pleas to let everyone make up their own minds.

"This is life and death, Dede," Amanda declared. "This is God's word we are talking about, not some special program on comparative religions on the educational network. You can talk all you like about Buddhism and Muslimism and sky worship and poetry, but this is people's immortal souls hanging in the balance. You just want to shut me up so you can be popular and talk about nonsense? Be just like everybody else? Well, go ahead and be like everybody else, everybody on their way to hell!"

Amanda did not pause for more than a day after the principal turned down her request to distribute leaflets in the homerooms. She simply persuaded a couple of girls from church to hand her flyers around. When she was told she couldn't use the cafeteria anymore, Amanda sent the girls to the parking lot behind the Bonnet and promised to arrange rides for everyone who missed the bus home. She had in mind putting together a militant antiabortion group that would link arms in front of the Marietta women's clinic on Tuesday and Thursday afternoons, the days the clinic made referrals to Planned Parenthood in Atlanta.

"You're minors, you won't go to jail," Amanda told the potential recruits who showed up for her first impromptu rally. "But think what an impact we could have on this town. We'd be standing there like soldiers for the Lord. We could put that clinic out of business in a month."

The problem with Amanda's notion was that most of the girls at Cayro High kept the clinic phone number tucked in the back of their diaries. The clinic provided birth control information, confidential counseling services, and those vital referrals to the clinics in Atlanta that would actually perform the abortions. Even though they hoped they would never need the help, most of these girls did not want the Marietta clinic put out of business. One small error in the heat of the moment and they might be slipping off to that clinic on a Tuesday or Thursday afternoon. Twenty-six days out of twenty-eight, the clinic was nothing anybody would want to think about, but every now and then those last two days could come on a woman the way hot iron came down on cold. Two days of terror and the world looked different. Two days of "Please God, no!" Two days of "If I have to, Lord, I will." Two days of praying you did not need what you suspected you did. Then blood and terror—the intervention of a merciful medical procedure—and you could draw a deep breath and think like a sane woman again. No, the clinic was terrible but necessary, a place where a woman could do what she had to do even when it was the last thing in the world she wanted to do.

The girls who came to Amanda's rallies were the ones who neither dated nor had friends who did. That was exactly five girls for the first meeting, and two of those dropped out after a couple of hushed conversations in the school bathroom. The three who remained were so nervous about linking hands for anything that Amanda decided the forces of the devil had come up against her.

The day came when Amanda found herself in the parking lot behind the Bonnet all alone. That night she dreamed of the crucifixion, her palms outstretched and pierced as she stared down at those who had betrayed her. Grandma Windsor covered her face with her hands while Dede wept and fell to her knees. A recovered, penitent Clint stood behind them, while Delia, wearing bell-bottoms, beads, and a red poncho, called out, "My God! My God, forgive me." A ragtag mass of teenage soldiers in camouflage pajamas and brown-skinned nuns in black smocks stared up at Amanda in awe. Lying back on the post as if it were a bed draped in linen and silk, Amanda looked down on all of them with tired compassion. The bruises on her body bloomed shades of purple while a thin trickle of blood crept down her left temple. She had come to them as a nurse and a teacher, and they had beaten her and hung her up to die. Through the ordeal she had clung to the name of Jesus, refusing to curse God and be set free. Her courage would be legendary, her example preached to young girls down the generations.

Amanda did not know exactly how all these people came to be there to witness her martyrdom, but it was right that they were present, that they saw her for who she truly was, a blessed daughter of the living God. Hers was a faith so powerful she could reach past the trivial categories of denomination, of Catholic or Baptist, of nation or race. After this day there would be a wave of conversions. Satanists would renounce the devil, and one after another the lands where her story was told would petition to join the United States. Reverend Hillman would preach a revival about Amanda's devotion to God. Reverend Call would come back from Arizona. The geography teacher at Cayro High would ask forgiveness for making fun of Amanda's desire to lead a mission to Cambodia when she didn't know where it was.

Amanda groaned out loud, and below her Grandma Windsor cried out her name. Delia dropped her poncho and reached out for the daughter she claimed she loved. Dede shook her head and looked up at Amanda as if she were waking from a daydream.

"Oh, for God's sake," Dede giggled and put a hand up to cover her mouth.

Desperately Amanda twisted her body and turned her face up to heaven. "No," she said, and her blood ran faster as the crowd stirred and the soldiers grinned and poked each other like boys in a school-yard.

"No, no," Amanda whimpered, and the nuns hurriedly lifted their skirts and scuttled away.

Dede rocked back and forth on her knees, giggling helplessly. "For God's sake, Amanda, this is too far. This is too much even for you."

Delia picked up her poncho and shook the dirt off it. "Well, maybe it's all for the best. I know you never wanted to come live with me." She looked around at the milling crowd and stepped back. "Can you see Cissy from up there? I don't see her anywhere."

"You get down from there," Grandma Windsor said, paying no attention to Amanda's increasingly violent struggles. She brushed dust off her skirt and scowled angrily. One of the soldiers lit a ciga-rette for the last departing nun, who pushed back her wimple and scratched absentmindedly at a mosquito bite under her ear.

"My God, my God!" Amanda cried out. "Why have you forsaken me?"

"**D**amn hippie bitch." Cissy heard it as she was leaving the Cayro middle school walking to her bus stop and reading Nolan's copy of *The Left Hand of Darkness*. She turned and found herself facing Marty Parish and two boys with hair so short their heads looked scraped.

"We know you," Marty said to her. "We know all about you."

"Like what?" Cissy said. Her heart was pounding, but she was not going to back down. Her daddy had faced people like this. She had heard stories about overturned plates and thrown bottles, sneer-ing, angry faces, men with crew cuts and rude manners. Why would anyone want to wear their hair so short that their ears stuck out and you could see the funny shape of their skulls? Randall's hair had been a soft river over his shoulders, glossy and sweet-smelling and framing his face like in those paintings of Jesus in the *Children's Illustrated Bible*.

"Your mama's a Commie, one of them libber bitches running the country into the ground. Your daddy was a hippie bastard stole another man's wife." Marty stepped forward. "And you," he said, stabbing a finger at her heart, "you're a bastard too."

Cissy closed her book and clutched it. The still air around her seemed to press on her skin. The three boys smiled and closed in on her.

"And you, Marty Parish, you're stupider than your stupid daddy and your moron granddaddy."

Suddenly Dede was walking toward the bus stop, notebook in hand and blond hair bouncing with every step.

"Least you an't as stupid as you are ugly, though." Dede grinned at her own wit.

Marty balled his hands into fists. "Don't you talk about me," he said.

Dede stopped at Cissy's side and looked at the other boys. "But you two, I wouldn't call you ugly at all. Give you a little time and a bit more meat and you might be almost pretty."

Skinny Charlie Jones flushed and dropped his eyes. The third boy, Junior Hessman, backed up a step.

"Don't go nowhere, Junior." Dede looped an arm around Cissy's shoulder. "I wanted to introduce you to my little sister and tell her all about you. Specially about that time you got sent to the principal's office for playing with yourself in homeroom."

"I never." Junior's face went as dark as Charlie's.

"Oh, you did. You still do it when you think no one's watching. You are everybody's favorite entertainment, Junior." Dede gave a lazy smile in the direction of Cissy's face but did not make eye contact.

"You better watch yourself, Dede Windsor," Marty said, raising his fists.

Dede stared at his pelvis and her smile broadened.

"You going to hit me, Marty? You going to hit me?"

Marty's face went white. "Damn you to hell," he shouted, and turned so fast he rammed into Charlie as he stalked away. Junior followed him. Charlie hesitated a moment, his expression shifting from embarrassment to awe and back, and then took off after his friends.

Dede laughed a slow, lazy laugh and let go of Cissy's shoulder. "You okay?"

Cissy felt as if the world were turning around her in slow motion. "Thank you," she stammered.

Dede looked at her with those blazing blue eyes. Her lazy smile went away. "You can't give those little snots an inch," she said. "Not an inch. You'll make us all look bad." She slapped her notebook once against her thigh and lifted her chin. "But do you have to wear those glasses all the time? They look stupid."

Cissy's mouth flattened. "I'm supposed to wear them," she said. "My eye is light-sensitive. It gets all inflamed if I don't wear the glasses."

"Well, then, for God's sake let's make Delia get you some don't look so stupid. Hell, those big old things make you look like Ray Charles." Dede frowned at Cissy's rigid face. "All right?"

"Yeah, all right. But you got to ask Delia."

"You scared of her?"

"No." Cissy was disgusted. "I just don't like to ask her for stuff."

"Is that a fact?" Dede looked more closely at her little sister. "Funny, it don't bother me at all."

Just left of the center of Cissy's left eye there was a tiny blemish, like a smudge on a photograph or a nick in a windshield. Almost imperceptible, it was the only visible evidence of the old injury Cissy worked so hard to hide. Cissy wanted the world everyone else had— shadows and light, depth and distance. Instead she had a dark orb that focused poorly, watered in bright light, and gave her terrible headaches if she did not wear her glasses. It was only after reading about the artist El Greco that Cissy began to understand her own angle of vision. There was a difference between the world she saw— flat, depthless, a photograph without perspective—and the curved horizon everyone around her saw. She could imagine the world as Dede and Nolan viewed it. They could not imagine hers. At least she hoped not. It was hard enough being Delia Byrd's rock-and-roll love child without any additional burden of pity and contempt. Cissy had spent the first part of her life cursing her glasses, but once she came to Cayro she wore them all the time, welcoming the dark tint that shielded her glance.

As self-conscious as she was about the glasses, Cissy never actually noticed the blemish in her eye until Mary Martha Wynchester's thirteenth-birthday-party sleepover. Mary Martha was the first of the girls who lived on the west Cayro school-bus line to become an official teenager, and her mother decided to make it an event. Cissy suspected Mary Martha had not planned to invite her, but Delia had been doing Gillian Wynchester's hair for a long time now, and the weight of shared gossip, thinning shears, and peroxide was just too powerful.

"Of course you will invite Delia's girl," Gillian said.

At the party, as soon as her mother left the room, Mary Martha produced a bottle of her daddy's bourbon and offered it around. Her best friends, Jennifer and Dawn, took quick gulps and pronounced it fine. Cissy took a small sip and nodded, though she didn't like it much at all. Lizzie Jones, Charlie's little sister, took a sip and made a face.

When half the bottle was gone, Mary Martha had an inspiration: they would watch the telethon and call in false credit card numbers. But the operators had unerring instincts or very sharp computers, and the girls never got past them. Finally, just after midnight, Mary Martha settled everyone in a circle. "I've been planning this," she said. She turned off all the lights and set one blue candle in front of the triple vanity mirror her mother had bought her at an estate sale. To one side she placed a blue metal bowl on a raised trivet. The bowl contained High John the Conqueror, she told them, ordered from a real bodega down in Atlanta. She got a discount because she bought their candles too. She lit the incense, and a foul smell rose in the room.

"All right. Each of us is going to look into the mirror." Mary Martha coughed. "You look at the candle, you breathe in the incense, and you pray to see the future. My cousin Barbara, she told me about this. She swears it worked for her. But you got to do it at the right time, you know, like around your first period, or anyway, before you, uh, you know."

"Before you have sex, you mean?" Lizzie's face was bright with interest. "You gotta be a virgin?"

Mary Martha nodded.

"Makes sense." Jennifer sounded like she had a whole theory on the subject.

Cissy's opinion must have shown on her face.

"Well, it does," Jennifer said.

"I read about those temples in Greece and Egypt where they had girls sit in the smoke and tell the future. Virgins. Vestal virgins. That's how it worked."

"Yeah. I read that."

Boyfriends, husbands, children, careers—anything might appear in those shadows in the mirror. Anything. You would only get a glimpse, Mary Martha warned, and took the first turn. She lit the blue candle with her left hand. Cissy ate the top off a cupcake and put the bottom half back on the plate. She was starting to feel slightly sick to her stomach.

Great wealth, two husbands, and two sons—Cissy was a bit surprised. She would not have thought Mary Martha would come up with two husbands. Jennifer took her turn next: a career in the movies, a statuette in her arms! Cissy bit her thumb, thankful the light was so dim that she did not have to hide her face. Lizzie took her turn but sat too long, insisting that she almost saw something but it just wouldn't come clear.

"I think it was a house, a big house."

Dawn had trouble getting comfortable. She said the mirror was at the wrong angle, so everything had to be shifted around. After a lot of dramatic peering and leaning in, she gasped and threw her hair back. "A race car. I swear I saw myself in a race car, with numbers on the side and everything."

"Oh my God! I didn't even know you could drive."

"I'm learning."

Mary Martha took another sip of bourbon and passed it around, toasting Dawn. "You could be the first woman to win at Darlington."

Cissy giggled before she could stop herself. It was a small giggle, but Mary Martha frowned.

"Why don't you try, Cissy?" Mary Martha's voice was stern.

Cissy had made a point of being unobtrusive and painstakingly appreciative until even she was tired of herself. She nodded and slid across the rug to the pitiful little candle's glow, settling herself in a cross-legged position and dutifully looking into the flame. She'd give it a minute and tell them she couldn't see anything. Cissy stared across the flame into the mirror. The candle was larger there, its light brighter, but around it Cissy saw nothing but shadows, a dark core, and the reflection of the dim room. She shifted a little and her face came into the frame, etched in candlelight in the glass.

The tiny flame moved, and Cissy turned her attention to the blue bead of heat at its heart. It was surprisingly bright close-up, not as small as it looked from across the room. Yellow-white, dancing in some slight breeze Cissy could not feel, the firelight hurt her eyes. Every flicker seemed to splinter and ripple at the edge of the pupil of her left eye. There was a flaw there, she saw, a crack in the smooth surface. Very small, but it was sharply delineated by the flame's movement. Cissy leaned in a little closer. Her eyes loomed larger in the mirror.

Beside her, Dawn wiggled and poked her. "Cissy?"

Cissy ignored her. She had never seen the wound before. She leaned in as close as she could get to the flame.

"You see something?" Mary Martha's whisper was husky with excitement.

Cissy watched the movement of her eye. The left eye generally followed the right unless she was very tired, and even then it just drifted a little. It did not roll up and around like Martin Nouvelle's did. Cissy saw Martin at the gas station every time Delia took her Datsun in to be serviced. Martin would look at Delia and smile while his left eye peered over in the direction of the ice machine. Cissy had to stop herself from turning to see if there was something that had caught one of Martin's eyes and not the other. Her affliction was nowhere near so obvious, but it was there.

"Shit," Cissy whispered.

"What? What!" Mary Martha was getting upset.

Delia never talked about the accident, the wreck in which Randall's left side was crushed, Delia's foot broken, and Cissy between them showered with glass. One of the few times it came up was right after Cissy started school in Cayro. The teacher had been very curious about Cissy's eye, and had sent her home with a note asking Delia to call her. Delia exploded. "It was an accident," she told M.T. "Cissy was so young. It's not a problem. She has minimal vision in the left eye, but it's no problem." She pounded her hands on the kitchen table and cursed. "Goddamn! None of her business. An't nobody's business but ours." Her rage had shocked Cissy as much as her brief comment. An accident. Cissy had no memory of an accident.

"Randall shouldn't have been driving," Delia said. "I never let him drive you again." Her face was stern with shame and apology.

"Shit," Cissy said again, her face cloudy in the mirror. She closed her eyes. She could remember Delia and Randall arguing, her daddy's slurred insistence. After they moved out, Randall would sometimes put his face against Cissy's and cry. She loved it when he did that, loved her daddy's touch even though it was bitter with grief. It was Delia who had been so angry at him. Now, for the first time, Cissy understood the expression on Delia's face. Horror and guilt were etched there. Randall had been driving, but Delia blamed herself.

"I remember," Cissy breathed. "I do."

"Remember what? Tell us, Cissy." Mary Martha could barely contain herself.

Randall had almost killed them. Stoned and careless, he had almost killed them all. Such a little thing. So much hurt. One careless drunken moment and everything came apart. One shard of glass, a splinter really, one little arrow of light had flashed into Cissy's eye and spilled blood down her cheek. Delia had screamed and pulled Cissy up into her arms. There must have been pain. She could almost hear Delia's scream, feel the shower of glass. Cissy had dreamed that scream. She had dreamed of that little bit of glass, that arc of light. The dream was terrible, but it did not feel. There was no pain when the arrow flew into her eye, and surely there must have been pain. Didn't eyes feel? And there were no scars. All that glass had left no mark.

At least Cissy had always thought herself unscarred. Now she saw the scar, the evidence.

Cissy kept staring into the mirror. The glare of the candle brought tears to her eyes. The tears made the surface of the left eye even more shiny, translucent, pearl white. That flaw shone deeper, brighter. A diamond. It was like the glitter off the edge of a jewel, her jeweled center. It was beautiful as cut glass. Cissy blinked and felt the warm tears against her lashes. She looked one more time at the small, pitted indentation at the edge of her pupil, and then turned her face to Mary Martha.

"What did you see?"

"A crack in the world," Cissy said. "I saw a crack in the world."

Chapter 9

Delia sat up, her heart pounding. She had fallen asleep on the couch, and for a moment she was back in California, drunk in that garden in Venice Beach. Her muscles ached with that old ghost pain, the need to take her children in her arms, and her heart was bursting with grief that she could not. But it was a dream. The girls in the back bedroom were so close she could almost smell them. She leaned back and rubbed her arms. Her mouth tasted sour. She wanted a drink, she realized. She wanted a drink so bad her need was like a knot in her belly.

"Jesus Christ," Delia whispered to the dark. "When does it stop?" It was going on two years now, two years since she had been drunk that last Thanksgiving in California. But her stomach still rolled and her mouth tasted of bitter cotton and old need. A glass of whiskey would clean it away, wash out the bitter and set her to singing again. Delia curled up and hugged herself. The worst mistake she had made was to put together her singing and her drinking. Now she mourned both of them, and dared not do one for fear of what would come of the other.

She could hear Clint muttering and shifting in his bed. The smell of that room was getting worse. She would have to haul him out into the sun tomorrow, scrub the floor again, and wash down the walls with vinegar. She could change all the sheets and spray Lysol in the corners, but the smell would come back in a few days. Was it the cancer that smelled so bad? Or was it Clint himself, the stink of his soul?

The first time Delia touched him was the worst. The feel of his skin made her tongue swell in her mouth and her lower back clench.

She had to concentrate to make herself touch him and not recoil. In time, though, she was able to put her shoulder to his to help him to the bathroom without flinching. Clint would set his teeth and fix his eyes in front of him. Delia focused her own eyes on her hands, the floor, anything not to look in his face.

"I'm sorry," he had said when she bathed him that afternoon. He might have been talking about how awkward he was, how slow and heavy, but Delia knew he meant more. She grunted and pulled him down the hall a little faster than was easy for either of them.

His hands shook, his legs trembled. Red-faced, he told her he'd been pissing in the tub more often than the toilet. "Sometimes," he whispered, "I sit down and I can't get up at all."

Delia nodded expressionlessly. There were railings now in the hall and the bathroom, two-by-fours with braces every few feet. One of the guys from the Firestone plant had done the work for a hundred dollars, but Delia could tell they would not be used for long. Clint could barely drag himself forward even with her help.

"You'd be more comfortable in the hospital," she told him once they got him into the bathtub.

"No hospital, you promised." Clint's face was stricken.

Delia said nothing. She pulled off his pajamas while he shivered and tried to help. He stood in the bathtub with his back to her, holding himself up on the railing with outstretched arms. Delia pulled the shower curtain around him, keeping a hand inside it to steady his body.

"This house goes to the girls," he said. "This house, the insurance. I sold the truck, but there's that boat out at Mama's, some furniture and old coins." His head was bent and his eyes half closed. He was trying not to look at her. There was a lot more gray than blond in his matted hair. His skin was so dry it flaked off at his shoulders and hips. "The papers I drew up for you are at the bank. They'll give them to you. When I'm dead, they'll give you all that stuff."

Delia turned on the tap. When it felt hot enough, she pulled the lever for the shower. Clint lifted his face. The muscles around his mouth and eyes went slack, the loose skin hanging in folds. He uri-nated gratefully as the water flooded over his trembling frame. As he relaxed a little, liquid shit ran down his legs.

Delia turned away. God had a hell of a sense of humor, she thought. She remembered lying on the floor of this bathroom, preg-nant with Dede, pissing herself because she was hurt too bad to stand. Clint was rubbing his left hip where the bone jutted out. She could not see his cock, but she remembered what it looked like. There had been a time when she loved him, a lifetime before he became the man she hated. He had been a different person then, and so had she. All those years ago, when she had bought that gun at the flea market near the Atlanta speedway, she thought she would have to kill him. She had come back to this house and sat at the dining room table with the gun in front of her. Clint had come in on her there and stood looking from the gun to her.

The guy who sold her the gun was a curly-headed Texan who did business from under a green blanket, no questions asked, cash on hand. It was about as big as a handgun could be, that .38 revolver, all blue-black and hot when he slapped it in her hand, laughing when she almost dropped it. Said, "You be careful now, honey. That's a real weapon, not some toy." She wanted to shoot him where he stood, but she paid and walked back to the truck. When she got home, she sat down and put the gun, fully loaded, on the table, and waited.

Clint didn't believe her when she said she was going to shoot him if he ever hit her again. If she had to shoot herself after, it wouldn't matter. And if he took that gun, she'd just get another. "There an't no slaves in the South no more," she said. "You been trying to make a slave of me." Clint just looked at her, his dirty blond hair hanging in his face, his jaw working, the hatred in him like a black light shining out of his eyes. He laughed a harsh laugh and turned and walked out. She wanted to go after him. She wanted to shoot him then. Instead she put her head down on the table and wept into her hands.

When people asked her why she had run, why she had left Clint

Dorothy Allison

and the girls behind like that, Delia was never able to explain. She
would think about that gun, the cool chestnut table under her cheek.
She would remember the despair that flooded her when little
Amanda began to sob and Delia couldn't pull herself up to go to her.
She had left her children long before her body left. She had been gone
long before she climbed on Randall's bus.

Clint swayed forward in the shower and groaned. His flanks
shook like a horse's after a long run. Delia wiped her face with the
back of her hand, reached for the soap bottle, and squeezed the gel
over his shoulders and down his back. She used a sponge to scrub
him, brusquely, her breath hissing as she breathed through her
mouth. Her eyes were unfocused, her motions automatic. I didn't kill
him then, she was thinking. I don't have to kill him now. I just have
to get through this little bit here. Next few days, a couple of weeks,
maybe a few months. With all I've done, I can do that.

When Clint groaned again, Delia turned him impatiently and
swiped the sponge down his front. Soap foamed and bubbled on his
flabby thighs and shrunken cock. The sparse blond hair on his chest
stood up in wet spikes. He put his head back and let the water run
down his chin. He was concentrating so hard on not falling that he
did not see how Delia looked at him. When she shut off the tap and
wrapped him in a towel, he collapsed into her arms like an exhausted
child. She staggered but held him until he could manage to struggle
with her back down the hall.

That's the last time I can do that, she thought when Clint finally
dropped back on the bed. She wiped sweat out of her eyes and saw
Amanda watching them from the hall, the look on her face grimmer
than the shame on Clint's. Lord, they were always watching, one or
the other of the girls, always looking at her with faces she could not
read.

Clint lifted his shaking hands and pushed damp hair back off his
emaciated features. "Thank you," he panted. "I could barely stand
myself."

Delia nodded and held the towel to her chest. Maybe she could
get a wheelchair, ask about a county nurse. At the door she heard a

half sob behind her. Stubbornly she did not look back. Let him pull
the sheet up on himself, she thought. Let him die wet in that bed.

It was after midnight when Delia finally lay down on the couch
again. Come morning she would have to be at the Bonnet early. She
had left everything a mess when she hurried away that afternoon.
M.T. and Steph were always picking up after her, but day by day
she was falling further and further behind. If she could put Clint in
the hospital, she would take two days and sleep straight through. She
would have time to talk to the girls, to rake up some of the trash that
had blown all over the backyard, go through the bills, and maybe
even write Rosemary. She covered her face with her hands. But if she
put Clint in the hospital, Grandma Windsor would be there in the
hour. She would have a lawyer with her, and Reverend Hillman while
she was at it. The old woman had not been to see the girls once since
they moved, but Delia could feel her eye on them. And Reverend
Hillman was probably upset that Amanda had shifted over to Tabernacle Baptist. No doubt he was watching them too. She could feel
them all watching and waiting, eyes on her at the supermarket, oily
tongues speaking her name when she passed, teenage boys grinning
at each other when they walked by the Bonnet every afternoon. If
Delia put Clint in the hospital, she would never get those papers from
the bank.

"It's a bargain," he had said to her, and she had thought she could
do anything she had to do, carry him bodily to the graveyard, bury
him with her hands and a teaspoon. But to care for him for week on
week, to watch the girls standing outside the door of his bedroom,
to see Cissy in there with her face fixed on that man's eyes. Delia
could smell rubbing alcohol on her fingers, the sweet, musty stink of
Clint's skin under it. Her whole body shook with exhaustion.

A dog barked out in the dark, a hound-dog howl as protracted
and melancholy as any song Delia had ever sung. In California it
would be three in the morning. Rosemary might be up. She was a
night person, she had always said so. She might be out on her deck
watching the moonlight on that stand of cactus she loved so.

"I'm a cactus rose myself," Rosemary told Delia once. "I'm

prickly and sweet-scented and dangerous to the unwary." Delia could hear her chuckle, a deep growl of satisfaction. "And I'm like you," Rosemary said. "I can survive on just about nothing. And nothing's enough when you know who you are."

"I need help," Delia whispered to the night.

She wiped her face with her palms. There was the sound of a door closing, one of the girls going to the bathroom, Delia thought. She pushed herself up. She would fill the kettle before she went to bed, save herself a little time in the morning. In the hall she saw a shadowy figure outside Clint's open door. It looked like Dede, but the hall was so dark that it was impossible to be sure who was standing there, hunch-shouldered, staring in at the dying man.

"Dede?" Delia whispered. The figure did not turn but walked the three steps to the other bedroom door and went inside. Amanda.

Why was she standing in the hall like that, watching her father in his restless sleep? Delia stood motionless for a moment, listening to the ragged breathing from the sickroom, the silence from the girls. What was this doing to them? What must it be like, watching this happen, unable to get away or change a thing? She had not expected Dede and Amanda to be so angry at Clint, so much banked resentment on their faces every time they passed his room. Some days it seemed they hated him more than she did. Some days it seemed only Cissy felt any pity for the man who lay and watched them all with his burning, desperate eyes.

Oh, Clint was suffering, she knew. He was paying for his sins. Purgatory, M.T. had called it, purgatory in life. But there was no purgatory hot enough for Delia's rage at Clint. She knew that Cissy thought her cruel. Cissy looked at her now like it was Delia who had sinned against Clint. Some days she wanted to shake the child, to make her see what she really could not be expected to see—that when a woman learns to hate a man the way Delia had learned to hate Clint, she cannot look at him like a human being again in this life. She cannot just forgive him and make peace without some miracle of the soul. What Clint had done to them all, that was the one sin she could not forgive him. Maybe God could forgive, but not Delia.

She walked through the house to the girls' room and listened to their breathing, steady and strong. Then she looked over to Clint's room. His door was always partially open, but she could hear nothing.

She went to the door and pushed it gently. It swung soundlessly wide, spilling light from the little lamp on the floor by the bed. The radio was playing so softly she could only make out the murmur of voices from some far-off station. She leaned in and looked at Clint. His head was thrown back and his mouth was open. She could see the stubble on his chin like a scattering of big black grains of pepper. He looked like a corpse. Delia gritted her teeth when she saw his chest rise slightly and sink again. No, he was just asleep, deeply asleep, and that was rare enough to be frightening. Maybe the cancer cells in his bones had undergone one of those miraculous changes, curled up like hibernating frogs and fallen asleep to drift back and forth in his bloodstream. Maybe the cancer was receding like the tide receded, shrinking and dwindling away. Miracles happened—even to evil sons of bitches who deserved to rot in hell.

"No," Delia whispered. No, not to him. Clint's mouth worked, gasping for air. His body shifted, and the racked breathing began again, the slow cadence of pain to which Delia counted off the weeks. For a moment guilt sang in her brain. Had there been a miracle starting and had she stopped it?

Delia hugged herself. She had joked one time that she felt as if she had been raised by bears. There was no way for her to know how real people raised their young, how they loved and guided and pushed the child into a civilized state. But if Delia had come from bears, Clint had grown up among wolves. Not even his mother had shown him a gentle hand. When she first met him, it was that need that had charmed her, that boyish hunger for a gentle hand. She had misread it. She had thought they could heal each other. Now she looked at him dying and felt nothing at all.

God will judge me, Delia thought, but she could not change what she felt. She rubbed the knots in her left shoulder. He had twisted her arms up behind her and beaten her head on the floor. She could remember it as clearly as the smell of her babies' newborn bodies. He had left her helpless on that floor, walked out, and left her with Amanda screaming terrified from the next room. She had to crawl across the floor to get to her girl. She had to swallow her own cries to comfort her daughter.

Delia's teeth ached. She had been grinding down so hard that her jaw was trembling. She opened her mouth and tried to relax her neck. That was where the tension always got her, in her jaw and neck and the torn muscles of her shoulder. God, she wanted a drink. She wanted to drink whiskey and listen to the old records. She wanted to lie in Randall's arms and not care when they might die. Delia shook her head and looked again at Clint. She was taking good care of him as she had promised, keeping her side of the bargain. Dr. Campbell told her he was surprised at how well Clint was lasting.

She looked around Clint's room. The walls were patchy and spotted from all her scrubbing. There was a sour smell of sweat and sickness in the floor itself. The whole room would have to be cleaned and painted. Maybe the floor would have to be sanded. She ran her toe along one of the boards at the doorjamb. She would get a carpet, something with a nice bright pattern. When he is gone, I'll polish this room until no one will know what it looked like when he was here, Delia thought. When it is good enough, I'll move Amanda in here. Amanda needs a room of her own. She looked across the hall. What had Amanda been thinking, standing here looking at Clint?

Clint moaned and stirred in his sleep. Bad dream, Delia thought, and watched him rock his head. He pulled his legs up just a little. He was losing the ability to move them much anymore. He wouldn't get out of that bed again.

"God," Delia whispered. Maybe she could find someone to help. Not M.T., who gagged every time she came in the house, and not Steph, who made endless terrible jokes about rotting bodies and the fate of men who drank. Maybe Delia could find the money to hire someone.

There had been something frightening in the way Amanda had stood at Clint's door, something terrible in the set of those shoulders.

Delia moved down the hall and gently put her palm on the door behind which lay her girls. Her mouth tasted sour, her eyes felt full of sand and heat. Her whole body wanted a taste of liquor, tequila like a jolt to the nerves, bourbon like a balm for the soul, ice against her teeth and the glass thick and reassuring in her hand. Delia put a knuckle to her lips and bit a fold of her own skin, tasting blood and bitter while her pulse pounded in her ears.

"You can't do everything on your own," M.T. had told her. "Let your friends help you. Let me do for you what you would do for me."

Rosemary had said the same thing. The last time they spoke on the phone, her friend got angry. "There's something you're not telling me, Delia. You tell me what is going on now. Tell me what I can do. I could be there in five days. Three, if you gave me reason." And she laughed full-out into the phone.

That was what Delia needed. Not a drink of whiskey but the sound of Rosemary's laughter. She went to the living room and dialed the number she knew by heart.

The first few moments Amanda and Dede spent with Rosemary Depau were blurred with embarrassment. Delia had told the girls that her friend from Los Angeles would be staying with them for a while, to help out when Clint was doing so badly and things at the shop so busy. She had not mentioned that Rosemary was the most beautiful black woman they would ever meet.

The day Rosemary arrived, she was wearing a pink crepe de chine blouse and a wide gold necklace that covered a scar on her throat, a fine blue-black line along the side of her neck from an inch or so under her chin to a point just below her left ear. Except for that scar, she was flawless, her face clear and glowing. She had dark mahogany skin that gleamed with reddish highlights, and a gorgeously shaped mouth, dark red and pursed like a rosebud. Her short brown hair glistened with sweet oil and showed the delicate shape of her skull.

When she climbed out of the rented car, Amanda was startled and intimidated. Dede was simply enthralled.

Rosemary's eyes were huge and black and glittered like her earrings, small gold scallop shells perfectly positioned on her lobes. Gold jewelry, generous proportions, full hips and breasts set off by that slender waist, makeup that made those eyes seem larger still and the lips dewy even with a cigarette dangling from them—if it were not for the fine crevices at the corners of her eyes and a sadness in the eyes themselves, Rosemary would have looked like a model in one of those glossy ads in *Jet* magazine. A fantasy creature, that was Rosemary, a chimera from a noir classic—Dorothy Dandridge in blue jeans and a pink crepe blouse.

"You were friends in California?" Dede demanded of Delia while Rosemary settled her luggage in Delia's room. "Real friends, like you and M.T.?"

"Like M.T. Like family." Delia nodded. "Rosemary kept me alive out in L.A. Every time I thought I would die, she was there for me. If you're very lucky, someday you will have a friend like that, a woman you can trust with your life. I've been lucky past that. I have two. No woman is safe who doesn't have one. Any woman who does, well, she an't never on her lonesome."

"What we need is God," Amanda said sourly.

"Well, God is good." Delia's expression was solemn. "But Rosemary and M.T. never seemed so far away as God."

Rosemary was perpetually wreathed in cigarette smoke, though in deference to the sick man in the back bedroom, she smoked out in the backyard. Cissy was surprised that she bothered. The first day, when Delia led Rosemary back to introduce her to Clint, Rosemary only nodded briefly in the direction of his strained features. She did not say anything, and neither did he. Delia did all the talking, nervously babbling her appreciation for Rosemary's coming to help while her friend's long, elegant fingers rubbed together like insect legs.

Back in the kitchen Rosemary turned to Delia and spoke bluntly. "I am not touching that man. I'll do anything else you need. Cook and clean for these girls, lend you money or fight any damn body you name. But I am not touching that son of a bitch till he's dead."

Delia leaned on the table. Her face was pale and her mouth rubbery. Exhaustion showed in the set of her shoulders and the bluish shadows on either side of her nose. "You don't have to stay," she said. "I'm glad you came, but you don't have to stay."

Rosemary put her arms around her friend. "Shush, shush." She hugged Delia close and rubbed her back. "I'm staying. You know I'm staying. You are about ready to fall out. Don't you think I can see that? You think I am going to leave you alone with these cranky teenagers and that horrible man? Besides, I need myself some peace and quiet, a little listen-to-the-mosquitoes time. This will be a vacation."

Delia relaxed a little and let her head rest on the silky blouse. "Oh, Rosemary," she moaned.

"Yes, darling. Yes." Rosemary stroked her fingers down Delia's back. "It will be all right. But you and I have never lied to each other, and I wasn't going to start now. I hate that man, and I couldn't take care of him. I'd wind up putting diuretics in his milk."

Delia giggled, then put her hand over her mouth. Rosemary grinned.

"You be the saint," she whispered in Delia's ear. "You do what I can't, and I'll do the rest. We'll be fine, just fine." She pulled Delia closer and grinned wider. "And when he dies, I'll get drunk for both of us."

"That Rosemary's quite a good-looking woman," M.T. said to Dede when she came by with a basket of beefsteak tomatoes the Sunday after Rosemary arrived. It was a smoldering hot day, and Rosemary and Delia had gone for a drive, a trip that was obviously a device so the two of them could talk privately. M.T. drank a glass of Coke and sat for a bit at the kitchen table, fanning herself to dry the sweat on her neck. Amanda was on the back porch with her Bible-study notes, and Dede was in her underwear ironing by the window. Cissy had been reading in Clint's room but came out when she heard M.T.'s voice.

"You knew her in Los Angeles?" M.T. asked Cissy. "What did she do out there?"

"I don't know." Cissy blotted sweat from her forehead with a napkin.

"How can you iron in this heat?" M.T. asked Dede, who shrugged and spritzed a blouse with the spray bottle. She squirted some of the water on the iron so that it sizzled and steamed.

"It needs to be done, and once I'm this hot it don't seem to matter." Dede turned the nozzle around and sprayed her shoulders and stomach. "Want some?" she asked, waving the bottle at M.T. with a grin.

"I'm wet enough, thank you." M.T. turned back to Cissy. "Rosemary was with the band, wasn't she?"

"Yeah, I guess so."

M.T. frowned. "Well, has she said how long she's gonna stay?"

"Long as Delia needs her." Cissy looked over at Dede. "Couple of weeks or a month, Delia said."

"Well, I don't know what kind of woman can just pick up and take off like that." M.T. sighed elaborately and looked around the kitchen. A stack of crisp cotton sheets leaned against a neatly piled mound of faded jeans and T-shirts on the shelf beside the washing machine. The dish rack held four glasses and one bowl. There were no more pots sitting around half full of the soupy potatoes that were Clint's mainstay, and the smell of blood and sick that was omnipresent from the first day Delia moved here had been replaced by a bleached austerity. The room looked clean for the first time in months.

"At least it looks like she's being a help while she's here," M.T. said.

"Rosemary's a house afire," Dede said. "She puts on the radio and gets to work first thing in the morning. Don't stop either. About the time I think she might be ready to sit down and rest, she starts making lists of things that still need to be done. Delia says she don't know what she's going to do when she leaves."

M.T. looked down at the material pulled tight over her thighs. "Is that a fact?" She drank the last of the Coke and stood up. "You tell her hello for me, say how glad I am she came."

Cissy and Dede watched M.T. walk out to her car. "It's eating her up, Rosemary taking care of Delia," Cissy said.

"Oh, she'll be all right." Dede went back to the ironing board. "M.T.'s as tough as they come." She turned the spray bottle up and squeezed into the air so the water droplets rained down on her up-turned face.

Rosemary's visit scandalized Cayro. Nadine Reitower told her husband that she was sure there would be a tragedy in that house, that if Delia Byrd wasn't going to smother Clint Windsor in his bed, then that black woman from Los Angeles surely would. "Just look at her," Nadine kept saying. Her husband shook his head, but he did look at Rosemary. Every man in Cayro looked at Rosemary. Men joked with each other about her at Goober's on Friday nights. "Did you see who's staying with that Delia Byrd?" "High-priced tail" was the general consensus. "Yankee nigger bitch," said Harold Parish, Marty's older brother. "Time was we'd have run her ass back to New York City."

"She's from Los Angeles," Richie Biron said, drawing out the syllables.

The men around him laughed. "Still a Yankee bitch," one of them said.

"Oh, come on, son," Lyle Pruitt said to Richie. "She's just helping out old Delia Byrd and Clint."

"That Delia's another one."

"Delia Byrd was born right here in Bartow County," the bartender threw in. "I knew her daddy before he died."

"Maybe he was born here, but his child got the soul of a Yankee."

"I don't know. You ever listened to that band, old Mud Dog? Woman could sound just like Maybelle Carter."

"Naaa, her voice is deeper. Reminds me of Rosanne Cash."

"Chrissie Hynde," Pat, the waitress, cut in.

"Who?"

"The Pretenders, you know that song. 'Got brass in pocket?' That deep-voice angry kind of song?" Pat whacked her order book against her hip and tried a Chrissie Hynde chord. The men snickered. "Well, that always reminds me of Delia on *Mud Dog*," Pat insisted, "like she sings on '*Lost Girls*.' "

"You crazy."

"I never liked that one."

"Still say she's just another nigger bitch."

"Delia?"

"No, dammit, that colored girl she's got staying with her."

"Oh, Harold, hell. Leave it alone."

Harold Parish's racial views didn't stop him from trying to flirt with Rosemary at the Piggly Wiggly one Sunday afternoon. "How you doing?" he asked her.

She gave his sweaty features and beady black eyes a carefully blank look. "I'm in the market for greens, pork shoulder, and red potatoes." Rosemary studied Harold's acne-scarred cheek. "Don't need any trouble or any big-shouldered men," she said, and stepped past him.

Harold went red. There was something in the look Rosemary gave him that made him feel not only big-shouldered but handsome and appreciated. He felt as if someone had finally seen past his gangly body and bad skin. After that Harold discouraged the vulgar talk.

"It an't as if I'd date a black girl," he told his friend Beans. "But if I was going to, that's one I'd go for."

In the second week of the visit, Stephanie bought herself a costume choker that was almost a match for Rosemary's gold necklace. "Everybody in Los Angeles has one," Steph told the women who came into the Bonnet and complimented her. M.T. was conspicuously silent. When Dede saw the choker, she blushed. She had been thinking about buying one for herself.

M.T. was polite whenever she saw Rosemary, but she stayed away from the house and even took a few days off to go visit her cousins in Tallahassee. "Ecological niche," Rosemary joked. "I would probably like M.T. if we'd met first, and she might even like me. But I can tell she's worrying I'm going to talk Delia into moving back to Los Angeles."

"Are you?" Dede was hopeful.

"Lord, no." Rosemary beamed at the girl. "M.T. would hunt me down and rip my heart out."

It was not simply that Rosemary was magazine-model gorgeous, with those enormous eyes and that fine neck. She was also outrageous. She ignored custom and prejudice, going around in a gossamer skirt. Sometimes she covered her scar with that gold necklace, sometimes with a creamy scarf. Once, when she saw Amanda staring at her as she was washing dishes in the kitchen, Rosemary confided that she was thinking of outlining the scar with eye makeup and glitter.

"It adds character to have a flaw in a precious stone," she said, and when Amanda hurried outside, Rosemary leaned over and yelled out the door after her. "Don't you think I'm a character?"

The two of them sniped continually. Amanda complained that there was not enough room for Delia's friend, and Rosemary talked out loud about how some people might do better to cut back on their praying and do a little more picking up around the house.

"I pick up after myself," Amanda huffed.

"Rosemary is our guest and she's helping us out," Delia said. "Don't be rude to her."

"I am not rude!" Amanda shouted.

"Maybe she's scared I'm going to steal you away," Rosemary said to Delia after Amanda announced she was going to yet another prayer meeting and stalked off.

"No," Delia told her. "I don't think Amanda would mind me

leaving. You just shake up her simple notions of how the world is supposed to be."

"Well, then, I am a blessing in disguise, because from where I stand, your girls are entirely too certain how things are supposed to be." Rosemary was forcing cooked potatoes through a sieve for Clint's dinner. She wouldn't feed him, but she had taken over all the cooking.

"No, Rosemary, that's not the problem. They're not certain of anything, anything at all." Delia, who had slowly been getting more rest, sounded tired all over again. "Think how they've grown up. As far as Amanda and Dede know, there an't nobody in this world they can trust to be there for them the way you are here for me now."

Rosemary frowned and went back to shoving potatoes through the tiny holes in the sieve.

Amanda could not get over the fact that Rosemary used suntan lotion. "I burn same as you," Rosemary told her. "Faster. My skin is finer than yours is."

"That's a fact," Dede said as Amanda left the yard in disgust.

"Thank God, I'm not that touchy." Rosemary smiled at Dede as Amanda left the room. "She's always on her way somewhere, isn't she?"

Dede grinned. She and Rosemary had bonded over teasing Amanda and then discovered a mutual passion for fashion and style. Rosemary had shown Dede how to highlight her eyes with a blue-black pencil and shape her brows to follow the line of her eyes. They had taken over the bathroom for hours and set up a mirror on the kitchen counter so Dede could check her makeup in daylight.

"See, you don't wear that blush before sunset," Rosemary told her. "It's perfect for night. Make you look like a clown in sunlight."

"Makes you look like a fool any hour of the day," Amanda said. "Excuse me, could I please get to the sink?"

Amanda grew steadily more furious the more Dede followed Rosemary around. Good Christian girls in Amanda's tiny universe went barefaced until they were married. Wearing makeup was just further evidence of Dede's intention to sin.

"She's fourteen, not forty," Amanda protested to Delia.

Delia did not see the problem. "It's perfectly all right to try things out at home," she said. "I'd rather she learned how to do makeup from Rosemary than copy some of the girls I see coming in the Bonnet."

"She shouldn't be messing with that stuff at all."

"Amanda, your sister has her own ways. She's not like you, and she doesn't have to be." Delia did not want to fight, but she had discovered that it was better to be firm with Amanda than to try to avoid arguments.

"Ways! What ways? The devil's ways!" Amanda pointed her finger at Delia. "See what you say when she's running the streets. See what you say when she comes home pregnant and can't even name the father." She crossed her arms under her breasts. This was something she knew about. She had been going to the special family programs with the Grahams over at Tabernacle Baptist. She sat with Lucy Graham and her brother, Michael, the young man everyone said was going to replace Reverend Myles when he was ready to retire. They shared the study guides on the power of prayer and the very real dangers the devil put in the way of teenagers. Michael wanted Amanda to be his partner in the young people's class on miracles in everyday life, and he had already told her how much he loved her bright scrubbed face and her disdain for worldly vanities, makeup and powder and flowery scents. Amanda knew she could never tell Delia and Dede about Michael, how he smiled into her eyes and how he made her feel. When he touched her, she knew in a way she had never known before the real danger that Dede was courting.

"Dede's going to get in trouble, just you wait and see," Amanda declared.

"I'm not deaf, you know," Dede yelled from the bedroom. "And I'm not going to get pregnant. I'm not a damn fool."

"She's not running the streets." Delia tried to keep her voice level.

"Wait and see, just you wait and see. I know what I know."

* * *

Dede giggled at Amanda's constant harping on sin, but it worried Delia. Amanda started going in to Clint every day to read to him from her Bible, beginning with the Book of Job and working her way through the Psalms. The night she reached Psalm 107—Such as sit in darkness and in the shadow of death, being bound in affliction and iron—Cissy came to the door twice and saw Clint with his teeth clenched and his eyes focused on the ceiling. He looked as if every word out of Amanda's mouth was grating on his bones.

"She keeps that up, she'll kill him."

Cissy jumped. Dede was standing in the hall behind her. "'Course, that wouldn't be such a bad thing, would it?" Dede nodded in Clint's direction. The man was starting to rock slightly under the impact of Amanda's implacable recitation.

"You hate him that much?"

"Oh yeah," Dede said with a blinding smile. "Grandma Windsor always said it took blood to know blood. My blood knows his blood and hates every drop that moves through his veins." Her smile flattened into a look of cold assessment. "You don't hate him at all, do you?"

Cissy looked back at the narrow bed and the body huddled under the sheets. Clint's head was turned to the door. His lips were pulled back from his teeth, and his eyes searched Cissy's.

"No," she said. "I don't hate him."

"More fool you," Dede laughed, "more fool you."

"**W**here are you from?" Dede asked Rosemary, who was looking into the bathroom mirror over her shoulder. Rosemary used a tissue to wipe away the excess foundation she had applied to Dede's cheekbone and smiled at the girl's pleased expression. "I was born in a hospital in New Bedford, Massachusetts. Raised in Los Angeles, Rio de Janeiro, and Ceylon. My father was an engineer for a petroleum outfit. He invented a process for purifying certain oils you wouldn't know how to pronounce." She drew one finger along her right eyebrow, then the left, smoothing the fine hairs. "I'm your granddaddy's worst nightmare, child, a black Yankee woman raised to be rich and bossy."

Rosemary laughed, a full, joyful tone that Cissy heard in the next room. She knew that laugh. For an instant she could see it all again, Rosemary in California in a tiger-striped bikini and big purple heart-shaped sunglasses. She went to the door of the bathroom, where Dede and Rosemary were still giggling.

"You were with Booger," Cissy said, not thinking how she knew.

"That silly man?" Rosemary waved an arm and Dede cocked her head expectantly. "I was never *with* that man. I let him hang out with me for a while, be seen with me. That was all. Booger had talent but he didn't have style. My men have style, always have had style."

"Amen," said Delia, coming down the hall with an armload of sheets.

What was she? Amanda wondered. Some kind of prostitute? In her mind, that was the only way Rosemary made sense. If not, where did it come from—the arrogance, the jewelry and clothes, the glossy look of that skin? Sin, it had to come from sin.

"Doesn't she have a job she has to go back to?" Amanda asked Delia, echoing M.T.'s question.

"Rosemary owns things," Delia said. "And she's always been good with money."

"Owns what?" Dede was fascinated.

"Shopping centers, mostly," said Rosemary in a bland, honey-coated voice. "I'm partial to commerce, not just property. I like my money to make money. That was what my father told me, that money is meant to be put to work or given away."

"You given a lot away?" asked Dede.

"Oh, honey, I've given away more than most people ever get." Rosemary put her arms around Dede's shoulders and laughed like a bird, high and bright. "Isn't that right, Delia, haven't I given away more than we could count?"

Delia nodded, and Amanda glared. Dede leaned back into Rosemary's embrace. Delia shifted the sheets in her arms and gave her friend a long look. Cissy wanted to ask about all that money and all those years in California, and all the things she thought she remembered from when she was a little girl, but the look in Delia's eyes stopped her. The gleam there implied a world of story behind the tale Rosemary was spinning. Treasured daughter, careful education, loving daddy, California shine—there was something else, another story, not so simple, from the look in Delia's eyes.

Rosemary picked up her glass of soda and drank deeply. "Can I have a sip?" Dede asked.

"You don't need none of *that*," Rosemary said curtly.

"**D**rinks a lot, don't she?" Cissy said to Delia a few days later. Rosemary had gone to the Piggly Wiggly, and they were cleaning up the kitchen after breakfast. "After we go to bed, Rosemary sits up and drinks like a fish."

"I've never understood that comment." Delia held a towel over the wastebin and shook out crumbs. She gave the towel one last flick and then folded it half over half. "It's just the strangest thing to say. You imagine fish absorb water like taking in air?"

"Maybe it's the way she consumes as much as she would displace if she was dropped in a pool."

Delia put the kettle under the faucet and ran cold water into it.

"Well, she drinks at night, don't she?"

"You don't know that," Delia said.

Amanda appeared in the doorway. "She does. I been keeping track. She did a fifth the first two weeks, another bottle half gone since last Saturday. Talks big, but look at what she's doing. That woman is drinking herself drunk every night after we go to bed."

Delia slammed the kettle down on the burner and then turned to Amanda and Cissy. "Rosemary is my friend," she said. "Maybe you haven't figured it out, but this is no place a woman like her comes to visit for fun. She's here to help me. If you'd look a little closer, you would see what kind of woman she is." Delia paused for a moment, her eyes dark in her pale face.

"God," she said, and it was not a curse. "God knows you could look a little closer, see yourselves now and then. While Rosemary is here, you will treat her with respect. You will not make rude comments on what you cannot understand."

Cissy dropped her eyes. Even Amanda looked abashed as Delia turned her back on them. Cissy sat at the table for a while trying to figure it out, why Delia would get so angry so fast. Amanda had said worse, far worse, many times over. But this was clearly the straw on Delia's back.

Cissy was still thinking about Delia's outburst that evening as she sat in Clint's room reading Tim O'Brien's *Going After Cacciato,* another loan from Nolan. She looked out the window to the shadowed backyard. A thread of smoke hung in a line above the stoop.

Rosemary was sitting on the third step, big eyes catching the reflection of the lights from the house. Cissy went outside to join her, took a breath, and smelled the liquor on the night air.

"You still have that striped bikini and the purple sunglasses?" she asked.

Rosemary laughed. "You remember that? But hell, why wouldn't you. Every woman in Los Angeles has a striped bikini, and for a while there we all had those sunglasses too." Rosemary stubbed out her cigarette and shook another out of the pack lying next to her hip. She tapped it on the back of her wrist.

"Yours were heart-shaped," Cissy said. It had been another hot day. The wooden step under Cissy's thighs was just beginning to cool as the night came on.

"Uh-huh." Rosemary put the cigarette in her mouth. With graceful motions she used her silver lighter to spark a flame.

Cissy watched her inhale, remembering when Delia gave Rosemary that lighter at a party in Venice Beach. It had an inscription on the bottom, Cissy knew, something about friendship and laughter. "Why'd you come?" Cissy asked.

"Well, Clint's dying, isn't he?" Rosemary blew smoke in a pale stream, then leaned over and reached for the bottle of bourbon that was between her legs. She took a sip. "That's cause enough for a party. And your mama asked me to come. She doesn't ask for help easily, you know."

"You knew Clint?"

Rosemary looked into Cissy's face, her eyes glittering. Then she turned and stared out at the yard. "I knew about him. I think I knew a little more than most. When he had that abandonment notice served on Delia, she just about killed herself. Your mama might have run off and left your sisters, but she tried for years to work something out with that man. He wouldn't even let her send presents to them, but she did anyway. Wouldn't let her have pictures or tell her anything about how they were doing. His idea was that she should crawl back here and beg his forgiveness, let him knock her around and use them girls against her all over again. A whole lot of reasons to hate a man I never met."

"He's not so bad." Heat rose in Cissy's cheeks.

"No? You sure of that?"

"He's sorry, anyway."

Rosemary's face did not soften. "Maybe. The preachers say people can change. Me, I don't know."

"People change." Cissy said it with more certainty than she felt. She remembered what M.T. had told her. "You the way to her heart. He can't get there through Dede and Amanda because they hate him so much. But you. You the way. Get you and he's got her. Don't you think the man knows what he's doing?"

"Maybe," Rosemary said again in a voice as dark as her eyes, as silken as her hair. "Mostly, though, I think people die and start over. Get another chance next time."

"Next life?" Cissy almost laughed. Another Buddhist come to Cayro. She started to speak, but Rosemary waved her cigarette in the air and the gesture stopped her. The brown cheek was wet.

"Go inside," Rosemary said. "Nights here are too hot to be sober. And I can't properly drink with you sitting there watching me."

She remembered Delia's angry words. You should look close and see. She looked close. Pain, and stubbornness. Who was Rosemary?

"This an't bad," Cissy said. "It's almost cool now. You should have been here last August. It was so hot I thought I'd melt out of my underpants."

Rosemary shrugged and took another little sip from the bottle.

Cissy propped her elbows on her knees and rested her chin on her hands. She listened to the crickets and the cars pulling into the gravel parking lot by the convenience store just past the Reitower house. Nadine Reitower had complained so fiercely about people using her driveway when they stopped at the little store that the owners had created the lot. No one ever turned in the driveway of Clint's house except Deputy Tyler, who sometimes idled there to watch who was buying beer. Delia swore one of these days someone was going to kill themselves pulling drunk out of that store on their way back up to the highway. The deputy seemed to agree.

Rosemary seemed to be listening too, as she hugged that bottle against her hip. Her head moved slightly, as if she were counting time to some music only she could hear, and her gold necklace glinted.

"How'd you get that scar?" Cissy asked suddenly.

Rosemary paused with the bottle lifted slightly. "Why do you care?"

"Just curious."

"You tell people how your eye got hurt?"

Cissy's face burned. "Nobody asks."

"Oh, people that polite around here?" Rosemary took another sip.

"I'm sorry," Cissy said.

"Uh-huh." Rosemary swirled the liquid in the bottle.

"Really, I'm sorry I asked."

"Yeah." Rosemary used the stub of her cigarette to light another and took a deep drag. "It was like your eye," she said after a long silence. "Stupid damn accident. I ran into a wire fence in Rio when I was a girl. Just about cut my throat." One finger traced the scar delicately.

"Most people see it, they think somebody did it to me." The finger stroked the dark line under the necklace. In the light from the house it might have been a crease of skin or a shadow's edge. "I always hated telling people I did it to myself. Used to make up lies about it, anything to avoid saying I got it doing something my mother had told me a hundred times not to do, running in the dark, just running in the dark."

"Must have been scary." Cissy watched Rosemary's long fingers wrap around her throat.

"It was not a good time," Rosemary said.

"It's kind of dramatic." Cissy wanted to comfort Rosemary in some way, give her back what she felt she had taken. "Dede thinks it's kind of cool, sexy even."

"Your sister has a lot of romantic notions." Rosemary flicked ashes into the grass, her voice without inflection.

"She likes you," Cissy said.

"I like her."

"She says you coming here is the best thing that ever happened, that you are just what Cayro needs. I told her I couldn't see why you came in the first place. You told Delia you would never come to Georgia."

"You remember that too? Didn't think you were paying attention." The tip of Rosemary's cigarette glowed brighter than a firefly. "But Delia warned me you never forgot anything. Trust a child, she told me, to remember what you want to forget."

"Why don't you have no children of your own?"

The cigarette drooped. Rosemary took it out of her mouth and exhaled smoke. "I just don't," she said. "And now I never will. Delia tell you about that?" She ground the cigarette out on the step and tossed the butt into the grass.

"No. She said you had your own reasons for coming."

The sprinkler at the side of the house came on. Delia or Dede watered every other evening in the height of summer. A cool pocket of air drifted over them, and Rosemary waved her hand again, in the same arresting gesture as before.

"All this," she said. "You with your hard little pinball eyes, that man in there eating her up every minute, Amanda with her pinched mouth and nasty looks, Dede like a big old sucker snake swallowing the air wherever she goes—all this, and still Delia is happy." She shook her head slowly. "Happiest I've ever seen her."

Cissy raised her chin. Pinball eyes. She did not have pinball eyes.

"Maybe there is something to all that stuff people say about making babies. Sure looks like it's pretty much taken over whatever it was that Delia wanted before you came along. I don't think she even remembers who she was before she made you girls."

"You don't know who we are," Cissy sputtered.

"And you don't know who your mama is." Rosemary cupped the neck of the open bourbon bottle in her palm and rocked it on the step.

"And you do."

Rosemary rocked the bottle again. "Maybe not. Hell of the thing is, I'm not sure I do know anymore. I look around at this, and it doesn't make sense to me. There isn't enough money in the world to make me do what Delia's doing."

"She's just doing what she's supposed to do."

Rosemary laughed. "Yes, exactly. Being Mama, and Lord knows I do not have any of that. Oh, I had a baby, you know. That was part of what your mother and I had together. She'd left hers and I'd given mine away. She was always talking about getting hers back, and I was just grateful somebody else was raising mine. For being so much alike, we were nothing alike, your mama and me."

Cissy was confused. "You lost a baby?"

"No, no." Rosemary tilted the bottle and spilled some of the bourbon out. Cissy wrinkled her nose. "What I lost was a life. One I wasn't intending to have anyway." The tea-dark liquid trailed down the steps.

"Damn," Rosemary said softly. "Goddamn. All that time I was saying I didn't want any children, I was thinking I could have them someday. When I was ready, when things got right for me. Now here I am, no children, no husband, no settled family. None of it. Just a curse in the belly and a song in the air. My grandma's never-to-be grandchild."

A door slammed behind them in the house. Amanda's voice and Dede's rose together. "You're driving me crazy," Dede shouted. "You're crazy already," Amanda yelled back. Then Delia's contralto spoke something low and soothing and unintelligible.

"Family," Rosemary whispered. "Sounds like a family sure enough." She upended the bourbon bottle and emptied it, shaking the last drops onto the grass. Then she extended the bottle to Cissy. "You want to give this to your sister? Let her add it to her list?"

"No."

Rosemary put the bottle down on the step, and they sat listening to the wet swish of the sprinkler as it got cooler and darker. When Cissy finally spoke, she surprised them both.

"Delia says you are her best friend."

Rosemary grunted.

"She says you are the only person in California she ever trusted."

"Only person she should have trusted. I was about the only one wasn't trying to get something out of her or off of her."

"You were in the band."

"God, no." Rosemary lit another cigarette. "I can't sing. Not all of us can, you know. I can dance, but why would I do that? No. But I gave her that yellow convertible."

"With red seats."

"Red leather seats."

"I remember." Cissy closed her eyes and saw the car, seats gleaming in the sunlight, the back full of boxes and bags with Christmas wrapping.

Rosemary looked at her. "You don't," she said. "You were a baby. But it was something to remember. Best damn car I ever owned."

"I do remember," Cissy said stubbornly.

Rosemary ignored her. "It was Randall's car first. He gave it to me, I gave it to Delia. Bothered the hell out of Randall."

Cissy was getting lost. "Randall gave it to you?"

"Sort of. Traded it for something I had that he needed. And don't ask, 'cause I am not going to tell you."

"Drugs."

Rosemary laughed. "You'd think that, but you'd be wrong. There was more than that going on. Ask Delia."

Cissy shrugged. "She won't tell me nothing."

Rosemary took a drag on the cigarette and stroked her forehead thoughtfully with her free hand. "Mud Dog's second album, the one called *Diamonds and Dirt.* You know that one?"

"The one where Delia sings 'Lost Girls'? The one that made all the money?"

"Made some money. Made some of us almost rich."

Rosemary ran her hand over her head. Her short hair had kinked up in the damp. As Cissy was thinking it was the first time she had seen Rosemary look less than perfectly put together, that hand reached out and touched Cissy's cheek.

" 'Lost Girls,' " Rosemary said. " 'Minor Chords of Grief.' 'Walking the Razor.' 'Tall Boys and Mean Dogs.' All of those songs are mine. I wrote them, the parts that Delia didn't write herself. It was another thing she didn't care about. It was Randall busy being the legend. We'd get a little stoned and she'd start it. It would come out of her like a river, and I would write it down. After, she wouldn't remember a bit of it, though sometimes she'd cry when she heard one part or another. It all came from what Delia said. She'd get to me so badly I'd go write my own version of it. I wanted her name on those songs, but Randall and the record company guys were all over me. Hell, it all had to be Randall. Another Jim Morrison snake-eyed boy poet with a direct line to a woman's heart. Shit."

Rosemary lifted both hands, then dropped them, like a conductor setting a tempo, music in the way her hands moved in the air.

"Delia didn't care. Randall did. I did a little. Half the songs say 'Randall Pritchard and R.D.' Nobody said R.D. was me, but I had a good lawyer. I got my cash. Delia got nothing. When she brought you back here, I was glad to help her with that damn shop. It was only a piece of her share anyway. It was us, you know. We were the 'poets with a feel for female grief.' " She sighed.

"But Randall was why the record made money. He was so damn pretty, and so good at working the game. The rest of us didn't even know enough to care. That's why Delia is here and not in Los Angeles. She never cared the way Randall did."

"She don't care a thing about Los Angeles."

"Oh yeah, right." Rosemary raised one classically shaped brow. "Like I said, you don't have any idea who your mama is."

Cissy flinched. "You never understood my daddy. He was special. He did understand the heart. He understood a lot of things."

"Oh, hell." Rosemary put her arms around her knees and pulled her legs up to her breasts. "It's probably just as well I can't make babies anymore. I'm not any good even talking to you."

"Delia's happy, you said so." Cissy pushed up off the steps. Her legs were all pins and needles from sitting still so long. She stood in front of Rosemary and scowled.

"Happier than she was in Los Angeles, yeah." Rosemary nodded. "She's doing what she always wanted to do. Doesn't make any difference to her that she could have walked away from Randall anytime, made her own music, and been more famous than he ever got to be. That wasn't what your mama cared about."

"She wanted to come home," Cissy said. "She wanted to be here more than she wanted any of that."

"Yeah. That's right, sugar biscuit. She wanted to drag her butt back to Georgia and pick up after you and your sisters till the day she dies."

Cissy's breath hissed between her teeth. "It's you don't know who Delia is," she said. "You don't understand her at all."

"Maybe not." Rosemary hugged her knees. "Maybe there's a whole lot I just am not designed to understand. Look at me here talking to you like you some grown-up, and you are nothing of the kind. Can't understand a thing I am saying."

"I understand plenty." Cissy felt like crying but was too angry to let herself show it.

"I swear, you are just like your daddy. You think Delia doesn't know what she threw away? You think she didn't throw anything away? You think all she amounts to is what you need her to be?" Rosemary's voice was hoarse.

"Diamonds and dirt, legends and rude boys, poets that are no poets at all, babies that never get born or get lost through no fault of our own. Life sweeps you away like a piss river. Saddest thing I know is that there isn't anybody who knows who Delia is, not even her girls. Saddest thing I know is that she is in there with that evil man, burying herself alive to save you and your sisters, and not a one of you knows what she is doing. Nobody knows who my Delia really is."

Rosemary stood. "Nobody," she repeated, and went up the stairs and into the house.

Cissy sat unmoving on the step. She heard Dede's cheerful "Hey, Rosemary!" and then a door opened and closed. "Where's she going?" Dede asked plaintively. Delia's voice said, "Leave her alone."

Cissy tilted her head back and looked up at the night sky, the stars that were slowly brightening as the dark became deeper. The stars in California had not been so clear and big. The night had not been so still. The sky was always glowing and the night full of noise and movement. Cissy used to sit out behind the cottage in Venice Beach and stare up at that bright sky and listen to Delia's low crooning inside the house. Drunk or sober, Delia moaned out melody, the words slurred and painful, that voice of hers as rich and strong as melted chocolate. People came to the house and offered her work, wanting her to sing with other bands or make her own records. Cissy remembered their eager expressions, the way they spoke Delia's name, and Delia's flat refusal. She could have done something different. She could have made a different life altogether.

Maybe Rosemary was right. Maybe Delia was a bigger mystery than Cissy had ever imagined.

Cissy started counting stars. She began at the eastern horizon above the pecan tree. She counted bright and dim, ignoring the constellations and working in quadrants, sixteen, seventeen, eighteen, stars in California, stars in Georgia, all the stars between, nineteen, twenty, twenty-one.

When I grow up, Cissy promised herself, I'll never have children. And if I do, I'll give them away.

Chapter 10

It scared Delia how much time Cissy was spending with Clint. She was in there every day now, and she refused to let Amanda anywhere near him. "Get out of here," she told her sister one Saturday in the middle of August. She took the Bible from Amanda's hands, closed it, and gave it back to her with a look so steely that for once Amanda didn't argue. She had never seen Cissy like that, but she recognized the determination in her eyes as a match for her own.

Cissy was already in Clint's room the next morning when Amanda left for church. Delia poked her head in. "Why don't you go outside a while?" Delia said. "It's gorgeous out, and it's so stuffy in here. Clint's sound asleep anyway."

"I'm all right," Cissy said.

Delia frowned. "Go on, I'll sit with Clint."

"I'm just reading. You go out, you look like you need some air."

Delia took a deep breath, visibly counting to ten. "Cissy, I don't want you sitting in there all day."

"Well, you can't keep me out. This is Clint's house, and he don't mind me sitting here. He don't mind at all."

"No," Delia said, defeated. "I'm sure he don't."

Sometimes Cissy thought that Clint was the only one of them who had finally figured everything out. He was the only one who had the time and nothing else to distract him. Thinking was better than drugs some days, thinking about how people really were, who he really was.

"It's like music in my head," he said to Cissy one afternoon as she was clearing away his tray. He was down to eating a few mouthfuls at a time, though Rosemary took care to send in heaping bowls of potato puree. "It's like Delia's music is always playing in the bones of my neck, that voice of hers singing out."

Clint's eyes were enormous. It had been a bad day, a bad week, the drugs never seemed to work right anymore. He was either a lolling doll with empty eyes or a burning bush, sometimes from moment to moment.

Clint's right hand, lying loose on the chenille bedspread, lifted a little as if counting time, like a skeletal version of Rosemary's.

"God, the way she'd sing." His fingers counted. "Lord, love, Lord, love," he whisper-sang in his scratchy voice. "You know when she sings that song, that kind of gospel thing of hers?"

"Delia don't sing that," Cissy told him. "It's on one of the records, but she don't sing that stuff no more."

"Yeah, I noticed. It's a shame." He smiled as if he knew something Cissy didn't.

Cissy put the tray down. She was thinking about that long drive cross-country in the Datsun, the headlights picking up road signs and the radio's tinny music under the roar of wind through the smashed back window. In California, Delia's voice was the one constant, a familiar resonant lullaby, but on that hellish trip the words had faded. Once they were back in Cayro, Delia gave up singing for crying. Only when she took over the Bonnet did she begin to hum and murmur, sometimes following out a melody, but she never did what she used to do—close her eyes, put her head back, and sing as if the song were all she knew.

"Shame," Clint repeated, slurring the word. His afternoon shot was kicking in, the morphine music overriding the pulse of pain. His mouth opened and closed, and his eyelids moved as if marbles were rocking gently in there. There was a slight hum in the room, and Cissy realized it came from Clint, as if the words Delia had abandoned were still sounding in his body. He opened his eyes and looked up in a drifting gaze. In the front of the house they could hear Dede and Rosemary giggling.

"Put on the radio," Clint said in that gaspy whisper. "Put on the radio and let me hear it."

Clint's face went slack. He was still making that humming noise. A little breeze moved the curtains, and Cissy heard an echoing hum from outside, just audible through the window. Delia was hanging sheets on the line, singing to herself, oblivious of who might be listening. Cissy looked back at Clint, the shifting marbles under the translucent lids, and felt a wave of rage and pity so intense that her whole body shuddered. She reached blindly and clicked the radio on. There was a squawk and Clint's hands twitched, settling again as Emmylou Harris's whiskey drawl came in soft and low. She was singing about rocking the soul in the bosom of Abraham and Clint's hands rocked with her.

Cissy looked back through the window at Delia. They both were crazy, she thought, always had been. She put her hands to her cheeks and felt the tears she had not known she was crying. Emmy Lou crooned and Clint stirred.

He was crazy, but he was like her, or she was like him. She was more like him than his true daughters. Maybe it was the silence they both wore like a long cotton shirt. Delia and Amanda and Dede were always talking or shouting or slamming doors, radiating outrage and crackling energy. It was only Clint who had nothing more to say. Cissy only spoke when she had to, but he had been turned by pain and sickness into himself, into a core of great silence. He had begun talking to Cissy a lot in his brief stretches of lucidity, but even then his silence was what she noticed, that and a passionate eloquence of the body. His limbs would twist in that bed and speak agony, his jaw clench with an awful endurance. All his strength was needed to stay in that body. None was left to waste.

Maybe he had been angry and full of hate at one time. Maybe he had been ashamed. But somewhere in that long dying, he came to some other place. Clint had lost the need to be anybody but himself, and he seemed to be constantly looking inside to see who that might be. It was as if he were creating himself over in that bed, a stark, essential Clint with no padding, no insulation, no pretense. Looking at him, Cissy saw suddenly a thing that was nowhere in the books she had read. She saw how demanding the act of dying could be. She extended her hand and took Clint's cold fingers in hers. He breathed out softly, and his body seemed to loosen in the sheets. Cissy wiped her wet cheek with her sleeve and held on tight.

If Clint knew what kind of anger he was provoking between Delia and Cissy, he gave no sign. To Cissy he talked about Delia whenever he was awake. That the talk was obsessive never became clear to Cissy at all.

"Delia tell you about me?" he asked Cissy over and over, as if he could not keep in mind that she had already said yes.

There was a stubble along Clint's jawline. His beard came in slowly and sparsely, speckled with gray and certain evidence that his body had little substance to spare. Half a dozen times he'd decided to let the beard grow. Each time it came in worse than the time before. Clint would run his hands over his cheeks and sigh, finally asking Delia to take it off for him. He couldn't shave himself anymore. His hands trembled too much to control even the electric razor. Part of the reason for growing the beard was his desire to make less trouble for them. It was a lot of trouble shaving him.

"He looks terrible," Cissy complained to Delia. "Tell him he can't grow no beard."

"He's not growing much of one, just working himself up to ignore it," Delia told her. "Let him do it at his own pace."

Cissy fumed; she didn't want to tell Clint how bad he looked either. The problem was that while Clint might whine about the itch, he rarely looked in a mirror, and so had no real notion how gaunt and gray his face had become, the bony nose and sharp chin growing steadily more prominent. The sunken hollows of the cheeks were wearing so thin you could see the movement of the tongue in his mouth. It was just as well that Clint didn't see himself very often, Cissy told herself. Lying in there with the radio on and the windows open, he could pretend he was resting, getting better. Looking in the mirror would have meant facing the mortality written on his bones. Maybe there would come a time when he didn't care what he looked like anymore. Maybe there would come a time when he didn't care that he was dying.

"Delia talk about me?" Clint said to Cissy. "Delia tell you why she left me?"

Cissy smoothed one of the towels she had been folding at the foot of the bed.

"Oh, come on now. She told you. I can tell."

Cissy looked up. Clint's red-rimmed eyes were fixed on her.

"She told you I beat on her, didn't she?"

"She told me some stuff."

"Uh-huh."

His hands were on top of the bedspread. His wrists looked too thin and fragile to hold them up. The knuckles were swollen, the skin oddly discolored. Already his hair seemed to have stopped growing, his nails lengthened constantly. Now the skin beneath them was blue-gray all the time.

"She was right to leave, you know." Clint's voice was matter-of-fact. "Wasn't much choice. The night she took off, I was past crazy. I even scared myself."

Cissy looked at him directly, right into those wide, stubborn, un-blinking eyes.

"It's hard to think about some things, but it's pretty much all I do think about these days. What I did. What I didn't do. What I said. What I was ready to do. You know, I think I might have killed Delia if we'd gone on. I was working up to it. So full of rage, you can't imagine. I wonder at it now, how I let myself get that far into it. A craziness. A literal, dry-eyed madness. I tell you, I was as ready to cut my own throat as hers. Every time Delia looked at me—that way she had, all sad and hurt and stubborn—I got crazier. It was like sliding downhill. If you don't catch yourself, you hit bottom. I just about hit bottom."

His hands lifted slightly, fingers spread. Bird wings trying to take off, featherless and sad. He was having one of his high-energy days, needing to talk, needing Cissy to listen.

"Lord. It's a good damn thing she ran."

Cissy's bones seemed to quiver to the reality of what Clint was saying, the frank admission that he had been as bad as everyone said. She wondered if he could see as deep into her as it seemed he was looking—X-raying those bones, memorizing the beat of her heart.

"Why?" Cissy hadn't intended to speak. The question came out of her on its own.

"Why?" Clint nodded. "Exactly. That's the whole point. Why? Why would a man go crazy like that? I loved her. Always had. Delia an't like most people. She's got something inside her—something hard and strong and beautiful. A man gets close to her and he knows."

He stopped and looked away. When he spoke again, his voice was lower, more careful. "Most people," he said, "most girls anyway, ones as young as Delia was, they're soft in the middle. You get close to 'em, you feel that softness turn to you. And that's what a lot of men want. Like a clay center, you can make it into what you want, fire it, harden it. You think you can make it fit you. I got to where I expected a woman to make herself over for me. All the women I had ever known, I could feel that center place turning to me, waiting and wanting. I couldn't believe Delia wasn't like that. I got it wrong."

Cissy's hands twisted in the towel, and her knuckles cracked loudly. Clint paused and looked at her again, his face flushed.

"Hell, I don't know. Maybe most men think like that. I was so young myself, not quite a man. I was still a boy, but I was working so hard to seem grown-up and tough. Maybe I was afraid Delia would see the soft spot in me, see how it turned for her. I was the one who bent myself on Delia. But Delia was just herself, as true as the links on a surveyor's chain. Beautiful and fine and herself. Guys got nervous around her, even when they wanted her. Hell, specially when they wanted her." He smiled, proud still of what he could see with his mind's eye.

Cissy knew what Clint was talking about. She had watched people get nervous around Delia for years. Delia was like a magnet pulling at everyone around her. When they first came back to Cayro, Delia had seemed kind of flat for a long time, all that jangly, powerful energy tamped down. Cissy didn't know if it was Randall, or leaving L.A., or coming to Cayro, or something else entirely, but that broken Delia was not herself, not the Delia Clint was describing. Maybe Randall *had* done that. Maybe Delia had bent herself on Randall. But if so, she had gotten herself back, become again a woman who made men nervous.

"Way back I think I truly believed Delia would change," Clint went on. "I think I imagined she was gonna go soft for me once I really had her, so I kept trying to really get her. It was like trying to bend light. Couldn't get hold of it. Kept reaching. Now I see it all, and it's like I'm on fire with the memory, just hot all over with shame."

Tears were standing in his eyes. "Damn truth is I ruined myself trying to break the woman I loved. Just broke myself, and Delia never understood at all."

A sob escaped Clint's lips, though it was so strangled it might have been a curse. Cissy stared at the towels in the clothes basket.

Clint cleared his throat, groaned, and cursed one more time. "Damn," he said. "Lord damn."

Cissy picked up the basket and headed for the door. "I got to put these away," she said. "Give a shout if you need anything."

She went to the kitchen and dropped the basket on a chair. Some days she felt like she was fading out. Her hair had lightened since they came back to Cayro, the sun bleaching the red out to copper. And her eyes seemed lighter too, more and more the pearly gray of Clint's. She was getting ghostly, like a wraith in a novel, the spirit of a young girl murdered in her sleep.

Delia came in from the yard with a pair of pruning shears in her hand. "Will you please get some air?" she said, looking at Cissy's haggard face.

"He should be in a hospital," Cissy said.

Delia sighed. "We've been through this before, Cissy. He wants to be here. And I promised him he could be." Delia hated these arguments; she felt like she was standing in front of Cissy's rage as she would before the throne of God except that God would not make her feel so guilty.

"And the hospital couldn't do anything more for him than we do," she added.

"We an't doing nothing," Cissy stormed. "He's dying. He's dying in there."

"Yes." Delia's face was smooth and her voice firm. "He's dying the way he wants. He's got the right to do it the way he wants."

Cissy wanted to hit her then, to throw herself on her mother. Save me, she wanted to say. Save me from this long, slow wearing away of my soul. She started to cry.

"You said you hated him. You said he was a monster. You said you'd have killed him if you could. And you wash him and feed him and hold his hand in the night. I don't understand. I don't understand."

Delia reached for her, but Cissy pulled away. "Baby, it an't gonna be too long," Delia said.

"It's too long now." Cissy wiped her cheeks and her eyes hardened. "He's in there because of you," she said. "He ate himself up for you."

"Cissy." Delia's face went white.

"Well, look at him. He don't care that he's dying. He don't care about anything but you. If you went in there right now and told him you loved him, he'd probably climb right up out of that bed."

It was true, Delia thought. It was what Clint wanted most in the world. Maybe it wouldn't cure him, but it might. It might. Wasn't there magic in love?

Cissy watched shock and grief work in Delia's features. "You promised, huh? That's the deal you made? He'll give you Amanda and Dede, and you'll see him safe into the grave. An eye for an eye. Two girls for bathing and burying a man you don't love."

Delia dropped into one of the kitchen chairs and clasped her hands in her lap. The moment stretched. "You're not a grown-up, Cissy," she said finally. "You think you know it all. You think it's all cut-and-dried, and exactly the way you say. But it's not. I wish it was. I wish loving someone was something I could just decide to do."

Clint started coughing, the sound hollow and echoing. Cissy pushed her palms across her eyes and back through her hair. Delia smoothed down the cotton of her skirt. Both of them turned their heads in the direction of the back room.

"I'm sorry," Delia said.

"Yeah," Cissy sneered. "You sure are."

Cissy stopped speaking to Delia. She avoided Rosemary, and talked to Dede and Amanda only when she could not help it. She spent her evenings in Clint's room, curled up in the armchair she had moved in there, reading her books and letting him talk to her when he wanted. When Delia or Amanda came to the door, she would look up angrily as if she were ready to fight for her right to be there. Dede stayed out of her way. Amanda prayed for her. Rosemary watched her with impartial black eyes.

When Delia came in to bring water or carry away the bucket that sat by the bed, Cissy left. Delia would change the sheets whenever she sponged Clint's body.

"Talk to me," Clint whispered each time.

"There's nothing to say."

"Tell me what you do. Tell me what you're thinking. We don't have to talk about us." He spoke in a breathy whisper, his eyes devouring Delia's face.

"There is no us," Delia said. Her eyes did not lift from the body she was bathing. She carefully rinsed the cloth in the alcohol and water solution she had made up, wrung it out, and ran it over Clint's wasted thighs.

"What about the girls?" Clint's voice was scratchy with desperation.

"The girls are fine." Delia pulled the sheet back up. Her eyes went to the doorway, where Cissy was watching her. "The girls are just fine."

Clint clung to Cissy like a lifeline. He talked when he had the breath to speak, or stared at Cissy while she read. "You won't forget me, will you?" he kept asking.

"No," Cissy said. "I won't."

Clint smiled at her, that infinitely gentle, infinitely pleased smile he developed while she sat in his room. For a moment he looked so satisfied, so settled down into himself. Then he started talking again and the other look came back, the uncertain gaze that wandered the room, searching for something it could not find.

"Worst thing," he said. "Worst thing is I have days when still, if I could, if I could get up from here, I would do something terrible. This dark comes down on me and I just lie here grinding my teeth like I want to grind bones. Delia's, yours, mine. Hell, I think I was born crazy. I've been trying to get right ever since. Some days I'm just crazy damn mad."

Clint coughed thickly as if he were blowing a pipe clear, and fell back on his pillows. His eyes had gone deep pink. "Damn," he gasped, shuddering with the effort to breathe right.

"Delia said Jesus spoke to your heart," Cissy said, mainly to distract him.

"She did?" His breathing eased a little. "Well, Jesus or somebody, I guess. Might as well have been Jesus. Though sometimes I think maybe it was the cow god." A goofy grin crossed Clint's face. "In the army I learned about people overseas, how some of them thought cows were holy. Thought that was something. I liked it, that notion. I could get into bulls, the idea of bulls. Bullheaded. Bullnecked. Bullish. Damn foolishness."

He growled low in his throat, another attempt to clear it. He relaxed a little when the need to cough passed. "Didn't know nothing about holy cows, just saw a picture once, one of them films they show you in the army. Big brass bull and we all joked about it. Bull dick. Bullshit. Jesus or bulls, I never gave a damn. Just came out that one day I couldn't stand myself no more, the stink of me."

He stopped for a moment and shot a direct look at Cissy, that scrawny head nodding only slightly, nothing else moving at all.

"You don't know, girl. You cannot imagine. It's bad, that stink. All the time drunk or crazy angry. Your sweat smells different when you're a long time angry, old and mean and sour. Couldn't stand it. Spent about a day in the bathtub at Mama's, crying drunk and running hot water, getting a whiff of myself and hating everything about me. It'd get cold and I'd run more hot. Mama kept coming to beat on the door and yelling at me to get my ass out of there. This was after Daddy died, you know. She would never have talked like that when he was alive. I ignored her, just put a rag in my mouth and went on crying. Chewed a hole in that rag trying to make no sound."

Cissy was watching Clint closely. He seemed to draw some strength from the memory of his wretchedness. He was breathing effortlessly now, and his color was almost normal.

"Thought I'd have to kill myself. Decided that I would come out of that tub and shoot myself in the head. Put it through the mouth and out the top. Do it right. Use Daddy's rifle just to make a point. I was getting ready. I pulled the plug and let the water out. I wiped my face, and I was ready sure as shit. But all of a sudden it was like the air in the room changed. I saw what killing myself would come to. I saw how it would be. There I was, sitting naked on cold porcelain with my knees pulled up to my chest, my skin all wrinkled and my belly empty." He laughed and shook his head.

"Lord damn, I saw how it would be. I saw how I would have to kill Amanda and Dede, and Mama of course. I couldn't leave them to deal with it all alone. And somebody might come by, and I'd have to kill them too. And then, I'd have to burn down the house. Hell, might as well burn down Cayro while I was at it." He stopped and looked down at his hands.

"Funny how you get one moment like that when you see it all clear. Crazy, maybe, murderous and black, but it all makes sense in your head in a way it never did before. You see how everything connects, what is meant to be. I saw what killing myself would come to." He put his hands together and laced the fingers as if he were going to pray.

"Maybe it's just once God gives you the ability to see that clearly.

It sure was clear to me, the awfulness of my life, the grief slate I'd made. Maybe God waits until you're so far gone you can survive seeing it and then he hits you with it. It hit me like a load of pure evil. Delia was the least of it. My daddy, my brothers, my girls, everyone in my life always looking at me scared or angry. There wasn't a look of love in my life, and I'd made it that way. I'd made my life hateful." He pulled his hands apart, his eyes bright and fixed on Cissy's face.

"I saw it clear. I saw that I could die and wouldn't nobody mourn me. People would be relieved, people who once had loved me. People would just shake me off and go on." His pupils widened. Clint looked as if he were pouring himself out through his eyes.

"Maybe God touched me," he whispered. "Maybe Jesus put his hand on my heart. Maybe the bull of somebody else's heaven looked my way. I hadn't never believed in nothing, and I an't sure what I believe now. Except that sometimes, just for a minute, I get a feel of it all over again. I was crazy. Then I was crazier. Then I came around sort of sane, sitting in an empty bathtub, wanting it not to be the way it was."

He was wheezing now, fighting off another fit of coughing. "Anybody asks you, you tell them that's how people change. Suddenly or not at all. Stupid, crazy, or just desperate not to be who they have been. Of course, then they got to live it, be changed in their day-by-day lives, and that's hell all over again."

His right hand came up, and the bony, raw-looking fingers wiped at his mouth. "Day by day, changing my life has been about as terrible as anything you can imagine. And like I said, there are days when I don't do it so well."

Clint closed his eyes. Tears slipped out from under the lids, and when he spoke again, his voice was so low that Cissy could barely hear him.

"Days I am just as terrible as I ever was. Days it is just as well I am dying, 'cause for sure God wouldn't want me to live to do what I would do."

"But you were touched," Cissy said, and knew she was really speaking for herself.

Without opening his eyes, Clint smiled. "Yeah." The emaciated chin nodded once. Then the face was still, and Cissy thought he was asleep. She backed toward the door.

"Sometimes it seems like something touches me and I an't so scared or angry. Just for a minute, but it's . . . it's something. Bull or bullshit, it's something." Clint's hands slapped weakly at the mattress, his eyes still tightly shut and streaming tears. "It's something."

"Yes," Cissy whispered, and opened the door as Clint's voice caught her again, weak but insistent.

"You won't forget me?"

"God, no," Cissy said.

"God, no."

Clint heard them, his woman and his girls. They were talking and arguing and moving around. For an instant he was angry, but morphine made anger tricky. He couldn't tell which was making him dizzy and confused. Things shifted on him, took on other aspects—Dede's face the exact replica of Delia's, Amanda speaking like his mama, Cissy looking back at him like his own mirror. Whatever he had been, he was not that anymore. A man could change. *A man could change.* He breathed hard. Air was like whiskey. Sweat was like blood. God would take him up, purify his bones, and feed him to the bulls. "God take me up," Clint whispered, and remembered how it was.

He had not known Delia before high school. They were thrown together by default, each too shy and stubborn to bother charming the other students at Cayro High.

Before Delia, Clint had dated without any real conviction. Something always seemed to come between him and the girls he asked out. He was good-looking enough, but he was shy and awkward, and he had a slight limp from the shattered knee joint that would keep him out of competitive sports. That the knee would also keep him out of the draft did not seem at the time the advantage it turned out to be when the Vietnam War became such a fearful presence in the minds of the boys who could play ball. At Cayro High, as in so much of rural Georgia, sports was everything. Even boys with money in their pockets and cars to drive around jockeyed for the real prize, a place on the team. Clint could never win that.

Clint smiled easily and that got him a ways, but he could not follow up the smile.

"That boy's nice, but it's like swimming in mayonnaise to get him to talk."

Girls would look at Clint expectantly. He would look back, then drop his head and smile at the floor. What was he supposed to do? Talk about his daddy, that man who never spoke himself? Talk about his mama, that woman who woke up with a prayer on her tongue and rarely said more: breakfast, dinner, mail's here. Nothing but phrases and grunts at the Windsor place. Mumbled phrases, whispered pleas, sudden hisses of indrawn breath.

"Sir, don't."

"Woman, yes."

Clint would set his teeth while dry atonal hymns blew through his head and scratched at his pride. Better not to speak. Better to smile and look away. Better not to see what he could not understand, his daddy's gray anger and his mama's thin-lipped endurance.

It was Delia's singing that caught Clint's attention that afternoon behind the gym. A light, cold drizzle was coming down, and he had decided to take the later bus home. He could tell his daddy he'd slipped in the rain and missed the first one, have a little time to himself for a change. It was a rare moment of freedom from the farm and his daddy's insistent demands. Clint sneaked off to smoke and watch the football players running their laps. He didn't want anybody to catch him watching and think him jealous or resentful, so he took care not to be seen sidling along the gym building with his signature limp. But he had barely positioned himself in the shelter of the overhang at the side entrance when Delia came around the corner, that soft reverberation preceding her at a little distance, a melody as tender as a prayer.

Surprise opened Clint's mouth. Surprise spoke.

"Lonesome."

Delia stopped, turned her head, looked Clint in the eye. A spark flared in his middle. Instant heat shone on her cheeks. They were like a photograph and its negative, Clint with his dark expressionless face and Delia's polished red-blond and distant features.

"I could die." Embarrassment prompted him. Heat and sweat. "So lonesome I could die. Hank Williams. I recognize the tune." His voice seemed raw after Delia's molasses notes.

"Yeah, I like those old records." Her drawl was as rich as her song, like burnt-sugar frosting. Like nothing Clint had ever heard. She rocked a little on the balls of her feet, both hands pushed into the pockets of her car coat. "But I always imagine it's a woman singing those words, kinda like Joan Baez would sing it—if she would."

Clint saw the fabric of the coat bunch and knew Delia had curled her hands into fists. She's scared, he thought. But Delia's head came up then and her eyes pierced him, stubbornly unafraid.

"She should," he blurted. "Joan Baez. She should. It would be good."

Astonishing. He had spoken. The heat eased off a little and he risked another look at Delia's pockets. Her head was tilted to one side as if she were considering him from some rare and special place inside, but her hands had loosened their hold on her coat. He smiled at her and was rewarded with a smile that seemed as easy and luminous as her song.

"You got one for me?" She gestured at the damp cigarette in his hand, forgotten but still carefully pinched between thumb and forefinger. Clint looked down at it, then back at her. A girl who smoked, a girl who didn't care that he knew. His mama and daddy would hate that. He smoked constantly, every moment he could get away from them, and they were always telling him how filthy the habit was, how much it said about his weak and shiftless nature. "Boy, you're ruining yourself."

You'll ruin yourself, he almost said to Delia; instead he fumbled in his jacket for the pack of Winstons. Delia moved to stand beside him, and he realized she was waiting for a light. His heart sank. He had used his last match for himself, and knew he could never offer the butt he had been smoking. Goddamn, he cursed to himself.

Magically Delia seemed not to notice his distress. In a careless movement, her pale fingers reached for him and drew his fist up to pull the glowing cherry from his cigarette to hers. Her cheeks hollowed and filled, hollowed and filled out, and then she dropped his hand and drew the welcome smoke in.

"Goooood," she breathed gratefully, leaning back against the wall beside him, ignoring the sharp intake of his breath. She blew smoke out in a thin stream up toward the gym roof. "So good. By the end of the day, this is all I want."

Clint kept his face turned to the football field, his eyes shielded from her glance. That she had cadged a smoke from him so easily and comfortably created as much of a sexual charge as he had known in his seventeen years. That she had drawn fire from his cigarette made him dizzy with desire. Unseen in the shelter of his jeans, his knees began to tremble, and a new source of heat began to pulse in his groin. All he could think was how magnificent she was, this girl who smoked beside him. Her cigarette flared again, and another stream of smoke peeled up into the sky. Clint raised a shaky hand and took a final drag, drawing nicotine deep into his lungs. The smoke seemed different, electrically charged and sweet. Beside him Delia went on puffing in companionable silence. She sighed once, and he felt the impact as her head knocked gently against the brick building.

"Look at them run," she said so softly it was like that murmured song. The team was staggering in the final set of laps, some of the boys stumbling as their exhausted legs came down heavy and flat-footed.

"Poor sons-a-bitches," Clint said, the words pulled out of him by her disregard.

"You got that right."

Delia rocked her head again and shifted her shoulders. He could hear the cloth of her coat dragging against the brick. All his senses had sharpened, it seemed, picking up the smell of her smoke distinct from his own, the small crackle as her muscles worked.

"Like they're training for the army, God help them. Like they don't know." Delia shook her head.

Clint's vision came back into focus, and he looked at the boys on the field, seeing for the first time how they were rushing at their fate, a fate he would not share. He realized he had no idea what was coming for him, what he would do with his life. He wasn't that smart, he knew. His daddy had told him often enough. Not scholarship-smart, no advantages at all. But he understood suddenly that he didn't want to grow peanuts or to farm. And if he did not work with his daddy, what else was there?

God help me, he thought, forgetting for the moment the wall at his back and Delia at his side. The bunched pack of boys turned at the near curve of the track, shoulders angling, and then they were running away, hips grinding, feet throwing up clods of damp red earth. Pitiful and brave at the same time, they staggered toward the coach, who was thumping his clipboard against his thigh and glaring at their progress. Clint felt his throat pull tight.

"Sad," Delia whispered.

"Run, you sons-a-bitches!" The coach's words were a roar, his contempt a palpable wave that lapped at Clint's heart.

"Damn!" Clint shook his hand where the dwindling butt had burned him.

"Yeah." Delia echoed his curse and tossed her half-smoked cigarette to join the others scattered on the ground. "Makes you wonder at the world, don't it?"

She turned to him. She was hugging her coat close to her midriff, the expression in her eyes warmer than a smile. You all right, that look said. We know what we know, don't we? Clint could not look away. I'm all right, he thought. An't nothing wrong with me. Delia gave him a nod and walked off, resuming that murmured scrap of song.

Clint looked back at the runners. Two of them had fallen. He shoved his hands into his pockets. "I'm all right," he said, and pushed off the wall.

In his fever-heated sheets, Clint tried to roll to the side. His hip locked up with the old shortened tendons that ran down to his knee. Pain surged through the morphine fog. Delia had talked Dr. Campbell into raising the dosage, giving him respite and dreams cut loose of time. He had dreamed forward and back, every moment he ever had with Delia interspersed with flashes of his life before her and splintered visions of what would follow after him. The world was getting ready to let go of him, to swing him free. It was lifting him high and he could see far, to the girls grown up and hateful, and then back to himself an infant hanging on tight to a breast he could not imagine his mama had ever provided. Delia would go on forever. But he would not, and that was all right. He knew it finally. That was all right.

"Goddamn," Clint moaned. His tongue was dry and stiff. Too much trouble to talk anymore. Damn, he said anyway. He said it in his head and felt himself start that journey again, swinging up and up. He heard the car coat drag on the wall and smelled cigarette smoke and rich wet dirt, the girl beside him and the years ahead, her blood on his hands and his own tears sliding down his face. He felt heat flare in his groin for the first time in so long he did not at first know it for what it was.

"Damn." He said it out loud and swung high, as high as he had ever gone.

And let go.

Chapter 11

Reverend Hillman officiated at Clint's funeral. The crowd was small, though not so small as M.T. had promised Rosemary it would be. There were a number of women from Holiness Redeemer who had come with Grandma Windsor, some of the men from Firestone who had once worked with Clint, and at least a dozen patrons of the Bee's Bonnet who no one had expected to come.

"Some of them must be here just to make sure he's dead," M.T. whispered to Rosemary as they stood under the canopy at the graveside. Rosemary covered her smile with her hand. M.T. had been cheerful and friendly from the moment she had gotten the call telling her that Clint had died, and Rosemary knew it was only partly relief that the man was gone. M.T. was not at all unhappy that Rosemary would be leaving in a couple of days, but neither was Rosemary. She had gotten her fill of the small Georgia town and been packed to leave for weeks. She had sworn to herself she would kick dirt on Clint Windsor's coffin and was waiting for the crowd to clear so she could do it.

"When I get back to Los Angeles," Rosemary whispered to M.T., "I'm going to one of those expensive day spas, get my whole body oiled and massaged and revitalized. You come visit me and I'll pay your way. You will not believe how good you can feel."

"Oh, I couldn't do that!" M.T. sounded tempted. She looked sideways at Steph, who was holding Lyle's hand and trying to look sad with no success at all.

"You should. Los Angeles is a hell of a town for women our age, full of handsome young men ready to appreciate us older women of substance." Rosemary smiled and put her arm around M.T.'s shoulders.

"Gigolos you mean."

"Uh-huh, fine, strong, good-looking young gigolos. Just what the doctor ordered for tired blood and general malaise, and I don't know about you, but after all these months I am suffering from malaise." Rosemary squeezed M.T.'s arm and angled her body away from Grandma Windsor's glare. The old woman had been giving her hateful looks since they left the church.

"The way you talk!" M.T. pressed her lips together to keep from giggling. Pity Rosemary disliked Cayro. She could learn to like this woman.

"Just like you," Rosemary told her. "I talk like you. Why you think Delia likes us both so much? We got a lot in common, Marjolene Thomasina. More than just our friendship with Delia Byrd." She turned her head and gave Grandma Windsor a big smile. Clint's mother glared back at her and started walking away from the grave.

Cissy barely heard what Reverend Hillman said. She was thinking about her daddy. She remembered the time they had all gone to a funeral for some friend of his in a chapel filled with big baskets of flowers tied around with colored ribbons. Delia wore a velvet vest with a starburst sewn on the back in bright orange threads. Randall had walked around the little church with Cissy on his hip, hugging people and trading reminiscences. At one point he had picked her up and put her in a hamper of flowers, yellow daisies and pink and white mums in a mound so high the blossoms almost closed over Cissy's head.

"Death is a change of circumstances," said a guy wearing leather-wrapped braids and a tie-dyed shirt. He took a sip from a thermos and staggered.

Randall pulled Cissy out of the flowers all covered in pollen and petals. "Death is death," he said angrily. He hugged Cissy close and glared at the man. "Funerals aren't about death, they're about how glad we are to still be alive."

At Clint's graveside, Cissy remembered the whole exchange clearly, though she hadn't thought about it in all the years since. Afterward Randall had taken Cissy walking among the tombstones and made jokes about all the cement angels and concrete cherubs. "I'm going to be cremated," he told her as they sat in the shade of a stumpy California oak. "Get rendered down to ash and bone and used as compost for some big old tree. I'll turn into flowers and green glossy leaves." He seemed cheerful about it, especially after all the solemn faces of his friends.

Cissy didn't understand what everyone was so sad about. Randall had said that his friend was better off out of this life, that sometimes it was good to go on to feed the trees. At the gate to the cemetery, when he led her back to the long line of waiting cars, one of the drivers said something about hippies, and Randall laughed at him. "Yeah, we're rich hippies," he said, and swung Cissy up on his shoulders. She remembered Randall's laugh and the way he talked about turning into green glossy leaves. That was what hippies did, she had thought at the time, throw parties for their friends and get turned into fertilizer.

It would have been good if Clint had had a little hippie in him. That last week before he died, he was constantly afraid. He had asked Delia to call Reverend Hillman, and cried while the minister sat with him. When Cissy went in, he had grabbed her hands in his knobby fists and held on so tight she thought he would crack her bones. At the end he had not been able to talk or sleep, just roll in the bed and groan until Delia got the doctor to give him more drugs. When he died, Delia shut the girls out of the room, and Rosemary helped her wash him and dress him in a dark wool suit. For the first time Clint looked like the man in Delia's old pictures, stern-faced and fully dressed in clothes far too big for his wasted frame.

"Should bury him naked," Dede said in a cracked voice.

"Should burn him," Cissy whispered, and Dede gave her a look. "Turn him into ash and bone. Feed him to the flowers and the trees."

Dede shuddered. "To the rocks, maybe. Feed him to the rocks and let the birds take the bones to use in their nests." She had not wanted to go to the funeral, but Delia made them all go and stand in a line at her side.

When they got back to the house, Rosemary put her hand on Cissy's cheek and smiled gently. "You okay, honey?"

The child reminded her of herself at that age, low on the totem pole in a house full of demanding, powerful voices. Cissy's face looked pinched and worried.

"I'm fine." Cissy shrugged off Rosemary's hand.

"Grandma Windsor looked terrible," Amanda said. "Her hair has gotten all ratty, and her neck looked awful, like a chicken's."

"Your grandmother is getting older, and it's hard to lose a son," Delia said calmly.

"I was thinking I should go out to see her." Amanda's tone was uncertain.

"If you want to," Delia said. She didn't look as bad as Grandma Windsor, but she looked bad enough. The shadows under her eyes were dark as the grapes in the basket of fruit someone had left on the porch that morning. Standing at the table where casseroles and foil-wrapped plates of meat crowded the fruit and several little pots of wilted flowers, she reached out to touch one of the covered bowls, then dropped her hand.

"I think I'll lie down for a while," she said. "I think I just need to lie down."

Rosemary put her arm around Delia's shoulders. M.T. came to the other side. Together they guided Delia down the hall. With every step Delia slumped a little more, until it seemed the two women were carrying her.

"What you want to bet she sleeps through till tomorrow?" Dede asked Cissy.

"Day after," Cissy replied. "Or the day after that. I thought she was going to fall right down into the grave."

"I thought Rosemary was going to fall in. Did you see how close she got after they lowered the coffin down?"

"I saw." Cissy lifted one of the foil wrappers. She wanted something but it wasn't food. Her head pounded and her eyes ached. "Allergies," Rosemary had told her. "Your eyes are all swollen." None of them wanted to acknowledge that she had been crying. Amanda had wiped her eyes a few times, but neither Delia nor Dede had shed a tear. Only Cissy looked and felt as stricken as Grandma Windsor. She kept thinking about Randall and his funeral before they left Los Angeles.

"You know what I want?" Dede had a piece of ham in one hand and a slice of white cake in the other. "I want a drink, a real drink, one of those mixed drinks people are always ordering on television. A gin and tonic or a whiskey sour." She took a bite of ham and nodded solemnly.

"Yeah?" Cissy lifted her glasses and wiped her left eye. The corner was so tender it burned at her touch. Her expression was so sorrowful, Dede had to work to keep from laughing.

"What is it Rosemary drinks, bourbon or scotch?" Dede asked.

"I don't know."

"Well, whatever. Everything goes good with Coke. Let's mix ourselves some drinks and have a picnic out back."

"Do you think we should?" Cissy looked down the hall. She didn't want to have to talk to M.T. or Rosemary, and especially not to Amanda.

"I think we damn sure should," Dede said emphatically. "We'll do it for Clint. He's probably the only one in the house who would appreciate it anyway."

There was scotch and bourbon left in the kitchen, though not much of either. Dede made the drinks and gave the scotch to Cissy, telling her she knew it was what Rosemary preferred, so it had to be good. After one sip Cissy suspected she had found the one thing that did not go well with Coke. After the second, she decided it was not so bad. It made the ham sandwich taste a lot better, and Dede announced that bourbon was going to be her drink of choice. They sat under the pecan trees near the garage, and after a while Cissy started to feel better than she had in a week. Maybe it was like Randall had told her, that death was not so terrible a thing. Dead, Clint had looked almost peaceful.

"What was your daddy like?" Dede was a little hesitant, but determined. "I seen his picture, read some stuff about him. Sounded like he was a crazy son of a bitch." Dede was sitting against the far outside wall of the garage, holding the stub of a cigarette between two fingers. Cissy had thought Dede just pretended to smoke, but sitting out behind the garage, Dede had already gone through two of the butts she kept in her little metal tin. "I've been smoking for years," she bragged, and the way she puffed it might have been true.

"He wasn't crazy. He was just like anybody." Cissy had her stubborn expression on, mouth pulled tight and eyes intent. "Liked to drive too fast. Got drunk too much. Was always on the move. Doing business, he called it. 'Got to do some business, Little Bit,' he'd say. 'Keep it dry.'" She gave Dede a careful look. "I never knew what that meant."

Dede shrugged. "You see him much?"

"When I was little, yeah. Sort of." Cissy thought for a moment. Had she known Randall at all?

"Sort of?" Dede said wryly, as if she suspected Cissy of lying.

"Well, it was hard, you know." Cissy frowned at the memory. "They were always traveling or in the studio, going places and doing things. When we still lived with him, there was Sonny and Patch. They worked for Randall, took care of the house, took care of everything. They'd look after me while the band was traveling."

"You didn't get to go on the bus?" Dede was disappointed.

"Not once I got older. Rosemary told me stories about when I was little and Randall and Delia would take me with them, how I would sleep backstage or in one of the bus seats. She even had pictures. There's one that's kind of famous where I'm with a bunch of other little kids and we're all naked off at the end of the stage with a drum set. I don't remember that at all."

"You don't remember much, do you?"

"Not what people wish I did." Cissy grimaced. "I remember stuff. I remember eating room service in hotels with Delia and Randall lying in bed on either side of me. And playing on escalators. I liked escalators a lot. I liked being with Delia and Randall, but I don't know, it was the way things were. It was just the way life was. I didn't know it was that different. And when I stayed home, that wasn't so bad. I liked Sonny and Patch. They were good to me. They had a little boy of their own, Wren. He was my age, but he didn't talk."

"Retard?" Dede asked.

"He was all right. He was smart, just didn't talk." Cissy remembered Wren's big smile and shy eyes. He was a sweet little boy, and Sonny was always carrying him around on his shoulders. When Delia and Randall were gone too long, she would pretend Sonny was her father and Wren her brother, that they were a family miraculously intact after some big earthquake had knocked out the rest of the city. Then, when Delia and Randall came home, she would feel ashamed and be mean to Wren until Delia scolded her. After they moved out of Randall's house, Cissy never saw any of them again.

"Grandma Windsor had Blanche to help her look after us." Dede seemed to know that Cissy did not want to say any more about Wren. "Blanche was a second cousin or something. Think she was only fourteen when she come to stay with us. I don't know. I was just a baby. Amanda didn't like her, but she always seemed nice to me." Dede swirled the flat Coke in the bottom of her glass, then drained it. She set the glass between her feet and took out a pack of cigarettes.

"What Amanda told me was that Blanche had had a baby of her own and got kicked out of school. Maybe the baby died or her daddy gave it away. After she come to live with Grandma Windsor, she never talked about it. She wasn't no retard neither, but she wasn't very bright. Had these big old moon eyes, pale blue and wide, pretty but empty. Black-headed and olive-skinned. Pretty enough to get in trouble. Stupid enough to get in more."

"Was she nice to you?" Cissy tried to imagine Blanche, fourteen and under Grandma Windsor's thumb, picking up after two angry toddlers and never talking about her lost baby. If she had been Blanche, she would have been mean to Amanda and Dede. She'd have pinched their butts and pulled their hair when no one was looking.

"She was all right. Played with us a lot. Don't think she'd have done that so much if she'd been smarter. We were boring, but she never seemed to mind. She just did whatever Grandma told her to do, picked up, cleaned, watched us. I liked her as much as I liked anybody." Dede grinned. "Hell of a lot more than some people."

"So why didn't Amanda like her?"

"I don't know." Dede picked a flake of tobacco off her tooth with a lacquered fingernail. "I've never been able to figure Amanda. When Blanche died, she acted like she'd been expecting it."

"Blanche died?" Cissy was shocked.

"Accident. Pressure cooker blew." Dede put a hand to her throat and tapped once to the left of her chin. "Cut her throat." Her fingers traced a line below the jaw and the ear.

"My God."

"It was the lid," Dede said. "Sliced a hole in her neck big enough to put a teacup inside." She caressed her throat briefly, and then the hand dropped. "It upset Grandma Windsor something terrible, but she said it was bound to happen. Blanche had never paid attention to how that thing worked. She was always letting pots burn up, bathtubs flow over, irons scorch sheets. Just didn't pay attention. With the pressure cooker, she didn't fasten the lid down tight, so it blew off. Bad luck she was standing right there."

"That's terrible." Cissy felt sick to her stomach. The black-headed girl she had been imagining looked back at her with a wide smile and a gaping hole in her neck.

"Grandma said it was a wonder Blanche didn't burn the house down. She was always staring off into space, always seemed to have some story going in her head, some adventure happening that was much more interesting than the life she was leading. Which was tedious as hell, being a day maid to Grandma and us."

"Were you there?" Cissy asked. "When it happened?"

"In the bathroom." Dede's voice was flat. "I heard the explosion. Come running out with my skirt caught in my underpants. Blanche was sitting on the floor with her hands up at her throat and a dark red river running down her front. Everything was dark red. She didn't even look at me. She just fell back hard. Grandma said she was dead already. You lose that much blood, you are dead before you know it."

"Lord God!"

Dede tapped her cigarette tin on her knee. "Hell, it's better than how Clint went, way better." She paused. "It could have been me easy as her. I'd been standing where she was just minutes before. Grandma Windsor said I must think about why I had to go pee at that moment, what I was meant to do now. But I can't think like that. Who knows what's meant and what an't?"

"It's scary to think about," Cissy said, watching Dede's hand.

"Yeah, for a while I would dream about it, about Blanche. Dreamed I went in and checked on the pot, fastened it down and she didn't die. Dreamed she called me in just as it exploded. Even dreamed she came and sat on the bed to talk to me."

Cissy shivered, thinking of how she dreamed about Randall coming to talk to her. She had had a lot of them in the last couple of months. He sat on the bed and called her "Little Bit" while he scratched at his mustache and looked around the room. "I know I wasn't no kind of decent daddy," he said. "I wanted to be, but I never had it in me. But nobody raised me either, and look how I turned out." Then he grinned as if he knew what he had said was not at all reassuring. "I'm kidding, Little Bit," he told her. "I'll keep an eye on you."

"Grandma told me that it was a dangerous thing, having a ghost in your dreams. She drew circles around the bedposts with salt, said that would stop the dreams. After a while it did, or they stopped themselves. Maybe they would have anyway."

Cissy wondered if she wanted her dreams of Randall to stop. Should she sprinkle salt under her bed? Would Clint start showing up in her dreams now?

"So tell me your happiest earliest memory."

"Happiest?" Cissy closed her eyes and pressed her lips together in concentration. Slowly a smile bloomed. Her eyes opened. "The fire show Randall made me when I was five."

"What's a fire show?" Dede was genuinely curious.

"Something he made up." Cissy's smile widened at the memory. "Randall had this big old statue of a bird out by his swimming pool. It was ugly, black metal and sharp edges. Delia hated it. But Randall used it to hang things up—wind chimes and ribbons and balloons for parties. That evening he taped all these old garbage bags Delia was saving all over it. She never threw nothing away and he said it was time to make use of her stuff. When the sun went down, he set fire to the bags one at a time."

"He burned a bunch of garbage bags? What's so great about that?"

"They burned in colors. All these colors. Some of them wouldn't catch and just made messy smoke, but some of them went up in a glitter of red and green and blue and gold all mixed together like oily water. The color would change as the flame ran up the bag. So then he took a bunch of bags and tied them to each other, and when he set fire to those, the colors changed as the flame ran up the strings of bags."

Cissy rocked gently, remembering. "It was all weird and strange and wonderful. When it got really dark it was even better, and Randall went all through the house collecting everything plastic he could find. Burned it all, even some of the curtains out of the pool house."

"Weird." Dede pried the lid off the tin, removed a butt, and lit it.

"Yeah, Delia was mad when she got home. There was black stuff all over the grass, and melted plastic on the statue and the flagstones. I had a burn on my foot, and Randall's jacket sleeves were all scorched. She was really pissed."

"I bet."

"But I liked it."

"Well, you were five. You would like it."

"It was beautiful," Cissy insisted.

Dede sucked smoke. "I like fire," she said. "Always have. Grandma Windsor wouldn't let me burn nothing. Made me rake up all the leaves and crap but wouldn't let me burn it. She'd make Amanda burn it. And Amanda hates fire."

Cissy thought about Amanda. Yes, Amanda would hate fire. "What's yours?"

"My what?"

"Best memory from when you were little."

Dede shrugged her shoulders and blew on the end of the cigarette stub. "I don't know. I liked the cows. Granddaddy Windsor had two really good milk cows, big old lady cows with swollen nipples hanging down. He kept them producing, and they had a great setup in the barn. Sweet-smelling straw and the walls all scrubbed down and whitewashed. That milk barn was cleaner than the house, and I liked to hide out in there. In the winter I'd sneak cups of warm milk from the buckets and climb up on the hayrack and drink it slow."

"Was it sweet?" Cissy tried to imagine warm milk fresh from a cow.

"Naaaa, not sweet. Frothy and funny-tasting. If the cows got spooked or ate something they weren't supposed to eat, it would taste kind of sour or get this strange tang. I didn't care, though. I'd put bread in it to soak it up and eat that for dinner when Grandma was mad at me. You didn't want to sit at table when she was mad."

"She looks like the kind would get mad easy."

"Yeah, but mostly she was tired all the time. Amanda said it was like she was used up and just wanted to coast till she died. Seemed like the only time she was happy was when she was alone. You'd come on her out in the garden or somewhere where she didn't see you, and she'd be smiling and relaxed, big old smile. Then she'd spot you and get all stern-faced and sad. I don't think she had too many happy memories."

Cissy thought about Grandma Windsor's face at the funeral and about Amanda and Dede growing up in her house. They had been standing within a few feet of her and she had never looked at them. "What's your worst memory?" she asked.

Dede didn't even pause. "Clint, he's all my bad memories."

Cissy flinched. Her face felt hot, and the skin below her eyes was sweaty. She remembered how scared and desperate he had been the last week. "What'd he do?"

"Do?" Dede sounded angry. "He didn't have to do nothing. He'd just come around, and everything would go bad. Grandpa Windsor would start cursing and being mean to Grandma, and she'd get all hunched over and start being mean to us." She shook her head. "Mostly Clint didn't do nothing. He'd show up drunk or looking like he just got sober. He'd say things to Grandma you couldn't make out, and stare at us like we were dogs in the road. He was just bad news, bad news always coming around."

The cigarette butt in Dede's hand had burned down to the filter. She crushed it out on a rock between her legs. "Grandma was always making us go over to see him. We'd get all dressed up and go over there and sit at the table, and he'd just look at us with that stupid expression on his face, like he'd got hit by a truck or something. Always smelled like he had been sitting in spoiled milk. Always looked like he had shaved himself raw. Wasn't nothing to do or say. We'd eat what Grandma had sent over, and we'd try to talk some, but it was no use. It was purgatory, sitting there waiting until we could get away. Worst thing was, everyone knew he was our daddy, and they'd look at us like we were gonna turn out as useless as he was. Like being some criminal's child or something. God."

Cissy licked her lips. "People used to stare at me that way. 'Cause of Randall and Delia and everything."

"That was because they were famous." Dede spat once on the ground. "It's not the same."

"Maybe not, but it would get bad sometimes." Cissy rubbed her temples, remembering the embarrassment. Once, when Randall was arrested for speeding, reporters came out to the house and took pictures of her and Delia through the windows.

"Okay, your turn," Dede said. "Tell me the absolute worst thing you remember."

"Fighting," Cissy said immediately. "Delia and Randall fighting. Yelling and breaking things and cursing each other and Delia crying and screaming. Before we moved out, they were fighting a lot."

Dede raised an eyebrow. "He hit her?"

"No. Randall never hit nobody." Cissy wiggled uncomfortably. "He broke things, though. Worst time, he got so mad he went through the living room kicking the furniture over. He smashed the little tables and the lamps, pulled down the curtains, and threw stuff in the fireplace—all the ashtrays and dishes and stuff."

"You were there?"

"I was up on the staircase. They didn't even know I was watching."

"Oh." Dede sounded disappointed.

"Randall kept shouting," Cissy went on, "and shoving things over. While Delia was telling him he was a sorry excuse for a man or a dog, he went to kick the big coffee table in front of the couch. Delia yelled, 'You crazy son of a bitch,' but he did it anyway. Broke his foot."

"Broke his foot?" Dede laughed.

"Yeah, had to wear a cast for two months. Told me it was a lesson for us all, not to let your temper run away with your good sense."

Cissy leaned back against the garage wall and watched the clouds bunching overhead. Randall had a fast temper, but his anger would go away just as fast, like clouds racing across the sky. His sense of humor was the same, sudden and wry and turning sad without warning. Changeable. Her daddy had been changeable. She still had trouble believing that he was gone, that he would not someday walk in on them and give that lazy smile, and hug her tight. He could not be dead. She could not keep it in her head. Some thoughts just did not want to stay.

"Broke his foot!" Dede rocked forward and came up on her bootheels. "Wish I could have seen that. Wish Clint had broken his sorry ass one time and I could have seen it." She tucked her cigarette tin in a back pocket and smiled down at Cissy. "You tell good stories, little sister. Really good." She kicked leaves up on her way back to the house, kicked them so they scattered before her.

Cissy looked down into the glass tumbler between her legs. It was empty now but coated with a sticky residue of Coke and scotch. Clint had told her he liked to drink whiskey, Wild Turkey or Jim Beam. He had talked about it like it was the best thing in the world. She tried to remember what Randall drank, but all that remained was the memory of some unlabeled red-brown bottle sitting at the top of his bed. Her eyes flooded again. This time she didn't know who she was crying for, Clint or Randall or herself.

Amanda had not been to see Grandma Windsor since a few weeks after she and Dede moved into Clint's house. The visit had been humiliating and brief. Her grandmother met her at the road with a couple of paper bags and told her to make herself useful and help pick up some of the windblown trash. Obediently Amanda trailed behind her, picking up cans, bottles, sheets of newsprint, milk cartons.

"Don't put them together. Sort them out," the old woman yelled at her, and when Amanda tried to talk about Delia, Grandma Windsor sent her to pick up on the other side of the road. "You going to help me, help me," she said, making it plain she did not want to talk about Delia or the move or Clint and what was happening in that house. Amanda finally crossed the road to kiss her grandmother's cheek, packed up her bags of trash, and walked back down to the bus stop. She didn't go back to Grandma Windsor's and wouldn't tell anyone why.

Three days after the funeral Amanda decided to try again.

"I brought you some pecans," she told Grandma Windsor, setting a paper bag of nuts on the kitchen table.

The old woman pursed her lips. "Those from them scrawny trees on Terrill Road?"

"From Clint's." Amanda nodded.

Grandma Windsor snorted. "Those make little mealy nuts, not fit for anything but feeding pigs."

Amanda flushed. She had not expected her grandmother to make a fuss, but did the old woman have to insult her? It hurt her that Grandma Windsor kept looking away. Grandma Windsor's neck seemed even scalier than it had at the funeral, and her cheeks and hands were red and chapped. It was fall, and the trees were dropping their leaves all over the yard and along all the ditches. Grandma Windsor led Amanda out to where she was shifting her flowerpots, knocking the old dirt out and lining the pots up to be rinsed with her hose. She had a pair of pruning shears in her apron and kept pulling them out to cut things—a blackberry vine that had crept over the fence, a weed in the vegetable flat, a few branches off the bushes by the steps.

"Grandma, I wanted to tell you something."

"Tell me something?" Grandma Windsor stopped working long enough to catch sight of Amanda's flaming red cheeks. Grudgingly she settled on the bench by the fertilizer bins, near a pile of branches that had been cut from the apple trees in the fall. Amanda remembered how Grandma Windsor always insisted the branches be pruned and clipped in the fall. Grandma Windsor pulled a couple of the long branches toward her and began to clip pieces off in short lengths to toss in her wheelbarrow. She liked applewood for her smoker, Amanda remembered. She looked at her grandmother's stern face and saw again how she had aged. Guilt shot through her. All this time and Amanda had not even visited.

"So what was it you wanted to say?" Grandma Windsor's eyes were on the pieces of wood she was trimming down. Maybe she meant to be kind, to let Amanda speak without pressure, but it felt to Amanda like impatience, just like her own. It was as if Grandma Windsor had cleared her mind of her granddaughters when they went to live with their mother and now she resented being faced with Amanda again.

I won't think that way, Amanda told herself. I will be a loving spirit. She made herself take several deep breaths.

"It's about Daddy," she said finally. "All those months I would sit with him and try to pray the way you taught me. You know—your will, O God, not mine, be done. Only I wasn't really sure what my will was, what I wanted." Grandma Windsor went on whittling branches and slowly filling the wheelbarrow.

"I didn't love him." Amanda spoke softly, but Grandma Windsor's shears stopped. "Sorry," Amanda said quickly, and covered her face with her hands.

When Grandma Windsor was silent, Amanda went on. "I used to be afraid of him. I've always had to fight not to hate him. I remember that time he hit you." She heard her grandmother's shears sniping again, faster now. "I knew he was drunk. I know you said he didn't mean it. But it seemed like every time we saw him, it was terrible. Either he was drunk or angry or fighting with Grandpa or being mean to you. I never thought about him as my real father at all."

"He was your father. I taught you to honor him." The words were faint but clear.

"Yes, yes. And I did what you said, Grandma. I pretended Jesus was with him, watching by and waiting for him. But when we had to go live over there in the same house with him—and with her—I just couldn't stand it. I realized that nothing stopped what I was feeling, that I hated him." Amanda's shoulders were shaking. "I was so ashamed," she said, "so ashamed."

Grandma Windsor looked at Amanda, her face impossible to read, the eyes red-rimmed and wide. "He was your father," she said, "my son. It's for God to judge him, not us."

Amanda started to cry.

"There's no need for that, girl." Grandma Windsor put both her hands in her lap, cradling the shears in one palm. "God knows your soul. Couldn't be expected to be no better than you are. You're your mother's making as much as you are Clint's or mine." She curled her lips. "I doubt she taught you much charity. Way she hated him, what else could you learn but hate?"

"It wasn't like that," Amanda said. "She took good care of him. She didn't ever say a word about him to us."

Grandma Windsor grunted. "She hated him."

Amanda leaned forward. "He was dying. I hadn't seen Daddy in almost two years, and the first time I walked in there, I knew it was not going to be long. He looked so bad and smelled so bad. It was like mice were breeding in that room, some grassy stink and a kind of old blood smell on that. I would go in there and read the Bible, but it made me gag to be in the same room with him." Amanda wiped her eyes.

"But she would go in there, her and Cissy. Delia would go in there and take care of him, and Cissy would feed him or just sit with him and talk. You could hear their voices, right through the walls of our bedroom."

"What were they saying?"

"I don't know. I couldn't make out the words."

"Telling lies." That edge of impatience was back in Grandma Windsor's voice.

Amanda took another deep breath and closed her eyes. She did not want to see Grandma Windsor's face when she said what she was about to say. She did not want to see pity or contempt or disbelief.

"I think I saw the Holy Spirit."

"The Holy Spirit?" Grandma Windsor's voice was careful.

"Yes."

The old woman reached up and rubbed her neck. Her eyes wandered from Amanda's stricken face to her garden. So much work to do, her look said. So much work to do and I'm sitting here.

"Grandma, I thought he was damned." Amanda spoke in a rush. "I thought for sure he was going right to hell. He wouldn't have no preacher in the house. Said it wasn't God he needed to make peace with. He asked us to forgive him. One night he got Dede and me to come in the door and asked us to say right out did we forgive him. So of course I said yes, but I knew I didn't mean it. I think he did too."

"What did Dede tell him?"

"She told him he was a fool and to leave her out of his mess."

Grandma Windsor smiled.

"After that I was afraid to go in there. When Cissy told me to leave him alone, I was glad. I didn't want to talk to him. But I kept going to the door and looking in. I figured I had to make peace with him one way or another. I knew God was talking to my heart. One night I went and stood in the door while Delia was washing him down."

"She was washing him?" Grandma Windsor sounded skeptical.

"With alcohol. She was wiping him down and toweling him dry. He kept saying, 'Lord bless, Lord bless,' and I was thinking how strange it was for him to say that. All he had on was these baggy undershorts, and he was lying in those sheets so they were in a kind of cupped shape all around him. It looked like a painting from the Middle Ages, like Jesus in the sepulchre before the angels came to get him." She stopped, shivering at the memory.

Into her silence Grandma Windsor said, "She washed him."

"Yes," Amanda said. "Yes, I know. It was all strange. It was like a dream. They looked like they were in some cave in that little dark room with only the lamplight, and him going 'Lord bless, Lord bless' in that deep hollow voice, and Delia saying 'Hush hush.' "

"I can't imagine her to wash him. After all that time, the way she behaved. I can't believe that." Grandma Windsor was looking into the branches of her apple trees. Amanda felt a wave of resentment go through her again. "But I haven't told you what I saw," she said. Grandma Windsor looked at her.

"Well, tell me then."

"I was standing in the door and I was looking at them like I told you. They were in this little circle of light from the lamp. And all of a sudden it went funny, it reversed. One minute they were in the circle of light surrounded by the dark, and then they were all dark and the rest of the room was brightly lit. I looked at the walls, and the walls were glowing. I looked up and the ceiling looked like it had taken fire. It was diamond-bright, and then it got soft and yellow as butter. It came down on them until they were lit up again, all yellow and warm. It lit them up so bright I could see the bones in their bodies, the light just pouring through their skin. Only Daddy's bones were trembling and moving, and I realized that when he was saying 'Lord bless,' he was not saying thank you or 'That feels good.' He was saying, 'Please. Please, God.' And God heard him."

Grandma Windsor frowned, but Amanda nodded firmly. About

this point she was definite. This was what she had wanted to tell her grandmother. This was the thing.

"It was just a moment, Grandma. Just a moment, but it was a moment full of light. I knew everything that was happening. I could see his soul in the trembling of his bones. I could feel God's love in that yellow light."

"Oh, Amanda." Grandma Windsor scratched at her forehead.

"No. Grandma, no. Listen. I saw it." Amanda's lips quivered with concentration. "When that light went from dark to bright and bright again, when the ceiling and walls burned with it and it came down on them, it moved between them like something alive. It moved from her to him, and it was inside them both, and then it lifted up. And I could see it reached through the ceiling and past the sky, right up to heaven, right up to God's right hand."

"You saw God's hand."

"No. I felt it. I felt God's hand and the light coming from it. It was the Holy Ghost, Grandma, and it was breathing on Daddy. I felt it. I knew it. And I knew right away that I didn't have to forgive him, 'cause God already had."

"Oh Lord." Grandma Windsor suddenly sounded tired. She looked at her granddaughter again and saw her face fall.

"I knew it, Grandma, it spoke inside me. It was a whisper from God's own mouth."

"From God." The old woman looked up at the sky. "Well," she said. "Well." She gripped the shears in both hands.

"She ever say anything about me?" she asked suddenly.

Amanda was wiping her eyes. "What?"

"Delia. She ever say anything about me?"

Amanda stared at her. "She told us to call you. Said we should come see you. Said she would drive us out here to visit."

"Humph."

"She doesn't talk about you, Grandma."

"Good." The old woman started cutting apple branches again. Amanda watched in confusion.

"Don't you have anything to say?"

"Say about what?"

"About what I saw. About the Spirit and the light."

Grandma Windsor sighed. "I think you think too much, Amanda. Way too much, and too much about yourself. Why don't you go home and do something useful instead of telling me all this nonsense?"

Amanda's mouth hung open. Her eyes flooded with tears. Grandma Windsor stood up, grabbed the handles of the wheelbarrow, and gave it a shove toward the woodshed.

Home, Amanda thought. Grandma Windsor called Delia's place her home now. She looked around the yard where she had lived for more than ten years. This was supposed to be her home, but it wasn't. Amanda swallowed a sob, remembering that buttery light, the way Delia's hands had moved on Clint's wasted body. With such great tenderness she had washed him, bathing him the way a mother bathes an infant.

There had been love in that room, Amanda was sure, forgiveness and acceptance. God had sent His love down into that room and made it safe for two people who had reason to hate each other. Amanda shuddered at the memory, the comparison with the cold she felt radiating from her grandmother. All her life it seemed she had been cold. All her life she had been alone. But God had made that room warm and full and safe. God could heat iron. God could warm even the coldest heart.

"Lord," Amanda whispered into the cool fall air. "Lord, forgive me too. Lord, bless my dark and bitter heart, and I will honor You as my Father. I will magnify Your name and spread Your light. Lord bless me, I will be Your child." She reached down and picked up a thorny scrap of dry wood, turned it into her palm, and gripped it tight. She rocked slightly, feeling her skin tear and imagining the blood pooling in her palm.

"I will be Your child," she said.

Amanda's sense of God's favor was heartfelt and absolute. She had been born in sin. She had been raised hard, but God had his eye on her. She would work to spread God's light, that light He had personally shown to her. She went to church the way some people went to bed, gratefully, happily, and with utter peace in her heart. She let Michael Graham take her hand in his, looked up at him, and felt God's breath mix with her own. The only fear she had was that she herself was not worthy of the light she had seen, that no one would take her dying body in hand, bathe it tenderly, and love it utterly. In the back of her head there was always the sound of her grandmother's voice, speaking her name with impatience. "Amanda, go home."

Amanda looked long and hard at herself, her plain face, her barren heart. God, teach me love, she begged. Make me worthy. She was Delia Byrd's daughter, Clint Windsor's girl. She was that child no one had loved enough to keep with them. She was one of the ones who would have to work to deserve the light, but life was full of hard bargains and hers was not as hard as some.

Amanda set her teeth and went about it, the pursuit of a love she only dimly imagined.

Chapter 12

Four months after Clint died, Emmet Tyler walked into the Bonnet with a large brown paper sack clutched under one arm and a look of infinite despair engraved on his face.

"It's my wife's. She's sick." He extended the bag to Delia tentatively. "I was hoping you could do something with it."

The bag contained Amy Tyler's second-best wig. The best one had suffered what the home care nurse called "an unfortunate accident" because she would not admit that she had left Amy alone long enough for the woman to fall asleep with a cigarette askew in her mouth, blackening a big hunk of the side of the wig. Amy wasn't supposed to be alone, and certainly not to smoke.

"Well, things happen," the nurse had told Emmet.

"They do, they surely do," he replied. His hands shook. He wanted to hit her, and he had never hit a woman in his life.

The second-best wig was now all Amy had, though she still spoke dreamily of the lost one, the one her friends from the insurance office had given her, a real-human-hair wig ordered from a specialty supply outfit in Florida. "Where is it?" she kept asking. She seemed to think Emmet had hidden it from her, or given it to some woman down at the courthouse.

Amy had a tendency to lose track of things these days. Between the haze the drugs spread over her brain and the slow eating away of her memory, a lot was slipping. Sometimes she remembered she had set the wig on fire, and should be grateful she had not burned herself too. Sometimes the wig and the cancer and even Emmet's face retreated into a reality she could no longer comprehend. Was she truly a grown woman with two dead children and a husband who worked too many nights driving along back roads and sipping black coffee? Or was she still the girl who had not yet decided to marry that sweet-faced Tyler boy, the girl who was thinking about going up to Nashville for LPN training? How had she wound up typing insurance forms, miscarrying until she thought herself cursed by God, and then getting so sick so fast? Wasn't this just a bad dream? Emmet could never be sure anymore which Amy he was talking to, only that his wife was frightened and confused and in pain.

"Dying is hard," the Baptist minister told him. Emmet knew he meant to be comforting, but somehow the words rang harsh.

"It's work," Emmet said. "It's more work than I ever knew."

He had come into the Bonnet wanting the wig cleaned and styled, but with no real hope that they could fix it. It was only a cheap backup the clinic had given Amy to use before her good one came. The nurse had told him just to get a couple of terry-cloth wraps from the Kmart, said they would do fine, but Emmet knew that would make Amy cry. He wanted this wig to be transformed somehow, to look like her real hair had before the drugs and lying in bed so long turned it to fine, sparse straw. He didn't want anything more to hurt Amy's feelings, to interrupt the moments in which she imagined the bed a dream and herself a girl giggling when he flirted with her. He wanted her to stay in that dream all the way through what the doctor warned was going to be a long and terrible progress. But if she was going to be awake, he wanted her to be as well taken care of as he could manage. He wanted to be ready, just in case she should come fully awake again; he wanted her to be able to put on that wig and see her friends once more without shame or self-consciousness. He wanted Amy to die without having to show her almost bald head to anyone but him.

All of that grief and hope was in Emmet's face as he held the bag out to Delia. When he stuttered his request, she heard an echo of the last months she had spent with Clint. She looked at him with the steely eye of a woman who was still not over burying two husbands. She understood immediately the exhausted love that motivated the man. *Can't do much, but can do this.* She knew the feeling. When she looked at Emmet Tyler, Delia was looking at an earlier version of herself.

When you are helping someone to die, there comes a point when everything but the necessary falls away. Old angers and resentments sharpen, then dull. Passion recedes. It took everything Delia had to keep moving forward during Clint's illness, and half the time she was moving forward to escape what she knew was inevitable—the shameful relief that would follow when the task was done, the body buried, and the real grieving begun. In the months since Clint died, she had finally begun to remember him as he was when she married him, and as she thought he was. Some days it seemed she was straining at the seams with realizations that before had been too painful to imagine.

"What is it?" Delia was sure that Emmet would know what she meant. It—cancer. It—emphysema. It—any of the dreadful ways there are to die slowly, draining those around you until they walk the way Emmet walked, look the way he did, the same way Delia had looked when Clint was dying. There is a place past exhaustion that is not numb but prescient, and Delia spoke to that place in Emmet.

"Liver cancer."

His eyes drew her in. She took the wig from the bag and shook it out. Behind her M.T. coughed and announced she was going to go sweep up under the sinks.

"How soon you need it?" Delia's tone was matter-of-fact. She kept her gaze on the wig, running her fingers through the tangled coils of dark auburn hair. She wondered if it had been chosen to match the hair Emmet's wife once had, or if it was just whatever was available from the clinic support group. She had seen women come in wearing the most astonishingly inappropriate wigs, all of them with that curiously imperious, brittle manner. You never knew if they were ready to snarl or cry, and sometimes they did both. The worst were the ones who tried to pretend they were not sick.

Delia looked up at Emmet. He was staring at the wig, as stricken as any woman who had ever burst into tears under Delia's cool fingers.

"You need it back quick?" she prompted gently.

With both hands he pushed his hair off his face. He spoke in a voice thick with the refusal to show how badly he was hurting. "Pretty quick. Yeah. If you could." He pushed his hair back again, though not a strand was out of place. He did not seem to know what to do with his hands. He dropped them to his hips, then shoved them into his back pockets.

"I can pay whatever, you know. I just . . . just want to get this to her as quick as I can." Every muscle in his body was locked tight, the slight bob of his head marking the only loose cord in a skein of knots. Delia felt a wave of heat go through her, not lust but rage. God should be paying attention, she thought, then bit her lip. She didn't want to start thinking like that again.

"Might be able to get it washed and set tonight. Then you could come get it tomorrow after I comb it out. You got any particular style in mind?"

"No. Just kind of wavy and loose. Amy never wore no curls or nothing. Hated permanents. Always said she didn't understand women who would go through that for something that didn't look any good anyway." He smiled for the first time. Delia wondered if he knew he was already speaking of his wife in the past tense.

"He's a strange one," M.T. remarked after he left. "Little bit soft as a deputy, they say."

"Deputy?"

"You didn't see the shirt? Uniform. He an't wearing his deputy jacket, but I know the shirt. Don't know him, but I know the type. So upright he don't know about sin, you know?"

Delia grimaced. A deputy, the law. She didn't much like the law. But she had liked what she saw in Emmet's face. Doing the best he could with an impossible situation. Upright maybe, but full of heart.

Delia stayed late that night to wash and set the wig. She treated it as if it were her own, shampooing it twice, conditioning the imitation fibers with a compound she had discovered in a beauty catalog, then setting it on big plastic rollers and putting it on a high shelf to air-dry overnight. The next morning she came in early, scented the wig lightly to cover the persistent sickroom smell, and styled it simply with soft waves. At lunchtime Emmet showed up looking as if he had not slept at all for fear the wig would be no different. Delia felt odd knowing she had done all this for a woman she would never see alive.

Awe broke on Emmet's face. "It's perfect," he whispered. "Thank you."

When Amy died the following week, Delia went to the Catholic funeral. She gave the deputy a nod and lit a candle before she left. Months later Emmet came into the Bonnet just as it was closing, moving unsteadily on his feet like a toddler or an old, old man. His hair was lank and hanging in his eyes, and the eyes themselves were red-rimmed and watery. Drunk, Delia thought, looking up at his sweaty face.

"Mrs. Delia." He slurred the name.

Numb-drunk, she amended, noticing that he wore no socks.

"Ms. Delia."

"Byrd, I'm Delia Byrd. What do you think you are doing?"

"I was thinking maybe you would like to go have a drink with me, or a bite to eat or something." His air ran out. He swayed on his feet.

Delia shook her head. "You going to shame her in the ground?" she asked him.

Emmet looked into her face. For days he had been thinking of her in the church, the way she had leaned over that candle so that the light reflected on her neck. It was like the gentle way she had put Amy's wig into his hands. He had imagined coming to her and leaning into her as she took him in her arms. She was alone, he had heard. She'd lost her husband the way he'd lost his wife. He had imagined that she would understand, that she would take him in and comfort him, that the touch of her mouth on his was what he needed. He had not imagined this, her face set against him and her arms crossed tight across her belly as if she knew what he wanted and hated him for it.

"Will you go out for a drink with me?" he asked.

"No," she said. "I'll have coffee with you, but not now. You come back in here sober, and I will try and remember what an upright man you used to be. Then I will go and have one cup of coffee with you."

Ashamed, he lifted his hands and ran them through his hair. "All right," he said. "I understand. All right." He managed to turn and walk fairly directly out the door.

Two days later Emmet returned, shaved raw and hanging his head like a boy who needs a mama to slap him on the back and tell him to stand up straight. Delia watched him come in the door, the loose way his body shifted on those strong hips. Randall had walked like that, and Clint. It was something she always noticed, the way a man walked when he was hungry for a woman. Emmet hadn't worn his deputy's uniform. He had taken care. Trimmed hair, pressed shirt, pegged trousers, polished shoes.

She sighed and saw Emmet's face go still and stubborn.

We'll see, she thought. Aloud she said, "All right, coffee."

Dede finally found the limits of the Datsun one summer night on the Bowle River overpass. She was allowed to drive the Datsun now and then, but only when Delia was with her. She was not supposed to go driving at night alone, but Dede had driving in her blood, and Delia seemed not to understand the risks of leaving the car keys on the hook by the kitchen door. The first few times she took them, Dede felt a momentary qualm, but the feeling passed. She wanted to drive on her own at night, to speed down the nearly empty roads and feel the cool, damp air on her face. She was fifteen, she was careful, and she knew what she was doing.

Dede waited until Delia was sound asleep, and carefully pushed the Datsun down the driveway until it was safe to turn on the ignition. From the first night, she was intoxicated. Night was the best time to drive, the very best. With the breeze swirling in the windows and the crickets booming, she opened her mouth and started to sing. She pretended she had run away from home, that somewhere ahead waited the man she loved, a man rich and strong and longing for her to lie down beside him and croon into his neck.

"Whoa, sinner man," Dede sang. In her voice, the hymn Grandma Windsor had loved became rock and roll, the best kind of blasphemy, call and praise for the sinner who waited for Dede's kiss. She had a select batch of tapes acquired secondhand or as gifts sent from Rosemary. Her favorites were the Patti Smith Group and Todd Rundgren, music she sang with raw passionate emphasis. "G-L-O-R-I-A!"

"They never play Patti Smith's best stuff on the radio," Dede complained to Delia. "Just that one she does with Bruce Springsteen, none of her kick-butt stuff. I think they're scared of her." Dede even tried telling Amanda that Patti Smith was a kind of gospel singer if you paid attention. "God is her subject. Listen to the words."

She might have had more success with that argument if she had not been so fond of quoting the introduction to "Gloria" where the cadence drawled and Patti dragged out the phrase "Jesus died for somebody's sins—but not mine!"

"You are demented," Amanda told her. "Seriously demented."

"*Jesus died for somebody's sins,*" Dede sang at her. "Must have been yours."

The night Cissy climbed into the Datsun, Dede had the tape of Wave primed and ready to play as soon as she got well down Terrill Road. They fought in raging whispers.

"I want to go."

"I an't gonna take your ass."

"You take me or I'll tell Delia."

"You damn tattletale whiny bitch. You better tell nobody."

In the end, Dede let Cissy come, but only after extracting a sacred promise. "You swear? You swear you will never betray me?"

"I swear." Cissy put one hand on her belly and the other on her heart.

Dede laughed but accepted the oath. It was easier with Cissy helping her push the car down the drive, though having a passenger was not as satisfying as being alone, and it took a while for Dede to adjust. Cissy was quiet but obviously impressed with Dede's driving. Every so often she would ask Dede to teach her.

"Not in this life," Dede swore. "You'll never be able to get a license. You couldn't pass the vision test."

"I could pass that test anytime." Cissy's mouth twisted in a devious grin. "I memorized the chart."

Dede laughed. "Getting ready, huh? Well, you ever manage that, you let me know. I am not going to want to be driving anywhere in Bartow County the day you hit the road."

Dede drove them all over Cayro, keeping an eye out for Deputy Tyler. She could fool Delia, but that old boy was nobody's fool. Some nights they went out to the Bowle River and parked below the crest of the hill where the bridge supports were lit up by the railroad company. Dede smoked and Cissy sat and sometimes they talked. It amused Dede that Cissy did not want to learn to smoke. At Cissy's age, Dede had been sneaking cigarettes out of Clint's jacket and smoking them in the fields behind Grandma Windsor's house.

"I don't like the smell," Cissy told Dede. "I bet you can't even smell it no more. But Delia always stinks of cigarettes, and you do too. You think she don't smell it on you?"

"She don't say nothing to me about it."

"She don't ever say nothing to you, or Amanda either. She's still trying to get you to love her."

Dede shrugged. "Feels to me like she's still trying to love us. She looks at us like we're some kind of creatures she found in the back of the woods."

"Yeah, well, she's been looking for you all my life." Cissy put her feet up on the dash.

"Oh, for God's sake. Smoke one." Dede tossed the pack at Cissy. "You're starting to get on my nerves."

"I don't want it."

"What is it? You scared of getting cancer?" Dede blew smoke at Cissy. "Or you scared of Delia?"

Cissy blushed. What she was actually worried about was that

Dede would think she was trying to copy her. Cissy took a cigarette out of the pack, lit it, and inhaled. It burned her throat and tasted awful, but she wouldn't embarrass herself by sputtering or coughing.

"Don't taste like much to me," she managed to say.

Dede grinned. "Well, it's probably like beer and whiskey—an acquired taste, as the Petrie boys used to tell me." She took another drag and thought about Craig. He was fun when he wasn't being so pushy. She would like to have him asleep or drunk. Helpless. It would be nice to have him helpless. She would like to touch that boy any way she wanted, to stroke him and get him as disturbed as the brothers had managed to get her. She wondered if it would ever be possible to have sex with a boy, not get pregnant, and not have him tell everybody and their cousin you had done it.

Maybe if he was unconscious? Could you have sex with an unconscious boy? She giggled.

"What are you laughing about?" Cissy asked.

"Driving," Dede said. "The sheer power of the machine."

Most nights Dede took them twice around the overpass. The first time they went up and over, the old Datsun peaked out at just under 60. Dede checked the gas gauge. She'd have to get more before going home or Delia would notice. Twice already Dede had siphoned a little gas from Mr. Reitower's car up the street. She was going to have to find someone else to borrow from this time, or maybe she could get Cissy to buy two dollars' worth on the way back. Cissy seemed to have money now and then. She stroked the steering wheel. It was a good car, sweet. It should be able to go faster. She turned to Cissy.

"I bet if we went back over the grade and came down from the train crossing we could get it up faster."

"You think?" Cissy seemed eager.

"I think," said Dede.

The Datsun topped seventy-five on the downhill side of the overpass, the body shimmying but the engine roaring along fine. When the speedometer needle crossed the line, Dede whooped, "Damn!"

and Cissy crowed with her. She did not see the needle, but she felt the car lift slightly as they passed the crest and gained momentum. She put both hands straight up in the air, her palms flat on the rooftop, and blew a whistle of happy surprise. The surprise was in the exhilaration, the marvelous rush of air pouring in the windows, the lights along the bridge approach flashing past. She had never gone so fast in her life, never been so afraid and unafraid at the same time. Dede's hair was whipping in the wind. The damp off the river was cool and sweet in Cissy's mouth.

"Damn! Damn!" Cissy yelled, beaming at Dede in full impassioned glory. Her stomach felt a little funny. The cigarette, she told herself, swallowing acid. Then the right front tire popped and the car made a terrible shrieking sound. The front spun, poles and trees sweeping past. Dede roared curses along the car's rooftop as she fought the pull of the steering wheel. They deadheaded a mile marker, then another, slowing with each post that went down. Dede was aiming at the little posts deliberately, Cissy realized, trying to stop the car.

"God, God, God!" Cissy screamed in a rush of adrenaline.

"God, yes!" Dede screamed back at her as the car slammed into a dogwood sapling and came to a sudden wrenching halt in the mud and weeds of a shallow ditch.

"My God," Cissy breathed.

"All right, little sister, all right." Dede was shaking, hands tight on the wheel. "You okay?"

"I'm fine," Cissy said.

"Oh Lord!" Dede put her head on the steering wheel. "Shit! No way Delia an't gonna find out about this now."

Cissy felt her stomach roll. "Damn," she whimpered, and threw up out the window. "I have always hated this car," she said, and threw up again.

Miraculously, the Datsun survived. All the damage was to the body.

For all Delia's shouts and accusations, Cissy never admitted how fast they were going. "I asked Dede to drive me," she said. "It was just an accident and Dede saved our lives." Cissy stared hopefully at Delia's stern face.

"You could have killed your sister," Delia said to Dede.

Dede looked over at Cissy, her face suddenly pale and frightened. "I know," she said, "I know," and began to sob like a child for the first time in her life.

Delia watched her and remembered all the times she had said the same thing to Randall. *You could have killed her.*

"But you didn't," she said to Dede, and took her daughter into her arms.

It took Amanda about a minute and a half to decide to marry Michael Graham when he proposed to her the Christmas after they graduated. At the time, she and his mother were decorating the tabernacle, carrying in great pots of poinsettias and piles of white carnations.

"Let me help you," Michael called to Amanda, rushing over and bumping his forehead solidly into hers. His mother laughed and went outside for more flowers. Amanda saw stars and the bright sheen of embarrassment that flooded Michael's already rosy features. He's gorgeous, she thought, and said yes almost before the question was out of his mouth.

"God led me to you," Michael told Amanda repeatedly, and meant it with all his heart. His daddy approved. His mama beamed. That Amanda was a good Christian girl, a little serious and unsure of herself now and then, but a fine young woman. People talked about her mother, but Amanda wasn't wild. She was a faithful member of the congregation. She'd make a fine preacher's wife.

At first the only question for Amanda was whether she deserved Michael, whether she was godly enough to be his wife. Her doubts on the subject made Dede stay out of her way, and sent Delia out to her garden and Cissy off on a long contemplation of the more obscure holdings of the county library. But once Amanda convinced herself that she could somehow make herself into the wife Michael needed, she became equally insecure about all the things she imagined would go wrong before the wedding. For weeks Amanda squalled through the house, certain that Michael would drop dead or the sky fall before she could be married. She became fanatical on the subject of church attendance, but neither Dede nor Cissy responded well to harassment. A few times Delia gave in and went with Amanda to Cayro Baptist Tabernacle, where she hadn't set foot since crying season. There she shifted uncomfortably in the pew next to Michael's uncle, a carefully benign expression on her face. That expression vanished after the service, when Delia stood outside the church talking and laughing with M.T.

"Lord God!" Delia exclaimed loudly at one point, ruining the good impression her numb endurance of two weeks' sermons had won her.

"You embarrassed me!" Amanda wailed once they got home.

"Why can't she just marry that boy and leave me out of it?" Delia said to Cissy when Amanda ran back to her room.

Amanda's hopes for Delia's salvation were sudden and constant. She seemed determined to bring Delia to God—specifically to Baptist Tabernacle, Michael's family church—as proof of her own worth, her destiny as a preacher's wife. Cissy doubted that even a penitent Delia would solve Amanda's problem. Amanda was never going to believe herself safely a part of the God-fearing, respectable family that had produced her Michael.

"You'd probably have to renounce me," Cissy told Delia with a smirk. "After you joined the church and all." Delia gave her a long calculated look, but said nothing.

Amanda got married on the second Sunday in March, a week after her eighteenth birthday. That morning she shut everyone out of the bathroom with the makeup mirror, and Dede kept going out back to smoke. Craig Petrie had reappeared at Thanksgiving with a determined smile and a little baggie of Panama Red. When he left, the smile was wider, and the bag and a packet of papers were safely hidden in Dede's boxes of secondhand books in the garage.

"Don't believe what people tell you about this stuff," Dede told Cissy when she offered her a toke. "It's like a bottle of beer but you don't get bloated or nothing. Makes you a little hungry, though, you got to watch that." She found another boy to sell her a bag at a good discount. She wasn't going to let herself become dependent on a Petrie for anything she liked so much.

Cissy and Dede were giggling at the awful dresses they were required to wear as bridesmaids when there was yet another crisis of faith.

"Wouldn't be too bad," Dede drawled, "if we shortened the skirt, dropped the neckline, changed the color, and pulled off this rickrack crap."

Cissy doubled over with laughter and noticed for the first time that Dede had already cut off the hem of her dress. "I think the best thing we could do is march naked behind Amanda, wiggle our butts, and remind everyone what a marriage is really about," she said.

Amanda came out of the bedroom with a towel around her neck and her makeup half done. "I heard you. I heard you." The big wire curlers all over her head rattled menacingly. Limp wisps were already falling around her temples. Those curls were never going to hold up for the ceremony, Cissy thought.

"This marriage," Amanda sputtered, "is about joining our souls before God, committing ourselves to the Lord's service."

"Oh, for God's sake, Amanda." Cissy knew she should say nothing, but she couldn't help herself. "You're getting married, not taking a vow of celibacy. God isn't keeping count of every minute of your life. I'm pretty damn sure he's got other stuff going on."

"You don't know anything about God," Amanda shouted. "God is the judge of our lives. Wait and see what you know when you're burning in hell, when the flames of God's judgment are licking at your crusty soul."

"What is going on?" Delia came out from the back.

"We were just joking about the dresses," Cissy said.

"She was telling me about God!" Amanda's mascara had started to run.

"Well, what did she say?" Delia's face was almost as pink as the tea roses pinned to the veil she was holding in her left hand. It was Amanda's veil, and Delia had been pressing it out when the shouting erupted.

Cissy stopped in the act of reaching for Kleenex. "I didn't say shit, but I'll tell you, she better start asking God to sweeten her soul. She has got to stop trying to run everybody else's life."

"If I was running your life, I'd run you right out of this house. I'd run you out of Cayro. I'd run you clear out of the state of Georgia. Don't you know you are going straight to hell?"

Cissy looked from Amanda's wrathful countenance to Dede's frank enjoyment of the fight. Then she looked down at the orchid and yellow bell-shaped skirt Amanda had insisted she wear. It was only one dress size smaller than Dede's, but Amanda did not seem to notice how much Dede had shortened hers. Now that Dede was standing up, Cissy could see that Dede had put in enough darts to make the dress cling suggestively at her hips and bust. Catching the direction of Cissy's glance, Dede produced a glassy smile. That is not the grin of a sober woman, Cissy thought. Can't Amanda see?

"Oh yeah, Cissy is damned if anyone is," Dede drawled. "No question."

Dede was no devotee of Christian dogma. She had even been known to declare herself a Buddhist when pressed, but she took her faith by spells, a fierce believer when she was in the spirit, even if she usually slept through Sunday services and sneaked beer with the boys at Sunday afternoon ball games. Christmas and Easter, Dede worshiped with utmost seriousness. Most of the summer she did not. Last Christmas, right after Amanda got engaged, Cissy found her stoned and supine under the tree weeping out loud at the fate of the baby Jesus. The Cross, Dede explained, was like the tree. It had cradled the Son of God. Dede's hands were deep in the fir branches and covered with scratches, and Cissy did not doubt either her sincerity or her grief. They might have been chemically induced, but Dede's doctrine was heartfelt, no matter that she picked absently at the almost invisible scrapes and shrugged off Amanda's invitation to a revival meeting two weeks later.

"I got faith," Dede protested in answer to Amanda's accusation that she did not. "I just don't always make a big stink about it."

At heart, Delia's first two girls were believers. Amanda worried about her own worth, but not about the possibility that there might not be a Nazarene to judge her. Dede's faith was seasonal but there was no blasphemy in her, while Cissy picked at the idea of God like a prickly abrasion on her soul. It was Cissy, they all agreed, who was the heathen.

"My Lord. Couldn't we just leave it alone for one day?" Delia shook the veil impatiently.

In a sudden rage Cissy stripped off the ridiculous matron's dress and threw it at Delia. She stalked down the hall in her slip and nylons and slammed the bedroom door.

"Cissy. For God's sake, Cissy. Please." It was Delia.

Cissy pulled on jeans and a blouse, ignoring them all. Dede started to giggle just as Amanda started to cry. Delia came to the door twice to plead with Cissy, but she refused to answer. When the house was finally quiet, Cissy came out to find Nolan sitting on the couch.

"You want a lift?" he asked. He had his black suit on but was clearly ready to do whatever Cissy decided.

"You look terrible," Cissy told him.

Nolan regarded his hastily polished shoes and his too-short, too-tight pants. "Yeah," he agreed. "You want to go over?"

"All right," Cissy said. She would go late to Amanda's wedding, but she would go. Amanda would whine about it for the rest of her life if she did not. When she and Nolan slipped into the back of the church, she saw that one of Michael's cousins had been drafted to take her place in the ugly dress. The girl looked as miserable as a female ever looked in this life, but past her shoulder was Amanda, and Amanda looked pretty good. Pancake makeup masked her tantrum's effects, and at moments she appeared almost pretty, almost happy. At her side, Dede appeared absurd but cheerful. In the short trip from the house to the church, she had gone beyond her earlier sins, ripping off the rickrack and acquiring yet another layer of chemical insulation. She looked like a Magdalene in a deflated inverted tulip, and appeared to have forgotten that she was supposed to be mad. She beamed out across the church and waved Cissy forward.

"Come on," Dede whisper-yelled. "Come on up here and say good-bye. After today you get your own bedroom."

As Cissy shook her head, she took in Delia's stricken face and Amanda's bowed form. Dede waved one more time and Cissy gave it up, moving forward until she was beside them. The heat at the front of the church was extraordinary. Cissy was overwhelmed by perfume, the smell of Amanda's bouquet, Michael's astringent aftershave, Dede's tobacco aura, Delia's hair conditioner. She found herself going weak with the desire to get this thing over with and get out of there. Amanda's makeup was streaked with tears. Dede was tugging at the few remaining strands of yellow material on her skirt, and then Michael looked up and gave Cissy a broad smile of welcome.

Family, his smile said. God's love, his eyes promised. That's why Amanda loves him, Cissy thought.

Amanda turned to her, tears gushing freely at Reverend Myles's pronouncement of her new status. "Oh, Cissy," she wailed. "What am I going to do with you?"

"Love is past me," Delia was always saying after Amanda's marriage. "Love is so far past me I cannot even remember how it feels. But sometimes," she would add, "I look at my girls and I get the notion—the notion how it should be. God knows they got a better chance than I ever had."

Once Amanda moved out, Dede kept after Delia to redo the Terrill Road house. It was not enough that she now had Amanda's bedroom, the one in which Clint died—something none of them ever mentioned. She wanted Delia to widen the back porch and screen it in, put in flower boxes off the kitchen windows, and have all the floors sanded down and refinished. What she really wanted was a new house, a home made over now that Amanda was gone.

"Too much money," Delia would tell her. "We can't afford that."

Dede was undeterred. She enlisted Cissy and Nolan to help her pull up the carpets and rented a floor sander from the B & B Hardware for the minimal twenty-four-hour fee. Together the three of them sanded and swept and mopped and sanded again. They kept the stereo on loud, playing Patti Smith and Kate Bush. Delia stayed out of the house, partly to avoid the stereo. She thought Dede's taste in music eerily ironic, her girl was a hard-core rock and roller, oblivious to the Top 40 and uninterested in dance music—she called Madonna a joke, though she told Cissy that Cyndi Lauper wasn't too bad. Cissy liked Prince and the Revolution. She played his tapes at night under the covers.

"Sounds like Mud Dog," she told Delia.

"No," Delia said. "It doesn't."

Nolan worked like a madman, but Dede never paid him a minute's notice, not even when he got down on his hands and knees to smooth the sealant over the floors with a cotton towel. It turned out that he also knew how to pop off the sanding disks and use the old polishing ring M.T.'s sister Sally still had from a job she had done. For the last few hours on the rental, Nolan and Dede took turns with the polisher, making those floors shine like something out of the decorating magazines M.T. collected.

"My Lord!" Delia exclaimed when they finally let her back in the house. "It's beautiful." She hugged Dede and beamed at Nolan and Cissy. "You guys could hire out, make yourselves some real money."

"Hell, no," Dede said. "I an't going to work this hard for nobody else."

Cissy and Nolan laughed but Delia nodded. "Tell you what," she told Dede, "you pick out the fabric and I'll make up new curtains, maybe even do a new cover for the couch."

"All right! Then all we'll need is some real furniture and a new television set."

"What's wrong with this furniture?"

"Delia!" Dede gave one of the battered wooden spool tables a kick. "This stuff is older than I am."

"Makes it antique, don't make it bad." But Delia looked again at what they had. The couch did sag, and the coffee table was another wooden spool that Clint had gotten from a friend who worked for the phone company. Delia had sanded it down and painted it when she was pregnant with Amanda. Maybe she could find something better. She had liked taking things apart and putting them back together when she was a girl. She could buy some old furniture and fix it up. "I'll think about it," she said.

"Well, while you're at it, think about getting some new sheets. It's embarrassing when you hang those sheets of yours on the line."

"Don't start about my sheets."

"What sheets?" Nolan whispered to Cissy as they went out.

"Kermit the Frog, Snoopy and Linus, Miss Piggy, rocket ships and trains. Delia got them on sale in the children's department at Sears, and Dede is always bugging her about them."

"Yeah?" Nolan looked back at Delia and Dede standing on the floor he had worked on so hard. "Cool."

Delia bought new end tables at a yard sale and a great wingback chair at the Saint Vincent de Paul. She hauled the old spool tables out to the garden and used them as potting stands. Under pressure from Dede she put up new curtains and yielded on the television set, but she continued to cling to her sheets. It did not bother her that they were designed for a child's bed. When she did not fall asleep on the living room couch, Delia went to her single bed in the smallest bedroom, narrow, hard, and solitary. If it had not been for the sheets and the cartoon-patterned quilt thrown over them, that cot would have suited a nun.

"I like bright colors," Delia said when Dede showed her an ad for pinstripes on sale. "Just because I'm a woman grown don't mean I have to sleep on plaid or stripes."

"But it looks so silly."

"Who sees it but me? And an't I the one that matters? I like colors, bright and loud and full of energy. Don't have to wash them as often, and they don't go that sad gray. Besides, they look cheerful out on the line."

It was true. Cissy did the laundry, but never Delia's sheets. She did not even go into Delia's room. Delia liked to do her sheets and hang them out on the lines strung from the back of the house to the ramshackle garage, where she kept her garden supplies. She got up late on Sunday morning and put a quick load in cold water while she drank her coffee. She did a little weeding in the small garden off the back steps through the spin cycle. Then she hung those sheets out in the sun and sat on the steps to watch the cartoon figures billow and flap. With her knees pulled up and one hand trailing through her loose hair, she hummed softly to herself while Dede and Cissy banged around in the kitchen. She could have been a young mother with small children, not forty years old and still mourning what she had lost.

Delia's bed was a joke awaiting comment.

"My bed suits me," she would say, "and it an't like I'm inviting company."

"You an't dead yet." M.T. did not approve.

"And I an't crazy. I like my bed and I like it alone."

After Clint's death, men looked longingly at Delia, but few had the nerve to approach her. Delia barely noticed. As far as she was concerned, that was over. Oh, she went out with Emmet, but there was nothing to that. She'd had enough trouble in her life, she told M.T., and when Rosemary called they joked about how many men a woman could go crazy over in this lifetime. One, maybe two, never three. "Well, I've had my two," Delia swore. "I've had all I can stand."

The secret was that Delia's sheets saw little use. Her insomnia had gotten so bad, she used her bedroom as little more than a storage place for her clothes. Her naps were brief and restless. Mostly she needed to move around. She strung Christmas tree lights along the back of the house and the side of the garage, and took to gardening at night by the dim light of the parti-colored bulbs. When there was nothing left to do in the garden, she started refinishing furniture. She sanded and sealed some lawn chairs Steph had given her, then worked her way through the tables and chairs in the house. She picked up a few pieces of furniture at the Goodwill, fixed them up, and gave them away—a dining room table for M.T., a rocker for Amanda, and a splendid cherry side table for Emmet, with little drawers set on two sides.

"You built me a table?" Emmet smiled at her when she brought it over.

"You don't have to take it," she told him. "I just liked the way the finish came out and I remembered you had that cherry armoire. Thought it would look nice with it."

It would, Emmet agreed. He said "It would" with his head down. His fingers stroked the finish. He had asked her to marry him when Amanda married Michael. He had thought she would stop seeing him from the way she had looked at him, but so long as he pretended the question had been a joke, pretended she had not been spooked. They went out almost every other week, eating greasy food at Goober's and seeing movies at the drive-in near Marietta.

"Wasn't nothing," Delia said. "You'd be amazed at the beautiful stuff people throw away sometimes. This treasure was just sitting by the road."

"Thank you," he said. He lifted his head.

"Oh, you're welcome." Delia was already looking back at her car. "Why don't you come over next Sunday and I'll show you what I'm working on for Stephanie's birthday."

"I'll do that," Emmet said, his fingers gripping the edge of the little table.

"Well, Lord damn!" Steph said when Emmet and Delia delivered her birthday present, an antique vanity. "Girl, you should go into business."

"I got a business," Delia said. "Anyway, sanding is like doing hair. Feels like something I know with my muscles more than my brain. It makes me feel good to do it, and I like the way the wood looks when you sand it down real fine."

"Just as long as you don't start building flats and compost bins like that crazy woman on television. This is the kind of thing you can take too far." Steph winked at Emmet.

Delia had a few moments when she thought about giving up the Bonnet and restoring furniture for money. She would never have to smile at a woman with her head in a towel again, and that might be nice. But the truth was she was just restless. Her hips hurt no matter what she did, and no matter where she slept, bed or couch or a mat out on the grass, things seemed to press on her.

One of M.T.'s new boyfriends, George, put a big antenna up on the back porch so Delia could tune her radio to stations as far away as Phoenix. After 2:00 A.M. there were several stations that came in from the Southwest and they all seemed to carry phone-in talk shows hosted by deep-voiced religious commentators. These were the very shows that Delia had never been able to stand before, but suddenly they were her passion. She set up a workstation for herself out back with the colored lights and the radio. Sanding, she would hum along to country rock, switching stations to find music that matched her pace. She tried to time her work so that she was smoothing stain or sealant by the time the talk shows started and got her all excited.

"I get so mad," she told Cissy. "Mad or disgusted. You can see it in the wood. Sometimes I come close to grinding the grain right down to nothing or gouging whole strips off."

"Then why do you listen?"

Delia looked at her daughter as if what she was saying was perfectly obvious. " 'Cause sometimes mad is what I need. A good mad or a good cry. Cussing out loud or kicking a bucket across the porch, just something. Something strong. Sometimes a woman just needs to get mad as sin."

What Delia could not have guessed was how closely the rhythms of her body were matched by those in Amanda. She could not have known that when she was sweating under her Christmas tree lights, grunting and cursing at some far-off preacher, Amanda was moving with her all the way across Cayro, ironing T-shirts and chanting her prayers. For every "Fool!" of Delia's, Amanda would whisper an "Amen!" Now and then, as if in harmony, they would stop together, hearts pounding in counterpoint, to lift their heads at the same moment and breathe "Lord!"

Chapter 13

At fourteen, Cissy Byrd loved folk music—especially Gordon Lightfoot and Delia's old Joan Baez records—the high school swim team, the sausage biscuits Nolan brought her from his daddy's early shift at Biscuit World, the straight-leg jeans Dede said were cool, and science fiction books featuring orphan girls with amazing hidden powers. She hated okra, the marching band—from which she was expelled after blowing spit on Mary Martha Wynchester—her sister Amanda, and the entire congregation of Cayro Baptist Tabernacle, where Amanda spent all her time. And Delia. In a completely matter-of-fact way, Cissy hated Delia and tried to make sure she knew it, but Delia never acknowledged the hatred, and sometimes Cissy almost forgot it herself.

The Saturday after Cissy's fifteenth birthday, Nolan came over early. "You free?" he asked when Cissy appeared at the back door. He had called the night before and asked the same thing.

"As a bird," Cissy told him. "What you got in mind?"

"It's a surprise. A birthday surprise. Did you tell your mama you're going to spend the day with me?"

"Yeah." Cissy put on the birthday present Dede had given her, a straw hat shaped like a tractor cap, with a red, white, and green ribbon tied around the brim. "She said to go and be damned."

"She did?" Nolan was shocked.

"No! Lord, Nolan. It's a joke. It's what she would say if she ever said what she was thinking. We an't getting along too good."

Nolan was undaunted. "Well, never mind. My cousin Charlie is coming in twenty minutes. He's going to give us a ride out."

"Out where?" Cissy was not sure she liked this bossy Nolan.

"Where the surprise is." Nolan grinned and shook his dark hair back. "Don't ask questions. Just wait and see."

Charlie was late picking them up, and not terribly pleasant about making the trip at all. "You're gonna owe me, cousin," he said. Nolan nodded and avoided Cissy's eyes. It was some kind of trade, she could see from the look of concentrated misery on Nolan's face. Whatever his surprise, he had gone to a lot of trouble. There was a big satchel of gear he had not allowed her to touch, a cooler filled with sandwiches and Cokes, and a blanket that Charlie boasted had been "seasoned by Keenan men for generations," whatever that meant.

"Pretty damn skinny, an't she?" Charlie said as Cissy climbed into the truck. She glared at him while Nolan flushed and sweat beads of hot shame.

"Don't talk about her like that," Nolan said.

"Oh, I won't hurt your girlfriend's feelings." Charlie winked at Cissy. "Hell, son, I'm just proud you finally got one."

On the Little Mouth Road they stopped to get ice for the cooler, and Nolan apologized to Cissy while Charlie bought cigarettes and gas with money Nolan had given him. "I'll get my license next year," Nolan told her. "Daddy said he'd sign for me to get a permit. Then I can start driving us wherever we want to go. Won't have to put up with Charlie."

"Don't worry about it," Cissy said. "He's just your cousin. Not your brother. You can't help it if he's a damn fool."

"I got it all planned," Nolan said. "This is the bad part. Once we get there and Charlie leaves, it will be fine."

But once they got there, Charlie did not want to leave. He drank two beers while Nolan hauled the cooler and gear into the woods. He kept winking at Cissy and teasing Nolan until Cissy thought her friend was going to lose his temper. Finally, Charlie asked Nolan for another five dollars. He'd be back at sundown, he said, but he was going to be low on gas, and it was better to be on the safe side, didn't Nolan think? Nolan gave him the money, and Charlie drove away.

"What a pain in the ass," Cissy said as the truck spit dirt and rock behind the spinning tires.

"Always has been," Nolan agreed. Then he smiled for the first time in an hour. "Come on," he said. "I got something to show you."

It was a hole in the ground, a deep hole in the ground. Cissy leaned over and saw that there was a meandering sort of path along one edge. You would have to hang on to roots and rocks, but you could climb down pretty easily from that side. Nolan pointed out a few places where the incline had been dug out or shored up, making a rough staircase.

"A very rough staircase," Cissy said.

"Wouldn't want it to be too easy," Nolan told her. "There'd be people down there all the time if it was. It's called Paula's Lost. We used to own it. My uncles shared the plot, almost two hundred acres."

"That's a funny name," Cissy said.

"Well, it was lost for more than a decade. Found and lost more than a few times, Uncle Tynan used to say. It wasn't put on the maps until they gave it to the state in the fifties. It's a reserve now. Too rocky and sandy to be any good for farming. Uncle Tynan got a deal passing it over for taxes, but the cousins have been holding target practice weekends down in here forever. It's famous. The sheriff keeps coming out and busting up the camp, but the hollow down at the entrance is a great place for shooting. Can't no bullets go astray and kill nobody down in that hole."

"Why is it famous?"

"Well, that's a story." Nolan wiped his face and beamed. He pulled open the cooler, handed Cissy a Coke and a sandwich, and smiled again.

"It was my uncle Brewster made it famous. He mapped the first three passages and then threw all these parties out here. Strung a set of lights down the hollow. Sent out invitations with detailed maps. Called the parties Lost Weekend Extravaganzas. They were free, and Brewster gave away a lot of beer and marijuana."

Cissy took a bite of the sandwich, egg salad with pickles. Nolan knew she liked egg salad. He had really thought ahead, she realized. She hid her smile with a bite of egg salad and watched Nolan enjoy himself telling the story of Paula's Lost.

Brewster had come home from Vietnam minus most of his teeth, three toes, half the cartilage in his left knee, and more than a few of the bones in his left foot. His buddies tried to cheer him up by sending him back with a large supply of marijuana. The idea was for Brewster to make a little money on that stash, but he was just not the business type. He shared what he had until his supply was gone and never complained when he was not offered much in return.

"Hell, you got to make do with what comes, keep your head level," Brewster told everyone with a laugh. "What comes around, after all." He laughed harder after the deputies raided one of the last parties and found none of the killer weed everyone had sworn would be there.

"You shoulda come here last month," Brewster told Emmet Tyler after the deputy snapped on the cuffs. "You could of put me away for life."

Emmet grunted but said nothing. He was new on the job and hadn't wanted to hike so far out in the woods in the first place, and Brewster was just too genial a man to provoke much indignation. There was only a few years' difference between them, and Emmet could not look at Brewster without feeling grateful that he had not come back from his stint in the army in the same condition—partly crippled and more than partly crazy. The whole raid was a joke anyway. There wasn't even an underage drinker at the party, and the county had to settle for a vandalism charge to put Brewster out of business. Technically the cave was on state-owned land, and Brewster's light sconces were hammered into the cave walls.

"Big damn hole in the ground, an't it, Emmet?" Brewster was cheerful as he was helped into the back of the green and tan cruiser. "How you imagine it was ever lost?"

"Country's going to hell," Emmet said. "We could probably lose most anything." He wiped his neck and waved a mosquito away, looking back at the incline that sloped down to the cave mouth.

"There was a bunch of trees and shit here, garbage people had thrown down before the dump opened. It all grew over like this, kudzu and stuff." He kicked at an exposed clump of red dirt and watched it crumble. Black and silver metal fragments glittered in the harsh light of the lamps.

"You wouldn't have known there was nothing here. Nothing. Ground's so ripe, you spit on it and it shoots up green."

The mystery of how such a large hole in the ground could be forgotten did lend Paula's Lost a mysterious aura. In the last few years trees had fallen and the entrance seemed to have dropped farther down the slope. The park service had to put up signs warning the curious just how dangerous amateur caving could be—the ground could easily fall in; crevasses full of rock and silt waited for the unwary, particularly people who had heard about Brewster's old parties and came around to see what remained. Most of them showed up with only a couple of flashlights, a six-pack, and no idea what they were risking when they climbed down into that dark and dangerous hole. The ones who climbed out did so gratefully, sucking clean air and whistling at the muddy depths behind them.

Cissy leaned over the edge again. "How far down does it go?"

"No one knows." Nolan was opening the satchel. "It goes on quite a ways. People say Paula's Lost connects to Little Mouth, but no one has found the connection. Little Mouth is bigger, better known. This one is just family." He pulled out flashlights with clip-on rings that fastened to your belt. He had even brought an extra belt, in case Cissy wasn't wearing one, and a couple of long-sleeved flannel shirts.

"It's cool down there," Nolan said. "Always fifty-eight degrees underground, like air-conditioning left on all the time. As hot as it is up here, it'll feel nice when we go down, but it gets cold after a while. Makes you tired faster."

He looked at her with an open smile. "You ready to go?"

* * *

The rock was loose on the climb down. Cissy almost fell twice, but after a few minutes she learned to handle the rope Nolan had strung from one of the big trees at the top. Good thing I'm a swimmer, she thought when Nolan had her hold on to the rope and wait for him to get a better footing as he went ahead. Her shoulders ached a little by the time they were at the bottom, but climbing was fun. Like swimming, it didn't depend on anything but your own muscles and nerves.

Cissy lagged behind Nolan. The cave was like nothing she had imagined. She had seen a movie once in which people went exploring in a cave, but they just stepped over a few rocks and walked right in. This was nothing like that. After the descent there was a mouth, a big, wide opening that quickly narrowed down.

"Brewster dug some of this out, Uncle Tynan said." Nolan kicked at the rough ground. "But the real cave opening is back here."

It was a narrow slice in the rock. Cissy turned to step through and then had to turn again. After about six feet, the slice took a sideways turn and they had to stoop. Soon they were crawling, holding the flashlights ahead of them. It *was* like swimming, she thought again, using her shoulders and hips and hunching over to keep from hitting her head. Every now and then the rock would open, then close down again. No, it was like nothing Cissy had ever seen.

They were both panting when they climbed through another gap into a little cavern with slanting walls and reddish sand scattered on the rock. Nolan got Cissy down knee to knee with him and produced a canteen. "Have a drink," he said, "and then we'll shut off the lights."

"Shut off the lights?" Cissy took a gulp from the canteen. Nolan was playing his flashlight over the walls. The surfaces of the slanting rock were as broken and rough as the ground. That was the biggest problem, Cissy thought, the rough ground. She had never realized how important a flat walking surface could be. She put her hand on the rock beside her knee. It was cool and smooth, but it felt as if it might break if she hammered on it. Limestone, most of the rock was limestone. Soft, easily shaped by water.

"You ready?" Nolan turned the flashlight up on his face, shining it under his chin so that he looked ghostly. His grin was broad and happy. "Turn yours off."

Cissy shut her light off. Nolan's grin got even wider for a moment as he reached to take her right hand in his. Then there was a small click and the dark came in completely.

Lord.

Cissy's pupils widened to catch any gleam. But the dark was absolute, a blackness that touched her nerves with icy shudders and broke a sweat in the pockets of her body. After a moment, though, there was a reddish shift in the blackness, burning specks in a spectrum of velvet night. Plush. Gorgeous. She could hear Nolan breathing. The air moved past Cissy's cheek, and she turned her head to follow it. Sparks. Light. Instantly she could feel the open space above her expand as synapses fired and sparked. A bead of colored flame lit as she clenched her teeth. Every sound made color. Sand shifted beneath Cissy, and that sound became a streak of sky, a tiny blue streak of sky. She pulled her legs closer beneath her, and the sand spilled loudly. Cerulean blue passed her in a wave. Cissy turned her head again, and the sound of her breath was a blood-dark ruby moon. She held her breath and a diamond glint of ice yellow bloomed behind her neck. Cissy laughed, pleasure rising in her throat.

"Nice, huh?" Nolan's hand on Cissy's arm squeezed once. "I remember when Uncle Tynan brought me here. He made it dark for me. Some people can't stand it, but for some the dark feels like home. I thought you would like it."

"I do," Cissy whispered.

"It's human to be afraid of the dark." Nolan's voice was slightly sharp, and Cissy heard the fear behind the edge, under control but there. The fear was lime green and bitter.

"I'm not scared," Cissy said, then laughed again. Her words were apple green and false. She was scared, but it was all right. She could master the fear, ride it like the current in the Bowle River, where she liked to swim. Delia complained when Cissy went swimming in the dark. And this was like that, scary but exhilarating. Her laughter sprinkled black on black, like ebony beads on a tuxedo jacket collar.

"Can you see . . ." Cissy hesitated. Would Nolan think she was weird?

"See what?"

"Colors." How would she explain? If she tried to see the colors, they burst and faded. They were more to be felt than seen.

"Oh, your eyes will do that, kind of hallucinate. It can get pretty intense. You have to learn to ignore it." Nolan sounded sure of himself, and Cissy wondered how many times he had been here. She licked her lips and wondered if she would ever learn to ignore the colors. Why would she want to? She shifted slightly in the sand, and her hips felt molten chocolate.

The cave roof was close above them. The sand had been gray and red in the light's glare before Nolan shut it off. Was it still, or had it flooded with night like her pupils? She imagined the sand with a pearly luster. Her eyes ached, she realized. She had been holding them so wide open that they were dry and strained. She let her lids fall and felt immediate relief, lifted them again and felt the stream of air coming from farther down the shaft.

If white was all the colors, and black none, which one moved across her dry, aching pupils now? She smiled and relaxed. Nothing here would hurt her.

"Listen," Nolan whispered. "Listen."

Cissy tilted her head back slightly. Her cranium felt like a drumhead, open to the most subtle strokes, ready to produce the most delicate tones, every note brightened with pigment. She closed her eyes again, and the dry ache ebbed with a purple murmur. She wanted to hum but was too self-conscious. It would have been good, though, to hum deep in her chest, the way Delia did sometimes, to let that sound come up out of her to assume color and shape in the dark. The back of her neck felt open and strong like the sounding board of some giant instrument. A tear ran down Cissy's cheek from one burning eye to her chin. She wiped it away. The words in her head were white on white: I am safe here. Nothing can find me that

I do not want to find me. If I do not move, the dark will fill me up, make me another creature, fearless and whole. This must be what Amanda feels when she prays so hard, like being held close in the hand of God. It certainly felt like God's country.

Nolan snapped the light on then. Grief flooded Cissy in a scalding sweep. Both of them flinched, and Cissy covered her face. The light was too big, too hot, and too painful. The dark was gone, the great beautiful healing blackness.

"You okay?" Nolan was blinking and peering at her. "You okay?"

"I'm fine." Cissy wiped away tears and kept her face expressionless while her eyes cleared.

The flashlights were battery-powered, intense and narrowly focused. Reflected light made a diffuse shadow pool all around them. Cissy was startled when it quickly became obvious that Nolan could not see any better than she could, that she was actually better at judging distance. The blackness and the narrow beams flattened perspective in the cave. You could not tell if there was a gap below you or if a shadow of rock meant a crevasse until you were right on top of it. Everything was close-up or invisible, black and white and relentlessly misleading. But Cissy had learned to judge distance by subtle clues, and instinctively calculated contrasts that served her as well underground as above. They crawled forward steadily, Nolan telling her what he knew of the cavern layout but mostly letting her find her own way.

"That's a ledge," she pointed out for Nolan.

"You're right," he said, and Cissy barely nodded in acknowledgment. This is my place, she thought. What she wanted at that moment she could not have expressed. She tightened her grip on the rock under her hand and said nothing. She wondered, though. When Nolan led them slowly back to the entrance, Cissy wondered what would happen if she ever came down in the cave alone, shut off her light, and sat with the dark all around her. What would it be like to stay here a while with the back of her neck wide open to whatever might come?

* * *

"You were great!" Nolan said when they emerged from the bottom of the cave mouth. He was huffing and panting. Cissy was shivering.

"It was terrific," she told him. "What a gift!"

Nolan sat in a waning patch of sun. They would rest a minute and then climb up the last bit of the way. There were more sandwiches and sodas and a thermos of tea up there. He spread his arms happily. It had all worked out as he had hoped, except for Charlie. What a bastard, Nolan thought, leaning back on his elbows. He was exhausted.

"It sure is work." Cissy rolled her shoulders until some of the ache eased. Her eyes were still wide and full of the awe the dark had induced. "Your uncle found this?"

"Found it, lost it. It's been in the family a while." Nolan looked up at the fading light. "We should go," he said. "Up top, I'll tell you everything I know about Brewster while we wait for Charlie." He reached to give Cissy a hand, but she was already scrambling toward the rope. She passed him the tag end and started up on her own. She is something, Nolan thought. Just like her sister.

When they were settled by the roadside with their tea, Nolan made good on his promise. "Brewster was married to my aunt Maudy," he told Cissy, "but it was one of those things didn't last. They stayed friends, though, even after they separated." Maudy was Nolan's daddy's sister, and she had lived in Cayro all her life until she moved to Arizona two years ago.

"Brewster marry her before or after he was in Vietnam?" Cissy reached into the cooler and brought a damp can of Coke to her forehead, letting the moisture wash away the sweat that had dried beneath her bangs.

"Oh, before. Most of those boys went off to Vietnam right out of high school. Eighteen and gone—one, two, three. Like Brewster's big brother, but his brother was one of those hard-luck types, dead three months after he got to 'Nam. So then Brewster was an only surviving son, got himself a ticket out. Everybody said he was lucky, but Brewster didn't see it that way. He married Maudy and started some college, but nothing he took up lasted, not school, not marriage."

Nolan paused and cocked his head at the sound of an engine, but when there was no sign of Charlie, he turned back to Cissy happily. Nolan loved to tell his family stories. In his own mind they were like those miniseries on television, where the characters were always revealing some complicated interrelationship, mother of a child that married a man who had a child who grew up and murdered the brother it never knew.

"Everybody is related to somebody," Nolan would say to Cissy now and then, meaning not that everyone in Cayro was actually related, but that any story you heard was probably like the ones you had not heard, and much closer to your own life than you would want to admit—a tragedy almost surely if you looked at it properly or told it the way it should be told.

"Daddy said Brewster reached a point in his life where he started to think nothing would go right till he did what he had been supposed to do. So he signed up and went. Everybody said he was a lucky man, all right. At least he came back. Lots of Cayro boys never did."

"Too dumb to keep their heads down." Cissy thought about Marty Parish and the other boys at Cayro High. She used a pinkie to strain a seed off the top of her tea, then drained the liquid that remained.

"Or too eager. Hot-dog types. Good old boys." Nolan gave the little nod that meant he knew Cissy would agree with him. "No different from what we got these days."

"Yeah." Cissy broke a piece of Styrofoam off her cup. "But it was a different time. Everybody says so. Delia does, anyway. She's always telling us that people forget what it was like."

"Oh, your mama's right. No doubt about it. You should listen to my uncles talk. Hell, you should hear my daddy. For a while there, he even grew his hair out a little. Started playing those Allman Brothers records, talked like only a fool would have volunteered for the army the way Brewster did. As if he hadn't been all hot to go himself. Aunt

Maudy says the only thing kept Daddy home was the herniated disk he got when he rolled his truck." Nolan rocked the empty thermos on the flat of his thighs and watched Cissy get to her feet.

"Like Clint's knee." Cissy picked up a few nubs of Styrofoam and looked down the dirt road. They would have to carry the garbage out. Wouldn't want to leave it here. "He never had to go 'cause he messed up his knee in an accident out at his daddy's farm."

"Yeah, the lucky legion. The crippled and the infirm." Nolan flashed a wicked smile. "Evolution in action, Aunt Maudy calls it. The truly crazy and the weak-minded, and, yeah, the unlucky. They went early and never came back. The lucky and the messed-up got to hang around to plant the next generation, like my daddy made me and Steve, and yours made you and Amanda and Dede. If things had been a little different, it could have been Brewster's sons hanging around here and you girls might never have been born."

"Wouldn't that have been terrible?" Cissy gave a sour grin. She did not bother to point out Nolan's error—that Clint Windsor had made Amanda and Dede, but never made her. Unlike Nolan, she had no wish to repeat family legend. Randall had earned his ticket out of the draft with a set of tracks up each arm and the spirited intervention of a record producer whose sole mission had been to keep likely moneymakers out of army green. Clint was like Brewster. He'd have gone to Vietnam if he could. It was a crazy decade. Clint had talked about that time in almost biblical terms: "Everything went back to front. Women fell in love with boys who looked more like girls than the girls did. And real men got treated no better than dogs."

By the side of the dirt road Cissy could see one of the invitational signs that Baptist Tabernacle had put up all over Cayro. "All are welcome in His house," it said in red and white paint. She thought about Clint and the way he had talked. "Real men" was one of his magic phrases. Every time he said it, even in his sunken whispery voice, it came out hard and strong. Real Men. Good Women. God and Righteousness. Wages of Sin. What a woman really wants. The phrases resounded like the lyrics of some song sung only by the righteous—Church of God incantations set to a bluegrass melody. In

Clint's exhausted tremolo, the words became staccato and insistent. He knew what he sounded like, his daddy or one of those men who drifted through Cayro with stubbled beards and caps pushed down to hide angry, blasted features. Sometimes he even laughed at himself.

It was as if Clint had split in two, become half the man he had been before his illness, half the man he was trying to be. He would speak those hard words, then snort and say them again in a mocking tone. Sometimes, listening to Amanda, Cissy heard the echo of Clint in her blunt, strong language, the echo of the man he had been that he did not want to be.

"My uncles swear Brewster is buried in one of these caves," Nolan was saying. "Maybe Little Mouth, maybe Paula's Lost. Aunt Maudy knows, but she won't tell me."

Brewster had taken a bad fall only a few weeks after Emmet Tyler made him pull down his lights and shut down the parties. Drunk and angry, he messed up his injured ankle. He went to the veterans' hospital for treatment, and the doctors said they could fix him, but with every day Brewster got worse. Nolan's uncle Tynan went to visit him and discovered that instead of fixing the ankle, the doctors had cut the foot off. Tynan threw a fit and tried to bring Brewster home, but Brewster stopped him. "Leave me alone," he said. "I'm not coming home."

It was the early afternoon, but Brewster's eyes were red and unfocused, and he could smell whiskey on his breath. "You drinking?" Tynan was shocked and angry.

"You can get anything in here," Brewster told him in a loud whisper. "Anything. Sometimes you don't even have to pay for it." His glance wandered away from Tynan's face to the next bed, where a half-naked man lay drooling and twitching.

"Oh Lord." Tynan turned on his heel and left.

Every time anyone from the family came to see Brewster, he told them the same thing. "Leave me alone. I an't coming home." With every visit, he was more shriveled, more distant. Always he was stoned or drunk.

"Where you getting the money, boy?" Tynan demanded.

"I got friends," Brewster said with a grin. "I got friends."

"Some kind of friends," Tynan cursed, but there was nothing he could do. No one at the hospital would listen to his complaints.

The doctors swore each operation would be the last, but the gangrene came back and the leg came off in sections. When Maudy finally came to see him, the doctors threw up their hands and said there was nothing more they could do. She lifted the sheet and saw the eight-inch stump where Brewster's leg had been.

"Oh, Brewster!" Maudy said, but he barely seemed to notice she was there. As Tynan had warned, he was drunk, not just drugged but whiskey-drunk in the middle of the day. "I'm not coming home," he kept saying. "Not coming home ever again."

"You're dying," Maudy told him, and finally his eyes focused on her.

"Yeah." Brewster licked his lips and grinned. "Ah, Maudy," he whispered. "You sure look good."

"You look awful."

"Yeah." He glanced around briefly, as if to make sure no one was watching, and reached to catch her hand. "You got to help me," he told her. "Maudy, please. Don't let them bury me here. Take me home to Cayro. Don't let them put me out under that lawn where sick men will walk on me when I'm dead."

Brewster squeezed Maudy's hand. He's raving, she thought, but she could see the graveyard through his window. It was unfenced, with no headstones, just little markers set down in the grass. Men were walking there, heads lowered as if they were reading the markers, stepping casually from one to the next.

"All right," Maudy promised.

Brewster's fingers relaxed in hers. He would be dead before the week was out, and maybe he had been raving, but Maudy brought his body home and buried it in the cave country.

"You think he's here?" Cissy looked at the slope of pines and dogwood.

"Maybe." Nolan's eyes were sad.

"Aunt Maudy said Brewster brought her out here when they were first married, to show her the bats, but they got distracted and forgot to watch at sunset." Nolan smiled. "It was about the only happy story she ever told me about Brewster. Sounded like she really enjoyed herself with him out here. Think it was his favorite place, and maybe hers for a while there."

Cissy was looking back down into the pit. The cave was whistling hollowly, tongueless and inarticulate. A cave could not cry warning, but this one seemed to. She stared at the mouth of rock, rigid, eternally wide in its broken, dirt-lipped howl. It breathes, she thought. It breathes like Clint or an old woman with emphysema. She closed her eyes and listened as the sun dropped a little further down the sky.

"Yeah, Brewster sure loved this place," Nolan said.

Cissy nodded. She could see it, that broken man falling in love with a hole in the ground. It made sense to her.

"It's marvelous. It's the best damn birthday I ever had."

People go caving for no reason anyone can predict. Mountain climbing is more exhilarating. Skydiving offers a better view. Skiing, fencing, or even horseback riding provide just as good a workout. Caving is not a sport but a dare, more a trial than an excursion. A dark, deep, pitched hole is the perfect place to test the nerves, the muscles, the survival instincts, but the risk is awful, the terror primeval. From those first moments lying on her back in the loose shale of Paula's Lost, Cissy knew she loved it as Brewster had, the dark and the safety, the risk and the unknown depths.

"Can we come back?" she asked. "Can we get some better lights and come back?"

Nolan saw the hunger and the fear in her expression. "Sure," he told her. "Anytime you want."

"Soon," Cissy said. Her heart was racing, and there was a sugary feeling of excitement all through her insides. "Let's come back soon."

"All right. We'll talk to my cousins and get some lights. We'll come back whenever you want." He forced himself not to frown. He was thinking about what his daddy had said about Brewster, the sad way he had talked about that boy who wasted his life. Should have known he was crazy, Mr. Reitower said, when he took to climbing around in that cave. It was one thing to throw parties, it was another to sit in a dark hole in the ground all by yourself. He was talking to Aunt Maudy, who nodded at him and spoke the words that stuck in Nolan's mind.

"The first question to ask anyone climbing down into those holes is always 'Why?' " Aunt Maudy said. "But I swear, don't ever believe the first reply."

Chapter 14

Nolan Reitower had two obsessions. He played clarinet and he pined for Dede Windsor. The first was new and he was extraordinarily gifted at it; the second went back years, and at that he was a dismal failure. From the beginning, Dede never looked in his direction.

"He won't never make a man," Dede said of Nolan. She had a way of saying what other people hesitated to say, but once they heard her, they knew they had been thinking the same thing. About Nolan she was deadly accurate. He remained baby-faced and boyish even as he grew to a man's height. But what bothered Dede was not only that he was more than a year younger than her, but that his idea of courting was to make moon eyes and gape at her in public. There was also the fact that Nolan was a fairly pudgy boy when he started following Dede around, and for all that he grew to be wide-shouldered, he stayed soft. The only nice thing anyone ever said about Nolan was that he was a good boy to his mama and daddy. Not much of a recommendation to the very particular Dede—good boys were not what caught her eye.

"He's too good," Dede said. "An't he got any wild in him?" No, Cissy thought. He did not. What was wild in Nolan was his passion for Dede Windsor. From that first run-in on the steps, when Dede called him "mama's little precious," Nolan was captured. Another boy would have taken offense. Nolan took fire, and never got over it. For him, there was simply no other female but Dede Windsor.

* * *

A few months after the birthday trip to Paula's Lost, Nolan started working with his daddy at Biscuit World after Mr. Reitower had what everyone described as "a little-bitty heart attack." "Nothing but a warning," Nadine pronounced it. "A warning to put your house in order, honey. Eat a little better. Get more rest. God's way of saying slow down." For reasons that Nolan could not understand, Nadine seemed not to worry. It was as if she could not picture any serious threat to what had always been, life going on as smooth as the surface of a china plate.

Nolan looked carefully into his daddy's pale face and immediately developed his own notions about putting their house in order. Like the good son he was, he quietly reorganized his days so that he could spend three hours every morning helping his daddy out before making the second bell for school. He'd come into homeroom smelling of baking powder, butter, and salt, steam rising off a little bag of sausage biscuits clutched in his hand. Before long, Nolan's eyes—his best feature, everyone agreed—had sunk into his biscuit-swollen cheeks, and he had to turn sideways to get through the door. From Cissy's viewpoint, the worst of it was that Nolan could no longer climb down the entrance to Paula's Lost.

"I'm sorry, I don't have time," Nolan kept telling Cissy, and it was true. Between Biscuit World and practicing the clarinet, the boy did not have a minute to spare.

The clarinet was Nadine's idea. She had pushed Nolan to join the school band, hoping it would draw him out of his bookish ways, and she had suggested the clarinet because she imagined it to be a proper instrument, not so heavy and ponderous as a tuba or as sexually suspect as a piccolo. And while she liked the sound of the euphonium, she was not sure how Nolan would look holding it close to his chest. He had his daddy's build and was going to be big and awkward. No, she decided, her boy could manage the clarinet and look good playing it.

Nadine had been sure that the clarinet would be a temporary hobby. Nolan lost interest in everything eventually. Music would be a useful but transient distraction from adolescent self-consciousness. She bought an inexpensive Vito Leblanc, a decent beginner's model made of plastic, with nickel-plated keys. "Resonite, Nolan, Resonite. That's what the dealer said," she kept repeating. What Nadine could not guess was that her shy boy would find his life's design writ in sixteenth notes, for once Nolan got his chops working, he discovered he could breathe through that clarinet. He could soar through and out of it into a world no one knew, a world suffused with the drunken glory his talent stirred within him.

Nolan practiced whenever he could, mostly after school, when his daddy was home. Biscuit World closed at one every afternoon, earlier on the busiest days. "Once they're gone, they're gone," Mr. Reitower would laugh, already thinking about climbing into his bed as he wiped down the counter. Nolan's daddy slept every afternoon from the time he got home until dinner. He worried about Nolan getting up so early to help out, never managing a nap until after school and band practice. "Growing boys need food, sure, but they need sleep too," he would tell the oblivious Nolan every few days. "Dream time," he complained to Nadine. "The boy is getting no dream time, no easy, unbooked, lay-around-and-think time. That's what a boy needs to make a man. Time to imagine himself what he is going to be."

Most days Nolan got no nap at all, just went drowsy through the hours until the moment when he could put a reed in his mouth and come fully awake and full of joy. What his father did not understand was that his music was dream time for Nolan. He did not take up the clarinet to pretend he was Benny Goodman, or even to hide behind black plastic and shiny keys. Nolan had always liked music well enough. Nadine set the radio dial dutifully on the classical channel in the early evening, and every morning his daddy would put on the jazz station from Atlanta while they cut biscuits. But that bland appreciation had nothing to do with what Nolan felt after the first six months with the clarinet.

Nolan's music teacher, Mr. Clausen, worried about him as much as his daddy did. Nadine had found the man after the school-band director told her to "get somebody knows what he's doing." Mr. Clausen taught at the community college and directed a little wind ensemble that practiced a lot but rarely played for the public. Cayro was not a place where people would turn out to hear a wind ensemble. He had been almost rude to Nadine when she first called him, but became remarkably polite after a few sessions with her son.

"It's a miracle. That boy, the way he plays, no one knows what he can do. I listen to him and I think I've gone crazy. I listen to him and I start to believe there is a God."

"Mr. Clausen!" Nadine was horrified. "Do not tell me you do not believe in God." Nadine was willing to ignore a lot for the sake of getting her boy a good teacher, but not blasphemy. She knew musicians were dangerous that way. Freethinkers, hippies, atheists, queers, intellectuals—all were of a type, and not a type she wanted Nolan to know too much about. She loved him and knew how much he loved his music, but she also knew how easily boys could be led astray. She had already lost one son, after all. If Clausen was a danger to Nolan, she would make sure he never got near him again.

"Yes. Oh, yes, I believe in God. Absolutely." A vision of losing his prize pupil lent sincerity to Mr. Clausen's profession of faith. "Who else would have sent me this prodigy right when I was ready to give up? You have no idea how many youngsters are sent to me as punishment. Mostly mine. But your boy could be a virtuoso if he got a little more sleep." Mr. Clausen hesitated, not wanting to offend Nolan's mother. "I just think we have to make sure he gets the kind of encouragement he needs." His words prompted a deeper frown from Nadine. She too worried about her child. She had erred with his older brother, Stephen, and she didn't want Nolan leaving home in a huff, only calling once or twice a year.

Nolan was the only one who did not worry. Except for his continual despair over Dede, he was a boy full of patient confidence. He slept when he could, daydreamed when he could not, and came alive to play the clarinet, first in the high school band, then in the orchestra, and eventually in Mr. Clausen's wind groups. Nolan saw no need for dream time because he lived in a dream. He had only two waking states, the one in which he drew pure and astonishing music out of the clarinet, and the other when he was watching Dede Windsor with his dark puppy eyes. Nolan had no ambition but to play his instrument in such a way that other people could feel the exhilaration it produced in him, and to win Dede's love.

Mr. Reitower died of a massive heart attack two weeks before Nolan's high school graduation, not sweating over his biscuit trays but lying in his own bed in a deep and easy sleep. His death ended any chance Nolan had to go off and study music. A scholarship might pay all of Nolan's expenses, but it would not take care of his mother. And what people had always said about Nolan was true. He was a good son. With Mr. Reitower gone, Nadine needed a good son.

From the moment of her husband's death, Nolan's mama fell into a stunned and furious silence. Like a sunstruck puppy, she could not seem to understand what had happened to her or what had to be done now. Her good husband, that reliable man, had the smallest insurance policy ever issued. They were not destitute, but damn close, and Nadine could not accept that.

"How could he?" she snapped, glaring at Nolan and the neighbors who came in to help. She might have meant his dying, or perhaps his buying that pitiful policy that did not cover the cost of the cheapest burial she could arrange. She might have been speaking of Stephen, who called but did not come, and sent a check so small as to be no help at all. Or she might have been accusing God. Nolan thought she was close to it, an outright complaint to a divinity she had never questioned before. But what he really believed was that she was accusing him. It was his fault, his failure.

Within a few weeks of the funeral, Nadine stormed out the front door, angrily shoving the screen door, which snapped back and whacked her on the forehead. She staggered once and fell down the steps, breaking her left arm and, worse, her left hip.

"The weak link in old women," the doctor said. That hip was the evidence that finally proved just how fragile Nadine had become. The doctor also suggested there might have been a mild stroke, but there was no evidence of that except for the rage, towering and unpredictable, that now burned in Nadine. Nolan did not hesitate. He had already taken over full-time at Biscuit World. He knew how, and no one was going to refuse him the job or that high school diploma everyone knew he deserved. He was determined and uncompromising. He would manage. He would support Nadine, take his time deciding what to do, and meanwhile play his clarinet all afternoon out on the porch, where he could look down Terrill Road to the convenience store. Dede was working there now, and if he got up the nerve, he could savor a cold drink that she would have to put in his hand.

When Nolan started to feel like he was going crazy, there were afternoon classes out at the junior college, and clarinet auditions for visiting band directors, who would stare at him in awe. None could believe that he could play like that and then ignore their advice about his professional future.

"My God, boy, you could do something."

"I'm doing something." He would smile then, pack up his case, and walk away. That tight smile told Cissy everything. Several times she had gone over to Atlanta with Nolan. Mostly she would hang out south of Peachtree and haunt the record stores looking for bootleg tapes of Mud Dog, but once or twice she sat in the back of some darkened hall and watched Nolan perform what seemed to be his only sin. It had to be sin, the awful satisfaction he took in those auditions, smiling that way throughout, playing like a wicked angel until the rest of the clarinet section turned sour and pale. It was as if he harbored a rage bigger than the one buffeting his mama and it came out in runs of staccato-tongued sixteenth notes alternated with pure, piercing tones. Maybe that was the way music really worked, Cissy thought. Maybe talent was a blade cutting hard through those who had less. Watching Nolan, Cissy saw him as a deeply hurt boy, made rich through an accident of fate and hoarding his wealth. It made her slightly dizzy, the way he smiled through the despair of everyone else at his auditions.

Afterward, though, Nolan would be himself again, shy and eager to hear what Cissy thought. He would take her out for a big rich meal and laugh gently at the frustration of the orchestra leader. This

Nolan was her friend, and a genuinely kind soul. It was hard then for Cissy to remember how he was in the audition. Only when he talked about the other musicians did the nature of his resentment become apparent.

"Oh, they always think they're something until I show them what I can do. Humility, that's what these boys lack. It's what I give them." He smiled wide, and chewed with a satisfaction that scared Cissy, startled her into speaking.

"You should get out," she said, her expression stern.

Nolan took a sip of water and looked at her inquisitively. Cissy truly cared about him, he knew, had from the first time Dede snubbed him. But Cissy was no musician. She did not know what he felt when he sat down with those little groups of overly ambitious horn players. Nor could he tell her. He tried to smile and wave her words away, but she caught his hand and spoke fiercely.

"I'm telling you right now. You should go to Atlanta or New York City or Boston or anywhere you can. Go somewhere. Do something. Audition for an orchestra for real. Take a position or get a music degree. You got to stop this and get out of here."

When Nolan just smiled again and shrugged, the weight of her own resentment almost crushed Cissy. Anytime Nolan decided to leave Cayro, there would be people waiting to welcome him. Anytime he could face what was happening to him and walk away from his mother, he could have a career that would vindicate every bad choice he had ever made. But no one anywhere was waiting for Cissy. Sometimes Nolan's smile would make her feel more debased than those sweating clarinet players he had just skunked so completely.

Who was she? Delia Byrd's daughter. No talent, not special. She was like those bugs caught in amber, stuck in time. She'd never been in love, never dated. No boyfriend, no friends except Nolan and Dede, and Dede didn't count. What did Cissy have? Nothing. Nothing but the caves.

Cissy had been out to Paula's Lost half a dozen times with Nolan before he stopped going, and a couple of times with Charlie, though she gave that up when Charlie got drunk and tried to wrestle her down in the first passage past the entrance. Cissy could not explain how she felt about the caves. Nolan was too busy, Charlie wanted to get her naked, and Dede thought the whole idea was silly. Cissy had managed to talk three members of the swim team into going caving with her that spring. They went out to Little Mouth with a park ranger as a guide, and he was impressed with Cissy. What she told no one, because people would have thought her frankly crazy if they knew, was that she seized every chance that came her way for a ride out to one of the caves and went down on her own. Mostly she hitchhiked out to the Lost and climbed just far enough down into the first passage to sit in the welcome dark, sometimes humming to herself happily, more often falling asleep. There was no sleep like the one she surrendered to while wrapped in an old blanket in the sand bed of the first chamber at Brewster's old party site. But sleeping wasn't a career, a future, a purpose, any more than caving was.

Faced with Nolan's bland smile, Cissy would find herself picking on him, being mean just to spite him. "Eat something doesn't come with gravy," she would say. Or, "Dede's going to marry that Tucker boy, just you wait." Nolan's smile would evaporate, and he would look at Cissy as if he could see down to where she hid *her* sins.

Cissy was stilled then, overwhelmed by the power she had to hurt Nolan. It was awful, knowing each other's weaknesses so precisely. Nolan was unfailingly gentle with her, no matter how frustrated and resentful she became. Maybe he had grown calluses dealing with his mama's rages, or maybe the dark angel she had seen in the rehearsal hall was not so sinful as she had imagined.

"At least you're good at something," Cissy told Nolan.

"I'm not that good," he would tell her carefully, waiting for the cruelty to turn to embarrassment, waiting for his friend to come back. "Not yet. I'm not near as good as I'm going to be." Then he would laugh, a deprecating little laugh, and shake his head. "When I'm good enough to pull your sister up Terrill Road to my porch, then we'll see. We'll see."

The music in which Nolan found so much grace was a mystery to Cissy, the clarinet an instrument as imperial and strange as the concept of a wind ensemble or a jazz combo. The daughter of Delia Byrd and Randall Pritchard understood guitars and drums and rock and roll. Lyrics. Words and music. Mr. Clausen had found a Buffet at an estate sale and bought it for Nolan with the help of the other members of the wind ensemble, a gesture Nolan had almost, but not quite, refused. What he played on that gleaming ebony and silver creation was of another order, a language Cissy had never learned to speak and did not even know if she heard accurately. When Nolan played for her, Cissy felt like a Baptist child at a Catholic mass—intimidated, awed, and suspicious. It was gorgeous and scary. The melodies, almost recognizable or fully familiar but extraordinary at the same time, sometimes sent shocks through her nervous system. More extraordinary was the fact that this music was coming out of Nolan, with his flushed full cheeks and puffy eyes. Baking-powder memories rose with the cascading trills of notes. Cissy's mouth would fall open, and she would feel suddenly small and stupid and completely Cayro, Georgia, while Nolan would enlarge and assume the guise of Bacchus or Orpheus, some mystical god of high, far places as remote from Cayro as Paris or New York. If she closed her eyes when Nolan played, Cissy imagined the lithe figures of ballet dancers against a diamond and velvet sky. With each trill they leaped and Cissy's heart sank within her.

Maybe Delia knew what that was like—the great, dark power of a melody that could catch your pulse, speed it or slow it, lift you right out of your natural state. She had lived in that outer world. There was magic there, magic that only musicians knew, magic that remade everything and might have remade Cissy. But it was a magic denied to her. Like Dede, she had a pleasant voice, pedestrian, ordinary. Sitting next to Nolan, knowing she had neither her mother's gift nor his, was torture of a high order. When Cissy got that small, only one thing pulled her out of it: the knowledge that Nolan too had something in life that he wanted desperately and could not have. It should have been the subject they avoided, but it was not. Dede was the one subject Nolan would invariably turn to, the one reference point for both of them.

"Who's Dede seeing?" he asked when Cissy came by during his afternoon session on the porch the day after their latest trip to Atlanta. His whole body communicated frustration and nervous energy that he could not dissipate. The reed was barely inches from Nolan's lower lip, his desire plain on his face. "She's not still chasing that Tucker boy, is she?" He put his tongue out, deliberately threading the reed's moistened fibers. He was trying to be casual.

"Oh, Nolan." The tune he had been playing was still sounding in Cissy's head. Gratefully she shook herself back into the moment, the mundane world of thwarted desire and sexual obsession. Even musicians were subject to the laws of heartbreak. "Give it up. Christ, Dede an't never gonna go out with you. Even if she wasn't seeing Billy Tucker, she wouldn't see you."

Nolan rubbed his lower lip with his right thumb. "I know, I know." His eyes were unfocused, distant, his face without the hope of a smile. "I'm just asking." He tilted the clarinet and looked down its length as if insight lay in the finish.

It was no game. He was not pretending. His misery never abated. Every time Dede broke up with another boyfriend, Nolan's heart caught fire again. He plied Cissy with questions, ran errands for Delia, and searched out gifts that he took by the convenience store— small things like fabric-covered hair ties or padded fingerless bicycle gloves that would protect Dede's hands when she opened cases of eggs and butter or slit the tops of cartons of jerky.

"You can't help who you love," Nolan told Cissy. He was talking about Brewster but thinking about himself. "Some people are lucky. They find the one for them the first time out. Some never find the right one. Daddy always said Brewster should have stayed married to Aunt Maudy, even if it was like he swore—that she wasn't his true love. He said true love is rare and a good home life is as much as most can hope for. And then anyway, Aunt Maudy could have kept Brewster a little better focused. He developed sugar diabetes, you know, made it worse drinking. Screwed up his circulation, Daddy said. Almost suicide, if you think about it. Kind of thing didn't have to happen. Just stupidity, really, and paying yourself no mind. Runs in the family, kind of." His head dropped.

"Evolution in action?" Cissy joked, but Nolan glared at her. You could never predict when he was going to get his feelings hurt, she thought. She looked at his fingers on the clarinet, poised delicately and with unfailing precision. Infinitely fragile, immensely strong, a force of nature in his profoundly human body.

Even before she graduated from high school, Dede had trouble finding a job she could keep. After she got out of high school, her search for work became desperate and ceaseless. Her problem was only partly the limited number of jobs in Cayro. The real obstacles were temperament and aptitude. Most girls came out of Cayro High ready to leave town or work at the electronics firm that had opened in the new industrial park on the Marietta side of town. But Dede did not want to leave Cayro—she claimed that outside the city limits lay chaos and bad drugs—and she definitely did not want to pull a paycheck wiring guidance systems for missiles and pinning her hair back to do it.

"The pay an't that good anyway," Dede complained. "Once you buy enough grass to keep yourself stoned while you're working that line, you can't be taking no nice vacations or buying a good car. And hell, I'd rather do my drugs for fun, not just to get myself through God's own boring workday." Delia nodded and hid a smile. God's own boring workday was all most people could expect, after all.

For a while Dede helped out at Benny Davis's Cayro Dog Shop, grooming poodles and shih tzus and giving flea and tick treatments to dogs so big Benny no longer had the nerve to face them. It was irregular work and didn't pay very well, but Benny let her come in when she wanted and didn't care how she dressed.

When a group of women brought a case against the Atlanta police department, Dede took an immediate interest in their struggle. The state announced open exams for deputy and traffic-control positions, and Dede tried to sign on for deputy sheriff. When she came in for the application forms, Emmet Tyler sat down on the edge of his desk and stared at her.

"You want to be a deputy?" He was astonished. "As many times as you've almost wound up in jail?"

Emmet Tyler had taken partial disability after he rolled his cruiser chasing a couple of drunk teenagers on the road to Little Mouth. His left arm was stiff, but he refused to let the doctors mess with him. Since the accident, he'd been working at the courthouse escorting prisoners and filing papers for the traffic judge. On the weekends he was supposed to rest and do his physical therapy, but mostly Emmet hung out near the courthouse or over at the café down from the Bee's Bonnet.

"Almost don't count," Dede said, "and traffic an't no never mind. I'm as street-legal as anyone. I got a high school diploma. I got the right attitude."

"Girl, you an't got the right attitude," Emmet said quietly. He had learned to like Dede the hard way, tangling with her repeatedly since she was fourteen. He knew her temper and admired it, though he prayed never to run full into it in this lifetime. "What would you do if you had to arrest a friend, some boy you dated? Huh? How would you feel then?"

"Some boys I've dated should be arrested." Dede laughed at the idea. "Others, well, it would be like Judge Winkler when he excused himself from sitting at his cousin's trial. Can't everybody have some cases where they excuse themselves?" She was thoughtful, a little frown deepening the line between her eyebrows.

Emmet pushed his hair back and took a deep breath. "Dede, honey, that number of cases might be more than you could handle." He raised his palm when her face stiffened, as if to block the protest that was sure to come.

"You're smart," Emmet said. "You are simply one of the sharpest girls I've ever known, and you have to see how hard it could get, walking friends of yours from court to jail, putting handcuffs on people you've known all your life." His look held her, open to her anger but firm. "I've done it. I know." His eyes flicked away. "I've lost people because of it. Lost people I've loved. I wouldn't want to see that happen to you."

Dede gritted her teeth. She knew Emmet was thinking about Delia, who was friendly enough but now refused all his invitations to dinner or a movie. She never mentioned that Emmet had twice arrested Dede—once for speeding and once for possession of a tiny quantity of marijuana—but both of them knew that was why she stopped going out with him. "I can't date a man put handcuffs on my child," Delia told M.T. "I don't care if she was drunk in the middle of the street."

Dede frowned again and scowled at Emmet, but when she left she did not take the application forms.

As he watched her go, Emmet sighed heavily. He had tried not to take Delia's rejection too hard, and to keep himself busy, but every time he thought about her his heart thudded so hard his throat seemed to close. He would, he knew, have given his soul to lie once more on Delia's body, to thrust once more as hard as he could and then lie spent on her shoulder—even if it were the last act he was ever allowed. But she was miles away from him, too far to reach in this life. The friendship she gave him was all he would ever get, and he clung to it. He hadn't asked her out in a long time, just found excuses to stop by and eat his lunch with her when he could. He worked all the hours he was allowed, went to Panama City when he needed a woman. Now and then he helped the park service boys out, posting a sign or two and telling stories the rangers hadn't heard yet. Some blamed his skills as a storyteller for the fools who kept getting lost at Paula's.

"Sometimes you go down into the dark, and sometimes you don't come back," Emmet told the youngsters who asked him about the old parties. His tone of voice was bleak, and he nodded, as if his warning should settle the matter for any sane man. He never seemed to see how those boys grinned at each other. He had lost the memory of being young and crazy and eager to jump directly into the dark.

* * *

"Thing is, I want a job driving, and that's the job I can't get. But I'm a great driver. Maybe I could deliver something—something not too heavy. I an't no fool." Dede lifted her skinny arms and flapped her fingers, grinning at Cissy. "I know I couldn't do sodas. No canned goods, no soft drinks. Could you see me handling cases of soup or dog food?"

Cissy smiled at the notion. At her peak Dede got up to 117 pounds. Mostly she stayed well under that. Bad times, like those months she was alternating uppers and B_{12}, she dropped below 100.

"Skeletal," Amanda told Delia. "The girl is skeletal."

Cissy agreed but did not say so. There was no use talking about Dede to Amanda. Maybe Delia, but not Amanda, who spent a solid year hounding Delia to put Dede in the Christian Rehabilitation Center over near Savannah. There was a bad patch when it looked as if Delia was going to do it, but Dede must have caught scent of that. She shifted over to what she called her wholeness regimen, dropping Xanax, ginseng from Siberia, and chelated calcium, and bingeing on a diet of complex carbohydrates and fresh leafy vegetables. She pumped up fast and talked loudly about how satisfying it was to be clean for a change.

Dede believed in matching her drugs with vitamins, as if good intentions neutralized wild ones, and sometimes Cissy convinced herself that she knew what she was doing. Except for smoking a little grass with Nolan and drinking a few beers after a cave trip, Cissy had no experience with drugs. She knew she couldn't judge the effects.

But Cissy did understand what Dede was talking about when she complained about the lack of job opportunity in Cayro. If you didn't want to style hair with Delia or get line work out at Frito-Lay or the missile-wiring plant, there wasn't a whole lot of choice, not for a girl with no family money. The last new businesses to be established in Cayro were the motorcycle repair shop near the Marietta highway and the Crafts & Stuff at the Stop 'n' Go Mall. Both had failed.

Dede's abiding desire to steer a big truck around on narrow streets had been a constant since before she got her learner's permit. Sexy, Dede thought being a driver was sexy—right down to the uniform shirts and pocket patches. Maybe she could deliver something like paper products or baked goods, she told Cissy.

"Maybe. Angel food cake?" Cissy teased.

Dede lost her temper when she found out that no paper products came in any truck she could drive. That kind of thing came into the Piggly Wiggly via huge semis, along with canned goods and giant bags of pet food. Even the baked goods came in on a big truck whose driver just laughed at Dede when she tried to talk to him.

It was a bad summer. Dede holed up in her room doing Dilaudid and megadoses of vitamin C. Cissy found her stretched out on her bed one afternoon, where she talked for an hour about the beneficial effects of vitamin C, how regular it was keeping her. "Better than beer." She lifted her head and giggled softly. "Thought you were Dan," she whispered, naming the boy she had been dating the previous month, whom Cissy had not seen in weeks. "Thought you were Dan. That's a boy needs some C." Then she closed her eyes and drifted away. Cissy sat and watched her for a while, worrying over whether it was time to get Delia involved. In the end she decided to wait.

For a while Dede was excited about long-haul driving and dated a couple of short-haul drivers as a way of sneaking up on the notion. One of them had his own truck, and Dede saw immediately that that was the way to go, though, as she told Cissy, it wasn't likely she could borrow enough to get a truck. And who would trust her with their goods? She did locate a few women drivers, but most were part of a team, married to their partners or doing runs now and then just to keep things running smoothly.

"Son of a bitch," Dede cursed as her dreams of driving receded.

One night she ran a long, complicated fantasy on Cissy. She was going to go down to Atlanta and find work driving a taxi, sleep with somebody or rent a tuxedo and get herself one of those modified hansom rigs at Underground Atlanta. She could cluck to a horse if she couldn't baby an engine. Her eyes were glassy, and the skin around her nose looked pinched and gray. Cindy watched and worried.

One early Thursday evening Amanda called the Bonnet to tell Delia there had been a shooting at the convenience store down from Nolan's house. Two women were sitting under the dryers, big pink and blue curlers steaming under plastic covers.

"What was it?" MT sounded frightened. "What was it?"

"Somebody stupid said the wrong thing to the wrong person."

Strictly speaking, it wasn't even a robbery. It was a boyfriend/girlfriend thing, and there were drugs involved. Some boy too tanked to take the time to think, some girl too high to care what that boy thought, another boy too glazed to pay attention. Then there was a gun and some craziness no one was too sure about. Nobody could say how it got started, but the boy died and the girl was messed up, blood everywhere and half a finger gone. In the confusion someone went back and rifled the cash register—not, as far as the police could determine, any of the people involved in the shooting.

Dede was sitting in Steph's chair examining a newspaper in hopes of finding a company or an idea she hadn't tried already. "I could have seen that coming," she said, and got up and walked out the door. There was a new temporary manager putting shelves back up when Dede arrived at the store. The regular manager had quit as soon as the cops drove up. "I an't working blood," he had said. "No blood for me."

"I got an eye for trouble," Dede told the new guy. He was holding a split box of ice cream toppings in his hands, small cans of butterscotch and chocolate. He looked up at her blankly.

"Very little people can do that I wouldn't know how to figure," Dede went on.

The guy just stared.

"I could be good."

"Good?"

"This place, this job. This is something I know a little about."

"What? You used to hang out at a 7-Eleven till all hours?" He laughed and shoved a few more cans onto the shelf.

"Well, yeah." Dede was not belligerent. She was telling the honest truth. Her eyes swept the shelves, the glass storefront, the stand of newspapers and magazines with half the covers obscured by brown paper wrappers.

"I could handle this."

The man put down the box and turned to her. "Girl," he said, "you are tiny." He seemed to want to be patient, but his tone was dismissive. "And don't you know that somebody died here tonight? Somebody got shot."

"I an't gonna get shot." Dede looked him right in the eye. "I know how to handle myself, and there's not too much that can stop me when I make up my mind. So, no, I an't no two-hundred-pound stupid jock, but I can get things done. I could run this place like you cannot imagine."

The man was intrigued in spite of himself, but he didn't know what to say. He tried to wave Dede away, but there was already a sign on the window and a stack of application forms behind the counter. When Dede insisted, he pulled out his manager's book to see if he could say no. Nothing there helped him. There was no requirement for height or weight. There was an age requirement, but Dede met it—barely.

She filled out the form and checked back twice to make sure he sent it in to the central office. Nothing would come of it, Delia warned, but all Dede said was "I can handle that job."

They put her on days to start, split days, the worst possible schedule. Early morning and early evening were the peak hours. The man who trained Dede didn't think she would last a week.

"We get some rude types in here," he said.

Dede smiled. "Uh-huh."

Delia worried, but Amanda was outraged. "Counter help! That what you want to be? Counter help?"

"I can do this," Dede told them both, refusing to be drawn into an argument. Her eyes were bright and clear. She was drinking black coffee and swallowing big iron pills.

Rude boys, teenagers, almost legal twenty-year-olds with smudged identification cards and bad attitudes. Winos of both sexes. Angry mothers running in from carloads of shrieking toddlers. No one scared Dede. She could size them up with a glance and predict what they were after. Beer and cigarettes, milk and white bread, peanut butter cookies or gallon containers of Rocky Road. False IDs or fast hands, Dede spotted them before they could become a problem.

She knew the tricks because she had done more than her share of them. She knew what was possible and how to handle tired, hopeful children. She had a quip or a joke to deflect anger, or a ruthless glare when the little shits needed one. She even stopped the girl who had been palming quarters off the cardboard Cerebral Palsy poster by the ice cream freezer.

"You don't want to do that," she said, and that was the end of it.

Dede knew the game and she liked it. Maybe steering a big rig would have been better, but this was all right for the time being, she told Delia and Cissy. This was her place now, and it was going to be run right.

It was six months before her superiors admitted what Cissy knew already. This little spit of a girl had talent, she had control. "She knows her stuff," the supervisor told Delia. "She's the best I've ever had, and who would have guessed, huh?"

"I can do this," Dede said. Her eyes shone with conviction, vitamin E, and beta-carotene.

She could.

Chapter 15

After the expedition with the park ranger, Cissy spent two years collecting monographs on caves, finding only a few mentions of Paula's Lost but three articles about Little Mouth, all written by competent amateur cavers pursuing expert status, good old boys with night eyes and no fear of close quarters. Caving is a nonlucrative occupation, a pastime for ex-jocks and the kind of intense skinny youths who can be seen doggedly swimming laps or racewalking while others pursue team sports. There are no medals for this hobby, no trophies but the regard of other experts. The monographs on cheap paper, hand-stapled or clipped together and only occasionally published in bound journals, were self-deprecating, matter-of-fact, and full of the kind of understated bombast that develops among a clandestine elite. What did you do this weekend? Crawled headdown through three miles of mud and gravel, mapped a passage where no one has ever been, and, oh yes, cracked a femur against a little old stalagmite. Cissy's ambition was to write her own such account, to watch Delia or Dede as they discovered her secret life, the Cissy who went down into the dark fearless, competent, and only a little self-consciously proud.

Five miles north of Paula's Lost, Little Mouth was a vertical pit with a slanting shaft, nothing special, a limestone cave with a spring-fed stream, little explored but much rumored. A lot of good stories came out of that cave, most often from people who had never gone farther than the first pit, the second rocky incline. Only one person had died in Little Mouth, and there was no reason to remember it at all. Except for modern geology surveys, it too might have disappeared for a few years. It was not a good one, experts said of Little

Mouth, not like the little caves to the north or the watery pits in north Florida. Little Mouth's descent was soft, as bad as Paula. Those walks tended to flake and collapse. Many of the stories were about miraculous escapes, boys who climbed out covered with dirt and boasting of how close they had come to not getting out at all. The rangers laughed at the stories until that boy was lost in 1972. After that, they treated Little Mouth like the sinks. Farther south the water table was higher, disappearances more likely, the sinks deep-shadowed pools of water as popular and risky as the quarries of the Northeast. Cypress roots bled tannic acid into the still water, producing a brown tea color and occasionally a deeper red. The dark waters reduced visibility for the cave divers who occasionally vanished into their depths. Such holes were ringed with chains solidly fixed to concrete pilings or the great old trees. Stark white crosses were planted in the earth overhangs, one for each diver who did not come out, though still the divers came. They called those holes Devil's Eye or Red Lady or Night's Own Hole, and the stories they told were all about looking up through the pulsing black water into a single red eye of light.

The caves of north Georgia sport fewer than a dozen crosses. Since 1972 there was always one above the descent to Little Mouth, though no one remembers the name of the boy that was lost. Teenagers swore the cross was a sham, that the deputies put it up just to scare people off the property. Boys nailed condoms and old beer-can tabs to the cross, signed it with curse words and nicknames, and every once in a while shot it full of holes or tore it out completely, but the rangers checked the site regularly. Each time the cross disappeared, they hauled out a fresh one and hammered it into the ground. Death, Emmet told Cissy one Sunday afternoon, is more than teenagers can understand, and it is too easily found at the bottom of a hollow like the half-buried mouth of Little Mouth. The look she gave him said plainly she knew more about death than he ever imagined.

* * *

Jean and Mim were dark and lean women, acquaintances of Nolan's from the community college. Their eyes lit up when he told them his Brewster stories, and they plied him for details about the caves. Nolan was happy to oblige, and happier still to introduce them to his friend Cissy. When Cissy met them, her first thought was that they did not look like they were from Cayro. They looked like those heroines in the science fiction books she used to share with Nolan. When Jean looked at her, Cissy blushed as if the woman could read her mind, and felt a kind of panic that made her say yes to everything they asked.

They'd heard from Nolan that Cissy had gone caving a lot. They were trying to start a women's caving group, and they wanted her to join them. With the two of them looking at her, heat swept right up her spine and flashed at the base of her neck. She could not believe it. They not only were talking to her but were talking to her about the thing she loved most in the world.

"If Mim and I do it, we get credit for physical education," Jean told her.

"And we won't have to go with the men's group. It's full of Neanderthal jocks who just want us to climb ahead of them so they can look at our butts." Mim had a fast drawl and ran her words together. Cissy found it hard to follow everything she said.

"We checked them out," Jean threw in. "Pretty wretched bunch. And they're just using all this old nasty equipment anyway, but they're so proud of it. Didn't want us to use any of their stuff. Can you imagine?"

"Yeah," Cissy said, though she was not entirely sure what she was agreeing with, or to. She had gone caving with Charlie, for God's sake. She could go with these women even if they did talk too fast.

Even before they went on their first trip, Jean and Mim started loaning Cissy books and inviting her to go to the movies with them. They behaved as if they had all gone to grade school together and had just been separated briefly, as if they had some common understanding shared only by young women who enjoyed caving and wore blue jeans every day. They also touched as easily as they talked. Mim even kissed Cissy right on the mouth when Cissy showed her the roughly sketched maps of Paula's Lost she and Nolan had made. Cissy was startled and delighted at the intimacy. She wanted to be that free, that easy in her body, that cosmopolitan and grown-up and exotic all at the same time—kissing people and cussing like a sailor the way Mim did.

"Where's that girl from?" Delia asked Cissy one day after Jean dropped her off and stopped in for a glass of tea. "She doesn't look like any of the families around here."

"Don't know for sure," Cissy said.

"She don't look remotely Christian to me," Amanda said as if she alone knew what "Christian" looked like. Amanda was visiting with her boys, one-year-old Michael Junior and baby Gabriel. Gabe in his little baby carrier was Delia's whole focus. Cissy glared and stomped off to her room to read *The Color Purple,* which Jean said was sad enough to convince you that women needed to arm themselves for self-defense.

Not Christian, exotic. Cissy knew what Amanda meant even as she resented her saying it. Jean and Mim were nothing like the sallow, towheaded, narrow-faced girls of Cayro. They had dark hair, high cheekbones, clear skin, and long necks. Thick, finely shaped lashes caught the light and drew you to their shining eyes. They looked like the girls in *Seventeen* magazine, and it was true that Mim was Jewish, though Jean was not. Jean was from Bartow County, born north of Cayro on one of those old truck farms famous for peanuts and fast-spreading potato plants.

If Jean's hair had been blond and stringy, if Mim had looked like M.T.'s sister Sally, wide-faced and complacent, Cissy might not have been so fascinated with the two of them. But Jean and Mim looked like Los Angeles or New York City, and they talked like it too, mentioning books and films and far-off places as casually as they hugged each other when they separated.

The three girls started hanging out together, though Cissy never became as comfortable with them as she was with Nolan. She always felt self-conscious. Jean and Mim knew things she did not know, and she wanted them to accept her despite that fact. It astonished her that it seemed they did.

Going caving with them would cement the friendship, Cissy hoped, thinking of the time after, when they would all sit around and talk. And to get to go down into the dark again! The thought of being able to do more than climb around in the first passage at Paula's Lost was a powerful lure. Cissy would probably have agreed to go no matter how shy she felt. She pined for the caves when she couldn't get out there, dreamed about them in her restless sleep.

Jean and Mim were having trouble finding two more women willing to go. People said caving alone was suicide and that to be safe you needed a group of five. Three was tight. Accidents happened. People got tired and made stupid mistakes. Carrying someone out of one of the deep caves was a job for four or more. Cissy called one of the girls from the swim team. "You still doing that?" the girl said. "Cissy, you ought to find another hobby."

"Oh, hell," Mim said finally. "You've been on the swim team, right? We've both done judo for years, and each of us can deadlift a good 120. We can do it. I don't want to mess around too long and lose the chance to do some mapping of our own."

"Well, we don't want to kill ourselves," Jean laughed, "but it an't like we're going to do totally raw caves. These are known caves. And like my daddy always said, life is better if you take a risk now and then."

Like flirting with God, Cissy thought. God or the risk of death, or just your own hope of transfiguration. Buddhists strove for nirvana. Christians aimed for heaven. But a girl who believed in nothing, who just loved the dark, where did she go? It was a risk Cissy would just have to take.

It was as good as Cissy had hoped it would be down in the cave again. Looking up into the rock ceiling at Little Mouth, she imagined she could hear gospel music in the darkness just outside of the light's little circle. Every time Cissy went into a cave, she found herself thinking about God, the God who stacked rock on rock and watched over fatherless girls.

God was Delia's voice in the darkness when Cissy was tired, so soft and clear she almost believed the voice to be real. God was the thing outside herself, that enormous desire to shatter into a thousand living pieces and burn. God was the moment past orgasm, lying spent, belly-down on her own bed with her hand over her mouth—nothing she wanted any of her family to know about.

When Cissy was younger, she had enjoyed shocking Amanda with her nonbelief, but these days that was no longer so satisfying. Amanda's sense of constant outrage seemed to have abated with the birth of her boys and the work of managing Michael's Sunday school classes. "It's a pity," Dede complained. "Amanda's gotten so settled. She used to be such a kick in the pants." Cissy agreed. Their manic evangelical sister was almost as settled as M.T.

I bet God misses Amanda, Cissy thought as she was hanging onto a rock slope in Little Mouth. I bet he misses her, all noisy and insistent and challenging everybody and everything. Any God Cissy could imagine would enjoy an attitude like that. Whenever Cissy saw the steadily more haggard Amanda, she remembered how powerful her sister had been when she moved into Clint's house on Terrill Road, the energy in her that burned so hot it had to be profane. Amanda had stormed about like one of those nasty Old Testament prophets in the desert, the ones Amanda would quote but did not seem to appreciate, men capable of cursing God and dying with the curse still on their tongues. Believing and blaspheming anyway Cissy understood intrinsically. There was no true blasphemy without belief, the kind of belief that Amanda had.

One of Amanda's favorite Bible verses was what Dede called the hot-water imperative, Revelation 3:16. "You are neither cold or hot," Amanda would say, "and hell is full of the lukewarm." God's contempt was for those neither cold nor hot, the ones He would spit out of His mouth, the ones like Cissy and Dede, and probably Delia. Lukewarm was the word for them all, Cissy knew, but Revelation seemed a reprise of the Old Testament God, the one who saw no problem when Lot's daughters were thrown to the roughnecks on the streets of Sodom. For mercy or understanding they would have to go to Jesus. The last big family fight had taken place when Dede had gotten stoned and started casting the made-for-television version of the Bible.

"Alan Alda as Jesus," Dede suggested. "But he's too old. Maybe Timothy Hutton or Richard Gere, one of those sensitive guys who has issues with his daddy."

Amanda had gone blue in the face. "Hell won't be hot enough for you," she said. "The devil will have to dig you a special pit and pack it with charcoal."

No, even pregnant and exhausted, Amanda had no lukewarm in her. Her notion of Jesus was the Christ who chased the moneylenders out of the temple. At Tabernacle Baptist there was a painted glass figure of Jesus, backlit by 60-watt bulbs that retracted into the ceiling when baptisms were being performed. It was a pastel Jordan River that picked up the murky green paint from the baptismal font below. At Amanda's wedding the painting had been pulled up into the ceiling near the brighter light, and Jesus' features were foreshortened into a comic mask, the cheeks too pink and the eyes obviously mascara'd—like a rock star in a music video with his arms open wide and sweat streaking down. Female, Cissy had thought when she saw that painted glass image. Jesus looked oddly female. Get Sigourney Weaver, she had almost said to Dede—get some dark-haired, hot-eyed woman to play Jesus. That might have upset Dede as much as it would have Amanda.

Female, Cissy thought, every time she tilted her head back into the chilly drafts that swept through the outer passages at Little Mouth. The dark was female and God was dark. God was dangerous, big, frightening, mysterious, and female. And blasphemous. Sometimes Cissy wished she could explain to Amanda how she thought about the divine. Not biblical but familial. Not Jehovah, but Delia with her head thrown back and that raw soaring song pouring out of her open mouth. That was spiritual, that was the power of the

Most High. But how could Cissy tell anyone about that? After fighting so long and so bitterly with Delia, how could she talk about any of that?

Amanda's God was not Cissy's God. Amanda's God counted sins and dealt out penance. Cissy's God breathed righteousness and fire. Amanda's God awarded fat babies and back porches. Cissy's God was the pure risk of some impossible expiation—Jesus on the Cross or the body in extremis, the chance of redemption in the awful dark. Her God was a grin in the darkness, the agony that rode her shoulders when she swam so far her muscles gave out, the great jolt that went through her when Dede wrecked the Datsun. Every time Cissy changed over into her mud-heavy boots and old clothes for another trip underground, she felt the anticipation of another encounter with the mystery. Probably, she told herself, God had to hide in caves these days.

In the dark anything seemed possible. Anything could be born there. The cave was a dim, curving stage full of unseen motion. In that dark Cissy was not Baptist or Pentecostal but surely beloved of God. The rocks waiting at Cissy's feet made her think of falling, and falling did not scare her at all. Climbing shale required absolute concentration, putting the feet exactly right, moving slowly and never allowing a slip. Controlling her body that way made Cissy yearn to stand up, throw her arms wide, and shout out loud. And the act of not doing so created a sense of power held back, a constant tingling sensation at the nape of her neck. In the cave Cissy could feel what she might do, what might happen, her body hurtled against the stone walls, or the walls themselves coming down inexorably on her fragile flesh, pushing her up into God's embrace, a mystery of darkness and glory. In the cathedral elegance of Little Mouth's third chamber, Cissy lifted her head and felt a breeze whisper past her cheek. God or ghost, Clint or Randall, the sweating innocent dead or the burning terror of a lifelong desire. Someone climbed behind her, smelling of smoke and her daddy's tequila. Someone ghostly and resentful coughed hollowly, whispered Delia's name, and breathed on Cissy's neck. Every echo wheezed. Every rockfall sounded a bass note. Jesus, magic, or death—anything was possible in a cave.

Cissy moved through the cave like a woman in a dream, loving the sharp taste of her own fear when the rope slid across the rock surface, the steady, distant sound of water dripping, the heat of the other women's sudden tempers. Every time Jean shouted at Mim, the rock would reverberate and Cissy would straighten her body to take that shout into her belly, to let it shake her inside and out. The beloved of God would shout like that, unhesitating and unafraid. Cissy opened her mouth and felt the echoes resound against her teeth. For their open, unafraid shouts, Cissy loved Jean and Mim completely. Love heated her blood, speeded her heart. For the first time in her life, she did not feel alone.

Her family didn't understand it, the usually reticent Cissy showing an interest in something besides books. Dede barely noticed, but Delia and Amanda found rare common ground in their concern over Cissy's renewed enthusiasm for caving and her equally surprising friendship with those strange girls.

"You're always going somewhere or just back these days," Delia said with a frown.

"What you trying to prove?" Amanda demanded. "You never talk to us anymore."

As if I ever did, Cissy thought, but said nothing.

Mim kicked roughly at the bundle of muddy clothes she had just stripped off after the third trip to Little Mouth. "Ugh. Red mud and yellow clay. Washing that out is going to be worse than washing Daddy's dog."

Jean laughed. "I say we put them in that barrel in the backyard and just let water run through them for a day or two. We put them right in the machine, we'll burn out the motor."

"Maybe use that spray nozzle we got to wash the car."

"Yeah, that, or get the guys at the fire station to let us use theirs."

Cissy had nodded and laughed along with them. Talking about

laundry and the sticky mud was part of the ritualized end of their expeditions. The jokes—the same ones told over and over, the same complaints—were a way to leave behind the concentrated exhilaration and fear of being underground. Laughter, nervous shaking, and slow relaxation—the aftermath of the expeditions was as predictable as the trips themselves were not. They did not talk about their claustrophobic terror or the appalling sound that skin made sliding across rock, or about the chafing of the helmet strap under the chin, or the way the slippery crawl spaces closed in around their shoulders, and the damp-rock smell clung to their clothes. Like drinking hot coffee and eating from discount bags of broken cookies, complaining about the filth of caving was a safe way of boasting of what they had done.

"Look at me! I am clay from head to toe."

"Lord, I got that grit in my hair!"

"Goddamn, we are just filthy!"

The apartment Jean and Mim shared was comfortably messy, books scattered about among clothes, shoes, and empty soda cans. Whenever they came back from a caving trip, Mim and Jean would strip in the entry between the back porch and the kitchen. All the muddy clothes they pulled off went into an empty tub by the door. Then they took a shower together in the little bathroom off the kitchen. Cissy would watch them with self-conscious awe. Trying to be casual, she would pull her own muddy clothes off in the entry, but slowly enough as never to be naked in front of Jean and Mim. As soon as they were out of the room, she would speed up, toweling herself down roughly and dressing in clean old clothes she kept just for the trip home. She would sit at the kitchen table drinking spring water and listening to Jean and Mim laughing under the shower. Eventually, she figured, she would get so used to the girls that she would take a shower herself—just walk in naked and take her turn under the hot water. It must be wonderful, to be so at home in your body that you didn't hesitate to stride around with your butt bare naked and your nipples out where anyone could see. Jean and Mim's carelessness made Cissy seem even stranger to herself.

Cissy had her own system for getting the dirt out of her caving clothes. Delia's laundry room had served as a photo lab when Dede was dating the boy who took all the pictures for the yearbook. They had broken up the double sink and mounted a third so that water ran down from the top one through the next two. Although Dede's infatuation with the boy was short-lived, Cissy had found the sinks very useful for hand laundry. There had been a moment when she thought about offering to take Mim and Jean's clothes back with her, to do their laundry as she did Delia's and Dede's, and Amanda's before she moved out. Before the words could come out of her mouth, Cissy stopped herself.

No, she didn't want to be that person with Mim and Jean. The Cissy who did her family's laundry was someone she did not want them to know. She wouldn't be able to laugh the same way if she became the person Delia and her sisters believed her to be. Neither Mim nor Jean teased her about her silences or her habit of dropping her hair down over her left eye, or about her shyness or her hesitant way of answering questions. For them she was not weird Cissy but simply Cissy. They behaved as if she were exactly like them, and because of that, Cissy began to imagine she was. The things they talked about on the way to and from the caves were the everyday, the expected—how long it took to drive from Cayro to Little Mouth, the grade and weight of rope available at the Bartow County army-navy store, the hopelessness of getting up after spending a day and a half underground. For Cissy, talking to Jean and Mim was like slipping on a second skin. It was luxurious not being Delia's daughter for a little while. She joined in with them to laugh at her own muddy jeans.

"Feel this. I think my pants have gained twenty pounds."

"You got rocks in those pockets?"

"Yeah, when I was sliding. Collected a couple of pounds of gravel between my pants and my ass."

Jean and Mim laughed, and Cissy basked in the glow of their appreciation. They were so different from her sisters.

"You are from another planet," Amanda had told Cissy repeatedly. "There is not an ounce of normal human being in you."

Cissy did not argue. She thought Amanda was right. Maybe Delia was not her real mama after all. Maybe she was like those changelings in the storybooks, a fairy-tale creature exchanged for Delia's real daughter. What else would explain how different she was from everyone she knew?

"You an't *that* different," Nolan always said. But Nolan? If there were changelings, then he was another one. The two of them were the next best thing to aliens ever seen in Cayro, Georgia.

Delia's old washing machine banged when it was overloaded. To get it to do sheets at all, Cissy had to sit on top of it, the weight of her body providing the necessary ballast as the engine churned and spun. She would brace herself with one hand on the cinder-block wall and one leg extended so her foot pressed the metal shelving by the door. Buttressed like that, the machine would hum easily, and one of her hands was free to hold a book or change the channel on the radio or grip the side of the washer when the load became unbalanced again and started to shimmy beneath her thighs.

Cissy liked the way it felt, that machine heated and pounding under her. In the steamy heat of the laundry room, she fell into a reverie so intense she could not say afterward what she had been thinking. She would load the machine and climb up as soon as it started to bang, becoming instantly transformed, like a dervish who has been spinning for so many years that he can fall into meditation effortlessly. The steamy air exuded rapture. The heat seeped mystery.

"You get off on it, don't you? Giant vibrator under your butt?" Dede accused once, and ran off to tell Delia, who ignored her so determinedly that it was clear she too thought she knew what Cissy had been doing. Cissy imagined what she must look like—riding that washing machine, pink-faced and glassy-eyed, legs spread and knees flexed, feet tucked up on the shelves across from her—but what she was doing was nothing so mundane. Not everything was about sex.

The laundry room was Cissy's retreat, that cinder-block chamber with its permanent scent of detergent and bleach and a floral overlay of fabric softener. More caustic odors came from the plastic milk crates of cleaning fluids stacked in one corner next to old bottles and cans of ammonia, paint thinner, and kerosene.

"None of that can go in the garbage, you know," Amanda complained to Delia. "You got to haul it out to the dump. Get rid of it before one of my boys gets into it."

"Cissy will take care of it," Delia said. "Cissy keeps track of things out there."

Cissy did not haul everything out until the spring Delia redid the house. With Nolan's help, she pulled the shelves and the machines away from the walls, washed the place down, then set up a fan to dry it out for a day. She put on two coats of white paint, flat white for the ceiling, a glossy oil-based paint for the walls, to resist mildew. She scrubbed the floor with a bleach solution and left it unpainted. Afterward the room was like a temple, purified and clean. There was nothing for the bugs to eat, no trash in the corners to gather dust and spiderwebs. When Dede or Amanda brought in boxes of junk or bags of old clothes, Cissy would take them directly to the dump. Nothing was allowed to remain if it didn't belong. What Cissy could not say in words she said in that laundry room, in those baskets of spotless white shorts and undershirts, delicate underwear in net bags, immaculate sheets for the beds, perfectly folded towels to stack in the closet, jeans bleached down to a pearly cotton that caressed the skin. Clean clothing, shirts and blouses and underwear made new under Cissy's hands, all of it breathed the longing she would not acknowledge aloud, the family connection that seemed so tenuous everywhere outside that room—the one place in which she knew where everything was and how it got there.

But laundry was part of home, that other reality, the reality that did not include Mim and Jean and Cissy's easy laughter with them. The only time Cissy felt herself to be the dutiful daughter, Delia's little girl, was when she did the laundry. It was another life, that yearning for the safe girl-child's place. In the life she wanted, she cared for nothing outside the reach of muscle or sinew. In the caves Cissy would brace a hip, bend a knee, or reach above her head to push her body forward, and see Mim's eyes on her over Jean's shoulder gleaming in pleased admiration. There she was nobody's baby girl. She was a grown woman, strong and able. Cissy feared bringing the scattered parts of her life together—Amanda's contempt, Delia's confusion, Nolan's precise friendship, Dede's caustic jokes, Mim and Jean walking naked through their kitchen. Between them all, who was Cissy? What was possible for her and who would she be—the proud Cissy who climbed down in the dark or the timid one who hid in the laundry room?

After their last caving expedition, they came out of Little Mouth at night so grubby Jean refused to let them in her car until they changed. They all stripped down by the trunk, Cissy hiding her blush under her loose hair, grateful the dark covered so much. When Mim poured water over her naked shoulders and Jean waited to towel her back, Cissy tilted her face up to the sky and felt the air against her skin like a satin weight, the pulsing energy of her bloodstream singing to her brain happy to be alive.

She had crawled down into darkness and out again, risked everything and come up into the starlight caked with mud and sand, bat shit and ancient dust. Washing the mud away was baptism. Cissy unbuttoned the second layer of thrift-store trousers and pulled off her dirty boots. Like Mim. Like Jean. She moved with deliberate unconsciousness, not looking down to see her own nakedness, turning to scrub Jean's back and rub it dry with a rough towel. The muscles under her skin could be trusted.

Pulling on clean, dry jeans that smelled of fabric softener and sunshine, Cissy laughed out loud. Every time she came out of the cave dark, she remembered the Sunday morning television shows she had watched when they first came back to Cayro. Between the sermons there were sermonettes, little one-act plays in which moral lessons were demonstrated with brutal efficiency—the cursing father developed throat cancer, the fornicator lost a child. Caving was like that. If you put your foot down wrong, you would find retribution. If you ignored the dust, it would choke your light. If you laced your boots too loosely, your ankle might turn or the wet find its way into your socks. If you sinned against the rock, the dark might call your name. But if you persevered, you would come out into the light. Everything would be made right. You would know with unquestioning certainty who and what you were.

Chapter 16

In the years following her husband's death, Nadine Reitower broke her hip three times. She hadn't been on the second floor of their house since Nolan started at the junior college. "She never will again," Dr. Campbell told Nolan. "She'll be in that wheelchair till the day she dies." For all that, Nadine was a happy woman. Something happened to her with the third fall, something terrible and wonderful. A little stroke, a moment of grace, Nolan called it, and maybe God did have something to do with it, the God that made fish without eyes and two-headed calves.

Nolan's mama went a little bit more than a minute and a half without breathing. The paramedics put her on oxygen in the ambulance, and she came to with her mouth open and her tongue out.

"Like a baby bird," Nolan told Cissy. "Like a happy baby bird."

A hungry baby bird.

It was a life change for a woman who had never consumed a full thousand calories in a day for thirty years. Her husband and her boys were fat, but Nadine made a religion out of being thin. Rail-thin, starved skinny, a clear-soup-and-celery-stick life. She was painfully proud of the way her hips and collarbone protruded, smugly contemptuous of her wide, soft men even as she fed them all the food she would never eat. Nolan's mama believed men should be big and women small, and she was sharp-tongued about it. She was sharp-tongued by nature anyway, given to cutting remarks and sudden cruelty, though she believed herself kindly. It was just that she knew how things should be and the world so rarely matched her convictions. Nadine Reitower made gravy but never ate it, baked cakes, pinched the crusts of pies and steamed puddings. She fed her men like a sacrament and starved herself matter-of-factly, until her bones went lacy and fine and fractured in thin, spidery lines.

"Should have put her on calcium and had her walking more for the last decade," Dr. Campbell grumbled. "Should have seen what she was coming to." He was chagrined because he had believed Nadine to be supremely healthy, anticipating her visits every time her name appeared on his charts—that fine-boned, ethereal creature he had almost adored. She was a devoted mother, a happy wife, maybe a little bossy and difficult now and then, from what people told him, but no more than should be expected. Her husband's death changed all that, and Dr. Campbell finally met the Nadine Reitower everyone else knew. From the doctor's perspective, the woman he admired had been supplanted by one he could barely stand to examine, an indignant, contemptuous woman grown suddenly old and fragile, one who told him he was a fool right to his face. When that creature altered again, he stopped talking with any certainty. What they had was what they had. What might come next was completely past his ability to predict.

"Nolan," Nadine said, waking up after that last ambulance trip. "Nolan, I'm hungry." And so she was. Nadine's disposition changed with that minute and a half of stillness, with the acquisition of the wheelchair, the ramps, and the visiting nurse. Her baby-bird mouth smiled often, and she waved at people from the porch, calling out their names.

Cissy. Dede. Amanda. Anyone who passed. Even Delia. Nadine liked everybody now, and the plumper she got, the more she said so. In a minute and a half, Nolan's life was remade.

Nadine Reitower was a new woman and everyone knew it. What was not so quickly apparent was the change in Nolan. Only Cissy seemed to see it, perhaps because she saw him so regularly. As Nadine widened in her chair, Nolan seemed to relax and brighten. His late growth spurt intensified. He started doing an exercise routine with a set of weights his daddy had kept in the garage. He swore it had nothing to do with his last run-in with Dede, when she told him she would never go out with a boy who looked like a biscuit on legs.

"I just feel like it," Nolan insisted to Cissy.

"Naaa, come on. You're working at this. Damn, Nolan, you're coming close to having a real physique!" Cissy teased him so relentlessly she was surprised he did not take offense.

"It's practical, that's all," he said. "I have to lift a woman who is just about a dead weight, and heavier all the time. Getting her from bed to bath to chair has been just about breaking my back. Her doc told me I had to get a whole lot stronger or I'd wind up with a hernia. Only other choice is to hire a nurse full-time, and the visiting nurse is all we can manage."

"Uh-huh."

"Besides, I need to do it efficiently and quickly. Moving Mama is not something you want to do slow. You want to get it done fast." Nolan's face was very pink.

"Yeah?" Cissy was curious. She had never seen him look so uncomfortable.

"She giggles."

"Giggles?"

"God, yes." The pink of Nolan's face went a deeper shade, almost rose red at the cheekbones. He closed his eyes. "Me and the nurse go to pick her up, put her in the bath, and she puts her hands up over her eyes and starts to giggle. She says, 'Don't look, son, don't look,' and she just giggles all the way through. Naked and all, and I never seen her naked before in my life. She would have died before she let me see her like that. Now she's teasing me and laughing. God, if she was as embarrassed as I am, it would be awful. I suppose if she wasn't so cheerful, I wouldn't be able to stand it at all. But even so." He stopped, and Cissy could not think of a thing to say.

Nolan kept his eyes shut tight. There was more, a lot more, that he could not say to Cissy. While he was working out to get stronger, he was also trying to persuade Nadine to diet—a project that was awful for both of them. The new Nadine hated diets, hated anything but food fat-rich and tasty. And Nolan loved this new version of his mama, this extraordinary woman licking her fingers and laughing out loud, wheeling her chair around the kitchen, humming along to

287

his music, telling him how handsome he was, how proud he made her, and repeating that to anyone who happened to stop by.

But the doctor kept telling Nolan that bone mass did not replenish. It would not come back, and another break could kill Nadine. "She gets much bigger, those bones will cave in all the quicker," the doctor said firmly. "Son, you got to be the man."

Nolan could see what he meant. Nadine's body was not designed to carry the weight she was adding, no matter the gentle open mouth that only wanted to chew and smile. The bigger Nadine got, the greater the risk. If Nolan did not take care, he would lose his mama, this new creature he loved almost more than his music or his dreams.

Nolan took care and steadily pumped his muscles stronger. He invented games to help Nadine exercise safely, made adjustments in the kitchen while she was at physical therapy with the nurse. Sugar substitute, no-sodium salt, fresh vegetables, low-fat soups. He refused to bring home biscuits no matter how Nadine cried, and finally used her mother love against her. "Mama," he pleaded, "you have to help me. How will I ever find a wife if you don't help me shape up?"

Slowly, steadily, Nolan lengthened and thinned while Nadine endured, mourning the loss of butterfat, ice cream, and chocolate pies, but admiring the alteration in her big, soft boy. She watched as Nolan's shoulders became broad and muscled, his hips and legs slim and powerful. He looked like a football player, a quarterback, strong and handsome, maneuvering his mama's fragile body as carefully and intently as he played his clarinet.

"Such a handsome boy I've got," Nadine told people when they came to visit. They nodded offhandedly, and then they looked over and realized that she was right. Big, strange, shy Nolan was not the boy he had been. Big, strong Nolan was a man lifting his mama out of that chair, feeding her orange sections and apple slices, dropping his glance when women looked at him, playing his music so sweetly that half of Cayro knew he could go anywhere in the world.

The one who did not look was Dede Windsor. The one Nolan

would do anything for, go anywhere to please, never glanced up at the porch where he waited.

"Oh, baby," Nadine sighed when she saw him looking down the road. Her face was tender, her eyes wise. "Oh, baby," she said, in that voice that could break his heart. Nolan pulled her up and held her to his chest. He thought, If my mama could become this, then anything can happen. Someday what I want might be.

"Someday," he said out loud, and Nadine pressed her mouth to his salt-sweet skin. Her boy tasted like apple pie, like a sugar dumpling made to bless her tongue.

After her sons were born, Amanda became obsessed with trying once again to organize another Christian Girls' Coalition. Her new emphasis was the high school itself, the girls who smoked outside Dede's convenience store and laughed into their palms when Amanda came in with her boys.

"They act like they're not afraid of God or anything," Amanda complained every time she came into the store.

"They're not." Dede was the only person allowed to smoke in the store itself, but she only seemed to actually do it when someone she did not like came in. As soon as Amanda put her hand on the metal bar that held the Camel Red Pack sign, Dede would pull out her pack and start rolling a cigarette between her fingers. "Except for me. All of them are just a little scared of me, and I work that. I work it for all I'm worth."

"They should learn a little respect."

"Oh, they're learning." Dede smiled slow and flicked ashes in the direction of the muscular dystrophy can. She kept her eyes on little Michael. "They're learning, I promise you." Dede knew why her sister came in, knew that Amanda wanted her to put up one of her little posters. Under her arm Amanda carried a set of the cardboard prints that featured Jesus with the crown of thorns biting into his brow and one finger uplifted to point skyward right in front of his nose. Dede actually had one of those up for a while. It made her giggle at the idea of a Son of God who would pick his nose—the kind of savior she could appreciate. But the joke was no longer so satisfying. Amanda seemed more and more to have lost her focus, to come into the store to buy a can of evaporated milk instead of to lecture Dede on the prospects of hellfire and damnation. Some days Dede missed the old Amanda, the one that pulled over the rack of adult magazines after some of the boys had deliberately pulled down the brown paper sheathes that were supposed to spare the Christian eye.

Nadine ate the strawberries Nolan had left out for her breakfast, but first she rolled them in soft butter and dragged them through the sugar dish. Smiling in the morning light with that butter on her lips, she was careful not to wake Tacey Brithouse, who lay asleep across her notebooks on the kitchen table. The rich cinnamon of Tacey's bare arms glowed in the sunshine coming in the windows. Tacey had moved in with the Reitowers after hitting her mama's boyfriend in the head with a garden rake—a story she was happy to tell anyone. She was working at Biscuit World at the time and occasionally helping Nolan out with Nadine. One morning she came into Biscuit World covered with dirt and blood and unable to stop shaking. It took Nolan a good hour to calm her down and find out what had happened: the boyfriend had burned one of her journals, and she had tried to knock his head in.

Nolan went over to talk to Tacey's mama, Althea, but the woman was full of outrage. She tossed a box of Tacey's clothes at him and told him to "keep her away from here till she's ready to apologize." Since then Tacey had been taking care of Nadine in exchange for room and board, moving into Nadine's old bedroom upstairs now that Nadine was using the sewing room on the first floor. Tacey had a partial scholarship to Spelman for the fall, and had a stack of unfinished manuscripts in a box under her bed. "You wait," she told Nolan. "Someday you'll tell everybody you knew me when." Nolan did not doubt her.

Tacey was supposed to make sure Nadine had a good breakfast

before she left for school, but she had a tendency to stay up late reading or writing in her notebooks, and often napped while Nadine poured sugar on her fruit or slathered butter across her toast. They liked each other well enough, though sometimes Tacey could barely believe the things the old white woman said. There was, for example, Nadine's assumption that Tacey was sleeping with the garbage men, the mailman, her teachers, and the preacher at her church, Little River Methodist.

"Black girls don't have to wait like us white girls do," Nadine remarked one morning not long after Tacey moved in. "My mama told me. It's in the blood, all that heat from Africa."

"That right?" Tacey drawled.

Nadine nodded. "Oh, you know. Black girls get to do everything. Me, I never got to do nothing." Nadine smacked her lips and sighed. "If I'd been born black, I could have been sucking men's titties since I was twelve."

"And why would you want to do that?"

Nadine looked surprised. " 'Cause they taste so good. Men's titties taste better than women's do, you know."

"Really? I didn't know that."

"Oh, course you did, with all the men you been with."

"Mrs. Reitower, I have never been with a man."

"Oh, you don't have to humor me. If I could get up out of this chair, I'd go sit naked on the garbage cans in the morning just to see if the boys would let me suck on their shoulders and put my heels up on their hips." She sighed again, a perfect heartbroken sigh.

Tacey snorted and shook her head. "Mrs. Reitower, you are scary."

"Oh, you should have known me before," Nadine said. "I was something, yes. I was."

Nadine liked to listen to the stories Tacey wrote, long romantic tales of black women fighting to become rich and famous and succeeding beyond their dreams. "Like that woman, what's her name," Nadine told Nolan. "Tacey makes you think you are just right there."

Tacey laughed. "That's me, the black Judith Krantz, Danielle Steel, Rosamunde what's her name. Lord, Mrs. Reitower, I'm going to have to read you some good black women, give you some better reference points."

For weeks Tacey read her favorites out loud while Nadine did her ankle lifts and stretching exercises. Sometimes Nadine would stop and say, "Read me that part again." Soon she took to mixing quotes from Alice Walker and Gloria Naylor with her standbys from the Bible. "Lord, son, the things I never knew," she kept saying. Nolan smiled. He liked to lie on his bed and listen to his mama and Tacey read together. In his dreams it was their chorus that lulled him along, their antiphony and Dede's laugh.

Sometimes Tacey brought Nadine little fried pies when she came home from school, and Nadine sneaked away to eat them in the bathroom with the door closed so that Nolan wouldn't see. Tacey knew she shouldn't do it, but the hunger in Nadine's eye was hard to bear.

"You stay out of the sugar dish," she scolded Nadine.

"Oh, I love you better than sugar, Tacey," Nadine promised.

"Sure you do, honey, and if you could fry me in butter you'd love me even more."

Dede loved her box cutter. Razor-sharp, it was not supposed to be used on things like boxes of cigarettes and candy—paper- and plastic-wrapped items that it could slice as easily as the cardboard. A little nick in a cigarette pack meant stale cigarettes and returns to be written up. But Dede wrapped her cutter in blue duct tape from her little hardware display and gouged her initials in the handle. She used it for everything, the perishable items as well as the boxes of canned goods.

"What I need is a holster for it," Dede told Cissy. "Need a holster for my weapon. Someone messes with me, I'll cut them bad."

The cutter was in her hand when Billy Tucker came in the door that Thursday morning in September. Dede was kneeling on the

floor, her knees cushioned by cutoff carton tops. She had been opening boxes and stamping prices all morning. First of the month,
Thursdays around ten-thirty or eleven, after the late-morning rush
was when she restocked. Candy and cigarettes she did weekly from
boxes she had already opened and put in the cooler. Bread came in
twice a week, along with milk and beer. Tampax, specialty perish-
ables, chips and crackers, and paper products were the secondary
sellers, which came in on the monthly schedule—Thursday morning
and first of the month, the days when the cutter was never out of
Dede's hand.

"Billy!" Dede was surprised to see him but not displeased. Although they had broken up, she still liked the way he looked. "What
you doing down here?"

Billy wore a work shirt with "Chevron" emblazoned above his
name on the pocket. He smiled and produced a little silver .38. "I'm
gonna to kill you ass," he said, and extended the gun straight out in
front of him, the trigger line-sighted directly between Dede's eyes.

"Lord, Billy!" Dede's hand tightened on the box cutter, but she
was more than six feet away from him and her weapon was no good
at all. She watched his fingers move to cock the gun, the little metal
piece under his thumb pulling back and clicking into place. Dede
shifted her gaze to Billy's face. "I didn't even know you were mad,"
she said.

His eyes flooded with tears, and his lips pulled back in a grimace.
"Course you didn't, bitch. You an't looked twice at me all these last
few months. You say we gonna be friends. You say we always gonna
be special, and then you call me but the once. And it's 'cause you
want to buy some grass! What am I supposed to think, huh?" He
shook the gun. "What am I supposed to think?" Dede started to
come up off her knees, and he waved the gun wildly.

"Don't you move. You stay right there. You look at me now,
bitch. You look at me."

"I'm looking," Dede said. "I'm looking at you, Billy. You say
what you mean. I'll listen to anything you say." She pressed the blade
of the cutter down through the cardboard she was kneeling on right

into the linoleum floor, keeping her eyes fixed on Billy's and her expression as gentle as possible. She had to think of something fast, but for the first time in Dede's life, nothing came to mind.

Althea Brithouse stopped in at Biscuit World that Thursday morning a little after 10:00 to see Nolan. She had been out to the house twice but missed him each time and had not wanted to speak to Tacey. After her anger subsided and the sting of indignation eased, Althea found herself worrying about her youngest. Next to Tacey, her boys were simple, she thought, sweet-natured and easygoing; they were just like their father, and like their father they knew exactly how to charm Althea and get what they wanted. For Jamal, that meant early enlistment in the navy. For David, it was permission to move to Atlanta and work for Althea's brother in his garden center.

Thank God David hadn't wanted to quit school. Sidney had never finished school, and if he hadn't been such a good husband and such a hardworking man, the Lord knew what kind of life they would have had. It was from him that David got his green thumb, that ancestral ability to suck a little dirt and know exactly what nutrients the soil required. A decade after the accident that killed him, Sidney's garden was still thriving, even though Althea had done no more than turn on the sprinkler every now and then.

It was a pity there was so little of Sidney in Tacey. The girl was her mama all over again, but smarter, Althea admitted. Tacey was the smartest of them all, and so headstrong she drove Althea to distraction.

"Mother-daughter stuff," Althea told Nolan. "It's old and complicated and predictable as spring. Why, I didn't speak to my mama for fifteen years, from the time I left school to the week Tacey's daddy died. It don't mean we don't love each other. I love my girl, I just can't stand her right now. Which don't mean I want to see her in trouble or wouldn't kill the man who would do her wrong." The look she gave Nolan was level and sharp.

Nolan nodded, unsure whether he was being threatened or reassured. "Tacey's in no trouble, ma'am," he said. "She's been saving my life, if you want to know the truth. She's helping me with my mama, and I promise you she has not missed a day of school."

"I know." Althea pursed her lips and looked around. "I checked." She had also checked on Nolan while she was at it. From what she heard, he did not seem the type to mess with her child. People said he was in love with some girl worked at the mini-market, said he was Christian and reliable and no worse than she should expect. But people might say anything. Althea had wanted to look the boy in the eye.

"I heard she wasn't working here anymore, that she was working at your house." Tacey had originally taken the job at Biscuit World to earn money for college, and while Althea knew her girl was bright enough to get a scholarship, she also knew no scholarship would pay for everything. Tacey had explained her carefully plotted scheme—the cash savings account that Althea promised to match. It was one of the things they had fought about, money and what Althea did and did not understand. Sometimes Tacey treated her mama as if she were dumb as dirt and nowhere near as trustworthy.

"She earns as much working for me." Nolan was thinking about Tacey's brothers. Big, Tacey had sworn. Her brothers were big as football players and seriously fast. Nolan didn't want Althea to mis-understand his arrangement with Tacey. "A little more, actually," he added. "And she gets along good with my mama—which I got to tell you is pretty much a miracle. Mama's been—well, different, since she had her last stroke."

Nolan felt the blush that crept over his face but could do nothing about it. "Different" was such an inadequate word to describe Na-dine. Nothing short of a novel would have done her justice these days. Alternately maddening and endearing, Nadine was totally ab-sorbed in Althea's daughter even as she continued to appall them both by saying impossibly rude things as sweetly as she professed her love.

"Strokes are awful." Althea ignored the blush. Boy was ashamed of his mama, that was only to be expected. "My granddad had a terrible time after his stroke. Your mama crippled much?"

"Pretty much. She broke her hip. She's had a bad time since my daddy died."

Nolan was relaxing. From Tacey he had the impression that Althea was terror incarnate, but this plainspoken woman reminded him of Dede's mama, Delia. She had the same watchful reserve, and she obviously cared deeply about her daughter.

"Tacey is wonderful with Mama. It's like I said, she's just saving my life."

"Yes, well." Althea hugged her pocketbook to her midriff. "I just wanted to be sure she was all right. The way she took off, I wasn't sure where she would wind up. Tacey has a temper, you know. Like me, I suppose." She smiled.

"Yes ma'am. She sure has a sense of herself. She knows what she wants."

"Oh, she does. She does." Althea smiled again. "Don't you tell her I came around to talk to you. Better she should just go on the way she is, come home when she feels like it. Probably when she can show me up some way, boast of how well she's done. She gets that big scholarship check, she'll come around to show it to me."

"Yes ma'am."

Nolan was exhausted. After Tacey's mother left, he had the run of his career at Biscuit World and sold out earlier than ever before. Even his daddy never closed so early. He checked his watch twice, and it confirmed the record both times. It was just eleven o'clock and he was on his way home.

"Damn," Nolan sighed happily. For a change he might even get in a nap. At the corner of Starrett and Terrill, he paused briefly. He always stopped in at the convenience store on Thursdays, said a few words to Dede, and then picked up some club soda and the little giveaway papers. Nadine and Tacey liked to read the ads. They swore they were going to start hitting the flea markets as soon as Nadine got stronger. That wasn't likely, but Nadine loved the lists of what people were offering for sale.

"A full layette set," she'd read. "No more babies coming to that house." Pool tables, "like-new" exercise equipment, and elaborate stereo systems prompted her to speculate on the kind of people who were moving into Cayro. "People who buy stuff they an't ever gonna use. People from Atlanta or Nashville, that's who we're getting. A few more years and no one will recognize this town."

Nolan wiped his neck and rocked his head from side to side, listening to the muscles pop. His mama was right, he thought. Things were changing so fast. Some days he felt as if he were constantly losing ground. He should go home and do his exercises, take a hot bath and lie down for a while. Get some rest. He could drop by the store later, when he wasn't so tired. And if he got in a good long nap, he could try the sheet music Delia's friend Rosemary had sent from California, a Tone Kwas duet for clarinets. If he had time, he could try each of the parts. He glanced over at the lot and saw only one truck outside the store, a Chevron emblem on the door.

"Billy Tucker. Oh, hell." Nolan almost went on by, but then he remembered how busy Dede could get in the afternoons. He rocked his head again. "All right," he said to Billy Tucker's truck as he pulled into the lot. He could see Billy's green shirt just inside the door as he climbed out of his car and walked toward the store.

On the third step he saw the gun. Nolan stopped. Billy Tucker was standing in Dede's convenience store with a gun in his hand.

"Oh, Lord," Nolan whispered.

He looked around quickly, up the road and back down toward Delia's place. There was no one around, no cars in sight. Nolan looked back to the store. He saw Billy take a step forward. The gun in his hand was angled down. Nolan went forward another two steps and saw Dede on the floor, her face turned up and expressionless, her gaze intent on Billy's face.

There was a shout and Nolan flinched. Billy was yelling. The gun in his hand wavered and shook. Billy's head rocked and swung. There were mumbled unintelligible sounds coming through the glass facade of the store. Cursing. Nolan listened to Billy cursing in a deadened monotone. He's gone crazy, Nolan thought. Billy Tucker has gone crazy and he's going to kill Dede.

"I said stay down, bitch!" The words were muffled and peculiar through the glass doors, almost rubbery and echoing as if coming from the other end of a tunnel.

Nolan moved forward carefully, quietly. A bird was singing in a tree at the edge of the lot. Dede's face was still upturned and empty. Billy had lowered the gun a little, and was holding it now in front of his belly, the sight still centered on Dede.

"You don't give a shit about me," he screamed. "You just always thinking about your silly-ass self."

Nolan put his hand on the right double door. A wave of dizziness swung over him. He looked down and saw his shadow, small and hunched, just visible in the patch of sunlight that shone through the glass-paneled door. He had no idea what he was going to do. I'm going to get killed, he thought.

Nolan opened the door.

Billy was completely focused on Dede. He was waiting for her face to show something, her eyes to widen or tear up or her mouth to twist. Something. He wanted to see his mark on her before he killed her. He wanted to know that she was afraid, that she knew who was doing this to her. In her next life, she'd take more care, he had thought, but that didn't make sense. God wouldn't let her out of hell once he sent her there.

Billy had been doing methedrine for three weeks. He had slept no more than two hours any night in weeks. He knew his boss was going to lay him off. He knew his daddy thought he was a damn fool. Margaret Grimsley had told him he was sick in the head, and ugly besides. His mama had suggested that he talk to their preacher, and this morning when he had stood in the bathroom looking at his face in the mirror, the solution to everything had become crystal-clear. He would shoot her. He would. And afterward he would shoot himself. Then he would sleep. Then he would sleep forever. I want to sleep,

Billy thought. God, I want to sleep. He felt the air move behind him, the door opening.

"You have to decide what you treasure," Mr. Reitower had told Nolan at four in the morning a few months before he died. They were at Biscuit World and the ovens had just made the low booming sound that signaled the gas was flowing and heat would soon start pouring against the baking racks.

"You need to take the time when you have the time, 'cause things happen sometimes so suddenly you won't have time to think. Like your mama and me." Mr. Reitower had leaned over the flour-dusted counter and given his son a slow inclination of his head. "I knew what she was like. I knew she had a temper. I knew that being married to her wouldn't be no bed of lilies, no easy thing at all, but I took the time to look close at her. I knew her. You understand what I'm saying?" He had nodded hard once as if everything he meant were plain. "That woman would take all of me and I was ready. It sure is something wonderful to know that—to know the woman you love as well as you know yourself. And the thing is, to know a woman deep, you got to know yourself. You got to know what you need. I needed someone just like your mama." He smiled wide. "Someone to kick my ass and keep me moving. Which she has, Lord knows. She has."

Nolan nodded back at his daddy, unsure of himself a little. Did he know himself deep? Did he know what he needed? It was a hard thing to be sure about when what he wanted had always seemed so far from possible. Was Dede the right woman for him? She would never be a bed of lilies, that was sure. And she would be hard, she would be demanding. She would surely be a woman who would kick his ass and keep him moving. Was that what he needed? Never mind what he wanted, was that what he needed?

The moment before Nolan stepped through that door behind Billy Tucker, that conversation with his daddy replayed in his mind. The tone of his daddy's cheerful fatalistic assessment, the certainty and the rueful self-knowledge it implied—all that replayed and altered. Nolan knew then for the first time what his life was worth, what he would give it up to save. Maybe Dede Windsor would never love him the way he had always loved her, but loving her was the best of him. It shaped him and made sense of his life. Loving her validated the decisions he had made about his music, his mama, and Cayro. She was the measure and the purpose and the standard he had set himself. Dede was his deep knowledge. Dede was his treasure. If Billy Tucker killed him, it would be worth his life to save her.

"Confidence," Emmet said later. "You didn't hesitate, did you, son?"

"No sir." Nolan was shaking and trying not to let it show too much. He had started shaking once it was all over, once Billy was on the floor, mouth spurting blood and hands clamped to his wounded face, another wound slowly seeping down the front of his jeans where Dede's box cutter had slashed him as he fought them.

"Well, that's how you do it," Emmet wrote in his little notebook, his head bobbing as he spoke. "You got to move fast, no hesitation. Take 'em down fast and mean, and don't let nothing slow you in the process. I'd say you did it exactly right. Though coming in here in the first place was crazy. That gun was loaded and Billy sure looked ready to use it. Coming in here was the craziest thing you could have done, but if you were going to do it, well, you did it the right way." He slapped his little book against the flat of his hand.

"You understand what I am saying?"

Nolan nodded, thinking of his daddy and how he had asked the same thing. You understand what I am saying? Yes, he surely had. Nolan looked out at his car where Dede was sitting, smoking nonstop and doing her own version of the shake dance. God, he thought. What if I had not come in here? What if I had gone home? He shuddered once and saw Emmet smile.

"It's all right, son. No reason to be ashamed. I'd shake too. First time I faced a gun, I lost my lunch. You go home, son. Everything here is going to be fine. We'll take good care of little Billy. He an't going to be waving no guns around here no time soon. He looks like he learned something here today, just about passed out in the ambulance. You know, that boy looked like he hadn't slept this year."

Dede sat in Nolan's car and smoked a Marlboro. She kept looking up at the trees and feeling the sun on her lap. She had talked to Emmet twice already, and was finally slowly relaxing. Nolan, bless his heart, had brought her a Coke and left her alone. When her relief had shown up to take over the store, Nolan had even brought out the register slip for her to sign. Smart boy, she thought as she signed it. She never trusted anyone with her receipts. Then she watched Nolan walk away. He looked different, she thought. Hadn't he used to be smaller? When Nolan came back, she offered him a sip of her Coke.

"You all right now?" he asked her.

"No." Dede lit another Marlboro from the one that had almost burned down. "I just nearly died, you know."

"Yeah." Nolan nodded.

Dede took a drink from the Coke and grimaced. She only drank diet Coke, she'd have to tell him that. She looked at Nolan again. He was just sitting there looking at her. No moon eyes, no sweat, just grown-up and steady and calm.

"Didn't you think he would kill you?" she asked.

"I was too busy thinking he was going to kill you." Nolan looked up the street. "I called home. Nadine said to bring you up to the house. Said there is beer if you want some."

"Beer." Dede watched Nolan's face. His mouth, she thought. It used to be soft, lips always wet and bubbly, skin damp. Eyes. She looked up into his eyes. Dark amber and deep as night, they looked back at her. His mouth was set, closed and steady. God, she thought. Goddamn.

"I want more than beer."

"I could get that for you."

"Could you?"

"I could get you any damn thing you need."

"I bet you could." Dede looked at Nolan's hands where they rested on the steering wheel. Big and strong, with long fingers, they rested easily on the frayed rubber covering on the steering wheel. She remembered the way he had held Billy, the way he had spoken into Billy's ear. "I could kill you," he had said. "Don't make me."

"I'm glad you didn't kill Billy," she whispered.

"He'll be all right." Nolan opened his fingers and pressed his palms on the wheel. "He was just crazy for the moment. He'll be all right in time."

"Yeah, probably. Or not. At least he an't dead."

"No." Nolan let his breath out and Dede could hear his shoulders letting go. He settled in his seat and shook his head. "No," he said again. "He an't dead and neither are we." He looked into Dede's face and smiled. Dede smiled back at him.

"Nolan?" His name sounded funny in her voice, but right. It sounded right to speak his name. "Nolan, do you ever get drunk?"

He hesitated. "Mostly not," he said, "but I could right now."

"So could I," Dede said. "I could get happily stinking drunk."

"You want to?"

"Yes."

The way she said it sent a little tingly shock through Nolan, a vibration that centered somewhere just beneath his heart. Dede was looking straight at him, her glance level and dark. She was really seeing him, he could tell. She was seeing him as she never had. In that moment, it didn't matter to her that he was younger, that he was the boy from up the street she had joked about from the first day she had met him. Finally, she was seeing him clear.

Nolan did not smile. He just returned her look, his face wide open and alight.

"Yes," he told Dede. "Yes. Let's."

* * *

When Tacey was a girl, before her brothers left home and things with her mother went to pieces, the family kept dogs. Althea raised them and sold them, mainly hounds and beagles and a few selected mixed breeds noted for loyalty, size, and demeanor. There was always a litter of puppies in the yard, and Tacey dreamed sometimes of being a girl again—five or six years old and rolling in the grass with armfuls of squealing little dogs.

In the weeks after Billy Tucker tried to kill Dede, she and Nolan reminded Tacey of those puppies, sleepy-eyed but always watching, and jumping up happily when the other approached. There was no doubt they were in season, tuned to each other and vibrating to the same measure. They were like dogs and children in summer, their tongues always hanging loose and their hair smelling sweet and slightly acrid at the same time, like sugar and piss and love. Sometimes Tacey would take a breath of them and laugh despite herself, but once in a while, coming in on them while they were pressed to each other, she would feel as if something hit her in the heart, stopping her utterly and making her whole life feel useless and uncertain. No one affected her like that, no one speeded her heart or altered her breathing. No one in her life had ever even made her think of changing anything. Watching two who in one moment had been remade rendered everything she had ever known questionable. Tacey pulled out some of her stories and read them through. With the smell of all that lust in the house, the stories seemed thin and bloodless. Tacey rocked on her mattress and tried to imagine what it felt like, the reeling passion that had overtaken Nolan. She felt cramped, uncertain and fearful that there were things she had not yet prepared herself to face.

Worse was that Tacey was not at all sure what to make of Dede— the cranky white girl who was all Nolan's heart. Dede was no romantic heroine that Tacey had ever read about. Skinny, barefaced, and almost always sweaty and dressed in jeans and a thin white T-shirt, Dede was shameless, caustic, and seemingly as surprised by what was going on as Tacey herself. To Nadine's delight, Dede did not sneak out of the house or pretend that nothing had happened; she gloried in the affair, spilling out of Nolan's bedroom while Tacey was fixing Nadine's breakfast, with her hair all tangled and her sneakers in her hand. Dede smelled moist and ripe. There was sleep in her eyes and a satisfied glaze on her features. She giggled at Nolan's mama and shrugged when Tacey frowned, pulled on her faded denim jacket and hopped out the front door with only one shoe on.

"Shameless trash," Tacey called her, and Nadine bobbed her head happily.

"Oh yes," the old woman agreed. "She sure is."

Tacey took to addressing Dede as "wildlife" and drawling the word rudely. Coming home from school in the afternoon, she would pick up Nolan's damp shorts from the bathroom floor, purse her lips, and sniff loudly. "Uh-huh, smells like a little wildlife around here." Nadine would giggle and Nolan would blush. Unlike Dede, Nolan was not sure that he should acknowledge what was going on. He kept thinking they should be more discreet, but when Dede was close enough for him to smell, his thoughts blurred and a happy buzz took over his brain. He would lean into her and lose hold of any conviction. They were in love. Love would make everything all right.

Dede's spoor was all through the house. Beer cans appeared in the trash along with wet cigarette papers and used condoms. Makeup was stacked in the upstairs bathroom. There was a set of combs, a new toothbrush, three kinds of colored hair gel, and a little box of shells for the pistol Craig Petrie sent over after he heard about the incident at the store. The girl was at the house constantly—at lunch or after work, early evening or late, showing up at midnight to sleep over after her late shift and getting up at four in the morning to drink coffee with Nolan before he drove over to Biscuit World and she could climb back into his bed until Tacey got up. The house smelled of heat and sweat and sodden clothing. Nolan altered daily, his face swelling with sensual satisfaction and his belly and thighs shrinking away as he forgot to eat or sleep or keep to any regular schedule. Some days he forgot to play his clarinet, and twice he arrived late for Nadine's medical exams. "Sorry," he said, his ears tipped with scarlet and his cheeks flushed only a shade lighter. He seemed in a constant state of shock, his lips chewed and swollen, his eyes watery and his pupils large. "Sorry," he began every sentence, though there was no sorrow in him. He was swimming in an ocean of his own making, riding a tide of yearning and delight, bubbling happy promises to his mama, and blushing hotly at every glance from Tacey's dark eyes.

"Sorry, I'll get to it. Sorry, I forgot. Sorry, I was busy." Nolan was never home except when Dede was with him. If he was not at work or asleep, he was at Delia's eating vegetables Dede had chosen, or helping her sort stock at the convenience store, or in the tiny silver Airstream mobile home that Dede had rented over at the trailer park where the two of them were always stopping off for an hour or two. Everywhere he went, Nolan trailed the scent of carnal desire.

"Damn, Mama," Nolan whispered to Nadine one evening. "I never understood." His eyes flooded with tears until Nadine patted his head and agreed.

"It's the life force," she told him. "It's why we are here."

Tacey glared at them. It was not why she was there. It was not enough reason for all the extra work that was falling on her, so much laundry it had to be done twice a week or the whole house reeked. Tacey did not dare stay late to talk to teachers or friends, or even to wander home slowly making up stories in her head. There was no guarantee Nadine would not be alone and covered in sugary grease when she arrived.

"I understand," Tacey complained to Nolan one afternoon. "You are living out one of the world's great love stories, but could you please buy the groceries before falling back into bed with the queen of heaven?" Nolan flushed and promised, and promptly forgot his promise as soon as Dede called to ask him to drive her over to Goober's for a plate of fried vegetables.

One afternoon Tacey came home to find a beaming Nolan sitting on the floor sucking a stick of beef jerky. "Dede gave it to me," Nadine told her. Tacey hauled the woman back up into the wheelchair. Nadine smacked her lips and grinned at Tacey's angry face.

"I suppose Nolan said that was all right," Tacey snarled.

"He said it was better than fried pies." Nadine had the grace to look shamefaced.

"Did he?" Tacey kept her face expressionless. "Did he?"

Nadine's eyes flooded with tears and she extended her hand, holding out the beef jerky to Tacey. "Don't be mad," she pleaded, and leaned her head forward into Tacey's stomach.

"Oh, don't cry." Tacey patted Nadine's crown. "I'm not mad. I'm not mad." She hugged the old lady tight, smelling the salty beef and the sweet apple smell of Nadine's shampoo. I'm jealous, she thought. I'm jealous of something I don't even want. This must be how people go crazy. For the first time in months, she thought of the way her mama had looked when Tacey had been throwing all her stuff in her bags. Behind the anger there had been a kind of awful patience. At the time, it had just made Tacey even more angry, but her mama had been in love at least twice that Tacey knew about—with her daddy for sure, and with the silly man who was living there now. I wonder what Mama would say if I told her about all this, Tacey thought.

Nadine sniffed and put both her arms around Tacey's hips. "He never thinks about us anymore," she mumbled into Tacey's dress.

"Oh, he thinks about you," Tacey told her, and smoothed down Nadine's tangled hair. "Mama love is permanent. It's just different from that other stuff."

Nadine looked up at Tacey with a serious expression. "Oh, it is," she agreed. "It surely is." Solemnly she put the frayed end of the stick of jerky between her lips. Unable to help herself, Tacey grinned at the sight. After a moment Nadine grinned back at her, as mischievous and sincere as a little girl.

Chapter 17

The dirt cradle, God's country and the devil's backyard. Cissy breathed in the cool, damp air belowground and chanted the words to herself. They were four hours down into Little Mouth, and she felt completely loose and happy in her body. Above her was not the dome of sky but a dome of earth, a tabernacle of mud and rock and pulverized stone that felt safely close and comfortingly familiar. I love it down here, Cissy thought. Down here, I know who I am, what I can do. Oh, this is the hillbilly hiding place, the secret haunt of haunts. This is where I belong. "I guess I'm just a cave dweller," Cissy told Mim. And one seriously demented child of God, she told herself. She laughed out loud and saw Mim frown.

"I'm glad to be here again," Cissy said, not hiding the intoxicated happiness in her voice. Mim smiled, only a little puzzled. She doesn't love it like I do, Cissy thought. She does it for the adventure. If there were mountains near here, she and Jean would climb them, but there are none, so they climb down here. Of the three, Cissy knew, only she would go out of her way to search out the holes in the ground.

"Yuck." Jean lifted her hand and shook thick, powdery algae from her glove. "Disgusting crap."

"Bat shit," Mim said.

"Or rats." Cissy gestured to the torn and scattered remains of paper wrappers in one of the hollows of the rocks. Near the surface small animals used the cave as a refuge. They hauled garbage in for warmth and left spoor on all the loose surfaces. Algae and fungus grew wherever the temperature rose above the usual chill. The cave was a laboratory of corruption. Sweat left on a rock layered with bacteria that might grow even in the chill. Things underground altered, underwent a terrestrial change. Without sunlight or heat to dry it out, the rocks grew phosphorescent and took on the gleaming imprint of handfalls and finger grips. In some of the deeper passages the bacteria ate at fragments of sandwiches, pickles, and butter. The residue went on gleaming and growing for years after the cavers were gone. The idea charmed Cissy. Sometimes she reached up and planted her sweaty palms on the rock above her, just on the chance that long after she passed through, that place would hold her imprint.

"I hate this stuff," Jean complained. She scraped the guano off her boot on a rock. "Rot," Mim called it. "Just bat rot."

Rot was not what Cissy saw. Consummation, the slow alteration of what people thought they knew, that was what Cissy saw in the cave. Down there everything ripened. In the dark, deep slow changes took place. That package of closely wrapped tissue paper provided the sack where pale apples were nurtured into red flush flavor. The unaccustomed heat of her body dried the dark mud on her jeans so that it crusted and flaked from her hips and thighs, marking her passage up the wedge in the rocks.

The farther they crawled, the more careless Cissy became. Sliding on the rocks and scraping her elbows and knees made Cissy feel not wounded but more powerful. She could take damage and keep moving. She was stronger than rock, more determined than the tides of sand and grit that moved along the underground creeks. Climbing out of the lower shafts, her body trembling with satisfied exhaustion, Cissy knew she had done something extraordinary. Every time she crawled up into the light again, she knew herself different. It was as if her passage through the dark offered Cissy what she had always wanted, confrontation with God in the imagined body of a woman, the mama-core, the bludgeoned heart of the earth.

Little Mouth was not supposed to be anything special. Paula's Lost was the cave everyone talked about. "Oh yeah, those parties," Jean said when Cissy talked about Nolan's family. No doubt a few of the people who talked so loud about Brewster's parties had actually gone to one or two—a few perhaps, but not as many as said they did. Once the girls got past the passages Cissy knew, Little Mouth was far more spectacular than anyone had ever hinted.

"Look at that, Cissy," Mim kept saying as they went through the back reaches of Little Mouth. "Look at that."

Cissy looked. She lifted her head and leaned back into the beam of the flashlight so that the stream of light swept up and past her, picking out the limestone edges of layered, overlapping rock. Glitter, height, pitch, and angle, the slope reared above them and shone with mica flecks like a shattered mirror on a flagstone floor. Looking at the rock was like looking at clouds. They saw faces, bowls and chalices, angel wings and dragon's teeth.

"Somebody could make a fortune down here," Jean kept saying.

"If they could open it up and tame it," Mim said. "Turn it into Disneyland underground, like Ruby Falls with those flat concrete paths and colored lights."

Cissy watched the pulsing beam of the light pick out pea gravel, marl, and alluvium. The air was sharp with the stink of bitter water. A scum of bone-white dust coated her upper lip. She had to keep wiping her mouth and sipping at the canteen on her hip. Mim complained about the dust. Jean borrowed Cissy's canteen. Finally, they all had to stop to rest. In the crisp shadows between the rocks, ghost light seemed to shimmer and move. Cissy could not imagine what it was. This far down there were no bugs, no butterflies or birds, no snakes or living things to be feared. Down here only microorganisms were dangerous, ancient viruses waiting for the warm medium of blood and human stupidity.

"Lord damn!" Jean cursed. "Every separate muscle in my hips and shoulders is bruised."

"Got to watch that bouncing off the walls," Mim teased her.

A vibration rippled out from Mim's gentle contralto and echoed in the belly bowl of Cissy's pelvis. The feeling was small, wonderful, and secret. It made Cissy want to smile, but she only repeated Jean's phrase in the sofest whisper. "Lord damn."

"Look up there." Mim waved one hand up into the light beam,

gesturing to the sparkling rise of stone and adamantine. "Like a cathedral, like a goddamned cathedral."

Cissy nodded, and then realized that the light was pointed away and Mim could not see her. She whispered. "It's like a church, like a secret temple."

Cissy thought that Little Mouth was the cave she loved best. In the old maps, it was described as a small narrow cavern, but in the last decade the grotto had been broken open. The little mouth had opened to the larger one, the deep behind the shallow trench, and that furrow had opened again so that a series of awkward climbs lured the girls through a linked maze of caverns and crawl spaces.

"I think," Mim kept saying, "it must connect to Paula's Lost. Something has to. It's all linked by water, and water moves along the flat until it can fall, then it will push anything aside. I've been looking at the topographical maps. There's no way the water would not move down; it would push through the limestone and open it up. I think the caverns connect from the southern pit of Paula's Lost to the upper reaches of Little Mouth, maybe not in a way we could get through, but maybe. We could try anyway, map from here to the old back passages at Paula's Lost."

"I don't know." Cissy closed her eyes, picturing the passages she had climbed so many times. Both caves were limestone, but there was shale and granite, and other qualities of stone behind that. Paula's Lost was slightly uphill from Little Mouth, but only by a few degrees. "It might connect. It might not. Remember how many people have been looking for the links between those caves in Kentucky? Isn't that how Floyd Collins made all those headlines? He went down in early January convinced he knew his way, and was going to show the world. The books say that when they got him out on February sixteenth, they had to cut off his foot to do it."

"I an't going to stick my feet in no crevices." Mim was indignant. "We're careful. When are we not careful?"

"It's not about careful. Things happen." Cissy was thinking about the back passages at Paula's. There was all that red and gray sand, unique to the site. Had she seen anything like that in Little Mouth? If there was, would it mean the water carried it from one place to the other? Water would move south and downhill, so nothing from Little Mouth would be carried to Paula's Lost.

"That pea gravel," Jean suggested when they talked about it over pimento cheese sandwiches and hot tea. "Pea gravel is loose, moves easily along in a stream. The pea gravel in the upper passages of Paula's Lost is all pearly-silver-looking in the arc lights. It should show up in Little Mouth if it got carried there."

Cissy sat with her sandwich in one hand, thinking. After a moment she nodded her head. "Yes," she said. "I've seen pea gravel here. Not much but some. In the far back northern passages on the dogleg's cutback." She looked at Mim carefully. "It might connect," she said finally.

"Then we could map it." Mim was thrilled. "And if we prove the connection, we could get in the record books. We'd be the most famous cavers in the Southeast!"

"We could start anyway. We could start mapping and see what we get." Jean sounded less excited than Mim. Cissy took another bite of her cheese sandwich and nodded. No reason not to try, if they were careful.

Exploring the southern reaches of Little Mouth proved torturous and challenging. It felt as if there were always something waiting, something past that little cut or through that sandy wash, something like a rocky death or a fast descent down an open chasm.

"It's a bitch," Mim declared. "Keeps pulling me on till I forget how many hours we've been crawling. I start losing feeling in my fingers and toes. I start wanting to lie down and nap."

"Oh, that would be a good idea," Jean laughed.

"Maybe it would," Cissy said. "We could bring sleeping bags and hot coffee. Go as far as we could, flake out, wake up warm and rested, eat and go on again."

"And again," Mim laughed. "No matter how far you go, there will be another passage. Always another reason to go a little further.

Sometimes I start thinking all it takes is stubbornness, but if you lose your blankets and your thermos, forget your path out or lose track of how many hours you been in, you're dead. You get stupid down here, you get lost. There's a reason expeditions set limits and go in organized groups."

"When are we not careful?" Jean asked, repeating their motto. They looked at each other.

They did it for the first time the next weekend, with bags, blankets, food, and a little Coleman for making hot tea. For Cissy it was a new revelation, the idea of staying so long underground. When she curled up in her sleeping bag, she realized how happy she was with the feel of the darkness close and safe around her. She had napped on her own, lain down for moments at a time, but this was different. The dark closed around her like a blanket. She curled into it with a sigh. This was bread and meat to Cissy, what she had always needed and never had enough of at any one time.

All her life Cissy had had trouble sleeping. She would lie awake in bed long after her sisters' breathing had stilled and shifted into sloop-sloop patterns, steady and quiet. She would turn, rock, twist, and drum her fingers on her hip bones. She would squeeze her eyes tight shut to watch the starbursts that followed. Moonlight on the windowsill. Bathroom light slipping around the frame of the closed door. When they had shared the room, she had been comforted by the green twinkle of Amanda's digital alarm clock, the tiny red gleam of the battery light on the radio Dede always kept by her pillow, earphone cord moving as Dede breathed, now blocking the ruby, now exposing it.

How was it possible anyone could survive on so little sleep? Cissy did not know. When her sisters slept, she told herself stories and cataloged the phases of the night, the slow way light altered as time passed, the way sound became somehow longer and thicker in the deepest part of the night. Dog barking slowed down after the moon set, howling receded to something more subtle and desperate. Grief rode the night air and thickened perception. Cissy could do nothing but endure, though some nights her restlessness got so bad she would get up and read a book or listen to the broken TV set out on the side porch, the one that got no picture but brought in the late-night stations' voices. That never helped. It was better to lie in bed and let the body rest while the brain ticked on like an old clock, to count minutes or years or indrawn breaths. More times than she could count Cissy had watched the dawn birth past Dede's shoulder. She had cataloged the shades of light from first flush to slow bright and plush morning white. When Amanda married and Dede shifted into her room, the room had seemed still and lonely. Even sleeping alone, Cissy lay awake more than she slept.

When Mim and Jean talked about the weekend expedition, Cissy worried about sleeping with them beside her. Mim and Jean brought sleeping bags and hot thermos jars. Cissy brought rope, extra lanterns, and a deck of cards. She grinned ruefully at the notion, but expected she would be playing solitaire while Jean and Mim slept. Were it not for the added weight, she would have packed her tape player to pass the time, but obediently she unrolled her sleeping bag and hunkered down. Pretend to sleep, she told herself. Rest. Mim flicked off her lamp and rolled over. The dark came in, and with it the silence. Far off something beaded and thunked, then thunked again. Water falling a short distance made a slow sound and then stopped. There was no light. Sound was slow or absent entirely, the breathing of the other girls, moisture pearling on rock in response to their warm breath. Bats, Cissy told her brain, but the dark pulsed color. Images moved across her retinas. Blind fish. Black butterflies. Larvae. Delia. Dede. Amanda. Breathe in, pearl out. Nothing.

Mim's hand was on her shoulder. A careful light purposefully shielded pointed away from Cissy's eyes. Mim's eyes were huge and bright.

"Girl! You sleep hard."

Sleep. Four hours like nothing. Four hours like four minutes. Let me sleep again, Cissy thought. She shook her head and pushed herself up. She looked around her like a blind fish who had suddenly grown eyes, opened her mouth, and grunted a laugh. Not a dream, not a pause, just an indrawn breath and simple unconsciousness, her body made new in four hours of complete rest. Heaven no doubt lay on the other side of a long cave.

Cissy did not tell anyone but she knew. If she made her home in a cave, she would never have another bad night, never miss another moment's sleep.

In the days after the overnight trip down Little Mouth, Cissy found herself thinking about the base of the last cliff they had passed in the northern passage. Pea gravel was there, and sand that was almost red. Something was there, something that called Cissy on. A little more endurance, a little more care, they could have found how far back it went. That was how you lost yourself in the big caves, Cissy kept scolding herself. You started thinking you could find the passage that had to be there, the northwest connection or the link to Mammoth Cave.

Cissy had been to Mammoth with Delia for her seventeenth birthday. They had rented a motel room where they could stay overnight, and done the whole tour. It had been spectacular but predictable, a tame cave, another walk-through with colored lights and plank paths, bigger than any Cissy had seen but still less interesting than the wild caves. They went with a group down predictable corridors of dim shade and reflected light. Cissy persuaded the guide to turn off the big lights and let them stand for a moment where once someone had lain on his belly, cold and exhausted and exhilarated with discovery. That dark had been tantalizing but too brief.

Light is defined by its edges, Cissy realized early on in Little Mouth. The beam of a flashlight was edge-sharp, cutting past rock so that you had to teach yourself to see it. It was so easy to see what was not there, miss what was. Diffuse soft daylight was kind. It helped the eyes. Cave light challenged perception and invited hallucinations. The light in wild caves was tricky and strange. It tricked the eyes, seduced fear, and manufactured terror. It made you feel yourself utterly mortal and at risk. Cissy loved it.

After Nolan took her down in Paula's Lost and Dede moved into

Amanda's old room and gave her the bedroom, Cissy had hung double-thick curtains over all the windows, sealed the edges of the doorjamb, and put a muffling quilt over the door itself. "You turned it into a tent," Dede had said of the room, but that was not true. Cissy had turned the room into a cave, a place where the dark was welcome but never deep enough. The deep dark was what she wanted, and it was under the ground, always waiting for her, a landscape of black and white and gray. Like the moon on video, the dark in the cave made color irrelevant. When color did appear in the cave, it startled Cissy so much that she went blind for a moment. What she saw burned on her pupils, yellow crust on an overhang, pink flush at the circular edges of a sunken bed of sand, gray-green shading into pearly, lustrous blue. What she saw in the deep places was too subtle to be noticed aboveground. Everything down there was a stage, a place where something was meant to happen. The dark waited for light but did not need it. The dark was ancient and sufficient and patient. If Cissy had not come, it would have waited for another—the eye that could take it all in and glory in the beauty. Down in the dark everything waited all the time, for all time.

"I want to be buried down here," Cissy told Mim as they sat with their lanterns dimmed down, the shadows close in and comfortable.

"Lonely."

"No. Quiet."

"Safe," Jean said. "Nobody could get you down here."

"Maybe," Cissy said. "Maybe not. Just quiet and alone. I like that idea. I like it a lot."

M.T. had gotten so fat her upper arms seemed to be part of her breasts, great soft mounds of flesh that moved together. With her broad face and small features, delicate and close together, she looked like Glenda the Good Witch, but Glenda with a glandular problem, her aura warm and enveloping, her rosebud mouth almost always pursed to smile or laugh. For all her size, M.T. seemed no less attractive to men. Men waited on M.T. as if for spring. She was always "with" someone, though she swore she would never marry again.

"Did it once," she told Delia. "Did it for real. Not like some of these children do it today. I married Paul, I meant it. And I just an't like that no more. Wouldn't mean it again, not like that, and won't do it without meaning it. So everybody should just be warned."

The warning deterred no one. M.T. kept company steadily, though never too seriously. The first surprise was always how she could blush, look over, and snare a man. The second surprise was how gracefully she could ease that man out of her bed. Men walked away bemused by the experience. They would say, "Yeah, we had a thing." Then they would smile in remembrance, shake their heads, and give the rueful grin that so clearly expressed their confusion about just how that thing had gone the way it had. They didn't talk bad about M.T. the way they might have been expected to do. Most took to calling her "good thing" as if that were her nickname. "Good thing," they would murmur in M.T.'s direction, and she would smile and put her hand out in that delicate gesture that acknowledged the affection but asked nothing further.

"Woman's got a hell of a talent," Stephanie would complain. "She should get her own television show and teach us all how to do it."

If pressed, most of M.T.'s old boyfriends would admit they thought about her and wouldn't mind seeing her again. It was almost as if she had drained off all their urgency and what she left behind was a kind of deep contentment. If called upon, they would come right over easily enough, help her out and do a job for her. Jackson Melridge cleared her gutters and checked her roof every fall. Garret Sultan would ride over on his riding mower and cut back the field behind her house, asking her solicitously how her allergies were doing. Charlie Peachhill would drop by to share a cup of coffee and take a look at the engine of her old Chevy. When she decided to buy a new one, he came along, saying, "An't gonna let no slick old boy do you wrong." After, he collected compliments for the deal he got her. "Got to take care of our M.T.," he replied to the men who teased him. "Got to make sure she's all right."

When M.T. went out on the street, men called out to her, mostly men of a certain age, near her age or older, men old enough to remember slow dancing with a sweet-smelling, softly round woman like her. The young boys practicing their sullen passivity at the gas station would watch and wonder. What was it about that fat old lady? But then they would pass close to her in the market, smell her perfume, and wonder again. So soft, so easy, eyes bright with confidence, a mouth that knew things. If they came too close, she would give that deep husky laugh, that laugh that had no cruelty in it, that laugh that was like a conversation, languid and unafraid.

"You be careful boy," the older men would tell them. "That's too much woman for you." It brought M.T. a new generation, though one everyone was sure she would never take to her bed. "That's a woman needs a man," the good old boys would say. But M.T. would just smile. The young boys would rake her yard, show her the new dances, tell her stories whose original versions she had long ago forgotten. Maybe she didn't sleep with them, but she made them feel as if she might. That was power of yet another kind, one she understood intuitively.

"How you doing, M.T.?" she'd hear as she went up the street to the Bonnet.

"Pretty good," she'd call back without turning around. "Hard for an old woman like me these days, but pretty good nonetheless."

"Oh, M.T., you an't old. You barely into the good part, woman."

M.T. would laugh, then put her hand back to touch a tanned dark arm. There was something in the way she did that, like a trusted older sister. Immediate family. Sexy as hell.

Cissy decided that M.T. had her own tribe, men who had been hers for a season and then took flight like butterflies lifting into the morning, but her scent remained on them. They were in some sense always hers, even those who married—perhaps especially those who married, those who could no longer flirt easily with her, and could only look longingly at the remembered heaven of her embrace.

"What is it you got, M.T.? What is it you do?" Dede asked the question as if she were teasing, though Cissy had no doubt she thought, as they all did, that M.T. knew something, had some magic or secret technique she would never share. It was a question that only got more persistent with the years. For no matter how loose and easy M.T. became, the men of Cayro continued to pursue her.

"You got some exotic skill only possible for a woman of size? You half smother them or something?"

"Dede Windsor, the way you talk." Steph looked over at M.T.

"Oh, leave her alone." M.T. wiped sweat from her temples and waved a hand in Steph's direction. "She got to learn the truth sometime."

With a growling harrumph M.T. settled herself in an empty pump seat, kicked the lever twice to drop it to a comfortable height, and carefully smoothed hair back off her brow while watching herself in the mirror. She easily had the attention of everyone in the Bonnet by the time she turned to Dede and spoke.

"Maybe," she began, "it's just that I know what men want." She smiled when Steph snorted and shook her head. "Or maybe it's just that I've reached the point in life where what they want is closer to what I want. So it an't no big struggle to give it to them. Maybe one thing men want is for things not to be so hard."

M.T. paused. A small grin crossed her face and she gave Dede a sly wink before she spoke again. "Course it also might be that with all my padding they know they not going to hurt themselves, you know? Not like some skinny sharp-boned things running around here. Hurt them or hurt themselves. Somebody in pain around here all the time."

"Well, that's a fact." Steph gave her righteous nod. "That's a fact for sure. Somebody in pain around here all the time." She looked over to Delia for confirmation but Delia was looking out the window, her face expressionless and tanned dark. If she was in pain, her face would never let anyone know.

* * *

A rock or a hard place, Delia knew where she had come down. Her hands in rushing water, her mouth pressed tight, she kept her eyes on the crown of Gillian's head and the hair she was washing, her attention on the talk in the shop.

"Emmet said there was another reporter hanging around at Goober's, asking questions about you. Wanting to know if any of Clint's people were still around."

"Ummm." Delia massaged the scalp gently, knowing that if she said nothing in response, Gillian would tell her more.

"Nobody had a word to say to him, a-course. He was cheaper than that guy came around two years ago. Wasn't offering to buy nobody dinner. Wasn't flashing no money or talking no trash. Little skinny fellow with straggly hair and a pitiful mustache." Gillian paused briefly as Delia reached to shut off the water and squeezed water through Gillian's hair until it ran off in sheets down the sides of the little porcelain sink. Only when Delia rocked her chair forward did Gillian resume.

"I hate a mustache on a man, don't you?" she said. "Always tastes like what he ate last, smells like dust, and looks bad no matter how it's cut. My Richard used to wear one, and it took me forever to get him to cut it off. Thought he had a weak chin, can you imagine? And that straggly thing was supposed to disguise the fact? Lord, what men think. I mean, can you imagine?"

Delia wrapped a towel around Gillian's damp hair. Guided her over to the pump-up chair and saw M.T. eyeing her in the mirror. You okay? M.T.'s expression communicated. Delia shrugged in reply and turned her full attention to Gillian.

"You want it just generally neatened up, or did you have something special in mind?" Delia's eyes in the mirror were steady and unblinking, her features impassive, her frame steady, posed behind Gillian's hunched wet head.

"Oh, just work your magic." Gillian patted at her wet temple with one hand and smiled into the mirror at Delia's face. "You always know what this old head needs."

Delia smiled and closed her eyes briefly. Here, she thought, I am right here and nowhere else, and this is what I am going to do. "Trim it up," she said, opening her eyes, "shape it a little more to the sides of your head." Her fingers caressed momentarily the temple Gillian had just touched. "If I cut it back just a little, it should fall just to the side of your ears. You used to wear it like that, didn't you? When you and Richard were first going together?"

Gillian sighed and nodded, closing her eyes as she did so, leaving Delia free to look again at her own face, the marks there of how many times she had shut her mouth on what she dared not say, the life she had walked away from and never regretted. Randall wore a mustache. It had always tasted sweet.

Delia thought the only pure thing she had ever known was how she felt in the middle of that roar of sound—Mud Dog onstage and Randall grinning like a man drunk on the reverberations of Delia's voice. A resounding bass note merged into 4/4 staccato downbeats. Booger's hands fused to his keyboard, and Delia followed behind, her voice becoming suddenly something separate, something like sex. That music was sex. Or sex was so much less than it was. For Delia, it was the only spiritual rush she had ever felt. Being music, the glory of singing out that predatory chord of need and exaltation, had taken her right up out of herself, her small grief and unrelenting shame. Her voice was made over into an instrument, her whole soul fell into the swell of chord and song. When she sang, Delia forgot what she had done, the baby girls she had abandoned. She stopped hearing the song of their breathing, endlessly reverberating in the back of her brain. The one life was cut off from the other. She could not have both. She had chosen, God knew, the only life she could stand. But she never forgot the other, not Randall and the business, but the music. She never ceased to mourn it.

When they first came back to Cayro, Delia spent too many of her sleepless nights lying on the couch playing the records with headphones on in the deep of the night. She imagined she could push through her despair with the sound of her own voice, but it did not work that way. There was a darkness in the music that called her name. It was as husky and biting as two ounces of honey in four of whiskey. Too sweet in the first heat of the swallow, it burned into the throat so purely a flush went down Delia's arms to her thumbs. Every time Randall's bass thudded into the rhythm, Delia rocked her head back against the arm of the couch, astonished all over again at the power of the music they had made, that thing so much greater than melody on vinyl. Every time the record played over, Delia's despair deepened and she hunched deeper into herself until all she could do was turn her face into the couch cushions and cry.

It was not that Mud Dog had been that good, but that they had made their music from the core of who they were—the guitars flexing Randall's raw anger and Booger's intractable anguish, that drum ricochet that was Little Jimmy's plea to move up front, and Rosemary's tremolo so pure it lifted Delia's growling song out of heartbreak and up to transcendence. The voice of Mud Dog was not just Delia's voice but some intimate cry from the voice box of God. As she listened to that music, Delia's heart would seize up again, as if blood were being wrung from her soul. The feel of those years would wash over her, the lyrics she and Rosemary had pieced out on brown paper bags, the chord changes Randall and Booger put together as resonating as the song they had made out of her restless, angry grief.

"Born on the corner of Nazareth and Calvary," Randall sang on the opening to *Diamonds and Dirt,* his voice high and thin. Then Delia took over "Nazareth and Calvary," dropping an octave while the drum's pulse resounded like a heartbeat slowing into death. It was a song not about crucifixion, but about guilt and expiation. Delia's song. Penance and rock and roll. Jesus and the Holy Ghost in leather fringe and high-heeled boots. It was their signature piece. The crowd would take up the theme and sing back at the band like the call and answer at Pentecostal Sunday sermons. Sing, mama. Sing, Delia.

On the couch, drunk on grief, Delia had hunched and sobbed listening to the live version over and over, her voice and Randall's intertwined, her memories darker than that room in the night. She had expected penance, been sure of retribution, and almost gloried in her own damnation. It was all part of the romance of the music, sitting up all night and weeping until she had no tears left. It was Cissy who stopped her. One night Delia looked up from the couch and saw her girl in the doorway, eyes wide as dinner plates and lower lip clamped between her teeth. When Delia pulled off her headphones, Cissy ran back to bed. But Delia had seen those eyes. She took the record off the turntable, carried it outside, and smashed it with a rock. Then she sat in the damp grass until the sun came up, wishing away the music, wishing away the pull at her heart.

What's it like? the women at the shop used to ask Delia. Being in a band, loving a rock star, going on the road? What's it like? What's it like? Delia would just look at them, shrug, and not reply. She could not have explained. It had been a dream, life as a dream. Every day bleeding into the next, stoned one night and drunk the next. Sex outside on the terrace with the lights of Los Angeles gleaming softly over the edge of a low wall. Sweaty, thick air like a blanket pulled too close. Hip bruised from the edge of a flagstone and dust spilling into the corner of her right eye, burning until she wept. From the inside of the bungalow music playing. A woman's voice made poignant by a low growl that was not meant to be so yielding. Janis doing "Ball and Chain" on a bootleg tape so bad the band was almost inaudible. But it was almost better that way. That voice carried the grief and guts of a woman riding her own nerves out into the unknown, like Delia on a good day. But Delia wouldn't sing "Ball and Chain" onstage. "That's Janis's anthem," she'd say, though it could have been hers. She had the drawl for it, especially when she had been drinking. But Delia preferred the smoother songs, not so demanding, not so tearing on the insides, the songs the audience might start singing along on. Everybody liked those. The drunks sang along with Janis, the drunks and the grief-stricken. The kids who came to hear Randall would sing with Delia. They would wind up and roar, and that was what Delia wanted—the group mind, the invisibility of being imaginary for a couple thousand people. All roar and lights—no discernible face or consciousness, she wanted to disappear into that huge mass of stink and noise and justification.

"I think they are sane out in California, which God knows they an't much here in Georgia," Delia told Cissy after they came back to Cayro. "But I was born here, so I was born crazy. And I want to die here, die with my hands doing something, not idle and spread. Not empty."

"But you could have been rich."

"I could have been dead. Like Randall or half the band. Heroin or speed or fast cars on wet streets. So easy, dying. So easy. And I was rich. For a day and a half or so, I was too rich to understand, so rich it didn't mean anything. But I wanted something different. The crowd, the noise, like a congregation." Delia closed her mouth, barely stopping herself from saying aloud the one thing she knew that might explain everything. "My mama left me and I left my own. Nothing I do will fix that."

What stops grief? What heals the heart? Delia did not know. She had tried to cure herself of hurting, but she thought all she had managed was to put it off. How long can you put off hurting? "A lifetime," Delia told herself hopefully. "You do it right, you can put off hurting forever."

"Gillian, you look like a new woman." M.T. sipped a bottle of peach-flavored iced tea and beamed into the mirror beside Delia's shoulder.

"It's nice, isn't it?" Gillian put one hand up to the gently curling wave that turned back toward her ear. Her face looked thinner with her hair cut close to her cheeks; the fine line of her temples stood out and drew the glance to big dark eyes. "Delia always knows what I need."

"Oh, anybody could cut your hair," Delia said, shaking out the smock she pulled off Gillian's shoulders. "Just got to follow the line of your face so it looks the way God intended. Nothing fancy, just a good-looking woman with a long neck." She did not look at her own face. She kept her eyes on her hands, long blunt fingers and carefully trimmed, unpainted nails. Nothing fancy. Nothing but her own hands.

Flowstone settles down at the rate of roughly two inches a year, the caving books said. It comes in shades from pure white to calcium yellow to mottled red. After her first trip down into Little Mouth, Cissy dreamed about flowstone, the slowly moving rock beneath the dirt. In her dreams flowstone was not hard but thick and soft as stale meringue. That white paste found in grade school libraries, dense and cloying and slowly stiffening against the skin, that was the flowstone in Cissy's dreams. She lay back into it and it took on the shape of her body, the warmth of her skin. It settled beneath her, gently crept between her fingers and toes, and rose to cradle her hips. Compressed. Viscous. Alive. Growing slowly, but growing. Flowstone made a white noise in Cissy's head, intimate and safe. She waited for it to wrap her around, slowly encase her body, and by that motion season her soul.

Like me, Cissy thought as she dreamed. Flowstone was like her—dirt pressed hard, unvalued and ignored. Kick it and it did not kick back. It crumbled, broke apart, and absorbed what came. It settled down at its own rate, two inches a year or not at all.

When Cissy dreamed herself into the cave, she felt the stone in her soul, the rock of her outrage. She knew who she was and where she belonged, the worth of her bones and the cadence of her heart. "Her place," Dede would call it.

My country, Cissy thought, and in the dream the cave shaped around her as steadily as mud took on the imprint of her heel. In the belly of Little Mouth, Cissy put her hand into sand as old as the earth, extended her fingers, and was not afraid. Whatever she needed, that thing she would find. Wherever she should be, that place was where she was.

The shuffling struggle of the others washed over Cissy and did not matter, their panting and pushing, creeping progress, and yelps of fear. "Shut up," she wanted to say, but didn't. "Listen," she did say sometimes. "Listen." Jean and Mim would look around in confusion, hearing nothing of what Cissy heard, the pulse of the rock, the heartbeat of the planet, the echo of the unknown and the mysterious. One could see only so far and then the night took over, the great dark where anything might hide. Anyone. Someone like Cissy or someone so different she could not be imagined.

Caving for her, Cissy understood, was like sex for most people. Though what other people thought about sex was nothing Cissy really understood. But in the dark she became for the first time fully conscious of her own body and curiously unself-conscious. Unseen, she moved freely. In the dark her body moved precisely, steadily, each foot placed exactly, while her hips rocked loosely on the pistons of her thighs. Is this what California was for Delia? That unknown country where no one looked at her, no one knew her, and she could become anything she wanted, do anything without worrying about what others might see or think?

When Cissy dreamed about the trip from California to Cayro, it was a nightmare with coyotes howling out in the desert and the wind whipping in the smashed back window, blowing grit in her eyes and stink against her mouth.

"You didn't stop to think about me, did you?" Cissy accused Delia in the dream.

"I thought." The Delia in the desert nightmare howled out the car windows like a maddened animal. The real Delia never talked about the trip. "We're going home," she had said in that flat, stubborn voice Cissy hated. "I'm going home. You are going where I take you."

"A hodag," Jean told Cissy on their first trip. "A hodag is an animal that has legs shorter on one side than the other. Imagine. It can walk on steep hills without bending over lopsided. Can't walk so good on flat land but moves fast on the steep." She winked at Mim.

"Course, this advantage—it has another aspect. The hodag can travel in one direction only." She spoke plainly without inflection or a smile. "It can never retrace its path, even when it tries."

"Uh-huh," Cissy replied. "Sounds like Delia to me."

Chapter 18

One of these days, Amanda is going to pop like a balloon blown up too full," Dede told Cissy. "Gonna go pop and spatter stuff all over Cayro. She's just too damn full of her stuff, you know?"

Cissy nodded sadly. "And when she does, the one person who is not going to expect it is going to be Michael. He's going to be standing there with Amanda all over him and never know she's been squeezing herself down for him."

"Maybe he'll figure it out after she blows up at him," Dede snapped. She had liked Michael when Amanda first started mooning over him, but from the day of the marriage Dede had steadily soured on Michael Graham and his open-faced, easy ways. "Can't he see what's happening? Amanda is like some black hole squeezing down tighter and harder all the time."

"He loves her," Cissy said.

"Yeah, and look how much good it's done." Dede was disgusted. "Love don't fix everything." She tugged at one of the little silver earrings Nolan had given her. "I can't stand women who give themselves up so completely. They just make it harder for the rest of us."

Amanda ignored her sister's teasing, their jokes about how she was raising boys, not an army for the Lord. They don't understand, she would think. Hers was an army for the Lord. Arguing with them, she never noticed how much like her grandmother she had become. Grandma Windsor chewed on Amanda Graham's soul. Since the old woman had not shown up for her wedding, Amanda had tried once every few months to visit her grandmother. But the aging Louise Windsor treated Amanda as she had once treated Delia, shutting her door on her granddaughter whenever she went out to the farm.

Amanda had taken the infant Michael out to the farm when he was six months old, but Grandma Windsor had hired a woman named Paterson to help her out, a red-faced middle-aged woman who turned Amanda away.

"Your grandma says to tell you she's lying down," Miss Paterson told Amanda. "Your grandma says to tell you she's not feeling well."

Amanda blushed to hear the woman speak those words, hearing in them a Christian woman bluntly determined not to lie. She did not say Grandma Windsor was sick or lying down. That would have been a lie. She said Grandma Windsor said it, and in those words Amanda could hear the echo of her grandmother's rage at Delia. She loaded Michael back in the car and drove away, determined not to try to contact the old woman again, but at Christmas she sent a poinsettia and a box of the cookies she knew the old woman liked. It might have been a good Christian act, but in Amanda's belly it felt like old-fashioned guilt. There should have been a way for her to reach the old woman.

To earn a little more to help out, Amanda baked sheet cakes for other women in Michael's congregation—sheet cakes for birthdays, celebrations, and parties, reassembled in elaborate shapes, Christmas trees, valentine hearts, a Jacob's ladder of alternating angel food cake and dark layered sponge cake. Her cakes were wonderful, and for a little while quite the rage, but there were cheaper sheet cakes at the Piggly Wiggly, so Amanda's orders were sporadic and mostly came at holidays or for church events. Amanda did not complain. She simply made more careful lists and plans.

Sometimes, in the middle of checking her lists, Amanda would stop and bend forward from her waist, pain in her middle like an earthquake at the earth's core. Unstoppable, irresistible, agony stayed her until it eased enough for her to pull up and pray out loud in a hoarse, demanding whisper.

"God, God spare my family." Since Gabriel's birth, it had gotten steadily worse. Cancer she knew. Death for sure. Her belly, no doubt, was eaten half through. And no, she would not pray to God to cure her. She looked forward to what she anticipated, vindication as certain as the fact that when the pain caught her she could not stand up straight. Sometimes, after a bad attack, Amanda stopped in at the Bonnet to look at Delia's face. Sometimes she went by the convenience store and bought some little thing she did not need at all, just to see Dede stick a cigarette in her mouth and glare. Once or twice she had even driven out along the old highway toward Little Mouth looking for Cissy's stubborn bent head. Her death, she knew, would teach them all what she had not been able to show them alive.

Delia had started running after her first grandson was born. She had not thought she would keep it up. It was just a way to be alone and fight off some of the desire to drink which had come back with a vengeance after Amanda married and moved out. Delia kept thinking she would stop running eventually, but the nagging desire for a shot of tequila would not go away, and after the first few months the pattern was set. Every time the urge to get a drink came on her, Delia would change her shoes and head out. Sometimes she would just walk, head-down, oblivious and intent. But sometimes her muscles would knot up so bad, running was the only answer, running until her pain was purely physical, a matter of muscles and ligaments and sweat.

Delia liked best to run at sunset, the time of day when her thoughts became so tangled that running took her out of the confusion. The dogs loved it, Delia running by just when they needed a little diversion, a little after-dinner exercise. She carried a stick and waved the dogs away, but eventually switched to early morning and the dogs lost her scent. Delia found that she liked the dawn, liked even the permeable darkness just before dawn. She told Dede how intoxicating it was, moving up Terrill Road with only the sound of her breathing and the smell of her sweat.

"Healthy," she said. "I smell healthy. I smell better all the time." Dede had blinked, uncertain if Delia was teasing.

Delia was fast. One of the high school boys timed her. He hoped to be able to tease her, that grown woman in the cutoff shorts who thought she was such hot stuff. The joke turned when he saw how fast she could go, as fast as he was and maybe a little better.

"I was a sprinter," Delia told Dede. Back in school, but never very seriously. Running again, Delia started to feel like she had more stamina, more than she remembered having when she was a girl.

"Back then it was all different. Nobody did it but the track-and-field guys, you know. There wasn't no track meets for girls back then. Didn't even have regular meets for the boys. Cayro has always been a pitiful county."

She wiped her neck, full of pride at this revelation of her earlier life. "They made us run laps in school gym classes, you know. I'd run for the pleasure of it. And then later I found out there were women runners in the Olympics. Thought about that for a while. I'd liked it that much, but what could I do?"

Dede nodded. What could you do?

"But I liked being fast." Delia gave a wry grin, a half wink. She dropped her head, embarrassed. "You never know," she said. "But I'm not so fast anymore. I just like it, the way it feels." She extended her arms, her skin flushed with the satisfaction of the speed she had managed, the three miles she had run, three miles without once thinking of Dede or Amanda or Cissy.

"You never know," Delia said again.

Dede smiled tentatively as if she wondered what she did know. In all the years she had known Grandma Windsor, that old woman had never moved faster than at a stroll, an arthritic woman's careful, steady forward motion, hips locked in grinding pain and teeth set in stubborn disregard. To go from shuffling along behind her grandmother to watching Delia step out all sinew and muscle ready to run was like jumping from a wagon to a train. Dede found herself looking down at her own body in a different way, seeing in her long leg bones the vision of Delia in motion, and in her small hard breasts the shape of Delia's, which were the same size but softer with babies and a hard life.

Amanda scowled when Delia went out to run in her cutoff jeans or cotton shorts. "You're too old to be going out like that," Amanda said, but Dede watched Delia go out with a face full of awe and longing. As hard as it was to imagine, that was her mother—flesh of her flesh and bone of her bone. My God. My God.

After Gabe was born, Amanda started doing her family's laundry every day, sometimes twice. She would collect all the dirty clothes every morning, strip the mattresses, and grope under the beds. By nine, or as soon as everyone had showered, she had the washing machine going. She never let clothes lie in the hampers. Sometimes she undressed the boys right by the machine, their little shirts and socks going directly into the soapy water. Two color loads, one white every other day. Sometimes there was another load to be done late at night.

"I like things to be done right," Amanda said when Delia told her she was looking tired, but it was more than that. Things had to be done exactly right. Bad days, days when the pain in her belly got so intense that her teeth started to echo its pulse, Amanda pulled the thermal blankets out of the closet and put them through a cold wash. The worst days, when the muscles in the back of her neck seemed to be pushing her head forward and down, she could not make her body lie flat, and as soon as Michael was breathing steadily, she would roll off her side of the bed and head for the laundry room next to the kitchen. She would turn on the iron, shake out the tiny boys' T-shirts, and set the radio to pull in a talk-show host from Phoenix, one known for preaching directly from questions raised by his call-in congregation. While the muscles in her neck burned, Amanda would slide the iron forward and back. Cotton, cotton blends, linen and rayon blends, while that voice echoed all the way from Oklahoma City, everything smoothed out under a fine mist of distilled water. The aluminum crescent of the iron pushed heat through the fibers, evaporating what could not be flattened and shoved aside.

Some nights, while everyone in her house slept, Amanda would drive over to the twenty-four-hour grocery on the Cayro highway. Her cupboards had index cards affixed to them, listing everything inside. Lightbulbs, four each: 60 watts, 75, 100. Toilet paper: an even dozen rolls. She always had more than the lists indicated; the indexed numbers were minimums. If the four-pack of 100-watt bulbs fell to three, Amanda went out in the night to bring back another pack, a little more laundry soap, another two or three boxes of Kleenex. She would move up and down the aisle with her list, looking past it to Band-Aids, Bisquick, canned hams. Her family needed something, and she wanted to have it to hand. Michael did not earn enough for backups and duplicates, but no matter. What Amanda had to have, Amanda had to have. She clipped coupons and hunted down discount sales. She kept notes, she planned ahead, but sometimes in the middle of the night she would go out anyway, looking for that thing not stored in her cupboards, not found on any shelf, the thing she had forgotten.

I am not going to be with them long, Amanda told herself. I have to do what I can while I can. Over and over again she prayed, "Help me, Lord, with my fear. Take away my fear of death and make me ready." Over and over Amanda prayed, never asking for the most essential, the most basic thing—the life she was sure she was losing. When she was gone, she thought, as she leaned over the open cabinet doors, they will know who I was. Praise God, then they will know.

It was Saturday, and Amanda could hear the boys babbling and Michael laughing. There was the clatter of plastic cups and bowls, a roar of giggles, and Michael's mock-stern voice: "Now, boys, Mommy's resting."

Oh yes, Amanda thought, lying in her bed. She wiped sweat off her face and pulled her legs up tight to her breasts. She was on her back, wrapped loosely in a towel, knees bent and bobbing above her as she tried to curl herself tighter still. She had showered twice, but the pain in her belly had not eased at all. She would catch her breath and stand up, and the scythe would swing through her again.

"Take me, Jesus," she pleaded. Tears trickled down her cheeks into her ears. Lord, how she hated crying. Amanda wiped her face and tried again to relax and pull a little more air into her lungs. She could not get enough. She just couldn't get enough.

"I will not put up with this," Amanda hissed, emphasizing each word separately. She set her teeth and rocked to one side. Slowly she unfolded her legs, sat herself up, and put her feet on the floor. She paused to breathe a few times, then pushed up harder and stood. When she was supporting her weight with her feet flat on the floor, Amanda managed to draw a full breath of air in and out, then in and out again. "I will not. I will not put up with this."

She was steady. She was breathing. Think on Jesus. She dropped the towel and ignored the dizziness. Anything was possible with faith. Deliberately she stood up straight and pulled on her bra. Will not. I will not. Slowly, slowly she got dressed. If God was going to take her, he could do it now. Dressed and ready, she inhaled deeply and gratefully. With a prayer of stubborn love, she swung her head and wiped her face again. Will not. Will not. She combed her hair back and looked at her plain features. Amanda knew herself to be ugly. She did not care. God knew her heart. When she got to heaven, Jesus would take her up like the sword she was.

"Praise God." Amanda whispered the words, standing upright with her back straight. She pushed her hair back one more time using both hands, then sighed deeply and put on her ferocious smile. "Praise God."

When she opened the bedroom door, she was holding that smile. Michael and the boys looked up expectantly. Proudly Amanda beheld her family, the boys messy, pink-faced, and beaming, while Michael mopped up milk and tried to look like he was in control. She said, "Now what are you all doing out here?" She stepped forward, holding that smile, and passed out cold.

"Gallstones." Dr. Brown said the word with dire emphasis. "Not that unknown in young mothers, specially women who have children close together." His head bobbed up and down. "I do not know how she has been walking around this long with them. Pretty big stones."

Michael leaned back against the green-painted walls of the hospital corridor. His face was pale and haggard. The last few hours had been a horror. He had been sure Amanda was dying. He had not known what to do first, whether to pray over her, or get the boys away, or call for help. He still was not sure which he had done first, but somehow he had managed. Somehow they were safely in the hospital and the doctor was going to take care of Amanda. She was going to be fine, the doctor had promised. He had said a lot, actually—that it was not even so bad a thing, gallstones. Just horribly painful, and there was no telling what Amanda had thought was happening, but Michael knew instinctively what it was Amanda had been thinking. She had been ready to die, ready to go to face her God. She was ready now.

"She's very strong-minded," Michael said.

"She's stubborn as a rock." Delia hugged Michael once and turned her full attention to the doctor. "You're sure you can fix this?"

"Oh yes." He nodded strenuously. "No question."

"Surgery?" Michael looked even more upset. "Amanda hates the idea of surgery."

"Well, fortunately, in this case it's not necessary. We can use the new procedure on these. Sound waves. Pulverize the stones. It's a very quick recovery. Best thing all around. You sign the forms and we can do it in the morning."

"Shouldn't she sign?" Michael was hesitant. "Amanda would want to be the one to sign. Can't we talk to her?"

"Michael." The doctor put a hand on Michael's shoulder. "Your wife has been in mortal agony for I don't know how long. Right now I've got her comfortable, and I do not want to do anything that would make her suffer one more moment of pain than is necessary. You can sign for her and she can do all those things tomorrow evening."

Michael nodded but looked over at Delia. He needs a woman to tell him what to do, Delia thought, understanding in that moment more about Michael than she wanted to know. "It will be all right," Delia said to him. "It will be fine." Michael smiled gratefully.

"All right," he said. "I'll sign anything, but I want a chance to pray with her before the surgery. Even if she can't hear me, the Lord can. And I know Amanda would want me to do that." He bobbed his head in unconscious imitation of the doctor.

Oh Lord, Delia thought, watching them nodding at each other. What has my girl gotten herself into?

Amanda was floating. An Ace bandage cushioned her arms while the metal frame that held the clear bag of saline and morphine swung above her. She knew the bag was there, just as she knew she was in a bed and the needle was pumping relief into her veins. At the same time, she knew she was somewhere else entirely, somewhere safe and happy and gorgeous past her ability to express it. It was a good place where she was, the outer gate of heaven surely. She rocked back into the surface on which she lay and thanked God for bringing her here.

Grainy pearls of sweet butter cushioned Amanda's hips, lifted her up out of the liquid beneath her. Mercury, silver sweet and cool, flowed under her. She liked that, liked the idea of it. Cool and silver and moving steadily past her thighs, that river was the river of God's love for the faithful, for the loved daughter. The butter balls swirled around her. Amanda turned her head. Each bead of butter was sculpted, chilled, and lustrous. She caught a handful and looked at them closely. They were perfect. She loved butter balls. Melon balls too. Melon balls in cantaloupe and Crenshaw, pale orange and green. Cool, she thought. Sweet and cool.

Amanda closed her hands and felt the fruit pulp push through her fingers. Oh, nice. Very nice. She whistled a long whistle and felt a giggle start to percolate under her ribs. Was it butter or melons in her hands? She didn't care. She wiggled down into the liquid metal surface and squished some more. The squeezed balls made a funny sound. She liked that sound. She turned her head to listen more closely, but there was something wrong, some sound droning behind her head. Something she knew was back there, some familiar sound.

Oh, Amanda thought. Michael was praying. Oh dear. She sighed. Maybe she should join him. She opened her mouth and a long gray pearl of song came out. Perfect carved butter beads of prayer. A bead for God, a precious sphere of her faith. Michael's voice receded. Amanda remembered the feel of his skin pressed to hers. He had such a beautiful body. God bless, she said, and the words became pearls while Michael's sweet mouth came down on her own.

Praise God, Amanda said. Let us both praise God. She rocked her hips in pulse to Michael's voice. Oh, thank you, Lord. I come to you with my hands full and open. It made no sense but it did, and Amanda loved every word that moved through her. Praise God. Praise God. I am dead and most heartily glad.

They took her downstairs in the morning, keeping the line in her arm feeding just enough magic juice to keep that sweet buttery feeling in her body. "Am I dead?" Amanda asked past a thick dry tongue. A nurse gave her a tiny sip of water. "No, sweetheart, you're fine, and we're going to fix you up perfect."

"Perfect," Amanda said. She looked around. Everything was white and bright. Dr. Brown leaned over her. Amanda knew him. She had never liked him. "Oh dear," she said.

"Mrs. Graham, Amanda." He had a fat tongue, Amanda thought. A smug expression. He thought he knew so much. "We're going to take care of those gallstones, Mrs. Graham."

Gallstones? What was he talking about? She had cancer. She was dying. It was all so obvious. So easy to die, Amanda thought, when you have faith.

Dr. Brown leaned over her again. "Now you're going to feel something. It's just sound waves. They will come in pulses and won't hurt you, but you will feel things. It's going to break up the stones, going to make you all better."

Metal moved. Machines. Amanda tried to sit up, but straps held her in place. Her abdomen, her thighs, her shoulders, everything was pinned to the surface of the table. Smite them, Lord, Amanda prayed. Something large and peculiar stirred the air, making everything electrical. God, Amanda prayed. Oh God.

The pulse came, a sound inside Amanda's body like no other. It moved the molecules in her bones. It moved the electrical current of her brain. It was like the morphine, butter-smooth and awful as the breath of God, terrifying and magical. The wave went through Amanda and stirred her soul.

Praise God, Amanda prayed, this cannot be a machine.

There was a low murmur in her mouth, a prayer and a song. The pulse came again. A deep, ivory-smooth shudder went through Amanda's middle. God was speaking, that was what she felt. She could hear him in her bones. It was like the moment when she and Michael had made their sons. Not sex but prayer, Michael's lips on her breast, his teeth touching her skin, his gasps feeding her own, and her name an invocation in his mouth. There had been that moment when every muscle in Amanda's body had tightened and throbbed in a psalm of joy. She had wept, held on to Michael, and known without doubt that they had made a child. Far past orgasm, that moment had been an incantation of love. This feeling brought that moment back, all trembling tenderness and impassioned satisfaction, but this was not the act that made a child, this was something acutely unsettling. Dr. Brown murmured above her. For an instant Amanda was offended by her body's betrayal. Her muscles tightened to struggle, but then the wave came again, speaking far down inside her, a reverberation that lifted as high as her heart.

Amanda turned her head. It was the only part of her body she could move. This is not the machine, she thought. This is something more. "That's good," Dr. Brown said, and Amanda stopped fighting. The wave came again, rolling and moving, talking to her bones. Jesus, Amanda thought. Jesus is speaking to my heart.

Yes, Lord. Yes. The oscillation was repeated and sang in her molecules, the voice of God was speaking. Amanda nodded. She understood. She knew what she was meant to do. Yes, Lord, she whispered. Yes.

Amanda woke to Michael's murmured prayer, his head bent over hers, his hands on the frame of the bed. She looked at his head. Michael could never get his hair cut right without her there to tell them how to fix it. She closed her eyes and felt inside. The pain was gone. Nothing. No pulse. No song. No pearls. Her eyes were wet.

Gallstones.

Lord, forgive my arrogance, Amanda prayed.

She opened her eyes and turned her head. Michael looked up, the prayer ceasing as he saw her open eyes. "Oh, my beloved," he said fiercely. Amanda nodded. She wondered what God wanted from her now. She closed her eyes. Whatever God wanted, she would think about that later. For now she just wanted to lie still and listen to the stillness within her own body.

While Amanda was recovering in the hospital, Cissy stayed over at Amanda and Michael's house. She did it with poor grace. Jean and Mim had wanted another overnight down in Little Mouth to map the dogleg and search out the section that Cissy thought might link several caves in the system.

"When's your sister coming home, then?" Mim had been impatient.

"Should be home already," Cissy told her. "They said she would be out and home today, but she's pretty wiped out. If it was anybody else, I'd think they were using her illness as an excuse for a little vacation, but Amanda isn't the type. I think she needs the sleep."

"When she gets home, we'll go." Jean's shrug was eloquent. "It'll wait. Cave's been there forever, an't going nowhere."

For Cissy, every day at Amanda's was a revelation. When she cooked the boys rice cereal, she read the index cards Amanda had taped to the cabinets. When she threw their jeans in the washing machine, there were more cards affixed to the shelves in there. Crab-bed handwriting recorded numbers and dates. "My Lord, she writes everything down," Cissy whispered. She tracked the cards through the house, each carefully annotated and pinned securely to a drawer or shelf or cupboard.

"Your mama is crazy," Cissy told little Gabe. "Just absolutely crazy." He bubbled milk at her with a smile. The two boys, Michael and Gabriel, were as sweet as their mama was sour. "Only Amanda would name her children for archangels," Dede teased when they were born, but neither Dede nor Cissy had ever spent much time with them. Amanda did not let her boys out of her sight very often, and did not care for the idea of other people watching them. "I get it now," Cissy told Delia. "She never wanted us to know what they were like." Cissy was sure that Amanda's boys were also the most exhausting creatures on the planet.

"You can't leave them for a minute," Cissy complained.

"You can't leave any baby, and toddlers are just a little bit beyond babies," Delia told her. "Amanda's boys are like anybody's babies, only cuter than most."

Cissy had not had the energy to argue, but she was sure Delia was wrong. Nobody could be as exhausting as those two. Little Michael was three and a half, and talked every moment he was conscious, telling stories that intertwined angels and truck drivers. He recited Bible verses in a chirping soprano, and sang "Jesus loves me" when nothing else came into his brain. The baby, Gabe, only fourteen months, barely spoke, though he clearly worshiped his big brother and worked his mouth like some baby guppy soundlessly echoing the endless stream that Michael produced.

"Bet Gabe doesn't learn to talk till he leaves home."

"Oh, he's learning. Just won't be able to get a word in till then."

Delia came over every day at noon to see if Cissy had lost her mind yet. She found the idea of Cissy as mom-substitute endlessly amusing, and her stint as baby-sitter a marvelous opportunity, letting Delia play grandma to her heart's content. Cissy had no intention of wasting any chance to take a minute away from the boys. Grandma and the boys quickly developed their own language and games, little rituals that the boys seemed to enjoy as much as Delia did.

"You just eat it up, don't you?" Cissy accused Delia.

"With a spoon," Delia said. "With a great big grandma spoon."

When Delia came in the morning, Gabe started to crow and wave his arms. Delia leaned over him and licked the spot just between his fine blond eyebrows, prompting a stuttering giggle. It was their way of greeting each other, and Delia loved the way Gabe's face would wrinkle and brighten at her kiss. Gabe was easily her favorite. He was not yet walking, so following after his big brother was difficult for him, but he did it anyway, accomplishing forward motion by hanging on to anything he could reach—furniture, tablecloths, people, or the dog. For every few feet the child accomplished, he fell or staggered sideways another few. The wonder was that for all his troubles, Gabe never cried when he fell. He merely pulled himself up and set off again in pursuit of his oblivious older brother. If Cissy had not snatched Gabe up half a dozen times, he would have split his head on the steps or the prayer stools Amanda had planted strategically all over the living room.

"It's no wonder Amanda has wound up in the hospital," Cissy told Delia. "I'm surprised she never put sleeping pills in their cereal."

Delia laughed. "I told you that you had no idea what Amanda's life was like. Raising babies is how God sorts us out. Only the strong survive. The weak call their mamas to come help."

"Well, I'm weak." Cissy wiped one last streak of dried rice cereal off the back door and dropped into a kitchen chair. "I give it up to you. I'm as weak as they come, and a damn fool for agreeing to stay over."

"All babies are angels," Delia said, and left it at that to lean over and lick her grandson again. Gabe cackled and flapped his arms so engagingly that Delia took a moment to rub her cheek on his little pink instep. "Baby skin," she sighed. "It just smells so good."

"Lord God." Cissy stared at Delia as if the woman had lost her mind. "You are just past yourself, aren't you? You talk like you are on drugs."

"You just wait till you have your own." Delia untangled Gabe's curls with gentle fingers.

"Oh, you can give that notion up right now. I'm with Dede on that. Amanda is the only one going to give you grandchildren. Far as I can tell, babies are shit factories, little industrial-waste sites. Rice and cereal and ca-ca just oozes out of them, and I think Michael is deliberately doing his business in corners and trying to hide it."

"Well, he was just getting the notion about the potty when his mama got sick. Three and a half is about right. With Amanda gone, I'm not surprised Michael is acting out a little."

"Three and a half is way too old. I thought two was when they learned to use the toilet."

"You've read a lot about it, haven't you?" Delia was enjoying herself.

"I'm doing on-the-job training, and I can tell you Michael is going to be a sneaky man. He hid his dirty underpants in the potato bin. Don't even know how long they'd been in there when I found them. I had to throw out the potatoes, pour bleach in there, and set the bin in the sun."

Delia smiled and carefully scooped warm water over the gleeful and struggling Gabe. She had him propped in his baby bath on the kitchen counter. Cissy was doing well at keeping the house clean, but was stark terrified of bathing the boys. She had nearly dropped Gabe, and Michael had pissed in her face while she was sponging him clean. "He laughed," she told Delia. "He knew exactly what he was doing."

Delia had told her then how Cissy had done the same thing when she was still a toddler, standing naked on the side of the tub and pissing as far as she was able. "It's just what you should expect," Delia told her. "It's a sign of spirit, not meanness."

Cissy was not so sure. Little Michael was waiting his turn while watching the Amanda-approved Bible cartoons, special-ordered from the cable evangelical program. The toddler's piercing soprano could be clearly heard over the deep bass of the announcer. "Watch out. Watch out." It sounded as if he were warning Daniel not to put his hands in the lion's mouth. Cissy sat back on her heels and cocked her head. "Did any of us talk that much? Did Amanda?"

"Not Amanda." Amanda and Dede were pretty much quiet. Early walkers but quiet. "You talked a bit, but I think that was Randall. He was always putting his face up next to yours and urging you on."

"Lord, why?"

"It's a daddy thing."

"It's crazy. I like these boys when they're sleeping. Unconscious, that's when they're at their best. Awake, they're enough to give anybody gallstones. Gallstones, hernias, high blood pressure. It's a wonder more mamas don't just up and keel over. Did you read those pamphlets Michael brought home from the hospital? Stress and bile, that's what got to Amanda. Pregnant women, diabetics, and folks with high cholesterol—that's who comes down with gallstones. I bet Amanda has been living on leftover baby food, applesauce, and butter gravy since Michael was born. And bile? Amanda was born with buckets of bile. I think it is babies that kill you. Having children, that's a life-threatening undertaking."

Delia pulled Gabe up to her shoulder in his warm terry towel. She shook her head at Cissy but said nothing. She remembered Amanda as an infant, eyes full of stars and mouth open and soft. Her hard-eyed oldest girl had been the sweetest baby. It was Cissy who was born grumpy—a little leaden-faced, angry creature. Sullen, resentful, every inch Randall's daughter. Colic at six weeks, croup twice, she was the most difficult of the three girls, but Delia knew better than to tell her that. She watched as Cissy emptied her bucket into the sink with Gabe's bathwater. No. She would never tell her. Gabe rubbed his face against her neck, and Delia clucked softly into his hair.

"Oh, you most handsome," she whispered to him, watching as her daughter swished dirty water around the sink. "You most precious precious baby boy, you just the best. Yes, you are." Cissy rolled her eyes in elaborate contempt, and Delia smiled to herself. Funny how sometimes being predictable was the best gift she could give to Cissy. But if that was what it took, she thought to herself, and shrugged.

"You just the most precious precious."

Gabe crowed again, and all of them were happy as they could be.

Delia told Cissy to get out of the house for a while. Amanda would be home soon and Delia wanted every hour she could get with the boys. Cissy said a quick thank you and was out the door. Delia put Gabe in his high chair, pulled over his bowl of applesauce, and settled in happily. I'm good at this grandma stuff, she thought happily. Very good at it. Better than I ever was at being mama. She looked out the door but Cissy was already gone.

Delia could cook up a lot of outrage and stubbornness about what she had done as a mother. There never seemed to be any easy way to talk about it, but sometimes she almost felt like everything made sense. She had read a bit of Betty Friedan. She'd seen *Up the Sandbox*. Most of all, she'd listened to music, Janis and Aretha and even a little Loretta Lynn. Sin was the boys' coin, she had told herself. Shame was the boys' game. A woman left lonely couldn't afford to think herself that kind of lost. Delia had taken it all in and worked out her own answers. No, she told herself, feeding Gabe brimming spoonfuls of his favorite strained apples, she had not been wrong to leave Cliff, to go with Randall, or to leave them both. She had made Cissy and gone after her girls. Everything she had done, she had done for a reason. What dogged Delia was the price she had had to pay, still had to pay—the way Emmet Tyler looked at her and how sure she was that she dared not look back, how hard it was to get Amanda or Cissy to talk to her, and the way Dede would stare into the distance sometimes when she thought no one was looking in her direction.

Sometimes it felt to Delia like she had Grandma Windsor in the back of her head, someone speaking God's big mean words—a Baptist God and a Pentecostal sin. She could shake a lot of it, but she couldn't shake it all. She knew that the first time Cissy shouted "I hate you," the first time she looked into Amanda's eyes, and the first time she saw Dede bite her lower lip and pick her fingernails. There was a cost, a cost to everything. Delia had paid all her life. When she looked at her girls, all she wanted was to have them not to pay as much. When she looked at her grandsons, she began to think that maybe it would all work out.

Chapter 19

Granddaddy Byrd died sitting up smoking a cigarette.

"Looked the same as he always did, sitting there on the porch while I took care of the house," Mrs. Stone told everyone down at the Bonnet. "Of course, it wasn't as if I checked to see how often he moved. He's been sitting on that porch near fourteen hours a day the last few years, but I always checked on him pretty regular."

Delia and the girls barely knew Mrs. Stone well enough to recognize her. The woman had moved in with Granddaddy Byrd about the time Amanda married, but no one knew how she had persuaded that old man to let her live in the house.

"You think they're doing it?" Dede asked Delia one time.

"No," Delia said. "I don't. She needs a place to live, and he needs somebody. Just glad it an't me having to drag out there and make sure he an't taken to yelling at the cars on the highway."

"He's a crazy old man."

"Well, she's a tough old lady." Delia had not wanted to talk about Granddaddy Byrd. She never did. "It's the best thing all around, Mrs. Stone watching him. At least it saves me the trouble."

Mrs. Stone was nervous when she came in to give Delia the news, but carefully polite. M.T. said it was good of her to come, and she replied that no one should hear about death over the telephone. She pushed her thin hair behind her ears and took a quick puff on her Salem when Delia sat down beside her on the couch at the front of the Bonnet. Mrs. Stone was a big-boned woman, though the loose skin on her neck and arms suggested she had once been bigger still. The way she sat on the couch, it looked as if she were trying not to put her full weight down. Used to be a whole lot bigger, I bet, M.T. thought to herself.

"It was a good death," Mrs. Stone said. "A good death." Delia nodded and took a drink of water from the little bottle she had taken out of the icebox in the back. The smell of Mrs. Stone's cigarette was making her mouth go dry. Six months since Delia had had a cigarette, and she still wanted one desperately. Why did I quit? she wondered, and tried to focus on what the woman was saying.

"Like I said, he was sitting up out there on the porch in that old rocker I'd put out for him. Took me the longest time to get him to use it and stop squatting on the steps. Always had nail holes in his britches right in the seat. Got him in that rocker and it made a world of difference. Think it made his knees hurt less too, but he would never say so. You know how he was." Mrs. Stone looked around for an ashtray, and smiled gratefully when M.T. handed her a souvenir glass dish from Stone Mountain.

"I've been there," Mrs. Stone said, putting out the cigarette in the dish where the peak of the mountain pushed up against the rim. She smiled again, reflexively, pushed her hair back one more time, and turned to Delia.

"Well, like I said. It had been a long time since I'd seen him light another cigarette. And I'd shaken out the rugs right by him, and he hadn't complained like he usually did, and that wasn't right. I was used to him always making his harrumph noises, spitting off to the side like I was driving him mad with dust. Only this time he was not moving. I was starting to feel grateful when I saw the ash fall off his finger, saw his finger was scorched. Man had died between one drag and another. That cigarette had burned to an ash between his two fingers."

Mrs. Stone smiled gently. "He died right," she said, her head going up and down emphatically. "Man just died peaceful and right."

Past her shoulder Cissy could see Delia's face, the hollows beneath her cheekbones sucked in tight, her teeth clamped together. She's going to cry, Cissy thought. But Delia only shook her head once and pushed her hairpins back in her twist. Cissy saw her lips move then, repeating an inaudible curse.

"Goddamn," Delia said. "If so, it's just about the only thing he ever did right." She turned around to get her purse.

Cissy drove out to Granddaddy Byrd's farmhouse with Delia. Dede pulled in behind them at the I-84 junction, driving the little VW, the one she called the turnip, that she had bought off Marcia Pearlman's nephew Malcolm. It was painted purple and white and had dirt crusted over the back bumper where Dede kept ramming it into the dried mud bank of the ditch by her trailer park.

"Got a call from M.T.," Dede told Cissy when she climbed out of the car. She was wearing cutoff jeans and one of the black and white Goober's T-shirts, emblazoned "Can Hold My Own" with two hands drawn in so that they cupped her breasts. She nodded at Mrs. Stone. "He died then?"

"He did." Mrs. Stone smiled. "He surely did. Went as easy as you please. Best death I ever saw." She glanced once at the T-shirt's legend and pinked up, but kept her smile and led them up the steps into the house.

For Cissy it was the first time she had been to the farmhouse since they moved to Cayro, and it looked as if it had barely changed, though Mrs. Stone must have been watering the bushes at the sides of the steps. They were fuller and not so brown and dry. Otherwise, the house seemed untouched, except that the porch steps had been torn down and rebuilt, the new wood making the rest of the place look even more worn and silvery. The pine siding seemed almost marshmallow-soft in places, and the entry was marked with greasy handprints and mildewed smudges shoulder-high along the pink wallpaper surface.

"I never could get that clean," Mrs. Stone said when she saw where Cissy was looking. "Mr. Byrd said it was from Luke dragging his wet self along when he'd come in late nights. Might have been. It's an oil stain, won't come off." She seemed nervous with the three women looking around.

"He's in there. I didn't do much, just cleaned him up and got him covered. That boy Jasper from the Texaco station helped carry him in for me." She waved toward the bedroom that opened off the side of the living room next to the arched fireplace. The headboard was just visible against the wall past the door—a big dark-wood headboard whose posts were cut off ragged so that the lighter core of the wood showed raw and dusty. The pillows had been taken off the bed, and Granddaddy Byrd's prominent chin was visible where his head lay tilted slightly backward.

"Amazing how heavy he was. The dead always are, though. I remember my husband Howard, how heavy he got." Cissy and Dede couldn't help but stare at Mrs. Stone. Delia ignored her, looking to the open bedroom and the body that lay there.

"You know this place is yours." Mrs. Stone was trying to get Delia to look at her. She stepped forward so that her body blocked Delia's view. "From your parents," she said. "Your daddy held the paper on it before he died. And he never left no will. I went through everything when I was helping Mr. Byrd get the Social Security started. No will anywhere. So it is all yours. Always was."

Delia said nothing. She stepped around Mrs. Stone and headed for the bedroom. Cissy hesitated to follow her, and Dede had already stepped over to the fireplace and the crowded mantel.

"I did him as nice as I could," Mrs. Stone went on. Cissy thought she was talking about the laying out, but it quickly became obvious she was not. "He wasn't no trouble once I got used to his ways. He always wanted it quiet. Said he didn't like to hear no hen-scratching woman talk. Well, I didn't put up with that, you can imagine. Told him I wasn't going to tiptoe around while I did my work. No sir."

Delia finally looked at the woman. "He always wanted it quiet," she said.

"Well, he was old. Old men are like that." Mrs. Stone was nodding again.

"How old was he?" Dede's voice was frankly curious. "He'd never say."

"Oh, near about a hundred for sure. When I got his Social Security going, they were real surprised to hear about him. Must have thought he was dead. Don't get too many men in their nineties going in to apply for benefits."

Delia had turned away toward the death room again. She walked to the doorway and stopped. Cissy was looking at Dede. "You've been out here?" Cissy asked.

"A few times." Dede's face was guarded, her mouth pulled back at one corner as if she were thinking something caustic. "I come out to see him a couple of times. He wouldn't never say much."

They just looked at each other. Mrs. Stone was going on about her accomplishment—getting that old man to do the paperwork for his Social Security. Delia looked back at the woman briefly with eyes that had gone hot and dark. The skin around Delia's eyes looked tight. Cissy felt a momentary pulse of anger. There was something Delia and Dede knew, something in their eyes.

"Course we only got them to pay $154 a month," Mrs. Stone went on. "Nothing really, but with the chicken eggs and the garden produce we would sell off the porch I managed. Managed pretty well." She looked pleased with herself, her face alight with achievement.

"And he got to die at home. He got to die right." Mrs. Stone beamed at Delia.

They all looked at her. Her moon-wide face flushed, and she looked hastily from Cissy to Dede.

"Well, think of the tragedy he endured. Losing his sons. That Luke's been in jail about all his life. And you daddy." She gestured at Delia and made a sad face. "So much loss," she said. "So much loss."

"Let me see him." Delia walked through the doorway, away from the suddenly stricken Mrs. Stone. She looked back once from the room and pushed the door closed behind her. Mrs. Stone nodded, took out a hankie, and wiped her eyes. She turned to the girls. "So much loss," she said again. Cissy could see no tears, but the grief seemed genuine.

Mrs. Stone blew her nose and shook her head sorrowfully. "He was all the family she had left, wasn't he? Except for you girls?" She clearly was not going to stop talking. It was as if all those years of taking care of Granddaddy Byrd had left her with an ungovernable tongue. Or perhaps she did not know how to be around people who were supposed to be grieving but seemed more curious than despondent.

"Oh, I heard a lot about you." Mrs. Stone waved her handkerchief at Cissy and Dede. "Delia's girls. Oh my, yes. Delia's two pitiful girls."

Cissy narrowed her eyes. If the old man had said that, he meant Dede and Amanda, not her. She could bet he'd never mentioned her.

Dede stepped over and put a hand on Mrs. Stone's arm. She said, "We'd like a minute too. I know you have things to do, stuff to get together. So don't let us stop you."

Mrs. Stone's mouth gaped a little. "Well, I wanted to talk to your mama," she said. "There are things . . . well, there are things I'd like to discuss."

She's going to want to stay here, Dede thought. She probably has nowhere else to go. Dede was nodding, her hand patting Mrs. Stone's arm.

"Yes," she said. "There will be lots to talk over, but there will be time later. I'm sure you have all kinds of things that need to be done."

Mrs. Stone's head bobbed fiercely. "Oh yes," she said. "Oh my, yes." And headed back to the kitchen.

The girls watched Mrs. Stone walk away. When the kitchen door swung shut behind her, they both sighed. "Big solid butt on her," Dede said. "How old you think she is?"

"Old enough to know better." Cissy's drawl was bitter, but Dede nodded in agreement, her face pensive.

"Lord. Don't ever let me get that desperate." Dede ran her palm up her neck to her chin. "Saddest damn thing in the world." She looked at Cissy. "What you think?"

Cissy shrugged. "You really came out here on your own?" she asked. She watched Dede's eyes track around the room, cataloging junk, tools, and knickknacks. A line of ugly ceramic dolls sat on the mantel in order of size. Each had the same painted black face with exaggerated features, red lips, and red aprons.

"What you want to bet those are Mrs. Stone's?" Dede waved at the dolls.

Cissy laughed. "No bet."

"Yeah," Dede said after a moment. "I came out here. When y'all came back. Before Delia came and got us." She looked around the room. "Give the old lady something. This is a lot cleaner than it was. It was awful."

Cissy tasted dust in her mouth, but the room was clean, more or less. The floor was swept, the rug was smoothed, the surfaces crowded but scrubbed. Still, the air in the room tasted old and bitter—woody, as if the grit of the pine walls had been sifting down a long time.

"You come out here alone?" Cissy watched Dede's eyes. They kept moving, lighting on one thing and then another. Something was wrong. Something was bothering her. Dede looked like she had been drinking a lot of coffee or holding something in too long. The muscles in her neck were jumping.

"Alone, yeah. I came alone." Dede turned around to face the mantel. "You don't know. Grandma Windsor, she never would tell us nothing. Never said more than Delia's name and a curse. Told me I was just like her, sinful and hard-hearted. Called me names like you wouldn't believe that old lady would speak, but she would say anything to us. Anything." She paused.

"And I heard enough. People love to tell horrible things. Heard this old man was out here. I hitchhiked out to see for myself who he was."

"I can't believe he told you anything. He was a damn hard man. You should have seen how he treated Delia." Cissy grimaced, remembering the first morning she'd spent in Cayro, the overcooked egg sandwich at the diner, and that old man with his crooked hands and evil eyes. "Harrumph."

Dede grinned at her. "I bet," she said. "I can just bet."

On the walls on either side of the mantel were black-and-white pictures in painted metal frames, most of them featuring cars and people standing around cars. There were different groupings in each photo, but the same figures recurred. Children, a woman, a man, and in many—startling for how little he had changed—the figure of Granddaddy Byrd. Dede pointed to one of the photos.

"That's our uncle Luke, the one she was talking about. He raced stock cars for a while. He was the one I always wanted to meet, but I think he's been in jail since I was born."

Cissy stepped closer and looked at the face. "He kill somebody?" she asked.

"Something." Dede's shoulders went up and down. "The old man wouldn't say."

"What did he tell you?"

Dede turned to Cissy, her face squeezed into a peculiar expression resembling awe. "He talked about Delia. He talked about her like she was one of the Seven Wonders."

"But he hated her."

"Maybe." Dede shrugged. "If he did, he was proud too. He was a strange old man."

Cissy looked back at the photos. In the center of the display there was one with a smudge on the bottom of the frame. A scorch mark showed on the wallpaper beneath the frame as if a candle had been held too close to the image. It was a family photo with everyone leaning against one of those fat-looking old cars with rounded bumpers. A woman held an infant in her arms while two little boys leaned into her skirt. Next to her was a handsome man with a tiny girl up on his shoulders, her knees jutting out around his chin. Just to one side of them all was an almost smiling caricature of Granddaddy Byrd, looking just enough like himself for Cissy to recognize the face.

"He talked to you," she whispered.

"A little. I had to be patient. You couldn't ask him no questions or he'd get all mean and clam up. Didn't bother me, though. I had grown up with Grandma Windsor." She laughed harshly. "Granddaddy Byrd had nothing on her."

Cissy shook her head. She tried to imagine Granddaddy Byrd sitting on his porch talking to his great-granddaughter like a real person. It was beyond her. She looked again at the photo—the old man had either just smiled or was about to smile when the picture was snapped. The shape of the mouth was proof.

Her eyes tracked across the other people in the photo. The woman was laughing. She had hair that looked to be the exact shade that Cissy's hair turned in late summer, light, almost blond, but the face looked like Delia's. Cissy looked sideways at Dede. No, the face looked like Dede.

"She looks like you," Cissy said to Dede.

Dede stepped close to the picture. "Maybe." She frowned. "More like Delia, I think."

"No." Cissy shook her head. "Like you."

Dede pursed her lips and shrugged. "That's them, you know. The lost family." Her finger tapped each figure. "Delia's mama, our grandmother. The daddy, Granddaddy Byrd's prize son. And the boys. And Delia herself." The finger stopped on the little girl. "All of them."

Cissy stared at the woman and the boys. "They died?"

"All of them, yeah."

"Damn."

"You knew." It was something between a question and an accusation.

Cissy frowned. What did she know? She looked again at the little girl, at Delia. The relaxed, easy face of a child who was happy to be where she was. The open mouth that was ready to smile, and it looked as if she smiled a lot. The small-framed body, thin face, big eyes, a girl no more than seven or eight. The boys had bruised knees, sharp elbows, and big smiles. The baby was cuddled up to the mama's neck. All of them were leaning into each other, a happy family. Delia's family.

Delia had been raised by Granddaddy Byrd, that was what Cissy knew. The family had died somehow. The story had been passed over, whispered or mumbled. She remembered Delia's face stern with grief and pain. Not crying season, some earlier time, some terrible story had been told and buried. Or had it ever been told at all? How had they died? A car wreck? Cissy looked at all the cars in the pictures. Then she looked again at Granddaddy Byrd with that almost smile.

The bedroom door swung open. Delia stepped out, her face wrung dry. Cissy flinched, seeing the bones of that little girl in her mother's narrow features.

"I'll have to talk to Reverend Hillman," she said. "Or maybe Michael. Maybe Amanda would prefer I asked Michael." She ran one hand through her hair and looked back at the kitchen door. "And I need to talk to Mrs. Stone, settle with her."

Delia's shoulders slumped as she moved toward the kitchen. She's getting old, Cissy thought. She looked back at the picture and the little girl. How long since it was taken? Thirty-five, forty years now? She thought about the old man on the bed, her great-grandfather, and the man in the photo. Little laugh lines around the mouth, crinkled eyes. Part of the happy family. Behind him the grinning dark-headed uncle leaned in over the bumper, one leg up, and he too was laughing. Part of the family she didn't know. Cissy did not know any of them. She shuddered.

"They all died," she whispered.

Dede was at Cissy's elbow. "Happens," she said. "Terrible things happen all the time." She crossed her arms over her breasts and clamped a hand down on each shoulder. "Let's go out. I need a smoke."

Cissy looked toward the kitchen, but Delia had gone through the door. She turned and followed her sister, still thinking about the photos. They belonged to Delia now, along with the house and everything else. Cissy trailed one hand along the stain on the wallpaper in the entry. All this had belonged to Delia's parents, to the family.

Dede squatted on the front steps and shook out a Camel. She lit it with one of the Day-Glo lighters she kept in a stand by the cash register at the store. The piercing blue color went opalescent as she turned it in her hand, then back to a shivery sapphire. Dede was always getting in new lighters, buying them for herself, and losing them everywhere she went. She tossed this one from one hand to the other and then laid it down on the steps.

Cissy dropped down beside her. The dimensions of the yard seemed to have altered. The sky had gone dark, and a wind was picking up. "It's going to rain," she said.

"Maybe." Dede looked at Cissy and then back out across the yard. "Nolan wants me to marry him."

Cissy turned to her. "What?"

"Marry him. Nolan wants me to marry him." Dede's face was pinched. She seemed angry.

"Well, don't you want to marry him?"

"I don't want to marry nobody." Dede kicked her feet hard on the steps. "Not Nolan, not anyone." She rocked her body forward and back fiercely while her fingers did a complicated spinning trick with the cigarette in one hand. She took a drag and then shot the smoke out in a long stream. "Goddamn."

"Don't you love Nolan?" Cissy said it carefully, but not carefully enough.

Dede jumped up. "Hell. Course I love him." She strode back and forth, waving the cigarette like a pointer in the air. "But marriage. Marriage screws things up. Think about it. Who do we know married and happy?"

"Amanda?"

"Oh! Amanda! Amanda an't happy."

Cissy watched the bright blue lighter rocking on the step's edge. "Dede, you love Nolan."

"Love has got nothing to do with it. Marriage is what's wrong. I'd sooner tattoo Nolan's name on my butt than marry him." Dede paused in her furious march, her face breaking up into a grin that Cissy had never seen before, half glee and half outrage. "I would too. Damn sight better to wear a tattoo than a wedding ring."

Cissy nodded. Dede would do anything, that was sure. Maybe it was the old man dying, but Cissy suddenly realized that Dede had been tightening up for weeks. She had thought the cause was Emmet, who had started hanging around Delia again. M.T. said Delia was having long lunches with him, something Dede had complained about the week before. The funny part was that Cissy knew Dede liked Emmet. It was just the idea of Delia liking the man too much that seemed to get Dede so upset. But Nolan? Dede loved Nolan, and Nolan surely loved Dede. Where was the problem with that?

"It's going to go to hell," Dede said.

Cissy looked at her sister. Dede was standing there with her head tilted back looking up at the storm clouds rolling high in the sky. Her eyes were red and visibly wet. She flicked her cigarette butt out into the grass.

"It's just all going to go straight to hell." Her tone was unequivocal and sadly defeated.

Oh God, Cissy thought. Don't let her do something stupid. Please God. Please. Let Nolan tell her he doesn't want to get married, that it was all a joke. She put her hands over her ears and pressed tight, listening to her teeth grind. Nolan had been so happy lately, so happy. He'd gone down to Atlanta and done his audition, and had just grinned wide when Cissy asked him about it.

"We'll just have to wait and see," he told Cissy. "Just wait and see. Dede and me, no telling what we might do."

He doesn't understand, Cissy thought, not sure she did either. The look on Dede's face was pure misery. That Cissy could understand. Dede was hurting. Dede was scared and hurting bad.

Granddaddy Byrd's funeral was at Holiness Redeemer. Michael brought Amanda, who barely acknowledged what was happening, not even bothering to chase little Michael when he ran over to Dede and Nolan. Jean and Mim stood with Cissy. Mrs. Stone had brought them the old white Bible from the farmhouse, but Delia pretended not to see it. Michael tucked it under one arm and pulled his boys up on his lap for the prayers. When they all walked away from the graveside, Delia remained standing by the massed pile of flowers. She came back to the Terrill Road house an hour after everyone else and went out to sit under the pecan trees out back. When he saw her back there, Michael took the boys out to her. He didn't speak, just nodded and took a seat on one of the chairs Delia had been planning to refinish. He kept Gabe on his knee while Michael ran back and forth from his father to the farthest tree. Gabe kept waving his arms and making "mmm mmm" sounds. After a bit Delia lifted one hand and waved it in Gabe's direction. Happily he tried to catch her hand. On the third try, he managed it and was transferred from his daddy's knee to his grandmother's arms. She pressed her face into his hair and hugged him close. Michael stood up and walked over to the tree where his oldest son was piling up pecans. He didn't return until well after he heard Gabe start to giggle and Delia finally laugh.

Chapter 20

The best thing about helping out at Amanda's place was that Cissy got to quit her job at the realty office. At the beginning of the year, she had taken the job doing data entry for the County Realty office three afternoons a week, but as the months passed she arrived late more and more often, slipping into the office long after everyone had left. There is nothing worse in the world, Cissy decided, than typing page after page of abbreviated notes, square-foot measurements and endless bland repetitions of the same few dozen sentences. Over and over she typed, "Secluded, 2 BR/2bth, fp, fixer-upper, grd vw, motivated seller, new roof, hdwd flrs, real sweetheart, new fixtures." Prices changed, brokers passed on different parcels, new properties were listed, and always there were the irritating little notes from the various real estate agents. Cissy forgot to include outbuildings, or the den that doubled as a guest room, or the decorative shutters, or the special enticements like the so-called English garden, which Cissy decided must mean a wild tangle untamed by Southern propensities for lawns and flower beds. Always there was something—spelling errors, missed measurements, a "special" property not put in the "special" category listings. Things were tight in the county. Property was not selling. There had to be a reason, and the notes made it clear that the problem was the way Cissy put in the data.

Cissy wondered if waitress work might not be easier. She hated creeping into the back of the realty office, trying to avoid the staff and sitting down to face the big jumble of marked-up forms and multicolored taped inserts. "You forgot." "You did not." "Please do not . . ." It was supposed to be an easy job, a favor to Delia's girl, who after all was living at home and just needed enough of an income to keep afloat at the community college, but there had turned out to be more buildings for sale than Cissy would ever have imagined, more lots and farms and abandoned shanties. All of them required Cissy to type and track and update their listings. Better, far better, to sit on Nolan's porch after turning the boys over to Michael, to drink seltzer with orange slices and listen to Nolan play music and repeat stories his relatives had told him.

Nolan had his prized clarinet on his lap, a Buffet R13 with a Selmer mouthpiece. He was rubbing the black surface of the instrument with a soft cloth, smiling with pleasure as the grenadilla wood polished up. "African black," Mr. Clausen had called it when he gave it to him. "Grenadilla and sterling silver. You keep it clean and polished, and it will last forever." The first time he played the new clarinet, Nadine had beamed at Nolan with such pleasure, the image had become imprinted on his brain. The weeks when he had to count quarters to meet the bills, Nolan would remember that smile when he looked over at the clarinet. He had sold his old one, the Vito Leblanc made of black plastic. ("Resonite, Nolan, Resonite.") It had brought in a desperately needed $200 the year before. He learned that the secondhand Buffet had cost Mr. Clausen and the group around $1,000, and as tight as things were, Nolan had only once considered selling it. That he had not been forced to do so was among the few things for which he was infinitely grateful.

"Is your mama all right?" he asked Cissy. "She looked so strange at the funeral."

"She's fine. Delia doesn't change. A mountain could fall on her, and she'd get up and go to work at the Bonnet."

Nolan nodded. "I got another audition coming up," he said. "Next week. I'm going to drive over to Atlanta for the day and meet with the director at Emory."

Cissy looked at Nolan. His eyes were trained on the clarinet, his voice careful. Why was he mentioning this audition? Nolan did lots of auditions, and she rarely went with him anymore. "You asking me to come?" Cissy frowned. She and the girls were supposed to make another try at Little Mouth next week.

"No, no." Nolan shook his head. "Just telling you. Just saying I'm going." He was quiet for a moment, buffing the wood of his instrument. "It's different, this time," he said suddenly. "If they offer me a job, I might consider taking it."

As often as she had encouraged him to do just that, Cissy was still dismayed at the idea of Nolan leaving her behind. "You'd leave Cayro?!"

Nolan looked uncomfortable. "Maybe. I might." He rolled the instrument between his fingers. "If I could figure things out, get a nice place down there, and get Mama set up. Of course it all depends on Dede, whether she likes the idea. She's been so restless lately. Been out practicing with that gun Craig gave her. She's taken to keeping it under the front seat of her car."

Nolan paused. He began the lengthy process of disassembling and cleaning the clarinet before putting it away. While slipping the reed into its case, he said, "Dede's unhappy, you know. Or maybe scared. We're happy, but . . ." He paused. "I think she's getting tired of the store and the same stuff all the time. Sometimes she talks about doing something different. She wants to learn about car engines, she says. Wants to do some driving. All kinds of things she could be doing. I want her to have the chance, and I could make good money in Atlanta. Play my music and get us a good place."

"You have lost your tiny mind." Cissy shook her head. "Dede an't going to move to Atlanta. And you don't know that you can get a job there."

"I can get a job," Nolan said. "If not this one, then another one. I'm good and I'm going to be better, and I know how to work for what I want." He looked thoughtful but determined. "I want to see Dede be happy the way she deserves."

Nolan sighed and closed his eyes. When he opened them, he looked directly at Cissy. "You're my best friend in the world. I just wanted to tell you what I was thinking. Wanted you to know. It an't like I'm leaving tomorrow. It an't like nothing has happened at all just yet. I just wanted you to know what I was thinking."

Cissy looked down at the shadows on the steps and then up at

Nolan's wide-open, hopeful face. "Well," she said, "like you say, it an't happening tomorrow. And when it does happen, we'll sort it out." She stood up and pushed her hair back. "You're my friend, Nolan Reitower. That an't going to change 'cause you're thinking of doing something different, but you talk real careful to Dede about this. She an't the kind of person likes surprises. And she an't that easy to predict. She might not want to go nowhere, you know. Then what would you do?"

"Stay in Cayro," Nolan said with a smile. "For Dede, I'd stay in Cayro and bake biscuits till the flesh falls off my bones." He made it sound like a cheerful prospect. He made it sound like the happiest thing he could imagine doing with his life.

Cissy spent every afternoon picking up after little Michael and Gabe and worrying about Amanda. She was still adjusting to the changes in Amanda since she'd come home from the hospital. Michael was pink and uncertain when he asked Cissy to stay a bit longer to help with the boys because "Amanda is not quite herself yet."

"You sure Amanda wants me to stay?" Cissy could not believe it.

"Yes, yes," Michael said. "She's a little fuzzy-headed right now. I'm sure she'll be fine once she catches up on a little sleep. If you could come over during the day for a while, it might help." He looked deeply troubled. "The doctor thinks Amanda needs a little time to rest and recover."

"She needs more than sleep," Cissy muttered, but the look on Michael's face was too tentative for her to confront. "Of course, I'll help," she promised. "At least it will give me a reason to take a break from typing for the realty company."

The week before Amanda went into the hospital, she and Cissy had run into each other at Delia's on a Saturday morning, and Amanda had made a caustic comment about Cissy's caving trips with "those strange girls."

"It an't debauchery we're engaged in," Cissy said. "It's exploration. We're mapping the system from Little Mouth to Paula's Lost."

"Uh-huh." Amanda put on her saintly expression. "And what's the use of that?"

"Well, then we'd know."

"And then?" Amanda asked. "What will you do then?"

"Plant seeds between my toes and grow marigolds! Mind your own damned business," Cissy shouted, and stomped out of Delia's kitchen.

As it turned out, that argument was the last conversation the two of them had before Amanda wound up in the hospital and Granddaddy Byrd died. Cissy worried that Amanda would return to their argument at the first chance. But the Amanda who came home from the hospital seemed to have no energy for arguing. She could barely be persuaded to get out of bed in the morning. Only when little Michael climbed up on Amanda's lap and demanded a story did Amanda show any spark. She had perked up enough to start retelling the story of Daniel in the lions' den, but when her son bounced excitedly beside her, she stopped and clenched him so tightly to her neck he had yelped. She had let him go with a heartfelt "Lord!"

"You all right?" Cissy asked. Amanda's color was odd; bright red circles stood out on her pale cheeks. She was staring at little Michael with enormous stricken eyes, and an expression that bordered on horror.

Amanda shook her head. "Going for a drive," she announced, and left before Cissy could ask her when she would be back.

Caught between resentment at being left with the demanding boys and relief that Amanda seemed not to want to argue, Cissy spent the day cleaning the already pristine house and preparing what she would say when the subject of her future came up again. She canceled everything on the schedule on the fridge—the home visits and the baking—and concentrated on caring for the boys, but it was still too much. In the late afternoon she realized she had managed to miss little Michael's judo lesson. He had been in the class only two months, taking it up after his Sunday school teacher suggested it would be a good way for him to work on his little problem with acting out.

"Kick butt," Dede laughed when she called to check in. "Amanda's boy needs to kick a little butt to even himself out. Makes sense to me."

Amanda came home shortly before Michael Senior and went immediately back to bed, where she pulled the sheet over her head. "Is she all right?" Michael asked Cissy. "Far as I know," Cissy told him. The next morning she came over a little late and found Amanda fully dressed, sitting at the kitchen table while the boys cried in the back room.

"Going out," Amanda said when Cissy opened the door. She was out the door before Cissy could catch her.

"When will you be home?" Cissy called after her. Amanda did not even look back.

"She leaves as soon as I get there," Cissy told Delia, but Delia merely nodded.

"Let her go," she said. "Amanda's never given herself a minute of her own, let her have a bit of time for herself."

"And what if she never settles back down?" Cissy demanded. "I can't watch these boys forever."

"You can watch them for another week," Delia said. "Give your sister that. What else did you have to do?"

Cissy grumbled, but not very seriously. She had the time. Mim and Jean were pressing her about another trip down Little Mouth, but Cissy put them off. "Next week," she promised Mim. "I told Delia I'd watch Amanda's boys one more week."

What she was thinking about was not the next week but the next year. Tacey bragged about what she would do at Spelman, and Cissy admitted to herself how pointless her classes at the community college were. The future was as unknown to her as the connecting link from Little Mouth to Paula's Lost. The guidance counselor had asked her what she wanted to do, and Cissy had stared at him blankly. She had no fixed goal in her life. The only thing that excited her was going caving, and no one took that seriously, not even her. She couldn't make a life out of crawling around underground.

"You could join the army," Dede told Cissy one Thursday night at Goober's. For months Dede and Nolan had been going over to Goober's at least two nights a week, ordering a pitcher of beer and a big basket of fried vegetables, and sipping whiskey shots out of Dede's bag when the waitress wasn't looking. Dede swore she didn't trust bar whiskey, though it was the price she truly resented, not the quality of the unlabeled bottles. It was like their fried vegetables. No one could guess exactly what those shapeless, crispy objects were before being deep-fried and covered with hot sauce.

"Get real, Dede. I am not going to join the army." Cissy was tired and irritable, more convinced than ever that she never wanted children.

"I would," Dede announced. "If I was you, just out of high school, with a clean record and all, I'd sign up in a minute."

"You wouldn't!" Nolan was appalled. "There's no telling where they'd send you."

"You wouldn't follow me?" Dede sipped at her beer. "You saying you wouldn't follow me wherever I'd go?"

"Course I'd follow you." Nolan poked at the pitcher between them. "I'd follow you to hell if need be, but I hate the idea of you going in the army. I've met some of those army boys, and they tell terrible stories about what happens to women in the army."

"What you expect is going to happen to me, huh?" Dede was red-faced and belligerent. Cissy wondered how many shots she had sneaked from the bottle in her purse. "You think I'm going to fall in love with some big old dyke drill instructor?"

Nolan's mouth fell open. "No, no," he said. "I was thinking about how much you'd hate it."

"I might like it. You don't know." Dede stood up suddenly. She swayed on unsteady legs. "I might like it a hell of a lot more than hanging out in Cayro till the day I die."

When Nolan said nothing, Dede headed for the bathroom, barely missing Sheila, the new waitress, who was bringing another basket of crispy vegetables.

"Oh, she's had a little, I guess," Sheila laughed, and set the basket in front of Nolan.

"I guess," Nolan said. He looked at Cissy with a mournful expression. "If you ask me, both your sisters are going through changes."

"Dede I understand," Cissy told him. She speared a fried mushroom out of the basket and chewed it thoughtfully. "It's Amanda I thought would never change."

Nolan picked through the basket. "Everything changes." He looked toward the bathroom. "Everything and everybody. Except me, of course. Dede told me that she wishes I would change, wishes I would show her what I'm made of. But I have, and she don't seem to know it. This is all I am. Hard work and taking care of the people I love, making a little music and being steady. That's all I know." He sighed. "I've asked her to marry me three times, and she won't say no, she won't say yes. She tells me I'm crazy, and then she fucks my brains out."

Cissy wiggled uncomfortably. "She loves you."

"Oh yeah, I know she loves me." Nolan took a drink of his beer. "I just wish I was sure Dede knew what that means, what love is really about. Some days I get the feeling she thinks sex is love, or craziness is love. That love has to be some big strange amazing thing, not the everyday all-my-life-and-then-some it is for me."

He picked up a nub of fried batter. "I think love's like this zucchini. Zucchini is what keeps Goober's in business, you know. Everybody thinks they know zucchini. Some like it, some hate it. They don't really know it. It's completely unrecognizable once they cook it up. Oh, they throw in a mushroom now and then, but you pay more for the mushrooms, so not too many of those go in. Put in a green pepper sometimes, or a carrot, but mostly it's all zucchini. Perfect cheap bar food, nondescript and usual. Half the people who eat this can't tell you what they ate. Always think it is something else."

"Whatever." Dede took her seat next to Nolan. "I eat it for the grease anyway. So I can drink more. Grease coats your stomach. You gonna drink beer and whiskey shots, you need lots of grease." She put her arm around Nolan and nuzzled his ear. "Why don't we go home?"

Nolan wiped his mouth and gave Cissy a warning glance, then stood up. "See you," he called back as they left.

"Whatever." Dede waved her hand at Cissy.

When they were gone, Cissy looked at the debris on the table, the empty pitcher and the greasy scraps. A pile of mushy zucchini lay on the salty wax paper at the bottom of the basket. Dede had picked the batter off her vegetables and eaten only the fried dough. Wherever possible, she stuck to fried bread and meat; her mainstay was hamburgers, pancake sandwiches, and the vitamins she still swallowed in quantity. "She's skinny now, but you wait," M.T. always said. "The way Dede eats, that girl is going to blow up like a walrus one of these days."

"If she don't die of a heart attack," Cissy said out loud.

"You want anything?" Sheila started clearing the table.

"Salvation," Cissy joked. She was thinking about what Nolan had said, that Dede did not know what love was.

"Well, you won't get that here," Sheila told her, and wiped the table clear.

The next morning Cissy went to Amanda's house early. She had fried eggs with sliced tomatoes on the table when everybody got up. Michael exclaimed over the plates and spooned soft-cooked eggs into plastic bowls for Gabe and little Michael. Amanda blinked down at her plate as if it held something unknown and strange. Before her illness, Amanda was down to eating only vegetables, fruit, and eggs. She would bake bread when the spirit moved her, using recipes from a cookbook published by a women's church group from Nashville— egg bread and cheese loaves mostly. Everything had to have some biblical reference or it was off Amanda's list. As she got sicker, Amanda would eat only eggs and bread, bread torn in half with a prayer and a blessing, and eggs almost runny on the plate. The eggs Cissy had made were soft-cooked but wholesome and sat on the plate next to creamy slices of white bread bare of butter or salt.

"Isn't this wonderful?" Michael said, but Amanda only sipped her milk and watched the boys smear egg into their hair.

There was some way in which the old Amanda associated eggs with Jesus, though Cissy had not quite figured that out. She thought it might have something to do with Easter. She had talked about it with Dede the night before.

"You can't figure these things," Dede said. "She's not rational like you and me. If it were me and I was thinking on Jesus, I'd be out butchering lambs. Or leading some women's group in prayer vigils out at the Piggly Wiggly, but with Amanda you can't predict. What's she doing now?"

"She's not doing anything," Cissy told her sister. "I mean, nothing. She gets up in the morning and goes out of the house. She comes home late in the afternoon and goes right back to bed. She don't talk to me even to complain, and it's making me nervous. I can't figure what she is doing. Makes me think about those people who go crazy and shoot up post offices or set off bombs in clinics. I can't figure what the hell is going on."

Dede's face went blank for a moment, and then she gave a bitter laugh. "Maybe she's finally living in the real world with the rest of us," she said. "Maybe Amanda's finally starting to see things clear."

Watching Amanda drink milk and ignore the plate of eggs, Cissy found herself remembering Dede's face in the bar. They were looking more alike, she realized. The night before, Dede's face had been so tense and strained that she looked more like her older sister than herself, and the blank-faced Amanda drinking milk and staring listlessly at her boys looked younger, like a girl who had fallen into a dream of having a family and did not know quite how to contemplate what to do with it all.

Before Michael could leave for his Friday home visits, Amanda grabbed her purse and was out the door and gone.

"Where's she going?" Michael asked Cissy. He had egg yolk all over the sleeve of the arm he had been using to prop up little Gabe.

"How should I know?" Cissy tossed Michael a dish towel.

"You're on your own," she told him. "I got to have a day off or I'm going to drown your sons."

Cissy was used to seeing Amanda everywhere—at the sewing shop on Main Street or the day-old bread store on Weed Road or the Quick Stop near the high school. Amanda had always had a set routine. A woman who was both wife to a minister and raising two boys had to have a system. Child care, prayer meetings, vacation Bible school, Sunday school, music lessons—with all that, Amanda was never on time and never where anyone thought she would be. Grocery-store runs were scheduled every weekend, but there was always something that Amanda had to do at the last minute. Casserole dishes had to be delivered to the sick and the bereaved. Clothing drives meant loads of laundry to be picked over and ironed nice and folded. The women's family committee had to have photocopied reports on abortion statistics, and grainy pictures of mangled fetuses in porcelain basins. The girls' auxiliary had a music group for which Amanda had even penned an original composition. Written in the voice of an aborted fetus, it was titled "I Forgive You but the Lord Does Mind."

Amanda's dirt-brown Honda plowed back and forth from the Christian Academy to the Kmart, from the A&P to the Little People's Music Emporium. Amanda was always stalking down the sidewalks of Cayro or angling through the doorway of the Bonnet in the afternoon, or even shoving through the midday crush at the junior college. Where does she get the time? Cissy had complained when she tried to keep track of Amanda's schedule. Where in the world had Amanda ever found the time?

On this Friday afternoon, Cissy saw Amanda's car in the one place she would never have expected to see it.

"M.T., stop!" Cissy yelled.

"What for?" M.T. was impatient. She didn't often run Cissy around, and resented doing it at all. Why couldn't Cissy just get her license and start to drive? "You got one good eye," M.T. was always saying, "which is more than you can say for some of the people driving around Cayro."

"An't that Amanda's car?"

"How would I know? You mean that muddy Honda? That could be anyone's car. Look, you want me to drive you over to those girls' place or not? I thought you said you had to get there by one o'clock." M.T. shifted uncomfortably. It had been a hot spring. She hated driving in the heat, hated it more that she couldn't afford to run the air-conditioning all the time. It used so much gas. And besides, people noticed. They'd say she needed the air-conditioning because she was so fat. M.T. was not bothered at all by being fat. She was bothered by people talking about it.

"If Amanda is going to Goober's in the afternoon, I need to know that too."

"Well, I an't got time to be checking on Amanda and running you all across town."

"Then let me out."

"Dede, Dede, Dede." Nolan nuzzled into the back of Dede's neck, his hands sliding around her middle to link over her belly. "You're my heart, girl. You're all my heart." He sighed happily, his hips flexing into hers and his toes curling in delight.

"Oh, for God's sake!" Dede abruptly flexed her legs and pulled Nolan's hands open. "Let me go." She kicked at him. "I said, let me go." She half fell off the bed and stumbled to her feet. Nolan sat up with a confused expression.

"What's wrong?"

"Nothing's wrong, damn it. Can't I get up when I want to?" Dede lit a cigarette angrily and kicked at the pile of discarded clothes on the floor. "Christ! Sometimes you just get all over my nerves, you know that?"

She pushed her hair back off her face and glowered at Nolan. Her body glowed in the sunlight pouring through the gap in the gauzy blue bedroom curtains. Nolan swung his legs over the side of the bed and tried a tentative grin. "Sometimes you like it when I get all over you."

"And sometimes I don't." Dede fished her underwear out of the pile of clothes. She dressed with rough, impatient movements. "Sometimes, you know, a woman needs a little time to herself. Not always having a man all over her butt." Dede pulled on her cotton shirt without bothering to put on her bra. It was a snap-front western shirt in yellow plaid with the sleeves cut off. She clicked the buttons together with the cigarette gripped between her lips. The smoke drifted up and made her squint.

"If you need some time to yourself, you know you can have it," Nolan said. He watched Dede hunt for her shoes. One sneaker was under the bench by the window, the other by the side of the dresser. When she had them both, she dropped to the bench and put them on, not bothering with socks. "Maybe we could go visit that place in Nag's Head that you went to that time?" Nolan suggested. "Have ourselves a few days' vacation." Nolan climbed off the bed and gathered his clothes. He pulled on his underwear, keeping an eye on Dede, and then stepped into his jeans. "You haven't any time off this year, have you?"

Dede blew smoke and hung her head. "I haven't had any time off in this life," she told him, and then reached behind her to put out the cigarette on the window ledge. "But I don't want to go to Nag's Head." Her mouth was flat and hard.

Nolan pulled his T-shirt on over his head. "You still mad at me?"

"Don't start."

"Dede, I told you. The way I feel about you, of course, I'm going to ask you to marry me. You know you can tell me no, you can tell me to go to hell."

Dede put her hands up in front of her face.

"Now, honey, I told you if you don't want to get married, I understand. You want things to go on just the way they have, that's fine with me." Nolan caught Dede's hands in his own. "I'll go on this way forever, I told you. And if you want I'll try harder not to get so gushy on you." He grinned ruefully.

Dede shook her head. "Nolan."

Nolan leaned forward and put his face down into her tangled hair. He breathed in deeply. "Oh, you smell so good," he whispered.

"Damn." Dede almost sobbed. She pushed him away.

"What? What is it?"

"Nothing." Dede wiped her eyes.

"Dede?"

"Shut up. Just don't say nothing, all right? Just leave me alone for a bit." She wiped her face again and ran her fingers through her hair. Her eyes searched Nolan's blank face. Abruptly Dede bent forward and pushed her mouth on Nolan's. She kissed him fiercely, her hands gripping his neck. "Damn you," she whispered to his mouth. She kissed him again.

"Oh, baby," he whispered back. "All my heart." He put his arms around her, kneading the tight knot of her shoulder muscles and massaging down her back to her hips. Dede pushed into him desperately, her mouth bruising his.

"Oh God!" Nolan moaned. He half lifted Dede, pulling her toward the bed.

"No." Dede pushed at Nolan until he stumbled. She swayed as he fell back on the bed.

"I got to go," she said.

"Lord! Dede!" Nolan's voice was shaky, his hands balled in fists on his knees. "Don't do me this way. Tell me what's going on."

Dede smoothed her shirt and stuffed her shirttails into her jeans. "I'll tell you later," she said. "I'll talk to you tonight."

Nolan sat on the bed and tried to catch his breath. He listened as she went out the kitchen door and pounded down the stairs. "I don't understand," he said out loud. "I just do not understand."

He heard the car door slam shut and visualized Dede slipping into the turnip-purple Volkswagen's bucket seat, her bright hair glowing against the dusty upholstery. He remembered her behavior at Goober's last night. Her mood swings seemed more and more extreme lately, though she said she was doing no drugs. He suspected he knew what was going on, but he dared not speak it. He would wait. He would let her tell him. He wiped his face and sighed. His pants felt too tight and sticky with sweat. Thank God Tacey had taken Nadine out to buy some new nightgowns in the handicapped van that made runs to Beckman's on Fridays. He had desperately needed to hold Dede closely, to make love to her and feel her wanting him the way he wanted her. It never stopped, that aching need for her, but lately it seemed they were both desperate all the time.

"She could be," Nolan whispered to himself. "Could be." He wiped sweat out of his eyes. He would not think about it. There was nothing he could do until Dede decided to talk to him.

Nolan scooped up the damp sheets and dirty clothes from the floor. He'd do a load of laundry and pick up a bit. It was still mid-afternoon, and he was not tired. He would get the house cleaned up some before Nadine and Tacey got back. Maybe for dinner he would get them all some fried chicken from that place Nadine liked on Yarnell Road. Tacey had been cooking all the time lately, she needed a night off.

When Sheila's pickup pulled into the driveway, Nolan was running hot water over dirty dishes. The washer was going, and all the windows were standing open.

"You doing housework?" Sheila asked with a laugh. "You are one major piece of work, Nolan Reitower, you know that?" She pushed open the screen door and gave Nolan her biggest smile. "I brought you that music book you left at Goober's last night. Thought you might need it."

Nolan nodded his thanks. He had soap bubbles all over his arms and hands, and a line of sweat running off his nose. "I appreciate it."

Sheila put the book on the table and looked around the kitchen. "You sure are industrious."

"Got to do it sometime," Nolan told her. "Place gets messy."

"And you're the type, aren't you? You see a thing needs doing, you just get to it, don't you?" She wrinkled her nose prettily. "Like I said, you are one piece of work." She stepped over to Nolan, looked up at him from heavily mascara'd eyes, and pushed up on her toes to kiss his mouth.

Nolan gasped and froze with his soapy hands in the air.

"Oh, look at you!" Sheila giggled. "I an't gonna bite you. And I know you're taken. Whole world knows that." She kissed him again, vastly amused at how he blushed and trembled.

When Sheila turned to go, Dede was standing in the doorway watching them. She had a bag of groceries in her arms, and a face as pale as the moon in the night sky.

"You son of a bitch," Dede said, "you goddamned son-a-bitch!"

Nothing in Cissy's life had prepared her for the sight of Amanda sitting at the bar at Goober's, her cheeks flushed and her eyes bright and glittering. Was she drunk? Was Amanda drunk in the middle of the day? She had one of those great big glasses in front of her, half full of one of Goober's famous fruitoholic drinks. Vodka, Cointreau, coconut milk, ice, pineapple juice, and slices of pineapple filled the tall, sweating glass.

Cissy sat down next to her. "So, what are you doing?" She was surprised to hear how much her voice sounded like Delia's. Mama voice, she thought. Here I am, talking Mama talk.

Amanda swung her head slowly to face Cissy. "Why aren't you watching the boys?"

"Michael has them." Cissy took a deep breath. She could smell the Cointreau.

Amanda shrugged. "Well, all right then."

"What are you doing at Goober's?"

"Becoming a regular." Amanda took a sip of her drink and rolled her eyes at Cissy. "You look shocked," she said.

"I am shocked. What's come over you? You been running out every day, staying away from home, barely looking at your boys when you are there. Is this what you've been doing? Sitting in Goober's every day, getting drunk on your butt?"

"No." Amanda shook her head. "This is only my second time. I've been to the mall. I've been to the peewee golf, and the video-games center down in Marietta. I went and had my nails done, and one day I drove all the way to Chattanooga to look at their bridge before I drove back home."

"Why would you do that?"

"I never saw it. Started thinking about how many things I had never seen, and just decided to go." She paused and took another sip. "And on Wednesday I was arrested," she said, each syllable distinct and precise.

"Arrested?"

"And released. The deputy wouldn't hold me no matter what I said. And I said something about it. I said a lot, but they just drove me around and ignored me. Put me out back at my car. Told me to go home and talk to God a little more." She leaned forward slightly and sucked at the pink straw that was stuck through one of the pine-apple slices.

"I didn't know that deputy. I never saw him before in my life, but he knew me. He told me he knew all about me." She looked at Cissy. "When I wouldn't get out, he pushed me out. He got in the back beside me, laughed real mean, and wiggled over until he shoved me out on my butt." She rocked her glass on the bar for emphasis. "Rude," Amanda said. "The man was rude."

Cissy twisted on her stool. "I don't understand," she said. "Where were you when you were arrested?"

"Over at the Planned Parenthood Center." Amanda sipped briefly and sighed. "I tried to bust up one of their typewriters. Didn't do any good. They were ready for me, I think." She sat quietly for a minute, eyes on her drink, and then spoke again very softly. "I felt like such a fool."

There were tears in Amanda's eyes, Cissy could see. She was not letting herself cry, but she was wet-eyed, sweaty, and limp. She looked like she had been wrestling somebody. She also looked like a woman who had never taken a drink before today.

"You know, I've never felt like a fool before." Amanda's voice was calm and slow. She seemed to be genuinely puzzling out what she was saying. "I've done foolish things, and I've done things that other people said were foolish, but I never felt like it was anything that had much to do with me, with what I was really doing. I always felt I knew what I was doing. Always felt like God was taking care of me, putting me where I needed to be, showing me what was to be done."

"Are you all right?" Cissy was unnerved by the spectacle of Amanda sitting at the bar sipping and talking.

"I'm fine." Amanda sipped again. "I'm just fine." Her right hand patted gently at her abdomen. "Gallstones all reduced to ash and guilt." She grinned as if she had not meant to say that, then took another sip and looked around the bar. She frowned at the framed photographs on the wall, all pictures of local girls in bathing suits.

"You know, it's intentional that God does not make things easy." Amanda's face became focused and sad. "Things are supposed to be hard. If they were easy, what would be the point? I always thought I knew what hard was about." She frowned and pressed her lips together. "I always thought it was like praying and climbing a hill. You just keep your focus and keep moving, asking God to help but keeping on. That kind of hard." She took a healthy suck on her straw, then pushed the glass toward the back of the bar. When she spoke, her voice was full of regret.

"When I thought I was dying, I thought it was all God's plan. All I had to do was do it right. Thought God was making me a living lesson. Thought I had cancer like Clint or something worse, eating me up from the inside out. Being proud and stubborn and suffering." She laughed bitterly. "Then to have gallstones. Just to hear the word about took my heart right out of me. Gallstones." She licked her lips and gave a little whistle.

"You think maybe God's got a sense of humor?" Amanda asked. She skimmed sweat off her forehead with two fingers and laughed again. "I've been thinking about that a lot, about God's sense of humor."

"I think you should go talk to your doctor." Cissy tried to keep her voice level but she could hear the crack in it. This was crazy. In Amanda's long, crazy life, this was the craziest yet.

"Well, anyway, this kind of hard," Amanda said, ignoring Cissy's comment, "seems to me it's a whole different kind of thing. This hard where you don't know what you're doing, what's the right thing to do, when you can't be sure you're not really a fool. I didn't know nothing about that. And I never wanted to."

Cissy sat there silently, her eyes fixed on Amanda's profile.

"I guess I am going to have to learn," Amanda said. She used the bar napkin to wipe her eyebrows. She looked at Cissy with an expression of great composure. "Guess I'm going to have to learn," she said again.

The bartender leaned over the almost empty glass. "You're the Byrd girls, an't you?"

Cissy stared at the man. She felt like she had just emptied Amanda's glass, like her blood was full of alcohol and confusion. She managed a nod and turned back to Amanda, but the man put his hand on the bar.

"Well, I hate to tell you this, but your sister's been arrested. She took a shot at Sheila, one of my barmaids. Missed, thank God, but she did shoot that old boy runs Biscuit World. Shot him two or three times, they say."

Cissy gaped. Dede had shot Nolan?

"She shot him?" Amanda said. She was right beside Cissy, her mouth mere inches away.

"Tried to kill him," the bartender said. "They just hauled her off to the jail. Had a call from Sheila's mama. Said that Dede went completely insane and shot up Nolan's house and all."

"She didn't kill him?"

"Well, not yet, but he might be dead by now for all I know."

"I'll drive," Amanda said. She seemed entirely sober. "Come on." She picked up her bag and her keys from the bar. "Come on," she said again, and took Cissy by the arm and led her out.

Chapter 21

Delia had paid off Marcia Pearlman with the money she received when Mud Dog's compilation tapes were reissued the year after Amanda married, but she still did her hair every Friday morning while M.T. and Steph opened the Bonnet. That Friday she was running late, but Marcia did not seem to mind. She smiled happily when Delia arrived, muting the television set and gathering a towel around her shoulders while Delia unloaded her bag of shampoo and conditioner.

Marcia was bone thin and more crippled than ever. She walked only with great effort, bent over and hesitant. She lost interest in food for months at a time and set an alarm clock to make herself eat, mostly the same thing, macaroni and cheese, steamed carrots, and fruit cocktail. "At my age, that's enough," she told Delia, "though I do miss fresh cucumber salad and pork barbecue."

"I'll bring you some barbecue anytime you want," Delia said.

"Oh, no one wants to be around me if I eat barbecue. Can't hardly taste anything anyway," she told Delia. "And Dr. Campbell tells me I shouldn't use salt or hot sauce. That takes all the joy out of it. Nothing tastes good without salt."

To comfort her, Delia brought bread pudding from the café downtown where they served a lemon sauce so strong you could smell it from the street. "Nobody else can stand it," Delia laughed.

Marcia took a bite and smiled. "Well, it tastes pretty good to me, and looks like they strain the seeds."

She ate part of the pudding while Delia set up a workstation at the kitchen sink. By now they had a comfortable ritual that both anticipated happily. Marcia even turned off her television while Delia was visiting, the only time it was ever turned off. Her nephew Malcolm, who was a mechanic for the Firestone people, had moved in with her after her stroke and bought a cable box that pulled in lots of channels. Marcia had grown addicted to jumping from channel to channel, watching bits of lots of things one after the other—old movies, nature specials, and any programs with music. "The kids look so young," she told Delia almost every week. "They don't know anything about what's coming at them."

"No," Delia agreed, "they don't, and that's probably a good thing, don't you think?"

"I don't know," Marcia said. "Some days I think life should come with a big warning label."

That Friday morning, while Delia had her hair full of suds, Marcia suddenly reached up and took Delia's hands in her own. Her eyes were bright that morning, and her skin translucent. "I had such a dream last night," she said. The pale skin flared pink and her mouth curved up slightly.

"One of those dreams, huh?" Delia grinned.

"Oh, not what you're thinking," Marcia said. "I have those sometimes, but this wasn't like that. I dreamed about my baby."

"Baby?" Delia's fingers stopped moving. So far as she knew, Marcia and her husband had been childless.

Marcia nodded and closed her eyes. A trickle of water ran along her jaw. Delia wiped it away with the towel. "I had a baby when I was a girl," Marcia said. "Fourteen and stupid as they come. Didn't go out of the house for six months and had the baby at home. My daddy took it to St. Louis and gave it to this lady who found good homes for babies like that. We never talked about it. Didn't even tell my husband when I married."

She let go of Delia's hands. "Fourteen is so young," Delia said.

"Yes," Marcia said. "It is." She opened her eyes. The faded irises were cloudy blue but not sad. "I never tried to find him," she said. "Never wrote. Never called. Tried to pretend it never happened, specially when I never had another."

"I understand." Delia triggered the sprayer to rinse the suds out of Marcia's thin hair. The water was warm on her fingers. She cradled the back of Marcia's head carefully.

"It was a boy with blue eyes," Marcia said. "In my dream he had the blackest hair and those pretty eyes. He came right up the steps and into the house, walked through like he knew where everything was, came right up to me and kissed my mouth. He wasn't angry at me at all. He was just happy to see me, and it was the strangest thing. I wasn't afraid. I was happy to see him."

"That's a good dream." Delia wrapped a warm towel around Marcia's head.

"It was." Marcia pushed the towel up for a moment to look into Delia's face. "I wanted you to know. Every time I look at you and what you've done with your girls, I think about my boy. I imagine him with a family who loves him, with children of his own that I'll never see."

"Oh, honey, I'm so sorry."

"No, no." Marcia shook her head emphatically. "You don't understand. I'm not sorry. I've been sorry. I used to imagine terrible things, people being mean to him, that he was hungry and cold and alone. Terrible things, but these last few years I've had the sense that he was all right, that he didn't fall among stones like the Bible said, that he fell into tender hands. He is loved, I know that, and he doesn't hate me."

Delia watched the skin move on Marcia's neck, the little freckles that spotted her throat. This woman had been good to her. This woman was her friend. "It was a good dream," she said again. Her chest hurt and her throat felt tight and sore.

"Yes," Marcia said, tugging at her collar and pushing at the damp hair that had come loose from the towel. "You think we should trim it this week?" she asked. "Seems like it's pretty much stopped growing, and all I really want is to look nice for church on Sunday. That's all I ask these days."

Delia put her hands on Marcia's head again. She closed her eyes and took a deep breath. It would be all right. She knew how to do this. The wall phone near the door to the parlor rang loudly.

Marcia looked at it unhappily. "We better answer it. You never can tell who it might be."

Looking at Dede across the scarred wooden table in the jail visiting room, Cissy thought, not for the first time, how like Delia her sister was. The hum of energy around Dede that was like the choral murmur that surrounded Delia, a slight charge to the air that made your skin tingle and the hair at the back of your neck fluff up. With both of them there was always the sense that something was about to happen, and when it finally did, people were not surprised but relieved.

That was what Cissy felt at the jail—a sense of relief. She was grateful that no one had been killed and that for the moment, at least, the storm was past, but she could see from the faint trembling of Dede's fingers that a charge was building up again, that already Dede was starting to vibrate with furious energy.

"I'm glad I shot him." Dede brandished her cigarette in the air and scowled at Cissy's dismay. "Stupid son of a bitch. Thought he could treat me like that. Stupid son of a bitch." Her voice was even, but loud, too loud, her gestures a bit too wide. Cissy could see that Dede knew the woman guard at the door was flinching every time she spoke.

"All my life seems like Nolan's been trailing behind me. All my life those moon eyes following me. All that time I treated him like some dog in the yard, and he just dogged me harder. Swore he'd love me forever, but I knew. I knew when we started seeing each other, knew it would go bad. Man runs after a woman the way Nolan ran after me, he always got to get his own back. Comes the time, he's going to make you pay." She flicked ashes in the direction of the little aluminum ashtray, looking around as if she expected someone to nod and agree with her.

"So I'd been waiting for it to come. Knew it had to, that he was gonna do me bad somehow." Her shoulders lifted and dropped. "That's how it is. I'm no fool. I know how it works."

Dede slumped in her chair, and Cissy wished she could take her hand. She had been told she was not to get up from the table and not under any circumstances to touch Dede. She had agreed readily, never imagining how hard it would be to see her sister looking so beaten down and not be able to reach for her. Her face must have shown what she was thinking, for Dede turned away, gritting her teeth.

"Damn! It was still more than I could stand!" She tilted her head and awkwardly brushed her cheek against her sleeve. "I mean, that little bitch! That Sheila! No damn beauty, and stupid besides. That he would use her. Fucking waitress that served me beer and onion rings, and he kisses her like that."

Cissy leaned forward slightly. "Dede, he wasn't—"

"The hell he wasn't!" Dede thumped her elbows on the table. "He damn sure was! You think I don't know?!"

"Dede, you are not making sense. Nolan never looked at Sheila. Most he ever did was go to Goober's to eat, and she flirted with him the way she does with everybody. They weren't doing nothing. She was just teasing him."

"Don't tell me that shit. Don't tell me no lies. I know how it happens. He could have told her to get her butt out of there. Saying he loves me, then kissing that bitch. And I've seen her over at Biscuit World, hanging on his truck, swinging that butt of hers, and laughing out loud. I know what I know." Dede's hands were shaking. She kept thrusting her head forward and huddling down in her seat.

"This didn't come out of nowhere," she shouted. "He wanted to leave me, he could have told me to my face, not done me that way. Lie to me. Ask me to marry him and then lie to me!"

"He asked you to marry him?"

"Damn right he asked me!"

"Oh Lord! Is that what it was about? Damn it, Dede, if you know so much, how come you don't know Nolan loves you?"

"Loves me?"

"Loves you."

"If Nolan loved me right, this would have never happened. He loved me right, he would have let things alone. I told him to let it alone. You think about how I felt, believing him, trusting him, letting myself love him, and him to do me like that? I trusted him. I trusted him!" Dede's face was white.

Cissy stared across the table in terrible comprehension. Delia Byrd's daughter had done the one thing she had sworn never to do. Dede had put her life in the power of a man, and it did not matter that Nolan loved her.

Never mind the rules, Cissy thought, and reached across to take Dede's hand. "He does love you," she said, and ignored Dede's grimace. "There he is, all shot up and trying to get you out. Says he won't press charges. Says it was all his fault. If he had his way, I think he would be the one in jail."

"He should be." Dede pulled her hand free and shot a glance at the guard, who had not moved. She hugged her forearms in close to her midriff. "He should be," she said again, this time in a whisper.

"Oh, Dede." Cissy clasped her hands together to keep from reaching forward again. "You doing okay?" she asked just for something to say. "You need anything?" She could not help but look over at the guard. The woman's face was stern, her eyes carefully focused on the far wall, but her cheeks were pink and her head was turned slightly so that she could hear every word they said.

"No, nothing." Dede picked up the cigarette pack and dropped it back on the tabletop. "Delia was here with some stuff for me. We didn't get to talk, but she brought me a whole carton of Marlboro 100s. Way it goes in here, I'm practically rich. They wouldn't let me see her, though, 'cause they weren't finished booking me. You should of heard her yell."

She rubbed her cheek against her shoulder and reached up to pick a speck of tobacco off her lower lip. Cissy was glad they had taken those handcuffs off after Dede had come into the visiting room. That had been bad, seeing her led in with her wrists cuffed to her waist.

Dede darted a quick glance at the door. "So, how is he?" Her voice was low as if she were not sure she wanted to know.

When the guard shifted a little, Dede sat up straighter. "He dead yet?" she said in a loud drawl.

Cissy winced. "He's all right. Delia's with him. She'll be back later. Said not to worry, that he an't going to die." Cissy heard her own voice, high and strained in the small room. How could you talk normally about such things in such a place? "You fucked him up, his leg anyway. Scraped the bone. Emmet's going to pack him over to Atlanta for an orthopedic man. Amanda and Tacey are taking care of Nadine." She hesitated a moment.

"Goddamn it, Dede. Why did you have to shoot him? You're not crazy. I will not believe that. You had to know what you were doing. Why did you shoot him?"

Dede pulled another cigarette from the pack and stuck it between her lips without lighting it. "It was either shoot him or cut his throat. And, hell, I don't know." Her voice dropped a little. "I just shot all the bullets that were in the gun. An't like it was no forty-four, just a damn little twenty-two. Bee stings. Just bee stings." She looked away from Cissy. "And I didn't aim worth a damn. It's a wonder I hit him at all."

"But you could have killed him. And we're talking about Nolan, for God's sake. You could have killed Nolan!"

"Naaa, I just wanted to hurt him. Make him pay attention. If he had loved me right, it wouldn't never have happened."

"Oh, Dede."

"Well." Dede lit the cigarette. "Well, you said he was going to be all right."

"Yeah." Cissy waited, but Dede said nothing more. The guard shifted again.

"He's going to be all right," Cissy said again, and saw Dede nod as she brought the cigarette to her lips. There was that slight trembling along her fingers, and a glitter in her eyes, but Cissy could see the stubbornness taking hold now.

"Yeah, sure. Damn son of a bitch. He better be all right." Dede pressed the heels of her palms to her eyes once, hard, and turned in her seat to glare at the woman guard. "He better be."

* * *

"**I** gave Dede's address as the trailer park and listed Amanda as the person to contact after you." Emmet handed Delia a little paper cup of water and sat down in the office chair in front of her. She blinked up at him blankly. "Thing is, Delia, there's been a reporter here already."

Delia swallowed two aspirin and shook her head. "What did he want? Where's my girl?"

"What do they always want?" Emmet ignored the second question. His voice shook with anger. "They want a story, a scandal. Girl shoots lover, lover gets hauled off to hospital yelling 'Don't hurt her, she didn't mean it.' That's their favorite kind of story. Redneck girls and foolish boys, reporters eat that stuff up."

"I don't care about that. I want to see my girl."

"Delia, you should care. This blows up into a big story, it could be trouble." Emmet clasped his hands together. He leaned in close to Delia. "You've done so good with those girls," he said softly.

"Good!" Delia's reaction was raw and bitter.

"Yes, good." Emmet nodded emphatically. "You've had them to yourself all these years. You've shown them how much you love them. Reporters been turning up here ever since you come back, wanting to make you into a story, but M.T. and me and the people who care about you been keeping them away from you. Giving you that time."

"You can't handle people like that." Delia was looking at Emmet skeptically.

"Oh yes you can. If people help, you can. And Delia, you got a lot of people here willing to take a reporter in hand, buy him a drink or drink the ones he buys, talk to him for hours, and never tell him nothing. And you've been pretty boring, the way they look at it. Haven't killed anybody or gone crazy or done much of anything. This could change all that. It's just too good a story."

"You can't stop them," Delia said.

"No," Emmet agreed. "You been in the *National Enquirer* once or twice, and you get mentioned fairly often in *Rolling Stone*, specially since they put out that Mud Dog CD, but that was that old boy fell in love with M.T., and he never said where you lived." He paused for a beat, then said, "You been safe, Delia."

"I an't felt safe."

"Well, honey, you never would, would you?" Emmet's smile was gentle. "You an't the type."

"Oh, for God's sake!" Delia stood up and walked over to the office door. "Emmet, I just want to see her. You bring her to me." She turned around and looked at him accusingly. "I don't care about nothing else. Bring me my girl."

"All right, all right." Emmet rose slowly from his chair. "I'm telling you what I think you need to know. I care about you, Delia Byrd. You know that. I'd eat dirt for you, and you know that too."

"I don't want you to eat dirt. I want you to bring me my girl. Bring her up to me in this office." Delia's gaze was level. "And don't you bring her in handcuffs. You know she an't going to hurt nobody."

Delia had thought it would be easier if she and Dede could sit together like two normal people, like mother and daughter, but when Emmet brought Dede in, it barely mattered that her hands were free, that the office had typewriters and chairs instead of bars and a guard. From the moment he opened the door, Delia's heart began to pound like a train engine.

Dede looked terrible. She had refused to wash up or even to comb her hair, and she kept her hands clenched together as if she were still wearing the cuffs Delia had been so afraid to see. "Mama," she said, and saw the expression that crossed Delia's face then. "Delia," she added quickly, but it was too late.

Dede went to Delia's arms. "I'm sorry," she said.

Delia hugged her girl fiercely, pulling Dede's whole length in close. "It's going to be all right." She stroked Dede's hair.

"Nolan? Cissy told me he was all right." Dede started to say more, but Delia stopped her.

"He's fine. He will be, anyway. He'll be here as soon as he can make that doctor let him go."

"I hurt him. Oh God, I could have killed him! I didn't want to kill him." Dede was shaking in Delia's arms.

"No, no. I know, baby. It's all right. Nolan is going to be fine. Don't think about the rest of it, you just think about that. Nolan is going to be just fine, and you're going to help take care of him. It will be all right, honey. I promise you. It will be all right."

"I can't take care of him!" Dede looked horrified. "I shot him. I can't take care of him."

Delia hugged Dede again and then held her at arm's length. "Yes, you shot him. That's why you will take care of him. You said you didn't mean to do it. Are you telling me you don't love him?"

"I don't know. I don't know. Seems to me Nolan should keep his distance. Hell, seems to me everybody should. I an't no sane person. I'm crazy."

"You an't crazy. Maybe you went crazy for a minute. And maybe it would all make sense if you understood what was happening inside you." Delia's voice was a hoarse whisper, her face lined and intent. She took Dede's hand in her own. "Listen to me. You been all torn up since Granddaddy Byrd died. I could see it, everybody could. We just didn't know what to do. Closer you and Nolan got, the more messed up you got. What I think, honey, is you don't know how to love Nolan. What I think is that the idea of him loving you scared you so bad you did go crazy, the kind of crazy that fights for its life the only way it knows how."

Dede dropped her head and shook it from side to side wearily. Delia leaned in to her and caught her chin. "When did you ever see anybody in love and happy, huh? You grew up on Clint and all that craziness. And you grew up on me, didn't you? You got every reason to be scared of love." Her eyes held Dede's.

"I don't know," Dede moaned. "I think I love Nolan, but it makes me feel like my heart is breaking to think about him. And every sweet thing he says to me, I start thinking he don't mean it. Then I saw him with Sheila, and I knew it was a trick all along." She shuddered. "Oh Lord, I thought he was just another boy wanted to wear my heart like a badge. The gun was in the car under the seat, that one that I got after Billy Tucker scared me. I don't even remember going out for it. Seemed like I was watching him kiss her and then I was shooting. I said, 'You want to marry me, huh?' and he shouted, and I shot him."

"Nolan wants to get married?" Delia stroked Dede's shoulder like someone trying to gentle an animal. "You never said nothing about that."

"I couldn't. It was like Nolan was some stranger I never knew at all. Felt like I had to get away from him, but then I couldn't go a minute without him. Started carrying that gun in the car, because I couldn't stand the way I was feeling. Thought that I'd be better off dead. Oh God, I don't know what all I was thinking, but I didn't want to kill Nolan."

"Shush. Shush." Delia pulled Dede into her arms again and stroked her hair steadily. "Just let it out," she whispered. "Just cry. We'll fix it, honey. It's going to be all right. You're going to be all right."

Delia could have been talking about the weather; Dede would not have known the difference. What she heard was the reassuring voice, what she felt was the cool balm of mama love. Nolan was not hurt, her mama had promised. It was going to be all right. Dede fell into Delia's arms and let go. For the first time in weeks, Dede let go of her fear.

Twice Emmet came to the door and heard the sobbing and stepped back again. Once, he heard Dede say clearly, "I didn't mean to hurt him." Thank God, Emmet told himself. If she saw what she had done, it might be all right in time. Only ones who couldn't be helped were the ones who never admitted what they had done.

Holding Dede, Delia was thinking the same thing. She remembered how she had sobbed in Randall's arms so long ago, that endless first year of tearing pain over having abandoned her girls. "It's all right," Randall told her over and over, and she let herself believe him. Not until he died did she finally see that there had been other choices besides running and drinking herself into oblivion. I can help her, she thought as she soothed Dede. I can show her how to get through this.

After a long while Dede fell silent, her cheek pressed to Delia's blouse. "Baby," Delia said, "Nolan's going to get you out of here."

Dede raised her head, unbelieving. "He can't do that," she said.

"Oh yes." Delia nodded calmly. "He can. He will. If things were different, you could go home with me, but it's going to take a little time to get this sorted out. But soon, I think, you need to see Nolan. You need to know he's going to be all right."

"I don't think I can talk to him." Dede's voice was small.

"You can. I know you can." Delia hugged her girl again. "Listen, honey, Rosemary will be here by tomorrow, and if you want, you can go stay with her for a while." Delia paused for a moment. "But I'm telling you now, I don't think that's what you should choose. I think, if you had been talking to Nolan, none of this would have happened. Talk to him now, baby."

"I don't know." Dede pulled away, wiping her face on her sleeves. "I don't think I can."

Delia groped for her bag and got out a pack of cigarettes. "Here," she said, and lit one for her girl.

"You smoking again?" Dede looked surprised.

"No, I bought 'em for you. Thought you might have gone through that carton already." Dede tried a smile.

Dede sat down in Emmet's chair and drew hungrily on the cigarette. Delia sat beside her and watched her smoke. Delia simply waited while Dede smoked and looked around the room. "We don't never talk, do we?" Dede said when the cigarette was almost gone.

Delia shook her head. "We an't the type," she said.

Dede took another cigarette out of the pack. "I've been thinking about you a lot," she said. "About you and Clint." Delia waited.

"What I never understood is how it all happened in the first place." Dede lit a match and watched it burn down. "How you fell in love with him. You must have known what he was like."

All right, Delia told herself. Talk to her. She took a breath. "I should have known, but I didn't. I had been so alone for so long. When I met Clint, I thought he was hurt like I was. I thought he knew everything I knew. I thought he could heal my heart and I could heal his, but Clint wasn't Nolan, baby. Clint was nothing like Nolan at all."

"I know that." Dede sat back down again beside Delia.

"No, I don't think you do. What did I ever teach you but how dangerous love is?" Delia dropped her eyes. "I never wanted to talk to you about all that, didn't want to say hard things about your daddy, but not talking about him, I never got to tell you the other part. How much we loved each other. How much pleasure we took in you and Amanda. How it was for a while, loving him and trusting him. Everything in Clint that was broken and mean cannot erase what was good. I wouldn't have had you if there hadn't been so much good in him. He gave you back to me, you know. As torn up and sick as he was, he did what he could. He gave you back to me."

"He nearly killed you." Dede's voice was soft and clear. "I saw how he was with Grandma Windsor, even with his daddy. How he was with us. He didn't know anything about love. When I thought about how it must have been with you and him, looked to me like the both of you were crazy."

"Oh, honey." Delia's mouth twisted. "That's what I mean. That's all you ever saw—the mother who left you, and Clint when his worst parts had hidden his best. But I loved him once, and he loved me, and who we were then was the best thing about us."

"You never said anything about loving Clint before."

"I had a long time to learn to hate him. When I came back here, it was the only thing I felt, but I've had almost as long to unlearn it." Delia touched a finger to the arch of Dede's cheekbone. Her daughter had lost substance in the last few days. Dede's skin looked as if it were ready to split. Delia reached for the pack of cigarettes but stopped herself.

"I used to tell Rosemary that marrying Clint was two parts the moon, one part loneliness, and the last part the dirty-blond hair that curled over the collar of his shirt. I loved the way his hair felt when I put my hand on his neck. So soft it always smelled of hay and sunshine." She blushed. Dede watched the rose spread slowly up Delia's cheeks. "And he had that smile, that lazy smile that promised me I would never be bored or lonely again. It lit him up." Delia stared at the tiny office window as if it were the past. "But if you want to know a man's heart, look at his mama. Look into her eyes, not his. That will show you what to expect. Look at Nadine. She truly loved Nolan's daddy, and she was good to him. I should have looked at Grandma Windsor, but I was so hungry for Clint's smile I couldn't see his mama when she put her face close to mine and told me right out she hated me, body and soul." Delia's hand crept toward the cigarettes again. "Hating like that, hating what her son loved. I should have looked closer at them all, but I guess that's how it works, how most families get started—a needy woman and a smiling man, or the other way around. A little charm and a lot of hunger, that's how most of us begin."

"You were crazy to marry him," Dede said, but Delia went on as if she hadn't heard.

"We got married at Holiness Redeemer, you know. That Reverend Call was the sourest preacher ever passed the plate at Sunday services. Clint wanted me to wear this lace veil his mama wore when she got married. I'd planned to make my own dress and I wasn't too keen on anything that belonged to his mama, and when I held that veil up to the light, I saw how badly it was made. It was just about the saddest piece of nothing, but Clint thought it was old and special." She sighed. "So I said I'd wear it. That should have warned me I was making a mistake, how quick I gave in on something I felt so bad about. There could have been signs and wonders everywhere, there could have been burning bushes all around me speaking in tongues, screaming 'Don't do it,' and I would never have known."

Dede's eyes were fastened on Delia. "I used to watch you when you were taking care of him, when he was dying. Amanda and me both watched how you fed him and bathed him and took such good care of him. It didn't make any sense. Sometimes I would see you in there after he got his shot and he went all empty. You would stand there and look at him with this strange expression on your face. I used to wonder what you were thinking. Do you remember?"

Delia closed her eyes, then opened them again. "Sometimes I hated him so much I didn't think about him at all. I'd think about you or Amanda, make plans or wander in my head. Sometimes I'd think about the way his mouth pulled up on one side, the smell of his neck, the way his hands came down on my shoulders." Delia lifted her own hands and looked at them as if they held something precious.

"It felt like when Clint drew breath my diaphragm moved. When his skin flushed, mine burned. If he put his tongue on my skin, I swear I tasted salt. Lord, and the way he used to kiss my neck and put his hands up under my blouse. Every time he did that, I'd come all over hot and stupid. Oh, baby, more has been ruined by hot and stupid than people ever want to admit."

Dede struck another match and lit her cigarette. "Yeah," she said. "That's what scares me."

Delia looked hard at her daughter. "I wasn't like you, Dede. I was nothing like you," she said firmly.

"You loved him," Dede said. She held the unlit cigarette in her hand and kept her eyes down. She could not look at Delia.

"I loved who I thought he was, maybe who he was trying to be." Delia stopped. When she resumed, her voice was softer, as if she could not say what she had to say too loudly. "It could have all been different, but he was his daddy's boy, his mama's vengeance. I never knew him or myself until it was too late. And when I ran, I was running for my life."

Delia's eyes dropped as if the memory were too painful to look at again. Dede never took her eyes off Delia's. Tenderly Delia reached over and laid her hand against Dede's cheek. "You don't hardly know yourself, girl, till you find yourself doing things you never imagined." She drew her hand back and sat up straight.

"You've got your Grandma Windsor's strength, Dede, you just got to use it right. I used to look at her sometimes and tremble at what I saw. She'd been beaten down so many years, she was like a lump of dough kneaded into a rock shape. I think she wanted me to hunker down like she had, to prove she had done right with her life."

"She was so hard. Amanda got that from her, all that hard, pushed-down stuff," Dede said angrily.

"I don't know. I think maybe it runs in all of us." Delia gave a little grin when Dede looked surprised. "Well, if we weren't so strong, how would we survive? Grandma Windsor was strong enough to get through what she had to. You'll see. You live long enough, you'll see."

Dede shrugged. "I see enough already."

"Dede, listen to me. Things happen and we change. We grow up. We get hurt. We become other people. I was a different woman when I fell in love with your father. That's what I'm trying to tell you."

"People change," Dede whispered.

Delia nodded. "Yes, they do."

Dede's mouth was open, her face earnest. Delia felt a wave of shame go through her, but she pushed it away.

"All we ever heard was how evil you were," Dede said, "how you ran off and left us for no reason. But I could see the reason. People said you went after Randall Pritchard for the money, that you left to get famous and rich and you didn't want to have to raise Clint Windsor's children. I knew it wasn't that simple."

"No, honey, it wasn't." Delia wiped her eyes. "It was the moon all over again, that's what it was. It wasn't sex or money or Randall being famous." She smiled. "Randall wasn't really famous until after he was dead, but he took me in, and he tried to help me. He just didn't know what he was doing."

"You did what you had to do."

Delia held on to Dede's hands. "If I had been in my right mind, I would have found a sheriff and gone back right away to get you and Amanda. Clint and Grandma Windsor would have fought me, did fight me every step. And by the time I talked to a lawyer in Atlanta, it was all over and done. I still had bruises showing on my face, but I was the criminal, the runaway wife. They wouldn't even let me near you. I thought I would die, but when the grief hit, Randall was there to pull me through it."

"He took care of you." Dede puffed on her cigarette.

"He loved me. Randall found it easy to love. It never lasted, but it was easy and simple for him. And he was never cruel. He loved me. He loved Cissy. He just . . ." She shrugged. "What do you want to know, Dede? I've tried never to lie to you, but there is so much I never wanted to say. Clint was a good man, but he lost himself. Randall had his own meanness, but he carried me forward out of my grief, and love that lifts you like that is never a bad thing."

"You left him too." Dede stubbed the cigarette out calmly. She was surprised to find that she wasn't angry, only curious. "Why'd you ever come back?"

"Every moment I was in California, I dreamed about you and Amanda. I mourned you with every nerve in my body, every drop of blood. I was so full of grief that drinking was all I could do. I drank not to be crazy, but I was crazy anyway." She leaned forward. "All the time I was in California, part of me was always listening for you. How could I sort it out? How could I fix what I had done? It took everything I had to get you back, and when I look at you now, I wonder if it was all for nothing. Maybe I didn't do either of you any good coming back." Delia stopped and rubbed her arms, as if the muscles had fallen asleep and pins and needles were pricking her.

"You shouldn't have come back," Dede said. "I've heard Mud Dog. You sound like nobody else. I've read stuff. You could have done anything."

"No, I could not." Delia's hands clenched on her biceps. "Dede, I loved singing, but I never sang sober in California. I was drunk on those records. I was drunk onstage. I never sang for more than four people when I wasn't drunk."

"You were special."

"Baby, an't nothing special about a drunk. I loved Cissy's daddy, and when I lost you girls, he saved me, but not the real me. The real me never wanted to be famous or live in that town that ate me alive.

The real me never wanted to make music for anyone but you and Amanda and Cissy and myself. The real me wanted to be right here."

Dede stood up and walked to the door, her back to Delia.

"You understand what I am telling you?" Delia's question was sudden and urgent.

Dede turned around. "Some," she said. "You been telling us stuff all my life."

"What I'm trying to make you understand is that you can't shut your life down because of what happened to me." Delia rubbed her arms again, her glance carefully averted. "You don't have to marry Nolan, but you can't deny what you feel. You love him, you get mad at him, you get scared. Don't lie to yourself or him. Don't run away anymore."

"Like you?"

Delia opened her mouth, then shut it. She stood and went to Dede. She put her arms around her daughter and her lips to her forehead. "Like me," she said in a whisper. "Like me."

Amanda was waiting for Delia downstairs at the courthouse. Delia walked toward her on leaden feet. Her face had changed, Delia saw. It seemed fuller, the mouth less tightly compressed, the eyes softer.

"Don't let them put her in the hospital," Amanda said in a rush. "I know Emmet was talking about it, and it's not a good idea. The state Dede's in, she could wind up committed, and we'd have a terrible time getting her out again."

Delia frowned. "She needs help," she said in a tired voice.

"Yes." Amanda nodded. "She does, but let's not get her in more trouble than she's in already." Amanda had a notebook in her hand and was turning pages. "I already called George Creighton from the Baptist Fellowship. He's a good lawyer, and he knows about these things. He said every hour that passes helps us. Dede has said she's sorry. Nolan's thrown a fit at Emmet. We handle this right, and Dede can be home in a week."

Delia looked doubtful. "I don't know. She did shoot him."

Amanda smoothed the pages of her notebook. "Yes, she did, and we all agree that she needs help, but Bartow County Medical won't do a thing but feed her drugs and make her worse. What Dede needs is for us to think clearly."

Delia studied Amanda's face again. "You're right."

"And I think she's pregnant," Amanda said matter-of-factly.

"What?"

"It's the only thing that makes sense."

"She hasn't said a word."

"Dede wouldn't, and I don't blame her. You take a look at Nolan. You'll see he thinks so too. I could tell when I spoke to him. He's waiting for her to tell him."

"Nolan said Dede was pregnant?" Delia wanted to sit down. She wanted to put her head between her knees.

"He didn't say so, but I could tell he thinks so." Amanda was losing her patience. "It had to happen sooner or later, you know."

"She didn't say a thing."

"Delia." Amanda closed her notebook. "I suspect Dede doesn't want to think about it right now. You know how she feels about marriage. Dede's turned living in sin into a matter of principle."

"Oh my Lord. No wonder she shot him."

Amanda smiled. "Almost makes a kind of sense, doesn't it? When you know Dede."

Delia looked at Amanda. "She might not want it," she said carefully.

Amanda dropped her gaze and drew a deep breath. "I know, and that's something I am not going to think about right now. Dede's difficult, but she's not evil. She'll do the right thing if we help her."

"Amanda." Delia's voice broke when she said the name. "Amanda, you never fail to surprise me." She put her arm around her daughter's stiff shoulders, holding on until the body softened slightly in her embrace.

"We have things to do," Amanda said brusquely, pulling free. "Lots of things."

Back in her cell, Dede remembered the picture of Mud Dog that she'd cut out of an old *Rolling Stone* she'd found at Crane's when she was nine or ten. She hadn't looked at it since she'd moved in with Delia. It was a shot of the bus with the equipment piled high and everybody standing around and *Diamonds and Dirt* lettered on half the drum covers. Booger and Little Jimmy were leaning against the rear of the bus, sharing a joint. Randall was up front in his suede fringed vest. Round tinted glasses hid his pupils, but his smile was huge and toothy. Delia stood next to Rosemary, hair down loose and long, belly swelling up against a patchwork skirt with a velvet waistband. It was the textures that stood out in that picture, the feel of stoned confidence and the nap of the velvet and the sway of the fringe over Randall's belt buckle. It was a cliché almost before it was published. For all the success of *Diamonds and Dirt*, Mud Dog was a second-rate band that became legendary only when it no longer existed. What was memorable about the picture was the time-capsule effect, a frozen moment in a fable. Dede had stared at it for hours— her mama with that man, the hippie prince and the runaway wife, and Cissy implicit in the swell of Delia's belly. She had shown the picture to Cissy once, but Cissy wasn't interested.

Dede wished she had a picture of Delia and Clint before she and Amanda were born—the two of them in one moment of happiness. Cissy didn't understand. There was something essential about seeing Randall and Delia like that, and Cissy there too, on her way before she was anywhere. It was as if Dede could see herself in that picture as well, her ghost there beside Cissy in Delia's belly.

It was a song, that picture. It was a piece of Delia's blues, the story of all of them and what they had made together. Dede looked at it now in her mind's eye and saw the past and the future, not a band on tour but a family in pieces, pulling itself back together out of one woman's stubborn determination. I an't Delia, Dede thought,

I an't that strong, and then she heard Nolan's voice. Yes you are, he was saying. You are as strong as any man can stand.

"You're all my heart," Nolan had said just before Dede shot him. Sitting in jail, Dede knew he was right. She was his heart, and God help her, he was hers.

Chapter 22

You know what my daddy used to tell me?" Tacey said to Cissy that night after they finally got Nadine to bed. "He used to say white people were simply crazy."

They were sitting at the kitchen table. Cissy had taken down the bottle of wine that Nadine told her was in the top cupboard. They had each had a glass and started on a second.

Tacey took another sip and leaned her head to one side. "He said black people were crazy too, but we weren't simple."

"Yeah," Cissy agreed. "God knows my whole family is crazy. Probably going to get Dede certified out of this, and Amanda is nuts for sure."

Amanda came in from the hall that led back to Nolan's room. "Oh, am I?" And poured a good slug of wine into a water glass.

"How is he?" Tacey was prepared to be diplomatic. "He asleep?"

"He's drugged." Amanda rolled her head, and the muscles in her neck made popping sounds. "But he's fine. Thank the Lord, Dede didn't have a really big gun. For being shot like that, Nolan's doing just fine. I think the swelling in his leg is starting to go down. We'll have a terrible time keeping him in bed tomorrow."

Amanda frowned down at her wine. "Is this stuff all right? Is it supposed to taste like this?"

Cissy shrugged. "Nadine say how old it was?" she asked Tacey.

"Never mentioned it to me before. Probably thought I'd drink it up and replace it with soda or something." Tacey sipped. "It might have turned. Seems a little bitter, but what do I know? I don't drink." She looked at Amanda. "Didn't think you did either."

"I'm taking it up," Amanda said. "Had a drink yesterday with

Cissy. Going to do it regular from now on. I'm studying on sin. I'm studying on how it works."

"Amanda, you scare me," Tacey said.

"I know. I scare myself sometimes, but I'm trusting in the Lord. Figure I'm human and flawed and need His help. I'm just figuring things out as I go." She took a gulp of wine. "Those girls called you here," she said to Cissy. "Called twice, wanting to know what was going on. Said you were supposed to meet them this evening."

"Oh Lord! I forgot to call them. We were going to map Little Mouth. We were going to stay out overnight."

Amanda shook her head. "I will never understand you, Cissy. What on earth are you doing, climbing down into what might as well be the outer gates of hell? And Mary Martha Wynchester said you quit your job at the real estate office."

Cissy nodded. "I did. I hate realtors. I hated that job."

Amanda sat down at the table. "Well, what are you going to do now?"

"I'm going to think about it." Cissy looked at Tacey and then at Amanda. "Before all this happened, Nolan told me Dede wasn't happy, that she wanted to be doing something different. It sounded like he was thinking the same thing. He was talking about taking a job in Atlanta."

"Yeah," said Tacey. "He told me that too, and I told him to look me up at Spelman."

"Well, it shook me." Cissy toyed with the empty glass. "Funny how you go along and you get settled and you never think about things changing. Then this happened, and I realized things were changing anyway." She raised the glass to Amanda. "I'm thinking. Studying on things, like you. Time for me to make some plans of my own."

"Long as you stop running around with those girls." Amanda's face assumed a familiar pinched expression. "There's something not right about them."

"Oh, they're just like everybody else," Cissy said. "They an't any more crazy than you or me."

"Is that so? Well, I saw them sitting in that truck the last time you went out with them, you know. I saw them sitting close together. That tall one put her arm around the other one, leaned over, and kissed that girl right on the mouth. Looked to me like they're considerably more crazy than you."

Cissy watched Amanda refill her glass. Kissing? Mim and Jean had been kissing?

"I think they're lesbians," Amanda said with authority.

"Lesbians?" Tacey snorted. "For God's sake, don't tell Nadine. She'll invite them over and ask them to talk about it. Bad enough she still thinks I sleep with the garbage men. She'll be sure I sleep with the lesbians too."

"You don't know anything about them, Amanda." Cissy felt sick. She had the strongest desire to lean over and slap her sister.

"I know what I saw, and I bet you know too. You been spending all that time with them. You tell us. Don't they live together? Don't they kiss and hug all the time? Didn't they ask you to start this club with them so they wouldn't have to join the one that has all the boys in it? You going to tell me I'm wrong?"

"I don't have to tell you anything." Cissy stood up and shoved her chair back. "You should be home with your own boys, not here telling me all this crap."

"Michael's got the boys. They're fine. Don't tell me about my boys."

"Don't you tell me about my life."

"I'm not talking about you. I'm talking about those girls."

"Well, don't. Talk about me." Cissy felt as if Nadine's wine had turned to poison in her belly. "Maybe I'm a lesbian too."

"Maybe you are," Amanda said flatly. "I always knew there was something wrong with you. Figured sooner or later you'd get around to telling us, probably at the worst possible moment—when your sister is in jail and we're all just about worn down to nothing."

Amanda rested her elbows on the table, the glass of wine in both hands. I really should hit her, Cissy thought, but she could not move.

"I think we should get some rest." Tacey put both hands flat on the table and pushed herself up. "I think tomorrow is going to be difficult enough without all of us going crazy on each other."

"I don't know what I am," Cissy said through clenched teeth. "I an't got God on my shoulder telling me to take a drink of wine and push my sister around. I an't got a gun in my pocket. I an't got nothing—not one notion what I am going to do with my life—but if you ever come at me again, Amanda Graham, I'll push you so hard you'll need God to pick you up. I'll push you so you'll know you been pushed!"

"I rented a car." The voice was soft and startling. All of them turned to the door. Rosemary stood there with an overnight case in one hand and the other against the doorjamb. "You going to invite me in or yell at each other some more?"

"Jesus Lord!"

"You must be Tacey." Rosemary stepped in and dropped her case on the floor. "I'm Rosemary. Delia tell you I was coming?"

Tacey shut her mouth and nodded. This was Rosemary! This woman was Delia's friend from Los Angeles.

Rosemary sighed heavily and pulled up a chair. "I think you should sit down," she said to Cissy. "And maybe one of you could tell me where Delia is. I went over to the house, but she wasn't there. Figured you would all be here."

Amanda stuttered when she spoke. "Delia's at Judge Walmore's, talking to him about getting Dede out of jail."

"So she should be back soon. It's pretty late." Rosemary opened her purse and took out her lighter and cigarette case. "Is it all right if I smoke in here?" she asked Tacey.

"Yes," said Tacey, who couldn't stand cigarette smoke.

"Thanks." Rosemary lit up and looked at Amanda and Cissy. "You're still fighting," she said. "Well, at least some things can be trusted to remain the same, huh?" She blew out smoke. "You want to come over to your mama's place with me, Cissy? Maybe we should be there to meet her."

Cissy lifted her head. Tacey was staring at Rosemary in happy fascination. The woman did not look a day older than she had when

Clint died. Her hair was beautifully styled and her skin glowing, her nails perfectly done. Around her neck was the same gold necklace, wide and gleaming in the light from the overhead fixture.

"Yeah," Cissy said. "We should go."

Both of them were silent on the short walk down Terrill Road from Nolan's house to Delia's. When they got there, Cissy ran ahead to turn on the porch light and promptly tripped on the bottom step.

"Shit!" she cursed.

"Hold on." Rosemary had a little flashlight in her purse. As she clicked it on, a car turned into the driveway and caught the two of them in its beam.

"What happened?" Delia called.

"Cissy took a fall."

"Rosemary!" Delia left her lights on and rushed over to help.

"Hey, honey." Rosemary gave her a quick kiss on the cheek and the two of them pulled Cissy up.

"She's not really hurt," Rosemary said. "She's just been drinking bad wine."

"Bad wine?"

"With Amanda and that sweet little girl over at Nolan's. I came in and they were all half drunk and talking trash at each other." Rosemary put an arm around Delia. "Honey, what's been going on since I left?"

Dede couldn't sleep. She kept thinking about Nolan and about everything Delia had said. When she did doze off for a moment, she dreamed Nolan was in the room with her, his hands outstretched and his eyes on hers. "Do you want to shoot me? Shoot me in the butt, why don't you? It'll make me feel better and it won't hurt you none," she said. "I'm yours," he told her. "I'm yours and you're mine." His words made her hysterical. She yelled that she belonged to no one, and woke up alone in the jail.

Emmet had told her Nolan would come see her as soon as the doctor would let him. Dede ground her teeth. She did not want to have to look into Nolan's face again. She wanted him to give her something to hate him for. It would be so much easier if she hated him. It was loving him that felt dangerous, all that talk about family and moving in together, moving to Atlanta, making it possible for her to do what she wanted to do. Were there really people who got to choose what they wanted, instead of just taking what they could get and making the best of it? Nolan had talked to her as if anything were possible. That was what he said—"With you, anything is possible!"—and Dede knew from the look in his eyes that he believed it. That was the way he loved her. She loved him too, but like that? Like the whole world could fall on her and still she'd be all right because he was with her? People like Nolan were sports of nature, loving so completely that their love satisfied everything in them.

He's better than me, Dede thought. Nolan could make a real career with his clarinet in Atlanta, but he told her that he would move or stay in Cayro, whatever she wanted. If someone offered Dede a two-hundred-thousand-dollar rig and a route from Georgia to Arizona and back again, she'd jump at it. It wouldn't matter if Nolan couldn't go. Hell, it wouldn't matter if he were lying in the street and she had to drive over him. She'd shift gears and crush his spine.

It might never have happened if she hadn't already had that gun, and that was Billy Tucker's fault. But then, if not for Billy Tucker, would she have ever taken up with Nolan at all? Maybe all of it had been predictable. That silly waitress from Goober's didn't matter. She was nothing. Nolan didn't care about her and Dede knew it. When he looked at Dede with the gun in her hand, his face said, All right, shoot me if you have to, kill me if that's what you need. What kind of man stood still for a woman to shoot him?

"He's crazy," Dede had told Emmet.

"Yeah," Emmet agreed. "He loves you."

Two parts the moon, one part loneliness—and the rest? Dirty-blond hair or the smile of the beloved, Nolan's smile when he lay on top of her, his chin between her breasts.

In the jail late at night, Dede heard women crying. Emmet had put her in a cell by herself, but that didn't stop her from hearing a woman down the corridor sobbing for her baby—her child? Some man?—and another woman cursing at her. Whatever they'd done, they couldn't be as crazy as she was. They were like Delia, Dede thought, the kind of woman who could screw up her whole life for love of a man, but then Delia sat at that table and spoke about Clint as if he were not what Dede had always thought he was, contemptible and evil.

"Don't you live your life the way I have," Delia had said. "Don't shut yourself off to love. Don't bury your heart in a hole."

Dede lay awake and listened to the women. My heart is a hole, she thought. I have never let myself use it for love the way Nolan does, never risked everything and known what I was doing. She curled up and pushed her face into her pillow. With that woman she had never seen, she cried for the one she loved.

When Cissy got up the next morning, Rosemary was in the back garden walking around Delia's worktables, admiring the potting bench and the vegetable patch. Cissy poured a cup of coffee and went out to join her.

"Didn't you sleep?" Cissy asked.

"I slept a lot, on the plane and here." Rosemary nodded toward the house. "I'm doing fine. Just look at what your mother has accomplished back here." She took out a cigarette. "Doesn't appear to me like she sleeps at all."

"She don't, not much anyway." Cissy sat on the steps and sipped her coffee. "She's always out here when she's not at the shop. She putters and gardens and refinishes furniture. Never idle, that's Delia."

"A happy woman." Rosemary looked up at the pecan trees.

"You think?" Cissy watched Rosemary walking carefully on the wet grass. "She keeps busy. She's always doing something."

"How about you?" Rosemary came to the steps and sat down beside Cissy. "You keep busy?"

"Busy enough. I guess you heard what Amanda said last night."

"I didn't hear much, just you and your sister going at each other as usual. Seems to me you're both getting too old for that, but it's not my business." She raised an eyebrow. "Delia told me you were going to the community college, working a little and crawling around under the ground whenever you got the chance. All that true?"

"True enough." Cissy rocked on her heels. "But I quit the job, and school is stupid. I took two classes, but not with anything in mind. I don't know why I bother."

"You could do something else."

"Like what?" Cissy said, but she looked at Rosemary hopefully.

"You could come back to Los Angeles with me. Go to UCLA, if you could get in." Rosemary gave her a meaningful look. "No sense even talking about it, though, unless you really want to. You'd have to think about what you're willing to be serious about, what you care about."

Cissy set the cup down on the step and dropped her head. "I don't know what I care about. If I knew that, I could figure everything else out."

Rosemary poked Cissy's shoulder. "Delia says you've been doing this caving a long time. Says you've been going out to those caves for years, long before you started doing it with these girls Amanda was talking about. Seems like you might care about that, about caves and all. What's that? Spelunking? Archaeology maybe, or geology, minerals and such. You could check it out, see what interests you."

Cissy stared openmouthed into Rosemary's impassive face. "Are you serious?"

"I am completely serious."

"How would we pay for it?" Cissy tried not to let her excitement show.

"We could manage something. You are Randall Pritchard's daughter, after all." Rosemary rubbed her temple. "Seems to me we have to make sure that Dede is all right, and then there's a lot of paperwork and preparation involved. You don't just walk out of one life and into another. It's a bit more complicated than that."

"This Delia's idea?" Cissy sat back on the step. "She ask you to talk to me about this?"

"Your mother and I discussed you, yes." Rosemary's tone did not alter. "She loves you. Maybe you don't know that. I remember when she hauled you back here, what you looked like after your daddy died. Like a half-drowned kitten, and Delia the mama cat that was going to drag you around by your neck till you dried out."

Rosemary stood and went up the steps. "You think about things. Delia said it might take two or three days to get Dede out of jail. She wants her to talk to Nolan, and the doctor won't let Nolan get out of bed yet. You go on your trip with your friends, but while you're down there, you think about things. When you decide, Delia and I will talk to you about how to get what you want."

"You'll play fairy godmother?" Cissy said to Rosemary's back as she went through the door.

"You be good to your mama," Rosemary called back. "You pay attention for a change."

Cissy walked to Nolan's house on uncertain feet. "How's he doing?" she asked Tacey.

"Better than me," Tacey told her. "Better than me. I'm going to the store. You stay with him for a while. And don't wake Nadine up if you can avoid it. She was up and down all night after you girls got out of here."

Cissy hesitated at Nolan's door, but she could see his feet moving under the covers. "You awake?" she asked, and he said yes right away.

She stepped in nervously, not sure what to expect. He had been asleep last night, and he looked terrible every time she peeked in. His face was pale, and a shadow of beard was already darkening his jaw. The way his eyes moved reminded her of something, but she could not think just what. The feeling was unpleasant enough to make her want to back right out of the room.

"Don't go," Nolan begged. "For God's sake, Cissy, help me get some clothes on. If you help me, I can get downtown before any of them come back."

"Downtown?"

"To see Dede." Nolan was trying to swing his leg over the side of the bed, but the bulky bandage above his knee made him clumsy. "If I get downtown, I can talk to Emmet, maybe see the people at the courthouse, find out how to get her out. She shouldn't be in jail. It was all a mistake." He got his leg off the bed.

Cissy saw that he was wearing only his underwear, that there was an ugly scrape on his left side, and that he was about to fall on his face. "Goddamn it, Nolan." She jumped forward to catch him and shoved him back hard.

Nolan gasped. "Don't," he pleaded. "Don't do this. You got to help me."

"I am helping you. Are you crazy?" Cissy pushed him back onto the pillows and pulled the sheet up. "Think for a minute. Is anybody going to listen to you if you go down there like a madman? You want to get Dede free, you got to act like a sane, thoughtful individual. You got to convince people that neither one of you is crazy."

Nolan gaped at her. "You think?"

"Yes, I do." His face was too pale, Cissy thought. He looked so pitiful. "You got to start thinking like a lawyer if you want to help Dede."

Nolan put a hand up to his mouth. His eyes swept the room. "Maybe," he said. "Maybe you're right." Then he sobbed, a hoarse, ugly sound. "God, maybe."

Cissy put her hand on his arm and patted him awkwardly. "You know I'm right. You don't want to get her in any more trouble. You've both used just about all the luck you have."

"I messed it up," Nolan said. "I pushed her. I made her do it. You know she didn't mean to hurt me."

"I know. I talked to her."

"Is she all right?"

"She's fine, Nolan. She's angry and confused and scared, and she isn't sure what to say to you. I think she's afraid to see you."

"She shouldn't be afraid of me."

"No, she shouldn't." Cissy sat on the edge of the bed. Nolan wiped his eyes with the sheet.

"I asked her to marry me."

"I know. She told me."

"Did she tell you that's why she shot me?"

"I figured it had a lot to do with it."

Nolan swallowed painfully and took Cissy's hand in his. "Well, when you figure it all out, you tell me about it. I'll take it on trust, but I got to tell you I don't understand it yet."

Cissy held his eyes. "She's afraid. Do you understand that? She thinks that marriage is the end of love, that it will steal her soul and make her hate you. She thinks that if she loves you that much, she'll disappear into you and become someone she despises. She thinks that you'll turn into her daddy and start to beat her, or she'll turn into him and beat on you. She thinks she's damned, and she's always tried to defy that. Kind of a *Paradise Lost* devil-resisting-God kind of thing."

Nolan shook his head. "All that?"

"And more," Cissy said.

"Well, then, it's no wonder she shot me." He closed his eyes.

Cissy smoothed the sheet over Nolan's hips. For an instant she wanted to kiss his forehead the way Delia used to kiss hers when she was sick. She repressed the impulse and stood up quickly. "Give yourself a little time, Nolan. Let other people handle things for a couple of days. You'd be amazed what they can accomplish if you give them the chance."

Cissy closed the door and called Jean from Nolan's house. "You girls want to go this afternoon?"

"Go? Can you get away?"

"I need to get away," Cissy said. "I need to go somewhere cool, quiet, and dark. What about you?"

"Hell, yes." Jean laughed into the phone. "I'll talk to Mim and get back to you. If she doesn't have to go to her mom's place, we could do it for sure. How long can we be down before you need to get back?"

"Nothing's going to happen for a while, they tell me, so we could go for an overnight."

"Yes ma'am!" Jean's voice was loud. "You get your stuff, and I'll call you at your mom's as soon as I check with Mim."

Cissy nodded to herself. A lesbian, she thought. She's a lesbian, one of two. I know two lesbians, and what does that say about me? She looked back at Nolan's room.

"I don't care," Cissy said out loud. "I don't care what they are. I don't care who I am. I can go to Los Angeles in the fall. I can be anybody."

In the books, when something goes wrong, they always note what led up to it, the clues and mistakes, the premonitions and warning signs. The list includes equipment not checked out, rope put away wet, batteries not replaced, people going down drunk or exhausted, and the more mundane mishaps, the maps stained with soda or mud so that the one essential passage is missed. Five hours down at Little Mouth, all three of them knew something had gone wrong, but none could have pointed to an omen.

Dede, Cissy found herself thinking. I should never have come down here with so much going on.

"I don't understand," Mim was saying. "We've been through this part before. I know it, and it's on our list, but nothing looks the same. I don't remember this much sand, and I sure don't remember that rock."

The rock was memorable, a hot dog in a bun or a phallus cradled gently between two breasts. "A dick," Jean called it. "A dick with a lopsided head."

A rock like that should have been in their notebooks or on one of the maps, but it was not. Somewhere in one of the initial passages they must have taken a wrong turn. The subterranean passage they thought they were following did not exist.

"Where do you think we are?" Mim whispered. Her words echoed hollowly along the naked rock above them.

"Somewhere new," Jean said. "Somewhere we haven't been before. We've got to go back, go back exactly the way we came, and look for where we went wrong."

"Or for something we know," Cissy said. "We need a landmark."

"It's not that big a cave," Mim sounded determined to be reassuring. "And how many times have we been down here, huh? We go back a hundred feet and we'll find something. You'll see."

Rock on rock, sand and shale, inclines of gray-black stone and sharp-edged slopes of knee-grinding pea gravel—there should have been something they recognized, they kept saying. On one trip they had found bright splashes of Day-Glo paint sprayed in arrows and circles in some of the first passages. Mim had complained about the kind of boys who would do that. "Got to leave their mark. Break something, deface something, mess something up that's been clean and empty for a million years."

At the time, Cissy agreed. The painted signs were ugly, and they burned behind her eyes when she turned away from them. Now, crawling hour after hour up a passage she could not chart, she started to imagine splashes of color and almost wept when none of them turned out to be real. I'm going to die down here, Cissy thought, then stubbornly shook her head.

An hour later Jean announced that she had to rest. "We could die down here," she whispered. Cissy flinched. Mim giggled explosively.

"No, we can't." Mim kicked sand at the other two. "There is too much I have not done. I have not been to New York City. I have not seen the Pacific Ocean. And I have never had so many orgasms that I did not want to come again."

Jean smiled, her teeth pearly in the indirect light of Cissy's flashlight. "Neither have I," she said. "Except for the last one. I have done that."

They all grinned. Mim had a chocolate bar. Jean had saltine crackers with peanut butter. Cissy produced string cheese and salami slices. They ate intently and sipped sparingly. All of them knew there was not much water left.

"We'll find something," Mim said again. "We keep moving up this way, we've got to come out sooner or later."

"My knees are killing me," Jean said. "We keep moving up this way, they're going to give out completely."

"Better up than down," Cissy said, though she was not sure of that.

Forty feet farther on, the passage cut back and reversed on itself. They began to crawl sideways, their boots slipping on broken shale and gravel.

"This is bad," Jean said when she bumped into Cissy's pack. She repeated it a half a dozen times in as many minutes.

Yes, Cissy thought. This was very, very bad. Behind her, Mim sobbed once and told Jean to shut the fuck up.

The next time they stopped to rest, Jean asked Mim to turn off her lamp. "We're gonna need the light. We should use just one at a time."

Jean's voice sounded funny to Cissy, hoarse and shaky. Her face in the dim light seemed to have narrowed in the hours they had been crawling along the mud inclines. Cissy hoped she didn't look that bad, but the trembling in her calves and the ache in her throat worried her. She wanted to lie down and pull dirt over herself, curl up tight and nap until God or some rescuer came for her.

"I'm cold," Mim said.

Cissy closed her eyes. She did not have the strength to turn her head.

"You'll be all right." The sound of sand grating against soggy pants was loud in the hollow of the rock as Jean slid closer to Mim.

Cissy thought about how they would sit around the stove at Jean and Mim's place afterward with the heat beating against their exhaustion while they sipped wine and repeated stories. Women made great cavers, Mim always insisted. It was the extra body fat and the endurance. Upper-body strength was important, but that could be developed. Women weight lifters would be great in caves, she said.

They were muscled, flexible, and full of confidence. That was what it took, that and sheer determination.

Cissy laughed to herself. It was always easy to talk about determination and discipline while sipping wine and eating slices of chicken and cheese. There were spelunkers who deliberately starved themselves to be better able to fit through tiny crevices in the rock, who went down into the dark so thin they could crawl into passages where no one else could follow. Cissy wiggled, and a piece of limestone cracked under her boot. An echo ricocheted along the passage.

"It's Floyd Collins," Jean whispered. Mim giggled.

Cissy put her hands in her armpits and grinned in the near dark. She'd found two books on the Floyd Collins story, though both were less about the poor Collins boy than about the circus that took place above the cave where he died. All the time he was shivering and starving down in the dark, his rescuers were drinking, picnicking, and selling souvenirs above him. The first time the three of them went down as a team, Mim had teased them about "doing a Floyd Collins."

"Don't put your foot wrong. Don't take any unnecessary risks."

Another crack echoed, and Cissy hugged herself tighter. She could imagine that pitiful ghost wandering eternally in the rocky reaches from Kentucky and Tennessee down through Georgia. It was a good-old-boy legend, a tale to scare the tenderhearted. Did you hear about old Floyd, famous Floyd Collins? He's a limping echo behind your left ear; it's harder now for him to get around without that left foot, but if you listen you can hear him stomping and stumbling along. He wants to pull at your shoulder, tell you his story, whisper about the reporters who dropped down notes that promised a glorious tombstone, a fortune for his daddy, anything for how it felt, dying in a hole while the world made a carnival above your corpse.

"I'm famous," he whispered, though no one spoke his name in daylight anymore. "I'm famous, and you could be too."

Cissy watched color bloom on the underside of her eyelids, imagining how he might have altered, the haunt-body moving over sand and rock. He would be so lithe, so essential. No bend or slope could hold him now. He needed no dynamite, no ax, no rope. A solid wall was not solid to old Floyd Collins. Dark was not dark. He could breathe around rock, swim through dirt. He led with his head, his mouth, his canine phosphorescent teeth. Dead but not gone, Floyd Collins lived in the wind. He breathed from the deep rock, was there in the stink of bone and bat shit and slow-settling dust. A legend. A threat. A joke that was never funny. People had to speak his name to outlive his fate, people who knew better than to go creeping into holes they did not know how to escape.

Like Floyd, Cissy thought. If I get skinny enough, I'll slide right through. How many calories does fear use? I'm scared enough to sweat off everything I ever was. And if I sweat enough, won't I grease my passage? Could I slide right over these rocks and up into the light, become as lithe and essential as Floyd or memory or hope? Could I?

"Cissy? Cissy! Are you all right?"

"Fine, I'm fine."

"You were mumbling something."

Cissy shook her head. "Nothing, just thinking."

She looked in Mim's direction. She could barely see the two girls in the dim glow of the one lamp. Were they truly lovers? Lord, she was stupid. Jean was breathing hard and the sound bounced off the sloping rock. There were broken edges of slate close above Mim's face. The curve of the rock turned between them so that there was more space above Cissy. Reaching up, she could almost extend her arm straight out. She turned her head and followed the slope as it widened out into the darkness, the ground dropping down to what looked like sand, and the rock roof rising until she could not see how high it went. There was more room there, they might be able to stand up.

Jean's lamp dimmed again, so that the shadows seemed to be closing in. The only sound was their anguished breathing and the muted echo of water falling in the distance. Cissy held her breath for a moment, wishing that Jean would turn off the light and let them rest in the dark. If they were not moving, the dark felt perfectly safe to her, but she knew that Jean and Mim needed the light, that the dark was not comforting to them. It was only Cissy who was bothered by the light. It caught in the rough grade above her in such a way that the earth's crust seemed to be moving.

"Hallucination." Cissy said the word carefully, and felt Mim shift closer to her until their hips touched.

"Like an oasis in the desert." It was as if Mim were reading Cissy's mind.

The bumps in the rock above Cissy were whitish gray and darker gray, damp in the weak light, like bubbles in meringue. Some of them had dimpled centers with drip points that looked like nipples. To Cissy's dazzled vision the bubbles were warm breasts sweating in the cool, damp air. She was tempted to slide back up the slope to a spot where the gap narrowed so steeply that she could lie back at an angle and put her mouth to one of those bulges. She stared at the glistening center of the largest teat. She could imagine grainy syrup filling her mouth. That tit would sweat sweet. It would be like rock sugar.

"Wouldn't taste good," Mim whispered into her left ear.

"No," Cissy laughed. "Was I talking out loud again?"

"You been doing it for a while. And that's limestone mud." Mim pushed herself up a bit on the rock. "Limestone would be salty and sour. Don't think about sugar. Think about getting out of here, about climbing up this passage and the one past it. Think about how close we are to the top. Think about staying warm."

Cissy turned to put her mouth near Mim's ear. "It's beautiful, though." Her words were startlingly loud. "Isn't it beautiful?" Her voice sounded fuzzy. Every syllable had a little burr added, a slight vibrato that echoed against the crags. "Look at the way the light plays over the stones, the way the water drops shine."

"Looks like ice being born." Jean's voice was rough with exhaustion, gravel under dust. "Ice babies looking for ice tits. No sugar. Frost."

"You that cold, Jean?" Mim's voice was sharp with fear.

"I'm freezing. I am just fucking freezing. My hands won't stop shaking. Even my armpits are cold." She cursed again, her voice lightening into something close to laughter. "If I could spit, I'd spit hailstones."

"Oh, honey." Mim crawled over to rub Jean's shoulders.

"Oh, shit." Jean started to giggle. "Don't do that."

Cissy heard wet material dragging over clammy skin. She crawled toward the sound. Mim's hands rubbed Jean's skin where she had pulled open the layers of clothing. Jean's laughter slowed and faded to soft protests.

"Oh, honey," she said in a teasing tone. "Don't get me started."

"You got to get that wet shirt off." Mim's voice was grim.

Cissy did not move. She didn't want to have to be the one to do anything. It was enough just to be still and listen to them struggle, to hear the dull echoes of the walls all around them, to feel the thud of her own heartbeat.

"Christ damn," Jean swore. "Here I am freezing and you want me to get naked."

"Cissy! Come on," Mim shouted. "Come help me."

Cissy sighed. She wasn't sure exactly what Mim had in mind, but she was clearly the most alert of the three of them, and her tone was insistent. Cissy made herself slide across the slate grade to Jean's side. When her hand touched Jean's shoulder, the girl turned to her, laughing. Mim was pulling frantically at Jean's clotted layers of filthy wet clothing.

"Help me," she said. "Come on. Help me."

"It's too cold!" Jean's voice was slurred with exhaustion.

Hypothermia, Cissy realized. That's what Mim is afraid of. Hypothermia could kill you in a cold, wet cave. She pushed Jean's icy hands out of her way, carefully unbuttoning the flannel undershirt beneath the outer layer of denim.

"We got to get this off!" Mim's voice was almost hysterical.

Jean's light winked out. The dark was suddenly thick around them. Cissy did not hesitate. She clicked on her flashlight and wedged it in a crack in the rock so that it shone on the other two women. The angled light illuminated Mim and Jean perfectly, but it was the phosphorescent shine of Mim's naked shoulder that shook Cissy out of her frozen passivity. Mim was half undressed, with her own under-shirt wadded in one hand and scrubbing at Jean's body. Jean's shirt was pulled up to her neck and off one arm but still tangled around the other. Abruptly Jean started trying to help Mim drag her britches down, but her fingers were thick and fumbling. Cissy crawled close and wedged her legs around Jean's torso. She finished undoing the last buttons on the jeans, pulling several off completely when they caught in the heavy wet fabric.

"I can do it. I can do it." Jean was still reaching for the flannel shirt as it was being pulled over her head.

"Everything off. Everything off." Mim's voice sounded strained with her effort not to stutter with the chill.

"Right."

Cissy worked the last layer off Jean's upper body. The gray-blue shirt slid off Jean's head in a soggy heap. Little pinpricks of goose bumps dimpled Jean's blue-white skin in the awkward light. Icy prickles shot up Cissy's midriff in sympathy at the sight. Immediately Mim was at Jean's left side, pushing her back into Cissy's braced thighs, scrubbing furiously at Jean's exposed flesh. Jean blinked sleepily and struggled weakly.

"Don't fight," Mim insisted. "Lie back."

"Tell me what to do." Jean's demand was spoken in the voice of a petulant, exhausted child.

"Help me." Mim was growing more desperate as Jean's shivering increased. Cissy tried to scrub at Jean's back and look around at the same time. The slight grade they were resting on sloped down to meet another layer of rock. Just ahead there was that shine of some white reflective surface. Sand, she had seen it before. It looked like sand. Abruptly Cissy pulled free of Jean's shivering body and grabbed the flashlight to shine the beam in the direction of the white glow.

"That's sand!" She started pulling Jean with her before Mim real-ized what she was doing.

"Tell me what to do," Jean said again. "Just tell me what to do. I can't think. Just tell me."

"Here, here."

Cissy pulled Jean along the rock, dragging the wads of damp clothes with them. Mim was falling and weeping but climbing down with them, still holding on to Jean's shoulder with one hand as if she could not bear to lose contact with her. Cissy pushed Jean ahead of her onto the sand surface, ignoring the girl's squeals as the rough silt abraded her tender belly and thighs. Roughly Cissy shoved Mim to the other side so that they sandwiched Jean between them. Then she began again the coarse scrubbing motions with the filthy clothes. When Mim joined in and began to scrub Jean's other side, the girl's squeals became sobs.

"It's okay, baby," Mim crooned. "This is going to help. We're going to warm you up. Oh, baby, we got to warm you up."

Cissy scrubbed hard, rocking her whole body against Jean's passive one. Gradually the exercise began to warm her as well, but it was fool's heat, adding another layer of sweat to her skin. The damp would invite more chill. Deliberately she scooped sand over herself, adding another layer of insulation. Her body felt both tremendously heavy and gossamer-thin at the same time, as if her substance were evaporating with her efforts.

"Scrub," she shouted, no longer sure she was talking to anyone but herself. "Rub harder. Come on."

Mim scrubbed harder, briskly massaging Jean while Cissy left them to crawl over and drag back the packs. They had one remaining layer of dry clothing. The maps were wrapped in plastic covers. That was what they needed, paper to make another insulating layer. She used the map case and then some small plastic bags. She split those, spreading them out. That gave Jean one dry layer beneath the outer layer of wet clothing. It was a pity to pull apart the maps, but there was no way around it. They needed every bit of heat they could manage, every layer they could add.

With Jean in the shape she was, they did not have as many hours as they had hoped. They had to crawl and climb without stopping. If they stopped, they would die, all of them down here in the cold and dark. For a moment Cissy considered. Would she leave them if she had to do it to get out? Could she? If it came down to it, would she leave Jean in Mim's embrace and crawl out on her own? I might, Cissy thought. If I have to, I might. I want to live. I want to get out of here alive.

"It's going to be all right," Mim whispered into Jean's tousled hair. "You're going to be fine. Just fine, baby."

Cissy prodded Mim. "We got to get going."

"She needs rest." Mim sounded as if she wanted to cry.

"Listen to me." Cissy put her lips up close to Mim's cheek. She dug her fingers into Mim's arm. "This is like being in a blizzard. It's like taking a nap in a snowdrift. She can't nap. We can't lie down. We have to move and keep moving."

"Please, Mim," Jean whimpered. "Just let me warm up."

"You won't warm up." Cissy felt as if her shoulders were tightening into iron posts. An iron core went up her spine from her tailbone to her brain. She was all ice and metal and cold determination. "You will die," she said, and heard Delia's accent in her own. Delia had talked like that when she had dragged them all the way across the country. She had pushed and prodded and forced Cissy to do what had seemed like sheer craziness. It had not mattered that Cissy hated her for it. It had not mattered that there had been no reason to believe they were going somewhere safe.

"She's right," Mim said, pulling at Jean's body. "Oh, honey, she's right."

Mim pushed up onto her own knees and pulled Jean with her. Cissy reached over and grabbed Jean's belt. "Get up. Come on and get up," she shouted.

Weeping, Jean crawled up until she was kneeling beside Mim. "I hate you," she said. She could have been speaking to either of them. It made Cissy feel light-headed to hear her say it. She smiled and her lips cracked as her mouth pulled wide.

"I hate you too," Cissy said. "I hate this rock and this sand and God and Georgia and the ghost of goddamned Floyd Collins, but I am not going to die down here. And as long as I can make you crawl, neither are you."

Cissy turned her body so that she could reach Jean more easily.

She looped a loose piece of the rope she still had wrapped around her middle through the woman's belt. Then she rolled around again and started crawling forward. She heard Mim moan and Jean cry out as the rope jerked and pulled her forward. It was harder still, crawling forward that way, dragging the reluctant and weeping woman behind her. Mim followed behind, sometimes cursing when she bumped her head against Jean.

Cissy paid no attention to the girls behind her except to kick at them when they stopped. She had a clear picture in her mind now. She knew exactly what she had to do, how far she had to crawl, how many times she would have to roll over and slide along on her back. This passage was lit up in her memory. It was the way out.

"Come on," she called back over her shoulder to Jean and Mim. "This is it. It's the way out, I know it."

"You don't know nothing."

"Oh yes I do." Cissy scraped a line of dirt off her neck where her collar was rubbing a raw spot. "I know this part. I know where we have to go. If you don't come after me, I'll leave you to rot down here."

One of them sobbed and the other cursed. Cissy did not bother to see who did what or to speak. The rope tied to her belt loop pulled taut and then slackened. They were following. That was all that was important. If they kept moving, none of them had to die down here.

"I hate you," one of them said in a hoarse, unrecognizable voice, and Cissy, still crawling forward, laughed out loud.

"Sure you do," she said, "sure you do." Light-headed and exhilarated, Cissy kept giggling to herself as she crawled stubbornly upward. The color of the sandy loam beneath her was buttermilk. The shale above was as dusty as a raven's wing. Her pulse was pounding a steady cardinal, her breath was sky blue. Randall was singing somewhere behind her right shoulder, "born on the corner of Calvary and Nazareth, but I an't gonna lay me down and die." No Daddy, Cissy promised. If Delia could drag me so far, I can damn sure pull these bitches up out of a hole in the ground.

When they finally found the Day-Glo paint splashes three hours later, Cissy was shaking with exhaustion, but her head was clear and her thoughts as smooth as ball bearings on a greased surface. Venice Beach, she thought, Los Angeles, Santa Monica, UCLA California, and all those places I don't even remember anymore. I can go there if I want.

"Daddy," Cissy whispered when the morning sunlight fell on her face. "Daddy, I'm going to go back. I'm not going to die here. I'm going to find out what I can do."

"Oh God," Mim sobbed behind her. Her face was bruised and streaked with mud. She climbed up into the light on her hands and knees. "That's the last time, the last time I ever do that in this life."

"Oh, you don't know what you'll do," Cissy told her. She was stumbling with exhaustion but full of happy exhilaration. "We don't none of us know what we might do."

Cissy looked back down past Jean's sodden, mud-encrusted body. The gaping mouth of Paula's Lost was half obscured by a sweeping hang of kudzu vines. "I don't think I can map the passage," she said. "We found it, but I don't think I could show anybody the way. An't that a hoot!"

Chapter 23

Delia sat in the coffee shop waiting for Emmet Tyler. There was a new waitress, a long-faced woman wearing a poorly styled wig. Delia kept looking at the wig, the way it fell around the woman's face and the constant small motions she kept making to adjust it. I could fix that, Delia thought, and realized she had been comparing it to Amy Tyler's wig, the one she had styled so long ago.

"God," she said softly. She had drunk too much coffee. She didn't think she could stand another cup.

"Did you hear anything from Emmet?" Cissy slid into the booth across from Delia. The scrapes on her face looked pink and raw, the knuckles of her right hand were bandaged, but her eyes were bright and clear.

"He an't been in yet," Delia said.

Cissy nodded. "Jean's still at her mother's place. Mim says she's going to be fine, but she's still pretty out of it. Says she plans to sleep the rest of this semester."

Delia's face collapsed. "Lord, Cissy, I could have lost you. You could have died down there."

"Yeah." Cissy smiled. "I know, but I didn't, and I think that's the whole point."

Delia struggled to compose herself. Her fingers twisted together. The muscles in her neck corded as she swallowed and shook her head. "It's nice to see you smile," she managed to say.

"Well, we did something nobody else has done, what we wanted to do in the first place. We found our way from Little Mouth to Paula's Lost. Only we didn't map it and we can't show it to anybody.

Probably no one will believe it, and Jean and Mim swear they won't go back, so I might not ever get to map it at all."

"Is it that important?"

"It's ironic," Cissy said. "It's like God's joke." She looked back at the café door. "Emmet was going to come here, right?"

"If he could get everything done. If he's not here in the next half hour, we should go over to the courthouse." Delia pushed the coffee cup away. "Lord, I almost lost you. And Dede shot Nolan, and Amanda's drinking, and I just don't know." Her voice quavered.

"I've tried to hard to be a good mother. I've stayed sober, I've taken care of you, but I've done something wrong. None of you seem to know who you are or how much I love you."

Cissy put her hands down flat on the table surface. "No," she said. "None of us know who *you* are. Or I don't, anyway. I don't really know you at all. You always hold everything back. Clint told me more about you than you ever did, and when we were out at Granddaddy Byrd's place, Dede showed me the pictures of your family. You never told me a thing about them."

"I told you they died. Granddaddy Byrd raised me."

"That's nothing. That's less that nothing. How did they die? When? What happened? You had a mama, a daddy. You had brothers. I saw them in the pictures. You never talked about them. You carry around this big silence, even when you go on about being so frank and all."

Delia looked around the coffee shop. There were a couple of people at the counter, the waitress with the bad wig in the back, and one man in another booth. God help me, Delia thought. She felt as if her backbone were slowly twisting and pulling free from her hips.

"I want a cigarette," Delia said.

Cissy was startled.

"I want a cigarette so bad I could eat my own tongue." Delia turned around in the booth and waved at the waitress. "Ma'am, excuse me. You wouldn't have a cigarette, would you?" Delia pushed her hair back. "I feel like I am about to die if I don't get one."

The waitress frowned, then gave a rueful smile and walked

toward them. From a pocket under her apron she produced a pack of Kool Lights. "I know what you mean," she said in a slow drawl. "They ever make this diner a no-smoking place, I'm gone that day." She extended the pack to Delia, shook out one, and pulled another out for herself. From the same pocket she brought out a lighter and lit first Delia's cigarette and then her own. She looked at Delia's shaking hands and Cissy's expression of dismay, and smiled gently.

"Hell, an't it? Us being addicts and all?" The waitress put the pack and lighter away, then pointed at the cup. "How about something else?"

"I think something sinful." Delia waved the cigarette. "To go with this. Why don't you make me a malt?"

"Double chocolate or vanilla, or I think we got coffee ice cream back there." The woman pushed self-consciously at her wig.

"Coffee, no. Chocolate would be good. Chocolate would be great." Delia took a long, happy drag on the cigarette. All this time and she didn't even feel the urge to cough. Hell, she thought, it's the worst drug in the world. She turned around in her seat to call to the waitress again. "Hey," she said. "You know the Bonnet? Down the way? The beauty parlor?"

"Yeah, the one with the spider plants?"

"I run it. You come in sometime. I know a style would look really good on you."

The woman nodded. "Why, thank you. I'll do that."

"She needs some help," Cissy said sharply as the waitress disappeared into the kitchen.

"We all do," Delia said. "We all do." She took another drag and put the cigarette out in the saucer of the coffee cup. Then she looked directly into Cissy's face.

"All right. There's something I want to ask you. How many people you tell about that eye?"

Cissy jerked back. Her face flooded color and her mouth fell open.

"Not many, huh?" Delia shook her head. "Most people don't even know about it, do they? You don't bring it up in casual conversation, do you? Say, 'Hey, my daddy nearly killed me 'cause he was doing drugs and didn't care that he had me and my mama with him in his car'?" Her face was stern. "Do you explain how much you loved him anyway? And how it don't bother you at all that you can't get a driver's license?"

"Why are you doing this?" Cissy looked as if she wanted to cry but was not going to give Delia the satisfaction.

"I'm explaining something." The waitress set a tall glass of chocolate malt before Delia, who gave a weak smile and peeled the paper off her straw. "Thank you," she said.

"Anytime," the waitress said, her cigarette still in one corner of her mouth.

Cissy pushed herself sideways in the booth as if she were about to bolt. Delia reached across the table and caught her arm. "No," she said. "You sit. I'm not trying to hurt you. I'm trying to talk to you about hurt."

Cissy shook free. "You aren't telling me anything."

"No." Delia licked her lips. "You're right. I never talked about my family. I said they were dead and that was hard enough, but Cissy, there are stories no one knows how to tell, things you don't tell your children. If I had my way, no one would ever tell you. I figure Granddaddy Byrd told Dede. Probably someone told Amanda, some of it anyway. It's one of those stories people can't keep to themselves, but I couldn't tell it. I couldn't think about it." She cupped her fingers around the malt glass. "You sure you want this?"

"Tell me." Cissy's face was as stern as Delia's, her mouth as hard. "Just tell me."

"It was late July. It was the summer I was eleven, 1959. We were getting ready to go on a trip, but I changed my mind. Everything followed from that."

They were going to drive over to Fort Jackson, the whole family—Delia, her mama and daddy, and her three brothers. They were going to pick up Luke, Delia's daddy's brother, who was finishing up basic training. It would take a day to drive there and a day to drive back, two hot days in the summer heat, but only in the last hour did Delia decide she wouldn't make the trip. She'd stay with her girlfriend Julia, eat snow cones and play with the litter of newborn puppies Granddaddy Byrd had discovered under his tractor.

"I was thinking about the heat, and those puppies," Delia said. That enervating summer heat would have seared four children driving across two states in the back of a run-down Ford sedan, and the brown velvet noses of a half dozen blind, scrambling rusty brown puppies. Delia's brothers, three stair-step boys all towheaded and sunburned dark brown, teased her for missing the chance to see the soldiers' parade and to sleep over in an air-conditioned motel. Her daddy picked her up and hugged her tight, praising her for giving up the trip to make her brothers more comfortable. Now there would only be three restless, sweating bodies rolling around on those plastic seat covers. Her mama kissed her forehead and pressed Delia's cheek to her pregnant belly. Come October there was to be a baby brother, or maybe a tiny girl, Delia's miniature blinking up like another puppy from the crook of her mama's arm.

They were supposed to be back in four days, but there might be bad weather or Mama might need more rest before beginning the long trip back. Delia was to stay with Julia one night, maybe two, and then go to Granddaddy Byrd's for the weekend.

"Give me another kiss," her daddy shouted from the car, and Delia put her head in the window, scraped her cheek on his freshshaven skin, smelled her mama's talcum sweat, grinned at her brother Tom, and pinched Max's shoulder.

Leroy yelled, "Pick me out a runt!"

The Ford pulled away, raising a cloud of dust in the driveway.

"Did you get breakfast?" Julia's mama called.

Delia shrugged, and looked back at the Ford. A hand waved from over the top of the faded blue car. One of her brothers or her mama? Delia didn't know. She didn't know anything. The car and her family had driven away in a blur of dust and rising heat, and disappeared. The absence was sudden and terrible and complete. There was no word. They never came back. The world closed down on all of them, and there was Delia standing alone with a puppy in her arms. After a week Granddaddy Byrd went to Fort Jackson to help Luke search. He came back with his features blurry and confused and as angry as Delia's. Nothing was known, nothing was discovered.

Delia had replayed it in her mind endlessly, that one white hand waving over the top of that car, the scent of warm seat covers and loved bodies, the image of a little brother or sister, her life changed utterly. She cried for the baby when she cried, the lost chance, the mystery. Granddaddy Byrd never cried at all. His silence enlarged and hardened until Delia felt the pressure of it on her bones. She would go to him, touch his arm, and feel him pulling away from her like the moon rising up to the sky, everything leaving her behind and alone. Granddaddy Byrd drowned the puppies, lifted them one at a time in his big, knuckled hands, thrust their open mouths under the scummy water of the old washtub in his backyard, pulled them out limp and silent to lie in a line on the other side of the tub, glossy black in the hot afternoon sun. Delia watched it all with dry eyes, biting the insides of her cheeks so she would not scream.

When the Ford was found just before Christmas in a dealer's lot in Savannah, Uncle Luke came home to stay for three days. Delia felt a stir of hope then—not for her brothers or her mother and father, but for herself, for word of any kind, someone to say, "This is what happened, this is the story." Luke did not have that word to give. He was Granddaddy Byrd's boy, nothing of Delia's daddy in him but grief and confusion. Luke glanced at Delia impatiently, grimly, as if he wondered why she was still there, still breathing and demanding something he did not have. He pushed aside the plate of macaroni and cheese she had warmed for him, and sat at the table drinking Granddaddy Byrd's Jack Daniels while Delia retreated to her cold sheets. Christmas morning, she found him passed out on the floral-print couch in the front room. She stood over him, looking down into his open mouth and shadowed eyes. She felt it then, the stonelike silence that lay on Granddaddy Byrd, felt it shaped over again in her uncle, felt it ready to creep up through her body, felt it like something animate and dangerous, an animal that wanted to eat her alive.

At eleven Delia Byrd did the only known thing she could do. She balled her hands into clumsy fists and hit her uncle with all her strength, punched and kicked his stubbled chin and knobby ear, slapped at his loose drunken body. All the time she made the sound a baby makes being born. She opened her mouth and it came out—a groan that rose to a scream, a lifesaving terrible shriek that grew and grew. It was a cry that pulled Granddaddy Byrd out of his stony bed and rocked her uncle onto the floor. Granddaddy Byrd came into the living room with his hands out and his mouth open. His cold hands could not stop Delia's howl. He lifted her up off her feet as easily as he had lifted those puppies, but she kicked at him until he dropped her and stepped back. The two of them—her uncle, her grandfather—vibrated in tune to her rigid, shrieking form, a wisp of a girl holding them off with a scream.

It was her stolen world that Delia mourned, loudly and desperately. That world lived in her always, no matter how far down she pushed it. Grief burned in her glance, trembled on her chafed and bitten lips, spread like a circle of shade around her. Delia mourned her lost life and the people she had loved with a constant croon of anguish. Years later, when she stood up on a stage and opened her mouth to sing, it was the mourning wail that came out.

"Delia Byrd sings like the angel of the apocalypse," a reviewer wrote. "She sings like she has been to the bottom of the river of life and come back full of the knowledge of death." Delia laughed when she read the man's words. She got righteously drunk and stayed drunk a long time. "River of life," she told Randall, and crawled into his arms. "I been bathed in the river of life."

"My sweet Lord," Cissy said.

"I cursed them. Uncle Luke and Granddaddy, but also my mama and my daddy, and whoever had stolen them. I would have cursed God if I could have confronted him." Delia smiled bitterly. "I been cursing ever since. Singing, making noise, humming in my throat. I can't be quiet. You know."

Cissy swallowed hard. The faces in those pictures, the happy family, suddenly loomed in the close confines of the overheated diner. That mama leaned over and touched Cissy's cheek. Those boys, whistling and wiggling, passed before Delia's pale face. That lost grandfather put a gentle arm around Delia's shoulders. Then they faded like the ghosts they were, and there was only Delia sitting across the table with the straw between two fingers.

She took a sip of the malt. "It's good," she said. "I forgot how good."

Luke Byrd went to jail on a charge of manslaughter shortly after Valentine's Day. The conviction was more than deserved, Delia told Cissy. "The man should have stayed in jail where he couldn't hurt nobody."

Luke was drunk, people said, had been pretty much since he left his daddy's place after the family disappeared. And drunk and stupid, he had smashed his truck head-on into another man's car just outside Atlanta, killing a stranger who knew nothing of Luke's rage. Through the trial, Luke stood numb and silent, blinking at the judge, who seemed entirely sympathetic and nodded when Luke's lawyer brought up the family's loss. But the dead man's family was not sympathetic, and neither was Delia. "More people hurt for no reason," she said. "Luke killed that man out of his own careless grief and seemed to feel nothing for what he had done." A few years later he killed again, just as senselessly, two men in a tavern in Memphis. It was for that crime that he was still in prison.

"He probably thought he'd get away with that too," Delia said. "You got to remember that people like Luke are always out there, crazy people who'll waste your life for no reason that has anything to do with you. Maybe that's what happened. Maybe whoever robbed me of my life that was meant to be and left me with this one, maybe they thought they were justified. Somebody had hurt them and they could do anything."

Delia turned away; a kind of growl reverberated briefly in her throat. "Things happen, and they have nothing to do with what we want or expect. Luke never expected to kill nobody, like my mama never expected to disappear, but do you think I should have told you any of that when you were a little girl? When we came back to Cayro? When Clint was dying? Do you think that is what a mother does for her children? Hands them a vision of a world as terrible as that?"

Cissy sat quiet so long that Delia got nervous. She reached over and took her girl's hands in her own. She said, "It's all right, baby. It all happened a long time ago."

No, Cissy thought. It's still happening, still going on. She thought of Dede, the way she wrung her hands and prophesied. "Something terrible is going to happen. It's all going to go to hell," Dede had said. Something terrible was always coming, always echoing down from what went before.

"I never imagined," Cissy said finally. "I thought a car accident or a fire. Something."

"Something terrible," Delia finished for her. She held Cissy's eyes for a moment and then looked back at the door. "I'm starting to think that Emmett's not going to make it. If we're going to get this plan in motion, maybe we better get over there. I don't want Dede to spend another night in jail."

Cissy nodded, but it was a moment before she could make her legs move. She watched Delia open her purse and count out the money for the coffee and the malt. Delia waved at the waitress, and the woman waved back.

Cissy forced her hips to the edge of the booth. She looked up at Delia's worn face, the sad brown eyes looking back at her.

"I love you," she said.

Delia's eyes softened, the corners crinkling though she did not smile.

"I know," she whispered and took her girl's hand.

*   *   *

Nolan kept bouncing on the seat of the wheelchair. If he hadn't locked the wheels tight, he would have been halfway to Atlanta by the time Emmet came out of the courthouse to talk to him.

"She's all right?" he said first thing. "Is she all right?" he asked again when Emmet pushed him inside and rolled him into the judge's antechamber. "Just tell me she's all right."

"No, she an't all right." Emmet was losing all patience with Nolan. "She shouldn't be all right, boy. She shot you, remember? She's lucky she's got people willing to stand up for her. I'm still not sure she shouldn't stay in jail."

"Dede don't belong in jail." Nolan was shaking but determined. "This should never have happened."

"No, it should not have happened, but I'm not sure where Dede belongs, and you should ask yourself a few questions about that while you got the time." Emmet pushed his hair back. "You love her, we all are agreed on that. And everybody says she loves you, but nobody who would shoot the man she loves is all right. You want to get her out of here, and I can almost understand that notion. But, I'd be a damn fool not to tell you that you're as crazy as she is. The first thing the two of you should do is get some help." He leaned into Nolan's face. "You understand me?"

"I understand." Nolan's head bobbed. "You just don't understand me and Dede. Nothing like this is ever going to happen again."

"I hope not, boy." Emmet stood up awkwardly. "I surely hope not, but you take my advice and think about things while I get her."

When she came through the door, Nolan felt all his air go out of him. Dede looked as if she had shrunk. Her face had narrowed, and the dark shadows under her eyes made her look years older. Most striking was the way her mouth and chin seemed to have softened.

"Nolan," she whispered, and he thought his heart would break. Dede had never sounded so cowed in all her life. "I'm sorry," she said.

"No, no," he pleaded. "I'm the one. I . . ."

"Nolan, stop it. For God's sake, stop it." Dede's mouth twisted and her chin shook. "I can't stand it if you act like that."

"Like what?" Nolan made himself look away from her. "Like I love you? Like I still love you?"

They were both silent. Dede shifted on her feet and then pulled a desk chair over to Nolan's wheelchair.

"We shouldn't do this," she told him once she was sitting in front of him. "You should stay away from me until you know what you're doing."

"I know what I'm doing," Nolan said. He kept his eyes on her hands where they gripped her thighs. There was a bruise on the back of her right hand, a small blue shadow. He wanted to cover that spot with his palm and try to comfort her, but he knew not to touch her. Nolan curled his fists around the wheels of the chair.

"I am not going to change, Dede. I am never going to change. I love you, and that's all there is to it."

Dede shook her head. "Oh, Nolan," she whispered.

Involuntarily Nolan reached for her, the hand stopping in the air when she flinched. He curled his fingers and closed the hand. "It's all I can say, darling," he told her. "If you were to shoot me again, I'd say the same thing, but I think it might be a whole lot easier on both of us if you didn't." He watched her lift her head and look into his eyes.

"I think we could try talking a little more," he said. "Maybe you could tell me what hurt you so bad."

Dede looked at him, her eyes searching his, her chin still quivering. Her eyes flooded as he watched. Her hand came up to where his waited in the air. Her fingers laced through his. "Oh, Nolan," she said again. "I don't know how you happened to me. I don't understand it, but if you are sure, then I'll try. I'll try to forgive myself."

"Yes," Nolan said. He pulled her hand to his chest and pressed her fingers above his heart. "Oh yes." Dede leaned forward and put her lips to Nolan's. Very gently she kissed him. With a sob he pulled her onto his body, dragging her onto his lap. "Oh, Dede," he sighed. "You don't have to do this. We don't have to do anything. We can just go home and hold each other until they all forget what happened."

"No, no." Dede kissed Nolan's eyelids, his temple, and each side of his face. "That judge does not like me, Nolan. He'd love to keep me in jail and I need to get out of here." She pulled back and grimaced. "You need to know one thing," she said. "I'm pregnant. I'm about three months gone and it looks like it's going to stick."

Nolan's mouth gaped. "Oh," he breathed. "Oh, Dede, how wonderful!" He kissed her again, but she searched his face closely.

"Are you sure?" she asked him.

"I'm sure," he said. "Our baby," he whispered then. "Our baby will be the best thing that ever happened to us."

"I won't marry you, Nolan," Dede said. "I love you. No lie and I'll live with you. But I won't marry you. I won't marry no one."

In reply Nolan put his mouth over hers and kissed her. His hands stroked her shoulders and slid down to caress her back. "Dede Windsor, you are the most difficult woman I ever met, worse than my mama. And you know damn well I'd rather live in sin with you than be carried off to heaven with any other woman in the world. Only thing you need to know is that I will want to be a real daddy to this child."

Dede shrugged. "All right, but you got to do the messy part 'cause I hate stink. You do the diapers and mop up after it. And once it's weaned and I'm legal again, I want to take that truck-driving class they offer up in Chattanooga."

Nolan sighed happily. "Deal," he said. His hands slid under her blouse.

Dede's hands caught his. "I thought about getting rid of it," she said, and put her hand on her belly. Nolan put his hand on top of hers. They sat for a moment, both of them looking at her belly.

"Oh, hell," Dede said finally. "We can't do no worse than everybody else, right?"

"No," Nolan assured her. "Probably not."

Chapter 24

You remember the day Randall died?" It was almost full dark and Delia was sitting at one of her spool tables behind the house under the strings of colored lights. She had a glass of water with sliced lemons floating in it. From up the street came the sound of a clarinet solo; from the house, Amanda and Cissy arguing, M.T.'s booming laugh, and little Michael teaching Gabe to sing "Jesus Loves Me."

"Oh yeah," Rosemary said. She smiled and fingered the glass in front of her, half full of scotch from a bottle Nolan had provided. She didn't want the drink. She wanted to sit here with Delia in the peaceful quiet. The air was still warm, the breeze through the pecan trees a smoke-scented comfort.

"I was pretty crazy."

Rosemary nodded. "Of a kind," she said.

"I don't think I knew what I was doing, packing Cissy up to bring her back here."

"You were thinking about Dede and Amanda."

Delia leaned over the table. Her face was tense, her eyes distant. "I was trying not to go crazy, but I did anyway. What kind of a woman drags a child that young all the way across the country when she's just lost her daddy?"

"You've taken good care of all of them."

Delia shook her head. "No, I've just barely managed to make up for some of what I've done. And even that's not certain."

"They love you."

Delia's mouth opened, then closed. She set her glass on the table. "I wish Dede would marry Nolan."

433

"She won't marry nobody, but I think she'll stick with him."

"Makes me feel so old."

"You an't old."

"Yes I am. I'm old as a rock." Delia sat back in her chair and shoved her hands down in the pockets of her jeans. "And I'm going to lose them. Cissy will go off with you. When Dede's probation ends, she'll move in with Nolan, and God knows where they'll wind up. This house will be empty."

Rosemary's smile broadened. "Grown and gone, and the mama left behind. Oh, it's a tragedy, it is." The screen door opened and swung back to close with a loud thwack. Little Michael stood in the light spilling out of the doorway. Behind him Gabe leaned against the screen, his arms up and spread, his fingers pushing into the mesh.

Rosemary nodded in their direction. "Something's always coming," she said.

Delia looked back at the boys and her face softened. Her eyes glittered. "Rude boys," she whispered. She smiled as her grandson started down the steps.

"We should write some new songs," Rosemary said. She picked up the glass and emptied it onto the grass. She watched as Little Michael ran to Delia and reached up to her extended arms. Rosemary turned the glass upside down on the table, tilted her head back, and nodded up toward the lush expanse of gently moving leaves.

"Yes, it's time for some new songs."

Acknowledgments

I am deeply grateful for the loving help and support of my friends and family during the completion of this work, too many people to thank individually. I want to thank particularly Carole DeSanti, Joy Johannessen, Jim Grimsley, Amy Bloom, Jewelle Gomez, Diane Sabin, Sydelle Kramer, Lillian Lent, and most of all, Frances Goldin. For any of them, I would happily climb into a hole and out again.

When I had run my family into the ground, there were three sites to which I retreated to work on this manuscript—The MacDowell Colony which helped me realize all over again that I am too old to run on ice, the La Rose Hotel in Santa Rosa, California, where they let me spread chapters all over the floor and hide out for days at a time, and the Sabin-Gomez home in San Francisco. Every writer should have such nurturing places to go.

Thank you, all of you.

ARKANSAS

David Leavitt

'David Leavitt's writing has a polish and suavity which can only enchant. In this collection of three excellent novellas, he tackles the surprising, painful emergence of jealousy between carers for an Aids patient, sexual pursuit among gay and straight Americans in Italy (rendered not with farcical energy but with honest suffering), and a novelist selling academic papers for sexual favours (deliciously funny). Perfect … Leavitt's best book for years'
Mail on Sunday

'A literary triumph'
Independent

'Leavitt is a real writer. He tells stories, creates characters and turns every human moment he touches, however mundane, into compelling fiction'
Scott Bradfield, *TLS*

'The dialogue is lively and readable, the moral engagement discriminating and humane'
Sunday Times

'Excellent … a pleasure to read'
Spectator

'A must-read book, linking wit and compassion to laser-sharp descriptions of the minutiae of life'
Marie Claire

Abacus
0 349 11042 5

THE BOOK OF LIES

Felice Picano

Bright, ambitious, handsome Ross Ohrenstedt is a high-flier in the fashionable field of Queer Studies, flourishing amid the backstabbing, resentments and petty intrigues of academia. After taking up a prestigious university post in Los Angeles, he has been appointed to oversee the collection of the papers and works of Damon Von Slyke, leading light of the gay literary salon known as the Purple Circle.

Sorting through the papers, Ross stumbles across a 'lost' work by an unknown author. His quest to identify the mystery writer and achieve the glory of scholastic tenure unveils the lives and wild times of a group of writers who in the 1970s and 1980s broke new ground in the creation of a gay literary sensibility. But the truth contained within *The Book of Lies* is even more surprising ...

With sharp wit, powerfully unexpected revelations and a luscious sense of place and character, Felice Picano explores the ties of love, friendship and betrayal with rewarding depth and emotional honesty.

'A hilarious *roman à clef* ... carefully plotted and suspenseful'
Guardian

'An absorbing Henry James-style comedy of manners'
Mail on Sunday

'A thoroughly engrossing tale of literary and academic intrigue ... fascinating'
Gay Times

Abacus
0 349 109991 5

Now you can order superb titles directly from Abacus

☐	Breath, Eyes, Memory	Edwidge Danticat	£6.99
☐	Geek Love	Katherine Dunn	£7.99
☐	Animal Dreams	Barbara Kingsolver	£6.99
☐	Arkansas	David Leavitt	£6.99
☐	Family Dancing	David Leavitt	£6.99
☐	The Book of Lies	Felice Picano	£6.99
☐	Like People in History	Felice Picano	£6.99
☐	The Weight of Water	Anita Shreve	£6.99

Please allow for postage and packing: **Free UK delivery.**
Europe; add 25% of retail price; Rest of World; 45% of retail price.

To order any of the above or any other Abacus titles, please call our credit card orderline or fill in this coupon and send/fax it to:

Abacus, 250 Western Avenue, London, W3 6XZ, UK.
Fax 0181 324 5678   Telephone 0181 324 5517

☐ I enclose a UK bank cheque made payable to Abacus for £ ....
☐ Please charge £.............. to my Access, Visa, Delta, Switch Card No.

☐☐☐☐☐☐☐☐☐☐☐☐☐☐☐☐☐☐☐

Expiry Date ☐☐☐☐   Switch Issue No. ☐☐

NAME (Block letters please) ....

ADDRESS ....

....

....

Postcode ....Telephone ....

Signature ....

Please allow 28 days for delivery within the UK. Offer subject to price and availability.

Please do not send any further mailings from companies carefully selected by Abacus ☐